ON MY WAY THERE

What Reviewers Say
About Jaycie Morrison's Work

A Perfect Fifth

"Large blocks of internal dialogue create intimacy with all the main characters. The reader may not agree with Constance's meddling or be frustrated with Nelson's cluelessness, but they will certainly understand why everyone does what they do. The author also uses the technique to show intentions and actions that are awfully important to Zara and Jillian but unknown to them. This has the effect of Hitchcock's bomb under the table. The reader knows something bad is coming and can only read on and hope for the best. It's a nail-biting ride, making the romance all the sweeter."—*The Lesbian Review*

The Found Jar

"It's a book full of unexpected depth and humanity. I really appreciated how Morrison manages to illustrate that trauma does different things to different people. Both MCs have experienced trauma and loss that has made them who they are and her characterizations almost depict the two opposites of possible reactions. Having them fall for each other despite the many things they have to work through makes for a really good read. This is Morrison's first foray into contemporary romance, and I hope this continues. I'd definitely recommend giving this book a go as it brings a different approach to romance than I've personally encountered before in the wlw arena and for that reason alone it's worthwhile giving it a try."—*LGBTQ+ Reader*

"The beach setting and Beck's pure heart help to offset the frustration I felt with Emily and her issues. Beck is an innocent and at times naive young woman who suffered a traumatic brain injury in her teens. Emily writes horror novels and battles nightmares and demons from her past. Beck's kindness and innocence are a balm for Emily's tortured soul. And there are kittens, and they soften some of the harsher scenes. It was interesting seeing the contrast between these two women as their relationship developed. One with a TBI who deals with her disability and tries to face her challenges with a positive attitude versus the other with so much emotional baggage that she can't see past her anger and disgust with herself to allow Beck into her life. Will their friendship develop into the relationship you know they deserve?"—*LezReviewBooks*

Heart's Orders

"I am so enamored with this awesome story! While I was reading this book I got so caught up in the struggles the characters faced—I felt as though I was experiencing all of the angst, confusion and elation right along with them. There is one thing that I know for sure; this story is going to stay with me for quite some time. These strong-willed women are truly unforgettable, and they will capture your heart and attention from the first page."—*Lesbian Review*

"Jaycie Morrison has captured the mood of an era really well in these novels, and the determination of the women who have signed up to the WAC to not only do a good job but to forge a place for themselves in the world. ...The romances are sweet and gentle, the mood is soft focus despite the harsh realities of the time. An excellent follow up in the Love and Courage Series, I look forward to book three."—*Lesbian Reading Room*

Basic Training of the Heart

"There are some great WWII lesbian romances out there, and you can count *Basic Training of the Heart* among them. It's well worth a read, and I look forward to seeing what's next in this series."—*Lesbian Review–Top 100 Books To Start With*

Visit us at www.boldstrokesbooks.com

By the Author

The Love and Courage Series

Basic Training of the Heart

Heart's Orders

Guarding Hearts

The Found Jar

A Perfect Fifth

On My Way There

ON MY WAY THERE

by
Jaycie Morrison

2023

ON MY WAY THERE

ISBN 13: 978-1-63679-392-4

This Trade Paperback Original Is Published By
Bold Strokes Books, Inc.
P.O. Box 249
Valley Falls, NY 12185

First Edition: June 2023

Credits
Editor: Barbara Ann Wright
Production Design: Susan Ramundo
Cover Design By Tammy Seidick

Acknowledgments

As always, I owe so much to the fabulous folks at BSB—Rad, Sandy, Cindy, Susan, and especially to the guidance of my endlessly patient and supportive editor, Barbara. I'm also lucky to have my amazing friend Julie R who, along with being an eagle-eyed proofreader, will let me drop my work into her lap at a moment's notice. In addition, my special thanks go to Kim, for her stories about being a truck driver, and MAK for his sensitivity reading of Ray. Any errors or missteps in these areas are strictly mine.

Thanks to my fellow writers for your encouragement and inspiration. And to my readers, my deepest appreciation for your investment in my stories.

Dedication

To those who contribute to our transportation economy—gratitude and safe journeys

To those who suffer from or are victims of the ravages of mental illness—strength and healing

To those who seek to live as their authentic selves—tenacity and triumph

To those whose search for love feels hurtful or futile—faith and courage

To the one who's given me safe travels as we've journeyed through sickness and health, while richer and poorer, and for better and worse—all my love always

CHAPTER ONE

2007
Age Twenty-five

After she came, I crawled up her body and laid my head on her chest. Normally, breasts were something I genuinely enjoyed about women, but Daphne's were quite a bit firmer than the ones God had originally given her. Still, I was drifting off, ignoring the risk of a crick in my neck, when she gave me a nudge.

"I gotta get going, Max. Bill may be an asshole drunk, but he isn't stupid. I can't very well show up an hour after the game's over and think he won't notice."

While she found her panties, I sat up, rolling my head around. A little pop eased the stiffness along my left shoulder. Yep, just in time. "Okay, baby," I said. "Let me walk you back." I was butch enough to think I should be a gentleman about these things.

"So how's Lena?" I asked as we strolled through the damp evening toward the truck stop and diner that doubled as a sports bar.

Daphne stopped walking within earshot of the hollering but in the shadows between illuminations cast by the streetlights and the assorted neon signs of Etta's Place. "I know you're asking 'cause you care about me, Max." For once, sarcasm didn't drip off every single syllable; it only lightly coated that last pronoun. "But Bill is starting to make noises about you being such good friends with Lena."

I sighed. She was right. Bill wasn't stupid. And, yeah, I had a big wide soft spot for Daphne's daughter. It was a personal goal of mine to be there for her, especially should she ever toy with the idea of coming out. Because how could anyone choose the straight and narrow if they ain't ever experienced the big ol' crooked? Quick as a snake, Daphne grabbed my earlobe—something she knew I hated—and pulled me closer. "Tell me I don't have to worry about you, Max. Tell me you're not making some depraved plans for my daughter's future." She squeezed enough to maintain my full attention. "Tell me your decadence hasn't sunk that low."

"Ow! Goddamn it, Daphne." I wouldn't get much wiggle room, either literally or figuratively. She'd always been able to read me. "It's not like that. You know I care for Lena like she was my own."

I was glad for the semi-darkness as she gave me a long look. "All right," she said, finally letting go. I rubbed my earlobe and scowled my best offended look at her. "I'm sorry." She gave the injured area a peck and a quick lick, something she knew I liked. Fact was, she knew everything I liked. "It's just that I have enough to worry about without throwing you in the mix."

There was something unaffected in her tone that made me take a second look. Daphne was almost four years older than me, but we'd been acquainted for as long as I could remember. Her family had lived next door to mine until I was eight. My dad had told me how fascinated she was with me as a baby and a toddler, and I had sweet memories of her playing in the backyard with me and my brother, Adam, before everything went to shit.

I'd come to understand why her family had moved while I'd been in the hospital. But that meant Daphne had attended the other elementary school in town when I'd resumed my education as the oldest kid in my third-grade class. We weren't in middle school at the same time, but had reconnected at the end of her high school years. She'd stood up for me a lot in those days and probably saved me more than one ass kicking at the hands of some jock. I'd returned the favor in any way I could, later spending enough time with her and the baby that I'd gotten totally attached to the little rug rat. And though our favors had turned into more mutual pleasure once I was old enough, I truly did care about them both.

Still, my next question came pretty much out of nowhere. "Aren't you happy, Daphne?"

"Happy?" For a second, she seemed to ponder the concept before snapping back to reality. "Hell no, I'm not happy. And neither is anyone else. That's why we're all so pissed. We're promised life, liberty, and the pursuit of happiness, and we feel like we're getting shorted on one-third of the deal."

Daphne had been a brainiac, though she didn't look it now. She'd been on track to be valedictorian before her folks had sent her off to church camp for one whole summer, where she'd learned to drink, smoke, cuss, and dress like a hooker so she'd be able to get a man and procreate as the good Lord intended.

She turned a shrewd eye on me. "Are you happy, Max?"

I shrugged. "Sure. I guess so."

She sniffed dismissively. "Why did I ask? You don't have the slightest idea what happiness is." Her gaze ran slowly up and down my body. "All you know about is pleasure. And that's two different things."

"You sure?" I grinned because this was getting much too deep.

A shout went up inside the bar. I could make out Bill's voice among the din: "Fuck, yeah, Longhorns! We're going to overtime. Bring me another beer, will you, sweetheart?"

Katie Abrams, the server who worked this shift, was old enough to be any of their mothers, even by the less demanding standards we had out here in Pokeville. Or Pokeyville, as we locals who had a love-hate relationship with the slow-paced small town, called it. Katie said she liked working games because the men tipped really well if their team won, and if they lost, they got quietly, morosely drunk to ease their pain, so it was fine for her either way.

"Overtime, huh?" Daphne said, and pushed me against the side of the building. She had my jeans unbuttoned in about five seconds and had her hand inside my boxers quicker than that. "Then we better hurry. Won't the first score win?"

I didn't have the heart to tell her that wasn't precisely the rule. Or to interfere with her intentions.

❖

Next morning, I met Lena at the stop sign the way I did most school days whenever I was in town. I knew part of my compulsion to check on her was because she was exactly the age I'd been when my world had fallen apart. "How's it hanging, kiddo?"

Daphne's eight-year-old daughter was the sweetest baby butch in town, and it was a matter of great interest to me as to whether the ugly duckling was going to suddenly swan on us or if this "phase" was something her momma was gonna have to take to Jesus. If Lena ever stopped grinning at my manly greetings, I'd know the swan had emerged. "Hey, Max. Still hanging loose. How you been?"

And I would be deeply sorry if this amiable youngster ever entered that two-word-maximum teenage mumbling stage, but I wasn't sure she would. She wasn't bubbly by any means, but she had a happy-go-lucky way about her that most people liked. Her natural sweetness hadn't been soured by the world yet, and I hadn't been lying about caring for her. Two of the older girls joined us as we walked toward the Pokeville School complex. Normally, high school kids wouldn't be caught dead talking to some elementary punk, but like I said, everyone liked Lena.

"Y'all been working on that history project?" Lena asked, and both girls grimaced.

The dreaded semester project was a rite of passage for every sophomore who had the luck or bad fortune—which depended on what kind of student they were—to draw Mrs. Blanchard for American History. The only thing closeted about me during high school was that I actually liked history. In fact, I'd liked almost every subject because I'd enjoyed learning. If something fired my imagination, I'd dig into it, reading until I'd satisfied my curiosity. My project on "The Three Most Important Supreme Court Decisions" had caused Mrs. Blanchard to look at me a little differently for the rest of the year.

'Course, I'd looked at her differently too after sophomore year, when I'd happened to see her dancing with Miss Harper at a gay bar about seventy-five miles away. Miss Harper taught freshman English, and I'd been captivated by her smoky voice reading the love scenes in *Romeo and Juliet* with an intensity that seemed powerfully real. "Deny thy father and refuse thy name. Or, if thou wilt not, be but sworn my love, and I'll no longer be a Capulet."

As soon as I'd confirmed to my astounded eyes that Miss Harper was not a Montague, and Miss Blanchard wasn't a Capulet, but rather, both were members of my church—so to speak—I'd left. Young as I was, I'd still known there were about a million reasons for them not to know I'd seen them, and not one good one why I should have sidled up and said howdy. Besides, I had some idea of myself as a potential heartbreaker, not as a heart attack giver. I'd wondered then how it would be to live in a part-time, secret relationship. Now I knew exactly how it felt.

"I'll bet you've already decided what your high school history project will be," I said to Lena, who nodded enthusiastically.

She shared my love of learning and had gotten a healthy dose of her mom's brains as well. "I want to write about how women are discriminated against in politics." She looked at me anxiously. "Will you help me with my research?"

My heart swelled at being included in her plans seven years away. "Sure, kid. I'd be honored."

She smirked and bumped me with her shoulder. "Oh yeah. Just what you want to spend some evening doing."

"Actually, if your mom will make her chicken and dumplings, I'll read, edit, proof, and submit it for you."

Lena looked down. "My mom and dad had another fight the other night."

Poor kid. "You gotta stay out of it, Lee," I said, using the butch nickname I'd given her. "The stuff that your folks go through doesn't have anything to do with you. Trust me on this."

She didn't look up. "Yeah, you've told me that before. But I think this one was about you."

Shit. "Well, maybe I won't come by for chicken and dumplings. Maybe I'll read over your paper at Nan's," I offered, referencing the only coffee shop and bakery in town as I ruffled her short hair. "It's no big deal, kid. It'll probably blow over before I'm home from my next run."

"You really think so?" She beamed with hope.

Time for big lie number two thousand four hundred and fifty-one. "Yep, I do."

"When will you be home?"

"In less than a month. What's your class working on now?"

"World geography," she said with a skip. "I want to do my report on China. Daddy said they're Commies, and I should do someplace else, but I think the Chinese people are interesting. Did you know they built a wall you can see from space?"

Had I mentioned that I genuinely liked this kid? "Do what interests you, dude. That way, it won't feel like work at all." By now, we were within two blocks of the school, and there were more kids on the sidewalks. That Lena was still willing to walk with me made me feel like I maintained a modicum of cool.

Giving her a little shove, I said, "Go on. I'll check with you as soon as I get back to town."

"Thanks, Max." We did our special handshake, and she darted off.

❖

Denver had always been one of my favorite runs, and now that it was a four-lane almost all the way, it was a cakewalk. I'd gotten everything packed the night before, so after my fifty-point pre-check, I went into Etta's Place for a jumbo coffee to-go. Daphne worked the register part-time. I used to cringe at the sight. With all that she had to offer, she should have been a lawyer or a teacher or something more… challenging. But once, after I'd fussed at her about her career choice, she'd told me, "Look, I've made peace with it, and you should too. Don't you have something else to worry about?"

So I'd let it go. The ability to do that was pretty high up in my skill set.

"You off?" she asked, casually waving my hand away as I reached for my wallet.

"Yeah. I'll call you in a few weeks when I'm back."

"Better let me call you." Her voice was tight, and it made me look at her more closely. There were dark circles under her uncharacteristically puffy hazel eyes.

"Why don't you come with me?" I blurted, surprising myself. "Denver's fine this time of year, and the aspen trees should have nice color. There might even be a dusting of snow on the mountains."

For a long moment, I thought she might actually say yes. Her gaze drifted to the window of the truck stop, and I knew she could see the purple cab of my eighteen-wheeler. She'd always talked about wanting to travel, but I knew for a fact she'd never been anywhere more glamorous than Dallas. Not like Denver was all that sensational, but it would be new for her.

She shook her head like she was trying to clear it, and the way she answered told me she'd truly given it some thought. "I can't, Max. My life may be shit, but this is where I live it."

I wanted to give her a long hug. I wasn't in love with Daphne anymore, but she knew me like no one else, and though she wouldn't admit it, I knew her too. Because of that, I understood that anything physical was out of the question if she was hurting. Instead, I searched for something that might make her laugh. "Well, you know what they say." She swallowed, and her face returned to its usual, slightly contemptuous expression as she waited. "The grass may be greener on the other side, but at least you don't have to mow it."

"Hey, baby, I'll mow your grass anytime."

I hadn't realized anyone was standing behind me, but I knew that voice right away. Striker Douglass, total jerkwad and the bane of all womankind. He was certain women adored him, especially when he talked dirty or used what he considered clever innuendoes, while being completely oblivious to the fact that often, like now, his verbal repartee made no sense.

Predictably, he hated me, not only because of his knee-jerk homophobia but also because there were those women who would smile at me while completely ignoring his incompetent attempts at seduction. My aspiration to whittle him into a toothpick with a dull blade was barely mitigated by the fact that Striker was a foot taller and at least a hundred pounds heavier than I was. But at least I could best him intellectually.

"Back off, micro phallus, this is a private conversation."

While he was translating my insult, Daphne leaned over and kissed me on the cheek, an unusually affectionate gesture, which probably meant she'd been touched by my offer. "You keep it between the ditches," she said, telling me to be careful with some trucker slang I'd taught her.

"Hey." Striker must have given up on the translation. "I never get a good-bye kiss."

"You might if you'd ever leave," I suggested. "Because 'some cause happiness wherever they go; others, whenever they go.'" I knew Daphne would recognize Oscar Wilde's quote, even if he never would, and I saw her fighting a smirk as I turned for the door.

His attention switched to me as I'd hoped. "Shut up, you fucking dyke."

"You're really stupid, Striker, if you think 'fucking dyke' is an insult. One, I am a dyke. Two, I'm sure I've been fucking more often and with more skill than you ever have, so it's simply a very accurate description."

Apparently having exhausted his verbal ammunition, he made a move in my direction with a fist raised, and I went through the door quickly. I could hear Daphne's strictest tone behind me. "Striker Douglass, I'm calling the cops if you go out that door without paying me."

Okay, yeah, I still loved Daphne, just a little.

❖

Some people gave me a funny look along with an echo after I told them what I did. *A truck driver?* While I admit to having used the phrase "mobile independent contractor" if I thought it would help with a seduction, I claimed the occupation with pride. And I loved doing it. True, there were parts that sucked, like any job, but rolling with a full tank and an open road, I was totally free, and it was hard to beat that feeling.

Plus, I had a really sweet deal as an independent. Because I owned my own custom cab and trailer, I could decide when, where, and how much I hauled. I'd been at it long enough that I'd gotten my schedule pretty well set with repeat customers, room for some freelance for a bigger outfit like United Furniture, if I wanted. Besides being in control of my own hours and weeks of work, what made this process even sweeter for me was my truck. I called her Nephthys—pronounced *neff thiss*—after the Egyptian goddess of death, service, lamentation, nighttime, and rivers. For those who thought it was odd to name a truck after such a deity, they didn't know the whole story:

I had my ninth birthday in the hospital while my skull fracture healed. But after my release, my dad, John Terrell—or JT, as everyone called him, me included—and I had done just fine on our own. That Mom was out of the picture was more than okay with me. JT was the best mechanic in town, so it didn't matter that he'd changed his hours over the years to accommodate the schedule of his daughter for the Odyssey of the Mind team or the second lead in the high school musical or the bench-riding soccer player. He probably liked it best, though, once I became his second mechanic. Folks likely thought it sad that he hadn't lived to see his daughter the truck driver, but if he hadn't died, that might not have ever happened.

He'd been pushing me about college, but we'd finally come to an understanding that I simply wasn't ready to spend four more years cooped up in a classroom. I intended to go. Only not yet. He'd suggested the military, but I wasn't real keen on taking orders every minute of the day. Usually, he was patient about letting me figure things out for myself, especially the stupid things, but for the months leading to my graduation, he'd seemed frustrated that we hadn't reached any conclusion on the newly urgent topic, "What will Max do next?" Granted, most of our conversations were cut short, either by a senior activity or by a phone call from some helpless sap whose car wouldn't start.

Over the years, I'd learned that when JT got upset, he'd turn on the tube and watch PBS. Oh, he was also a sports guy, but the soothing or informative tone of the narrators on Channel 13 seemed to enthrall him, and pretty soon, he'd forget what troubled him. In mid-April of my senior year—class of 2001!—it registered that he was regularly sleeping in his recliner as I'd tiptoe past on my way to bed. Where was the fun in breaking curfew if your infraction didn't get noticed? And our breakfast conversations had no longer included discussions on PBS topics like the mating habits of the spiny lobster or the history of ship building in Portugal, suggesting he wasn't really paying attention to his programs anymore.

Finally pulling my head out of my typical, self-absorbed teenage ass, I'd become aware that he'd taken more afternoons off for "appointments," and there'd been more leftovers than usual. He'd bought a new suit, "for Easter," he'd said, which was weird because neither of us was the least bit religious, and I'd wondered if something in the cut of it made him look smaller.

That night, after I'd eased past his sleeping form, I snuck into his bathroom, and the number of pill bottles on the counter had twisted my guts into a knot of fright. I'd woken him, and we'd had a long talk about what he was going to do after I finished high school.

As it turned out, he'd gotten increasingly sick after the summer was over and had died a little more than a year after my graduation. The funeral was on a miserably hot day, and I'd pretended it was sweat and not tears running down my face. Daphne couldn't have been the only one who knew better about that.

My dad and I had lived comfortably. The house we'd moved into after my hospital stay was modest, but the neighborhood was nice. JT had never said, "We don't have the money for that," but I had never asked for crazy stuff like a pony or a prom dress. He'd traded some off-hours work for my motorcycle, and we'd rebuilt it together. With no plans for college, I didn't fill out the FAFSA form, so I'd never seen his tax returns, which meant I'd had no opportunity to know how well he'd invested or how much he'd saved.

When the office of Mr. Vittum, JT's lawyer, had wanted to set an appointment for the reading of the will a few days after the funeral, I'd told them I wasn't ready. The next week, Ed Vittum himself had called. I'd told him to go ahead with whatever he needed to do, and we could talk after probate. He'd hesitated for a few seconds before telling me that would be fine.

Right then, everyone was being nice. For a while, it seemed like casseroles and hams filled every shelf in the fridge, and pies and cookies were on every surface of the kitchen and the dining room. At my request, the hospice nurse had continued dropping by about every other day to take stuff to other families in her care until everything was eaten or had gone moldy.

After she'd stopped coming and the cards and phone calls tapered off, I'd have these weird bursts of energy where I'd obsess about alphabetizing the pantry items or vacuuming the carpeted part of the house for days in a row. In between, I watched TV, although I was very picky about my choices. No sports, PBS, or fucking Hallmark Channel. Most game shows were safe, as long as the winners didn't get all emotional and bring their families onto the stage. I felt like I was waiting for something, even something besides probate. Like there was evidence that had been overlooked or some sign that was forthcoming. A warning. A direction. This restless anticipation would keep me awake if I didn't drink, so I began drinking every night, though I was careful not to start until it was 5:00 o'clock somewhere.

I hadn't been at it for too long the evening that Daphne had knocked on my door.

CHAPTER TWO

2002
Age Twenty

We hadn't spoken for well over a year, since Lena was still a baby, and our last parting had been very unpleasant. I knew Daphne had visited JT at the cancer treatment center over in Clearmore a few times when I wasn't there. Somehow, her perfume would transcend the smells of antiseptic and illness, lingering just long enough to offend me before it vanished. After they'd sent him home, she'd mailed him cards or little notes every so often, and the sight of her handwriting on the envelope had infuriated me to the point that I had to break something, like a bottle in the recycling bin or some tree branches that had fallen in a recent storm. Two can play at this game, I'd decided, and had bought a set of small thank-you cards. Whenever something arrived from her, I'd print an overused or mundane phrase and send it by return mail. "Your kindness is greatly appreciated." "Thank you for your support during these difficult days." I'd never signed them because that would have made it real.

Before opening the door that night, I hadn't seen a live human in more than two weeks, and the sight of her made me close my eyes for a few seconds. I'd been unable to tolerate the somber expressions of people I'd run into if I went out. What reason did they have to be sad? I was his only kin. I was the one who'd lost him. I was the one who knew how wonderful he was. So I'd been holed up for a couple of months, paying the neighbor kid a few bucks a week to bring over stuff from the Sav-Mor.

When I looked again and Daphne was still there, I chose anger as my opening salvo. "I don't want to see you."

"I know you don't. But there's someone here who wants to see you. She wants to show you something. Then we'll leave."

Besides being angry, I was in a morose mood where I truly didn't want to feel better. I didn't want to see anything compassionate or sweet or enjoyable. I had reached a slightly buzzed stage of wallowing, and it was comfortably miserable there. "No," I said, but Lena peeked around her mother's side.

"Here, Max," she said clearly and held out a scribbled drawing. There were three heads with ovals for bodies, one much shorter than the other two.

"Wow," I breathed, remembering a promise I'd made to myself: no matter what was between Daphne and me, I wouldn't let it hurt this child. "Who made this beautiful picture?" I tried to bend to her level but swayed until Daphne caught me by the shoulders and propped me against the doorway.

"Me!" Lena said as Daphne assessed the extent of my drunkenness.

"So will we be invited in, or is this to be a threshold art critique?"

Her movement had been accompanied by a rustling sound and an incredibly mouth-watering aroma. At another glance, I saw a big handled bag weighed down with what looked like casserole dishes. My stomach growled loudly, and Lena giggled. "Uh…" I turned carefully and looked around. The house seemed surprisingly clean, so I gestured them in. "Sure."

After getting a nod from her mother, Lena tottered confidently into the room. My mouth opened a little. "She's growing."

"I see your powers of observation are as keen as ever," Daphne pronounced wryly.

I turned to her, my resentment returning. "Why are you here?" I demanded. I didn't want this. I didn't want her back in my life. I didn't want to see Lena and be reminded of how much I missed her.

"We were bored with eating at home, so we brought our dinner over here. There's plenty if you'd like some, but don't feel obliged." She lowered her voice. "But if you want to interact with Lena, please stop drinking until we leave. We don't have alcohol at our house anymore, and I think the smell of it upsets her."

I'd truly been out of the loop on town gossip if I'd missed the news that Bill Polk was on the wagon. We stared at each other for several seconds until her expression turned my antagonism into a slight feeling of embarrassment. "Please excuse me for a moment," I said finally, my voice sounding stiff even to myself.

"Certainly," she replied in the same tone. "We'll be in the kitchen if you don't mind."

"Fine," I said over my shoulder. One look in my bathroom mirror confirmed my fears. I looked like shit. Mindful that a shower would take too long, I did the best I could. Face washed, hair combed, I gargled and brushed my teeth thoroughly.

As I was coming down the hall toward the kitchen, I heard Daphne talking softly. "And remember, we're not going to talk about her daddy, okay?"

A sharp gash of pain shot through my chest, taking my breath away. I leaned against the wall, unable to stop the flood of thoughts that I'd been successfully avoiding for the past several days. *My father is gone. He's never coming back. He's dead. I have no one. I'm alone.* Daphne must have heard my wheezing attempt to resume breathing because she said, "Oh shit."

"No-no, Mama," Lena said disapprovingly.

I turned and staggered back into my bedroom. I'd cried like this once before, twelve years ago after I'd arrived at the hospital in bloody agony and heartsick horror. Now, I couldn't seem to stop sobbing despite Daphne stroking my back. She didn't shush me or tell me it would be all right, but I wanted to shake away her touch because it felt good, and there shouldn't have been anything good left in the world.

I cried until I threw up into the wastebasket she held for me. Afterward, I turned my face away, trying to get control of my breathing and deliberating how I could nicely ask her to go. Lena's small voice asked, "Max is sick?"

Daphne answered, "Yes, honey. Max is a little bit sick. But she'll be okay."

No, I thought. That's not true.

Daphne continued, "Did you finish your dinner?" Lena must have nodded because Daphne said, "Can you wait five minutes for dessert?"

Lena must have edged closer into the room. I could hear her more clearly. "Max be okay?"

I wanted to tell her no. I wanted to say I'd never be better. But how could I say that to a child, even if it was true? Didn't they need to believe, at least for a few years, in a world where there was love and healing and happiness, though it might be so fleeting they'd better not blink?

I groaned, and Daphne said, "Let's go get Max some water. I bet that will make her feel better."

I was sitting on the side of the bed when she returned, but I didn't look at her. I heard her put the glass on the nightstand. "We're going to have our dessert before we go. Lena would be thrilled if you could join us, but I'll understand if you don't."

I couldn't manage a response. After a time, I heard dishes clinking, followed by the sound of the dishwasher door. Bags rustling. Lena's voice again, "Bye bye, Max." She sounded almost as sad as I felt.

Suddenly, I was desperate to see them. I needed to be around life, even if it hurt. "Wait," I called. The sounds stopped. I realized my throat was raw, and I'd only made a croaking sound.

"Did you say something?" Daphne asked.

I swallowed. That was a nasty experience, but I repeated, "Wait a minute, please."

There was a murmur of conversation. "May we turn on your television?"

I took a sip of the water. "Yes. Help yourself." Returning to the bathroom, I wasn't surprised to find I looked worse than before. I repeated all my preparations from earlier, but it didn't help much. I heard Lena laugh and trusted that would be enough.

❖

I saw them once or twice a week after that, usually at my house but occasionally out somewhere. Daphne's home held a problematic history, but Lena's presence made us both happy. I started going by my dad's shop each week, but it was hard to stay around for long. JT's longtime friend Pete was running things now, and he always had such a woeful expression when he saw me. But on my third visit, there was an eighteen-wheeler rumbling out front, and since we didn't normally do diesel work, I was curious about it. The driver's name was Josh, and we exchanged pleasantries for a few moments. He seemed different from the good ol' boys I generally met at Etta's Place. He was soft-spoken but articulate and didn't look askance at me the way strangers sometimes did. He told me that he had known my dad and had come by to offer his condolences.

I bit my lip really hard and kept my head down as I nodded. Josh told me they'd met at Etta's, and JT had found him two cheap replacement tires after hearing that he had passed on a job trying to get home to see his new baby girl. From the things he said, I got the sense that he was a lot like my dad, the kind of man I missed having in my life. I wanted to hear him talk a little more, so I asked him to tell me about his work. He smiled, his eyes shimmering with contagious devotion, and an hour later, I had the names of three truck driving schools in the area and the promise of another ride around during his next pass.

Now that I had a mission, the days seemed to pass more smoothly. Three months later, we'd gone through probate, and I was in the lawyer's office for the reading of the will. By then, I knew that Daphne and Bill were in counseling together in the next town over, and she simply couldn't miss their appointments, though I had all but begged her to. That meant it was just me, sitting in a big leather chair, sipping my first Pellegrino, finding out that I was a millionaire. One million, six hundred thousand and change, Mr. Vittum said, when I'd asked him to repeat it.

Apparently, he said a bunch of other stuff too, about financial planning and tax issues. The main thing I remembered was, "This kind of money changes people."

That snapped me out of my fog of disbelief. "I'm not gonna change."

He shook his head somewhat sadly. "I'm not talking about you, Max. I'm talking about it changing the way other people act toward you. You may find that even your best friends won't see you the same way anymore."

Having read a couple of stories about the misery of former lottery winners, I believed him. That was why I decided never to tell anyone, including Daphne. But contemplating it gave me a sense of freedom that was both exhilarating and frightening. I still liked the idea of driving, feeling like it would ease my restlessness, so I let everyone else in town think that I'd used insurance money for my training fee. School-wise, I chose Lubbock because I had some fantasy about cruising the campus of Texas Tech for hot student bodies in my spare time.

In reality, spare time was pretty hard to come by, and the one day I spent at the campus, things turned out way different than I'd imagined.

❖

2003
Age Twenty-one

It was a fall afternoon, which in Texas meant it was still moderately warm. I'd been exploring the Tech campus for about an hour, checking out the dining halls, the University Center building, and the library like any potential student might. What finally caught my eye was a group of sorority girls going through some very enticing stretching exercises on the edge of a playing field. They wore matching silver shirts and blue shorts, and I'd been watching long enough to have started an exceedingly nice fantasy when I was distracted by a slight buzzing sound. I frowned and heard a throat clear before the droning turned into words, but all I could make out after the hum was, "...are you?"

"What?" I'd been actively imagining a scene featuring me as a strict RA, disciplining a naughty undergrad. What could I say? I loved the classics. My annoyance grew as someone who was evidently the queen of the nerds stepped into my field of vision, blocking my view of the two most voluptuous girls.

"I asked if you were a Tri Delt," she repeated.

"I'll try pretty much anything as long as it doesn't involve dick," I answered.

The queen blinked, and from the group behind her, I heard a few gasps and a somewhat muffled laugh. Thinking the laugher might at least be sympathetic to my loveless plight, I looked over the newcomers, but I almost couldn't distinguish one girl from another.

They were all wearing the same yellow shirt with a black stripe—probably where I got the bee idea—and their hair was mostly brown and straight, parted down the middle and pulled back. From the midst of them, a more well-built gal with shorter, reddish hair, stepped out and asked, "Are you GDI?"

I grinned, hoping for a kindred spirit. "I think I'm SOL, if you wanna know the truth."

No one laughed, and the queen took over again. "Let me try to explain," she said, and I could imagine her using those words regularly to whatever clueless lab partner or study buddy she'd been assigned. "We're short a player, and we'll have to forfeit if we can't get one more. We can only recruit people who aren't participating in the university's Greek system. And a forfeit means we have to spend the evening doing chores for those Tri Delts."

Everyone groaned a variety of lamentations, including, "They're so mean," and "I've got a paper to finish, test to study for, early class tomorrow."

"So you want me to play football for your team?" I wasn't really that dense, but I was getting into the act. The queen nodded. "Against them?" I pointed across the field. More nodding. "Is it tackle?" The idea of wrapping my arms around a tapered waist, bringing a long-legged beauty to the ground where I'd be prone with her—even for a few seconds—had definite appeal.

The short-haired gal spoke again. "It's flag football." She pointed to a belt she'd wrapped around her waist. Velcroed to it were two dangling strips, one on either side.

I amended my fantasy, placing myself—the strict RA—on one team and the wanton temptress on the other. Enthralled by this vision, I almost forgot that the bees were waiting for my response. I cleared my throat and said, "Sure, I'll play."

"But you're not in a sorority, right?" the queen was obviously one of those by-the-book types.

I shook my head. "No time. I'm in the International TDS program, and it's all I can do to keep up with their curriculum." They didn't need to know I was attending the Nationwide Truck Driving School.

The queen looked me over, and I could hear a little murmur from the rest of the swarm. "Oh," she finally said. I was certain there would be some extensive research on that name before the evening was done.

"Here." The auburn-haired gal, who had a nice face in addition to not being a toothpick like the rest of them, handed me a jersey. I stripped off my Indigo Girls T-shirt and pulled on the bee outfit to the sound of embarrassed chuckles. I was wearing a sports bra, but immodesty was clearly not a trait of this group.

"Who plays what position?" I asked, stretching a bit. I'd been doing a fair amount of sitting on my ass lately, and I didn't want to pull a muscle and embarrass myself right off. Although, one of the sexy Tri Delts might be in nursing...

"Trillian usually throws the ball." The queen pointed at the non-toothpick. "And the rest of us try to catch it."

"Uh-huh. And who's your best receiver?" I asked, feeling like I might find a place among the nerdy bees after all.

"Olivia caught one once. And Coraline did too."

"I almost did," piped up an eager-looking bee who struck me as the sexy librarian type. Without the sexy, though.

"What's your name?" I asked her, trying to be polite.

"Persephone."

So far, I had Thrill, Olive, Cora, and Perry. There was no way I was going to remember the rest of them. "Turn around," I said. Thankfully, they all had numbers I could refer to, although some included decimals. A guy wearing a striped shirt swaggered onto the field and blew a whistle. The queen went out for a parlay with the glamour girls, and I turned to Thrill. "Can you really throw a pass?"

She gave me an intriguing half-smile. "Can you really catch one?"

"Yeah, I can. Do y'all ever run plays or just..." I made a series of moves intending to represent how a freaked-out person would act if a bee was flying around their head.

She snorted a laugh and nodded. "More like that. A small group of us tried to design plays once, but it didn't work out."

"Too many cooks?" I suggested, and she nodded again, gesturing at the queen, who was pointing in my direction. The hotties were giving me the once-over, so I did a bodybuilder pose. They laughed and turned to each other, whispering behind their hands as they walked off the field.

"Tell her you'll only play if you can be in charge during the game," Thrill urged. "Otherwise, we spend all our time in the huddle arguing about what to do and then we..." She made the same bee-around-your head gesture.

"Good idea." I nudged her lightly with my shoulder. "Thanks, Thrill."

She blushed, and I noticed she had a sweet sprinkle of freckles on her nose. Cute.

The queen accepted my conditions and told us we had the ball first. I squatted and drew lines in the dirt. "Olive, you run a shallow cross to the right. Cora, go about fifteen yards and run an out to the left. Perry, you run a buttonhook at about ten yards. The rest of you, try getting in the way of one of them." I looked at Thrill. "I'm gonna be running a skinny post. Can you throw it that far?"

"We'll see," she answered.

The other girls were studying the dirt as if memorizing the solutions to humanity's most challenging questions. "Not much into commitment, are you, Thrill?" I elbowed her as the two of us made our way onto the field.

She looked at me earnestly, and I noticed that her light green eyes had a touch of brown in them. Almost the opposite of Daphne's. "I could be. If I met the right woman." We looked at each other, and for a moment, I felt like I was on a first date. She was decidedly intriguing. And when she licked her lips, attraction sparked between us.

I gave her an easy grin. "Let's see if our passes connect."

She underthrew me slightly on the post, but I jumped over the shoulder of the babe who was trying to guard me, made the catch, and bounced over into the end zone. The bees swarmed around me, screaming like we'd won the Super Bowl. I quickly learned they hadn't scored a single point in the last two years of intramurals.

As I was dusting myself off, the Tri-Deezy sneered at me. "I didn't know it was bring your own butch day."

"You should pick one up," I suggested, tossing her the ball. "We're available at finer dive bars everywhere."

In my new fantasy, the RA's won handily, but the actual game got pretty ugly by the second half. The hotties put enough people around me that both Perry and Olive had a catch, but running afterward hadn't been a part of my instructions, so that part didn't go too well, especially when Olive ran in the wrong direction until Thrill stopped her. One girl tripped me twice as I was running my pattern, so the third time I ran in her direction, instead of making a cut, I headed straight for her. She backed up so fast that she tripped over her own feet. After the whistle, I helped her up, saying, "Why'd you run? From the way you play, I thought you liked getting close to me." She rolled her eyes, but I held her hand for an extra few seconds, watching color come to her cheeks. Coverage got a little looser after that.

Defensively, the bees hadn't quite grasped the concept of getting in someone's way as they grabbed for a flag. We worked on it, but then Cora's glasses got knocked off and she lost a nose pad, and things went south in a hurry. I didn't know the final score, but I did detect that my halftime pep talk on taunting opened a door to creativity that the bees seemed to really enjoy.

"Keep your hands off me, you cane toad," Thrill snarled as some tall chick tried to push past her to run a pass pattern. She was truly attractive when she got riled up.

"I'm monitoring the seventh answer in the simplest Fibonacci series," Olive instructed as the hotties tried to confuse us with motion. Okay, not exactly a taunt but a flaunt, at least.

Following the babes' final touchdown on the next to the last play of the game, one of them confronted our queen: "Looks like your walk-on butch didn't help much, Princess Leia."

The queen bee was actually named Leia? As in *Star Wars*? Thinking of the years of merciless playground bullying she must have endured, I tried not to grimace, but our girl made me proud. "Somewhere out there is a tree, tirelessly producing oxygen so you can breathe." Leia managed to look haughty, despite being completely disheveled. "I think you owe it an apology."

Mercifully, the game ended, and I tried to talk the bees into going for a beer, but they were busy discussing their assignments and tests and papers. I gathered that this group was mostly very serious seniors, most of whom were working toward graduating Summa Cum Laude.

"Trillian," I called as I watched my best chance walking away. "Not even Madagascar?" I was hoping to change her mind by referencing a line used by the character named Trillian from *The Hitchhikers Guide to the Galaxy*, a book I had read and enjoyed in high school.

She gave me a knowing smile, and my stomach did a quick twist. "I thought you'd be too busy with your International TDS work, Kim." Somewhere along the line, I'd told them my name was Kim, playing incognito, certain I'd never see any of them again.

"I've already worked ahead enough to have this evening off. That's why I could play." I gestured at the field. "It was fun, wasn't it?" Kinda pathetic, but I'd have taken a pity fuck at this point.

"Where are you from, Kim?" she asked. She seemed to be genuinely interested. Plus, I could tell by her accent and the way she phrased the question that she was a Texas gal too, so I wouldn't have to be embarrassed at my small-town roots.

"I'm from Pokeville. It's about ninety miles from here."

She was already nodding. "I know exactly where that is. I've driven past there often on my way to Vernon."

I laughed. "Why would you be going to Vernon?"

"That's where my grandparents live."

"What about you?" I asked, wishing we were sitting somewhere with a brew between us so I could really turn on the charm.

"Tell me more about your International TDS work," Trillian countered, crossing her arms. "I'm curious."

I tried to think of a way to translate what I was actually doing into something that sounded collegiate. "Right now, I'm working on analysis of a particular shipping situation that involves safety issues concerning weight and balance."

"Trying to create leverage for the tandems to take a little weight off the drive axles?"

My mouth dropped open. That was the correct answer to one of two questions I'd missed on yesterday's quiz. At my truck driving school.

"I'm from here, Kim," Trillian continued. "In fact, we live about three miles from the Nationwide Truck Driving School. My dad's a former trucker, and he was an instructor there before he retired." She cocked her head, unsmiling. "Nice bluff, though."

"Look, Trillian, let me buy you a beer, and I can—"

She shook her head. "I meant what I told you about commitment. That's what it takes for me. I'm not interested in someone who's here today and gone tomorrow and lying about it the whole time. Kim."

I puzzled over the sarcastic tone she'd used on my fake name until I realized I'd put my shirt on inside out. Daphne had the habit of borrowing my T-shirts for yard work, and once Lena got ahold of them, I'd never get them back, so I'd written my initials on the tag inside the collar in permanent marker. M.T. Just the way I felt right now. Empty.

"I'm sorry," I said faintly, but she was already into the shadows, and I couldn't tell if she'd heard me or not. Like it matters, I tried to tell myself, switching over my shirt as I walked.

I heard laughter from the porch of the nearest building and realized I was in front of a sorority house. Across the doorway, three triangles, the Greek letter Delta, indicated these were my opponents from the game. The hotties. Sure enough, one of them called, "Who are you flashing out there? Don't tell me you struck out with the nerds?"

It was the girl I'd scored on at the very start of the game. I angled toward them. "Yeah, as a matter of fact, I did." I put on my most confident expression. "Guess they're not as smart as they think they are."

The girl and her buddy laughed hysterically. I could see several empty beer cans lying around. I changed my angle to a direct approach. "You wouldn't have an extra one of those for a vanquished foe, would you?"

They laughed some more and waved me over. Soon, I was alternating shoulder rubs on the two of them. Untold numbers of beer later, when all but those same two had staggered off into the house, I was led to Ashley and Amanda's room. Sometime during our encounter, I switched beds, having no clue as to which girl was which. I didn't think it mattered one bit, though, because we were all getting what we wanted. They got their college experience with a woman, and I got my pity fuck. Perfect, right?

Chapter Three

2003
Age Twenty-one

As it turned out, the best thing about choosing the Lubbock school was that I got to meet Zelda Butler. She was one of those grizzled ol' gals of indeterminate age who Daphne would have said was "rode hard and put away wet." She was an instructor who made an impression from the first day, telling us, "I know some of you got a romanticized, 'modern-day cowboy' image in your head about this life. But driving a truck was among the most hazardous occupations in the United States last year, according to the government's latest workplace fatality census. Thirteen hundred and ten driver deaths, three thousand nine hundred and thirty-five passenger vehicle occupants."

It had gotten quiet enough to hear the squeak of her marker as she wrote the numbers on the whiteboard behind her.

"And do you know why?" No one spoke. She continued, putting more numbers on the board. "Because you'll be sitting atop fifteen-plus gallons of oil and between one hundred and twenty-five to three hundred gallons of gas, in an 80,000-pound vehicle that takes forty percent more time to stop than a car." She underlined the forty percent.

Turning to face us, she asked, "Any of you ever had a close call where you barely managed to brake hard enough to avoid an accident? Or maybe what could have been something more serious ended up as only a fender bender 'cause you had slowed enough before you hit?" Obviously, enough heads besides mine nodded because she went on.

"Now add another forty percent on there. Wouldn't you be fried to a crisp if you hit someone carrying that much fuel?"

I swallowed. Dying in a fire was the death I feared most, which was kinda weird because I should have been afraid of water after what had happened to my brother Adam when I was a kid. But the thought of burning to death made me shudder. I hadn't put that possibility together with my newly chosen profession.

"So this talk about safety, cautioning you against certain behaviors and reminding you about others, take it to heart." She dropped the marker into the tray below the board. "I've already been to two funerals this year." She motioned to Chuck, who moved around and began his speech, outlining our schedule for the next seven weeks.

I tried to be objective and not give Zelda extra points because she was a woman and looked like a lesbian, but she really did know her stuff. Even the guys—the ones who were serious about learning and not into macho bullshit—tended to gravitate toward her during demos or stayed after class to ask her questions. She didn't cut anyone any slack, including me, the only other female in the room who always sat up front and smiled every chance she got. I wasn't trying to get her to sleep with me, mind you, I was simply making sure I stayed on the teacher's good side.

I guess I was lucky that there was just one genuine asshole in the class—Martin—and one instructor who was clearly opposed to women drivers. Wade was tougher to deal with because he was the one who gave points on certain exercises, and those scores could potentially affect whether or not I graduated. His way of discouraging me was to constantly put his hands on me in either threatening or inappropriate ways. At first, I thought he was trying to gauge if I was easily rattled, but after four or five instances, I wondered if my lack of reaction had made him think I might be into it. The next time I saw him walk through the break room, I made a point of raising my voice as I mentioned my make-believe girlfriend to the guys sitting around my table. Martin glared at me and left, muttering something about "perverts," but the rest of the guys pretty much took it in stride, and we ended up talking about women for the rest of our lunchtime. But Wade continued his groping at every opportunity. Speculating that he was combining his disapproval with an opportunity to get a free feel, I began knocking his hand away or turning so that it would be blatantly obvious what he was doing.

This only seemed to spur him on, so I resorted to my smartass personality. "Not getting any at home, Wade?"

He looked at me with his eyes flat. "What are you talking about, Terrell? If you don't feel capable of completing this assignment, I'll have to—"

"Maybe I need clarification on exactly what the assignment entails, Wade. Because if offering my tits to rub against your arm is part of it, I frankly don't see the connection between that and a pre-trip inspection."

His face flushed red. "Get out of the vehicle, Terrell. You're done for today."

Determined to make him move enough that he wouldn't brush against me again, I jabbed him hard in the gut with my elbow, mildly satisfied when I heard a grunt. As I stormed across the lot toward our classroom building, I heard Kevin call, "Where you off to in such a hurry, Max?"

"The nearest bar," I yelled as I saw Zelda's head come around.

I wanted to go to a gay bar, but I hadn't done any research on Lubbock yet. I rode my bike past the pay-by-the-week motel where I was staying to the first place I saw with a lit Budweiser sign. There were five or six guys already at the counter, so I took a booth, hoping to avoid any more unwelcome offers. I wanted a drink, and that was it. After two shots of bourbon and three beers, I was staring out the grimy window, about to decide that being a motorcycle rider in the circus would suit me fine, when someone slid into the seat across from me. I turned my head, my face fixed in a scowl, just as Zelda's face came into focus.

She pointed at the empties in front of me. "If you're gonna drink like that every time someone pisses you off, you're gonna end up dead or at AA."

"Not every time," I growled defensively. "Only if it's an asshole who gets to decide whether I drive or not." Maybe she disapproved of drinking in general.

Zelda signaled and the server came over. Shelly and I were already on a first-name basis. I was like that with servers. "Beer on tap. Not Coors. Whatever else is cheap," she ordered.

Shelly turned her gaze to me. "Something else for you, Max?"

I was tempted to order another shot but checked myself. "I'm okay for now."

While we were waiting, I filled Zelda in on the details of Wade's behavior and what I'd done, including today. She nodded occasionally as I spoke. Her beer came about the time I was winding down, and she took a long drink, finishing almost half of it. Okay, so not a lightweight.

"I learned to drive from my momma," she said after a minute. "She was probably one of four or five women on the road in her day. You should hear the stories she used to tell about how the men treated her before I got old enough to ride with her. And it wasn't but just a little better once I was along." She finished the remainder of her beer.

"How old were you?" I asked.

"Eight," she answered, and a smile creased her face. "I was homeschooled before homeschooling was cool."

Eight. The age I'd been when my mom…

Her voice put a stop to what would have been a very unpleasant recollection. I definitely didn't need to drink more if I was going there. "Momma died about three years ago. She hadn't driven in four decades, but her last words were, 'check the four-way flashers, Zelda.'"

I said, "Sorry," but she cut me off with a gesture.

"There ain't enough hours left before sunrise to bore you with all the things men have done to me since I was eight, though I know you were about to ask."

"I was." I tried to look sincere.

She lifted the right corner of her mouth. "I wanted to tell you that you're doing real good, and I think you'll make a fine driver. But you gotta find another way to handle Wade."

"Like?" I turned my palms up.

She looked out the grimy window. "When we had this problem before, the gal was a lot more…girly, so I'm frankly surprised that he's going after you."

"You figure I'm more your type?" I cocked my head, trying to show I was simply getting that issue out of the way.

She toyed with her empty mug, not meeting my eyes. "It got to where we had to get Mrs. Wade involved."

"There's a Mrs. Wade?"

"Oh yeah. A jealous Mrs. Wade."

"Really?"

She stood and reached for her wallet. I stood too, a little unsteadily, and put my hand on her arm, stopping her motion. "I got this."

She cocked her head. "Who died and left you rich?"

It was just something people said, but I froze. Between the stress over Wade and the liquor, my face must have shown more than I normally would have allowed. Zelda looked puzzled for a second, and then I guessed she replayed what she'd said and pulled me into a hug. "Oh shit, kid. I'm sorry. Me and my big mouth."

Maybe it was the roughness of her jacket or the fact that she was about the same height and had a wiry frame like JT. But something brought him so powerfully to my mind that it made me gasp. I followed with a shaky sound that was intended to be, "I'm fine," but when I heard myself, it made me burst into tears, something I hadn't done in many, many months.

She started walking me toward the door. "Give me a couple of waters to-go."

I didn't look, but I could hear the smile in Shelly's voice. "Sure thing, Zelda."

Apparently, I wasn't the only one who was good with servers.

❖

We sat in her car and talked for another three hours. I learned that her longtime "companion," Janey, had died a year after her mother, and Zelda still owned their place outside Isabell, Texas. Janey had been a schoolteacher, so she'd kept busy with that for nine months out of the year, riding with Zelda in the summers and during breaks. For years, they'd been regulars at the Dinah Shore Weekend in Palm Springs and at Women's Week in Provincetown, Massachusetts in the fall, two iconic events in lesbian life, neither of which I'd ever attended.

Zelda's voice cracked as she murmured that they'd had a real fine life for what she described as "a lot of years." She hadn't driven since Janey had passed, taking the first offer she'd gotten to teach at a driving school and was content for now to, "keep more fools from getting killed out there," and live in an unremarkable apartment near the school while she was teaching.

She looked at me like it was my turn, and I spilled some of my guts. Even though she was an instructor, my gut told me Zelda was trustworthy and nonthreatening. I talked about JT and hinted about insurance money. She nodded sympathetically. I'd have needed a whole lot more liquor if I was going to tell her about my mom and Adam, so I filled in the gaps with stories about Daphne and Lena. When the water was gone and we'd both yawned twice, she said, "Now, at school tomorrow—"

"This never happened. I'm cool, Zelda, I promise."

She turned her gray eyes on me for a solid minute. "I know that, Max. We wouldn't be sitting here if I didn't know that. What I was going to say is, I'll get you out of Wade's group for tomorrow only." I started to protest, but she stopped me with a raised hand. "You'll be tired and still a bit…sensitive, I'm thinking. After that, you're on your own. Deal?"

I shook with her and held on. "I'm not normally, I mean, I don't usually…"

"Yeah." She held up a single finger. Wait or a caution? "Don't be late tomorrow, Max."

"Thanks, Zelda."

She started her engine, and I opened the door. She looked out at my bike. "You be careful on that crotch rocket."

"Yes, ma'am."

❖

In spite of her telling me I'd be on my own, Zelda and I worked out one carefully choreographed moment for her to escort Mrs. Wade outside during her surprise visit. There, she got a clear look at the mister in action, and my troubles at NTDS were over. I insisted on taking her out to celebrate, and we began going somewhere once every week or so. We chose different bars on the other side of town where we weren't likely to run into anyone from the school, intending to avoid any question of favoritism or suggestive comments about something more personal.

We didn't have any other big, emotional talks, only easy chats sprinkled with her stories about life on the road and my contributions of amusing incidents during my high school years. I would never talk so candidly with a woman I was trying to go to bed with, but over time, I began to see Zelda as somewhere between a confidant and a mentor. She would occasionally make reference to something that she and Janey had done or planned to do. Those recollections got me thinking that maybe my life's ambition to be irresistible to as many women as possible might not be as satisfying as a long, committed relationship with a genuinely decent person who knew me completely and loved me anyway.

"How did you know?" I asked her once. "About Janey? What told you she was the one?"

She sighed, and her expression grew wistful. "You ever hear one of those big, fancy-made bells? One that rings with a tone that vibrates all the way inside you 'cause it's just so true? That's how you know. You meet someone who's the kind of right that vibrates inside you." She shot a meaningful look downward and added, "And I'm not talking about inside your pants, hotshot. I'm talking about inside your heart."

I was incredibly grateful for her friendship, and it dawned on me that she might be glad to have a friend too.

I'd done well in my driving classes, and the first few short runs went fine. I was feeling good about my career choice, but I was still incredibly nervous during my first long run, where I would drive real freight about thirty miles, deliver it to a dock, and return empty. Chuck was riding with me, and he wasn't given to conversation or any habit, like whistling, that might have put me at ease. But when a kid pumped a fist, making the "honk your horn" sign, I was reminded of all the times I'd done the same riding with JT on the familiar Highway 287. I remembered reading a funny bumper sticker: "I get paid to stare out the window," as we came upon an eighteen-wheeler. My dad had said how this would be a very different country without the semis delivering everything from Fritos to lumber to television sets. Looking over at the kid with a grin, I obliged without thinking, only consulting with Chuck after the fact.

He shrugged. "Some do, and some don't," he offered in his typically laconic style. "You decide, but just don't scare some four-wheeler in front of you."

I knew I always would.

The school held job interviews for us during the last week, but I didn't sign up for any. I'd spent many nights designing my custom cab and was already in negotiations with a couple of different manufacturers. I knew the RV-style layout in the cab would limit the quantity that I could haul, but I'd already planned to find a niche for myself by transporting smaller amounts of fragile or valuable cargo. Being a woman who was meticulous about details should work to my advantage if I could get the word out to the right people: museums with small traveling exhibits or custom-car companies or pricey furniture makers or antique dealers; businesses who took limited quantities of items to industry trade shows or bands going to musical venues—if they didn't have too much scaffolding or huge special effects machines. Making a custom contract for each customer didn't bother me. I'd get bored working my whole life for one corporation. And I was ready to be my own boss.

My plan to be in charge didn't mean I couldn't be surprised, however, as evidenced by the day we graduated and got our Commercial Driver's Licenses from NTDS. There were chairs for visitors, which was probably more meaningful for those four or five guys who had family nearby. But when my name was called, a voice yelled, "Way to go, Kim." I looked out into the very small audience and saw Trillian, the cute redhead from the flag football game.

My mouth dropped open wide enough to catch a whole swarm of flies. As soon as I could, I made my way over to her. "What are you doing here?"

"I have Sunday lunch with my family every chance I get, and my dad keeps up with things here. He mentioned that this was the last day for this class, and I drive past here on my way back to campus, so I thought I'd…" An adorable blush stole across her cheek. "I just wondered if you'd finished."

I was certain my face would have split clean open if I'd shown the grin I felt inside. She'd come looking for me. I'd always been the pursuer, never the pursued. It felt kinda nice to have the shoe on the other foot. Then, a different notion crossed my mind. "You weren't sure if I was actually here. Because I lied to you about my name." I shuffled my feet. "I knew you were mad about that."

"I asked my dad to check. But it's not an easy program, so congratulations on making it through." She nodded slowly. "And you're right. I was mad. My sisters used to—" She swallowed audibly, making me anticipate what was coming next. "When I was little, they made my life miserable with their pranks and hoaxes. I don't like feeling manipulated."

The way I often felt with Daphne flashed through my mind. "I don't like it either. And I wouldn't have lied if I'd known you then."

She tilted her head. "So you only lie to strangers?"

"Well, maybe sometimes to people I think I'll never see again." I swallowed, casting about for a rationale. "Because hey, you never know what kind of psychos you might meet."

"Like ADPi psychos?"

After a few seconds, I realized that was the name of her sorority. The bees. That made me smile. "Definitely like them. Scary on all counts."

She laughed. "But I'm one of them, you know."

"In the smart way, yeah. But not scary." Someone called my name, but I didn't turn. "When do you have to get back? Can I take you to dinner?"

"It's three o'clock, Max."

"Okay, how about a drink?"

She gave me a look. "It's three o'clock, Max," she repeated more emphatically.

I decided to go with dumb. "Oh, *three* o'clock. Right. Coffee?"

Kevin appeared at my side. "Hey. Are you coming out with us or what?" He noticed Thrill. "Oh, I'm sorry." I introduced them. Kevin studied her for a few seconds. "I thought you said your girlfriend was a blonde named Ashley."

Trillian paled and her eyes narrowed. "So it's true what the Tri Delts were saying about you and Ashley."

"No. Well, not exactly. See, I—"

She stopped me with a forceful shake of her head. "Good luck, Max. Maybe after a few hundred thousand miles, you'll figure out what it is you really want. And who you have to be to get it." She was out the door before I could utter a word.

"Sorry, dude." Kevin was staring at the floor.

I took in a deep breath. "No problem, man. Let's go get wasted."

❖

I arrived home with two contracts for next year, Zelda's address in Isabell, and her numbers there and at the school on a slip of paper in my wallet. Back in Pokeyville, as I always thought of it, I felt like I was going backward in time, though everything looked the same. Still, I needed to check on things at my dad's shop and settle some other business while I waited for the delivery of the sweet, custom-made Peterbilt 379 that I'd ordered. I went to visit Daphne, but she wasn't home.

"Gone to Dallas with those gals she hangs out with." Bill gestured imprecisely in the direction he imagined Dallas might be. "They'll be gone for a few days."

I made a vaguely affirming sound, hoping that Lena might venture into the den so I'd have someone intelligent to talk to. At almost five years old, she already had it all over Bill. Crushed pizza boxes and empty beer cans were strewn around, and he had the TV on at enough volume to be heard on Mars. "Do you mind if I say hi to Lena?" I knew he wouldn't care, but I was trying to be polite.

He gave an indefinite wave, and I headed toward her room. Lena looked up as I entered. Shrieking like I was Bruce Springsteen, she came running into my arms. "Max!"

"Hey there, mango tango." I'd taken to calling her after crayon colors, partly because she loved to draw and paint and also because she'd laughed really hard when I'd suggested that hues could be named after things in her house, like Daddy's House Shoe Black, or Lena's Bedspread Pink. I wished my high school counselor had mentioned devising crayon names as a career option.

She pulled me into the room and shut the door, allowing us to talk at a normal volume. "Did you know it takes the Earth three hundred and sixty-five days to orbit the sun?"

I liked that she opened the conversation by trying to impress me with her most recently acquired knowledge, though the vocabulary was slightly off. I put on my best pondering expression. "You know, I think I heard something about that when I was in school." I sat on the floor beside her. She was pasting beads and feathers onto the head of a

Disney character in a coloring book and doing a darned good job of it. "Do you know what that means?"

She cocked her head. "I'm not sure. What do you think it means?"

This kid cracked me up. I wanted to take her home with me. "I think it means that in three hundred and sixty-five days, the Earth will be in exactly the same position that it is now, relative to the sun."

She looked at me doubtfully.

"Let's act it out," I suggested.

I assumed the part of the Sun, and Lena was the Earth. I fast counted to three hundred and sixty-five, which meant I muttered my way through about three hundred and fifty-five numbers while she circled around me. "Does this happen over and over again?" she asked.

"Uh-huh. And each time it happens, you'll be another year older."

"What?" Her voice went up, filled with such incredulity that I wanted to laugh.

Instead, I nodded. "Yes. We start from the day you were born and after three hundred and sixty-five days, we have a birthday party."

She looked skeptical, so I went and got the calendar Daphne kept in the kitchen and we counted the days. Well, I counted, and she followed along. We got to three hundred and sixty-five, and she looked at me with great respect. I hoped it would always be that easy.

"I guess I'd better go so you and your dad can have dinner."

Lena's face darkened. "I don't want pizza again."

"What do you want?"

"I'd like some fruit. And maybe a hamburger."

This sounded completely reasonable, but Lena was like that. I held out my hand, and she smiled as she took it. "Let's go see what your dad has planned," I suggested as we walked back toward the roar of the TV.

Bill was snoring loudly with his mouth open, an open beer can wedged between his leg and the side of the couch. Lena shrank back, looking worried. "You better not wake him up," she whispered unnecessarily. "Sometimes, he gets real mad at Momma when she does."

"I bet he won't get mad at you," I reassured her. I found the remote and lowered the sound to merely blaring. "Okay, Lena," I said loudly. "Let's ask your dad about dinner."

Bill snorted and struggled to sit up. "I'm watching that," he protested to no one in particular.

"Oh hey, Bill." I tried to act casual. "Lena and I were talking about getting dinner. You interested?"

"We got pizza," he offered, rousing somewhat.

I leaned closer, keeping my voice sympathetic. "You know how picky kids can be. But I don't mind picking up some burgers."

"Knock yourself out," he muttered, rubbing his eyes and yawning loudly.

"Thing is, I only have my motorcycle." Everyone in the room knew it wouldn't be pretty if I let Lena ride on my bike. "Did Daphne drive her car to Dallas?"

"Nah. It's in the garage. Keys are by the kitchen door there. You can take it."

Motivated by the way he slurred his words, I went and knelt by the side of the couch. "Um, listen, Bill. I'm just back in town, and this is my first night in my dad's house since I've been gone. So I was wondering…I mean, it's fine if you say no, but…do you think Lena could keep me company tonight? She can have her own room, of course. I'll call Daphne for you and ask if it's okay if you want."

"Hell no, don't call her. She gave me strict instructions not to call unless the fire department or the ambulance was on its way." He looked over at his daughter. "You wanna go stay with Max tonight, honey?" Lena nodded solemnly. "No parties or anything, right, Max?"

"Oh, God no. I wouldn't do that, Bill."

He looked at me again, his expression showing a surprising few seconds of sobriety. "No. I don't guess you would."

"Thanks, Daddy." Lena came forward and hugged his arm briefly.

The days Lena stayed with me were a reminder of what it was like to live with a child's sense of wonder and joy. We had picnic lunches at the creek and explored the woods. We spent time at the library and visited the Dollar General for new drawing supplies since she'd forgotten to pack hers. I bought her a blank pad of drawing paper and told her I liked the pictures she made best of all. You would have thought I'd given her the keys to Disney World. Late in the afternoon before I had to take her home, I drove out to the highway and pointed as we came upon an eighteen-wheeler.

"See that big truck, inchworm? That's what I'm going to be driving all along this road." We came alongside, and I showed her the arm-pumping motion. "Do this, and he might honk his horn."

She did. He did. She laughed, but then her face grew serious. "Will you be gone away when you drive your truck?"

"Yes, for a while. But I'll always come back."

"You promise?"

I held up my little finger. "I promise. We'll pinky swear on it after we stop."

She was quiet on the way back. When we passed the Pokeville courthouse on the small downtown square, she sighed. "I wish you could marry my momma."

I concentrated on driving. "Your momma's already married."

"I know." Her voice seemed to shrink with disappointment, and a quick glance in my rearview mirror showed her short legs kicking anxiously.

She obviously wanted to talk about it. "Don't you like the daddy you have now?"

She was staring at her shoes, and I could barely hear her answer. "I don't know."

"It'll get easier, jazzberry jam. As you get older, you'll understand grown-ups better."

Her warm brown eyes met mine in the mirror. "Will I yell like they do?"

I pulled over at Jordan Park "Let's go swing for a minute."

We settled on the swing set, and I tried to downplay her daddy's yelling, but she told me that sometimes her momma yelled too. "Here's what I want you to do the next time that happens." I worked to keep my tone light. "First, I want you to remember being extra happy."

She closed her eyes for a second. "Like when we were playing by the creek?"

"Yep. And do you like music?" She nodded. "Can you play it in your room?" More nodding. "Well, if you feel upset, you go to your room and put on your music and think of us at the creek or whatever it is that makes you feel good. Will you do that for me?"

She scuffed her feet in the hollow of dirt below her swing, seeming to give my suggestion serious consideration. "Okay," she said, finally. "But could I maybe come over to your house again too?"

I felt my heart contract. *Don't overplay it*, I told myself. *It'll be worse if you show her you're upset.* Holding out my arms, I asked, "Would you come swing with me, Lee?" She grinned at her real nickname and stepped over to me. Facing out, she settled onto my lap, and I held her as I kicked off. "I want you to know that you can come over to my house whenever you want to. You are my very best friend, and very best friends are always welcome, okay?" She nodded. "I'm going to give you a card with my number on it. You get your mom to show you how to use your phone at home, and anytime you call, I'll come get you."

"Really?"

I worked hard to keep my tone normal as I felt her body relax. "Really." I showed her how to pinky swear.

"I love you, Max."

God. How long had it been since someone had said those words to me? "I love you too, Lena." Maybe it was the waver in my voice or the fact that I used her real name, but she turned to look at me. After a few seconds, she smiled, making me sigh as I saw her mother in that expression, though Daphne's smile was almost never that genuine. "Higher," she shouted. "Let's go higher."

"Anything you want, fuzzy wuzzy."

❖

I was a bit worried about taking her home, since Bill hadn't returned any of my daily calls. But we entered from the unlocked garage door to a spotless house, and I understood why after the rustling sounds coming from the master bedroom turned into Odie Mae Jeffing, who had worked for Daphne's family since Wonder first started selling sliced bread.

"Odie!" Lena cried, and I tried not to be jealous when they hugged while Odie Mae murmured something about her being the sweetest girl in the world.

"Hi, Odie Mae," I said, and she bobbed her head, still holding on to Lena.

"Miss Maxine."

There wasn't any reason to correct her. I'd done it dozens of times to no effect. Lena giggled and ran back to her room with the treasures we'd accumulated during her stay.

"Bill home?"

"No, ma'am. But Miss Daphne called to say she's in town. She's at the grocery."

I nodded. "You'll stay with Lena till she gets here?"

She looked mildly offended. "'Course I will. Cain't leave a sweet baby girl like this one all alone, can I?"

I gestured at the tidy room. "I'm sure Daphne appreciates you, Odie Mae. Please tell her to call me when she has a minute."

Odie Mae looked me over, and I had the sense that the details of my message would not be delivered. "I'll let Mrs. Polk know you were here."

Hanging the keys to Daphne's car on the hook, I yelled "See ya, bluetonium," and headed out to my bike. The echo of Lena's giggle brought a smile to my face on the way home.

CHAPTER FOUR

2005
Age Twenty-three

By the time I actually saw Daphne, I was the talk of the town—or at least the part that hung around Etta's—as my new truck had finally been delivered. Behind the traditional driver and passenger seats was a pass through to a kitchenette, four-person dinette, loveseat, queen-size bed, and dry bathroom. Outside the back wall was the hydraulic lift for my bike. The trailer was like a custom closet, able to adapt to various configurations, depending on what I was hauling. Thanks to the full hookups I'd paid to have installed on the far edge of Etta's parking lot, I had a place to stay when I wasn't on the road.

Lena's influence inspired me to dry out and eat better. My days had developed a routine where I ate breakfast at Nan's Coffee Shop and Bakery, casually flirting with whichever gal was behind the counter. Afterward, I hung out with the guys at my dad's shop—the sign still said "JT's," so to me, it was still his—or visited my CPA or attorney or whatever business presented itself, including writing to Zelda, who refused to do email except at work. I spent most of my evenings reading and accepted another contract for a job, which filled almost all of the upcoming year. All the while, some annoying part of my mind was hoping to hear from Daphne.

I spotted her in the midst of the latest group who had come to admire my custom rig, looking like a rose in a patch of weeds. Before I could greet her properly, she started pitching a fit about how much my special-order semi must have cost. I told her I'd put up the house to get

JAYCIE MORRISON

a loan and that I'd taken over a repo, so the bank had given me a good deal on it. My big lie numbers were probably still in the low 1,900s at that point. Plus, I explained that I was intending to live in it full-time, and renting out the house in town would help with the monthly payments, which I knew she was trying to calculate. Explaining it would be like rent and a car payment put together, I invited her inside. She declined, replying that she had to work in a few minutes.

Standing there in the parking lot, she looked into my face, speaking in that tone she generally used when there wasn't anyone else around. "You've grown up a little, I think."

I stupidly reacted to the flutter of hope in my gut. "It's because I've spent so many months pining for you, Daphne."

She rolled her eyes. "Perhaps I misspoke." Watching her walk away, I was struck with the memory of our first time together. And how it had led to the biggest lie of my young life.

❖

1999
Age Seventeen

It was Friday, the night of Daphne's bridal shower. Because she knew I was distressed over her upcoming marriage to Bill Polk and wouldn't come to any other gathering, she'd insisted I host the party at my house. Her friends must have thought it strange for a sophomore in high school—and one of the weird ones, at that—to be throwing the party, but Daphne, somewhat atypically, didn't seem to care what anyone thought. After a call with the future bride, JT had taken care of the booze, while I'd made snacks and used my fake ID to purchase a porno movie from the highway sex shop by Clearmore.

Because he was a wise man, my dad waited until Thursday to announce that he was going fishing for the weekend, and promptly disappeared. I knew he'd be home by Monday, the start of my spring break, but I refused to consider that Daphne would be a married woman by then.

I had told Daphne's friend Jeanette that anything specifically bridal was on her, so there were lots of stupid games, and the more we

• 54 •

drank, the funnier they got. Gag gifts followed, including a strap-on dildo because, Katelyn announced, everyone knew Daphne was going to wear the pants in her and Bill's relationship, so she might as well have the equipment to go with it. Of course, I knew such things existed, but seeing one being clamored over by all these straight girls made me incredibly uncomfortable. Someone commented that it wasn't particularly big, causing Katelyn to declare that a good wife would never make her husband jealous that way. All of it made me drink faster than I should have, being the hostess and all.

The other girls didn't seem to mind me taking on the role of the disapproving kid as they cheerfully covered all the things I should have been doing. We played one last game, a sort of Trivial Pursuit about Bill and Daphne, in which I got every Daphne question right, followed by the "real" gifts. She oohed and ahhed while I sat scowling in the corner, trying to come to grips with the reality of her marrying this loser. She'd asked me to be in the wedding party, but I'd declined, completely unwilling to wear a bridesmaid's dress or to witness what I considered to be a total travesty. She could do so much better. There was a place in my mind where I finished that thought with, "like with me," but I was more likely to announce that I was trying out for cheerleader than to say that out loud.

When the last present was opened and everyone had filled their plates with cake and freshened their drinks, I staggered to my feet. "And now for the rest of the evening's entertainment," I announced and turned on the movie. I'd cued it to a scene between two women, smirking at the predictable reactions of Daphne's friends: "Gross," "Oh no," and, "What happened to the real action?" were among them.

I couldn't bring myself to look at Daphne. Soon enough, the male character and his dick were introduced. Daphne's friends hooted and hollered until the money shot, after which things began to break up. The girls were vaguely pleasant, assuring me that it was the best bridal shower ever as I stood solidly in our small front hallway, while Daphne said her good-byes. There was so much hugging and kissing, anyone would have thought it was a family reunion or something. I avoided most of the giggling and whispered honeymoon talk by bringing the empty plates and cups into the kitchen. I was merely tipsy by then but figured I'd start all over after everyone was gone.

The door finally closed after one last round of leave-taking, thank-yous, and love-yous, and I thought I was alone. I'd put everything but the bourbon back in the liquor cabinet when I caught sight of Daphne leaning casually on the doorjamb, her hands behind her back. Genuinely startled, I gasped, which made her laugh.

"You didn't think I'd leave without saying good-bye, did you?" Her voice was husky from all the shouting that evening.

Returning to my kitchen duties, I tried to cover my surprise with disdain, which had been my go-to attitude with Daphne recently. "Well, you're marrying that sorry-ass Bill Polk, so there's no telling what you'll do, is there?"

"Give it a rest, Max," she said without moving into the room. An odd tone in her voice made me look over, and for a second, I thought I saw a glint of tears in her eyes.

"Hey." I took a step in her direction and stopped. There was something about her that looked peculiar, strained somehow. Typically, I tried to lighten the mood. "I know you're upset because I haven't given you my gift yet."

She waved, indicating the whole of my small but pleasant home. "This party was your gift, Max. Your dad and I agreed on that."

It was true that I'd paid for everything with the money I'd made working at JT's shop, but I had something else in mind. I pulled a wrinkled envelope from my pocket and handed it to her. "You can read it on your way home or, uh…whenever." How fucking eloquent. But I had to finish. "Just not, you know, in front of Bill, okay?"

She looked at me for a long moment, and I couldn't quite read her expression. "How about now?" she finally asked.

I knew she'd read it immediately if I asked her not to, so I shrugged, hoping she'd put it off. While my heartbeat begged, *please don't, please don't, please don't*, I remained outwardly cool. Moving back to the counter, I asked, "How about a drink instead?" She had curiously refrained from drinking during the festivities.

"Sure," she said, but I heard the envelope ripping as I finished putting ice in a glass. Splashing in a healthy amount of bourbon, I busied myself pouring her red wine as I tried not to think about how ridiculously goofy my words about our friendship must sound to her and how the two of us in Paris—France, not Texas, as I'd told her—would doubtlessly be the last thing that a woman like her would find appealing. I could feel the blush of embarrassment on my face and was steeling myself to face her.

"Max," she began softly, her hand on my shoulder, but I cut her off, talking fast without turning, pretending to fuss with the drinks.

"Listen, I was probably high when I wrote that, so don't take anything in there seriously. I mean, I don't even remember what's in there, really."

Her fingers tightened. After a few seconds she asked, "Are either of those statements you made true?"

I gritted my teeth, preparing myself for the scathingly sarcastic teasing she was always capable of. Goddamn Daphne and her goddamn marriage and goddamn my stupid, romantic inclination that reared its head at the worst possible moments, like when I'd written that goddamn note. "No, they're not true."

Her hand relaxed but didn't move. "Do you say such sweet things to all your girlfriends?"

I made a scoffing sound like I'd heard something ridiculous. "All what girlfriends?"

By way of reply, she moved closer, pressing near enough that I could feel the slightest brush of her breasts on my back. "Am I the only one who wants to see how that intriguing movie ends?"

I swallowed, wanting to laugh but not quite able to with the warmth of her body heating me up inside. "I've already seen it. It ends in another three-way."

She backed off for a second while she turned me and pushed me against the counter. In her best southern lady voice, she said, "Well, aren't you the ol' party-pooper? Now we're going to have to think of something else to do."

Knowing my face was still flushed, I looked down. Daphne was close enough that I could smell her breath. It was kinda sweet, like the cake, and sort of tangy from the alcohol-free punch she'd been drinking. I'd dreamed about kissing her a thousand times, but with her this close and me on the edge of being loaded, I sure didn't need to go there now.

Luckily, she remained oblivious to my thoughts. "Which reminds me. I want to give you your hostess gift now."

A jingling sound made me look up. She held the strap-on dildo in her other hand. "Shit, Daphne," I sputtered.

She grinned playfully. "I know this would technically be regifting. But don't you want it?"

Hell yeah, I wanted it. But I sniffed, going for cool yet again. "I guess. You know I'll have more use for it than you would."

She brought the tip to her mouth, making kissing motions. Damn if my clit didn't twitch at the sight. "And do you know how to use it?"

Shrugging, I braced my hands on the counter behind me. "What's to know?"

Her expression grew serious. "Maybe that mindset is why you don't have a girlfriend."

I had to look away again. This conversation, along with her mouth and the dildo and the memory of her breasts against my back, was beginning to affect my breathing, not to mention the condition of my denims. She put the dildo between us, exactly where I could imagine it would be if I was wearing it, and pressed her body all the way into mine again. "What if I told you that your gift came with instructions?"

Okay. Either this game was gonna end right now, or things were about to get real. I brushed my lips up her neck and whispered in her ear, "Instructions? Or a lesson?"

I could tell she liked that because she shivered a little. Still, she pulled back enough to look at me. "A lesson. One. Only this one. You have to know that first."

"Uh-huh." Eloquent, like I said. In shock, actually.

"And listen, Max. I'm not kissing you, understand?" She ground herself into me again until I had to close my eyes for a second. "Not on the lips anyway."

Her words sunk in. No kissing? "Why not?" I barely recognized my own voice as I looked up.

She sighed and took a step back. I caught the dildo before it hit the ground. "Because I'm getting married in three days. That's my offer. Take it or leave it."

Part of me wanted to protest, but then I considered that everyone had their limits. This was Daphne's. I tilted my head and let my gaze wander upward, pretending to consider whether or not to accept. She ran her hands along my sides and over my chest, moving them all the way up until she was holding my face, staring into my eyes. "Do you expect me to beg, Max?"

I let one corner of my mouth rise into my classic crooked grin. "God, I hope so."

"Don't bet on it." She bit me hard on my neck. "Give me ten minutes." She ran her hand down the shaft of the dildo. "And don't put this on yet."

❖

I used the ten minutes to turn off the lights in the front of the house and lock all the doors. In JT's bathroom, I used a new toothbrush I found in his cabinet. Carrying two glasses of water, I slowly opened the bedroom door. Daphne was sitting in my bed with the sheet tucked above her breasts, naked beneath it, I assumed. I tried hard to keep my cool, though my heart was beating fast enough to power half the town. How often did a seventeen-year-old kid get to have their wildest dream come true?

"No fair," I said, crossing my arms after I handed her a glass. "I didn't get to watch you undress."

She took the water and shook her head. "Try again."

Oh, she wanted romance? I could do that too. "Seeing you there in my bed is my best ever fantasy."

She nodded and waved me over. "Come here." I stood beside her. "Bend down." I obeyed, watching her start to unbutton my shirt. Her eyes swept over the undershirt I was wearing, and she smiled slightly, pushing the Oxford over my shoulders to the floor. My nipples were so hard, they almost hurt. She opened the top button on my 501 jeans and stopped. "Do you go commando to school, Max?"

"Not usually, no."

She opened another button. "Then you did this just for the party?"

"Yeah."

When her fingers grazed my skin to undo the next button, I sucked in a breath. "Are you wet right now? Really wet?"

"Yeah. And you?"

She grabbed my breast. Not hard, but it wasn't a tender caress, either. It wouldn't have mattered because any kind of touch would have been fantastic. "I'm asking the questions. Got that?"

"Yes, ma'am."

She squeezed rhythmically for a few seconds. Not hard enough to hurt but enough that the pressure went straight down my body and concentrated between my legs, making me bend and stifle a moan. "And don't act smart. Act respectful. I'm your elder, you know."

"Yes."

"Yes, okay, or yes, you like that?"

"Yes, both."

"Mmm." She let go and finished opening my pants. "Slide them off," she ordered. I did. "Now, take your undershirt off and walk over to your side before you get in."

I did as she asked, lying on my back after sliding under the sheet but being careful to stay on my side.

"You have incredibly nice breasts and a perfect ass, as I always suspected. If you were after the boys, I'd tell you to lose those baggy jeans and put on some tight pants and a close-fitting sweater. You'd have to beat them off with a stick."

"That's an image I'd rather not consider." I squirmed, squinting as if trying to forget something awful. She seemed to realize what she'd said and pinched my earlobe. "Ow! That hurt."

"You goof. You know I meant fight them off, not what you thought. I told you to be respectful." After a few seconds, she giggled. "You would use a stick if you had to do that other, wouldn't you?"

I nodded. "A thorny stick, if possible."

Her giggle turned into a laugh. I turned on my side to look at her, although what I was feeling wasn't humor. After her laughter played out, she ran her hand through the longer side of my hair. "You don't know how often I've wanted to do that. And it feels exactly like I imagined it would."

If I'd been a cat, I would have purred, but I had to settle for leaning into her caress. I wanted so badly to touch her, but I sensed the moment wasn't ideal.

She swallowed and crossed her arms. "I'm not young and perfect like you, Max."

I blinked. "Not to be disrespectful, but you're only four years older, not four decades."

She rolled her eyes. "All right. But not perfect, certainly."

"You are to me." The words were out before I could stop them, but she waved them away with a flick of her wrist.

"Have you ever been with a woman before?"

Leave it to Daphne to get right to it. "Uh, not quite like this, no. What about you?"

I didn't think she'd answer, but she did. "Once, in college. We were both loaded, and it was, you know, fun. Real nice but only for kicks. But it got weird. She was way more into it than I was. Later, she'd try to hit on me whenever we'd drink. I finally had to tell her to back off, and it hurt our friendship." She sighed and looked at me, touching my face with surprising tenderness. "I don't want that to happen with us, Max. Tell me it won't."

"No, hell no. It won't. I promise." Of course, I would have offered anything imaginable to get her to pull down that sheet.

She smiled knowingly. "So let me guess. You've gotten to... second base?"

"Yeah, pretty much," I mumbled.

"Well, look, there's something I need to tell you. What I said about not being perfect? I meant it." Her eyes looked past me while my mind went to the most unusual thing I could think of, like if she might be intersex or something. Not that there was anything wrong with that. I was just fishing for what on Earth she could be so hesitant about.

"Daphne—" I started, but she interrupted.

"No, don't say anything, Max. Let me finish." I closed my mouth obediently. She took a deep breath. "My breasts...they're...they're different."

Different? "Like, green or something?"

She swatted my arm. "No, you goof. They're different from each other. One is much larger than the other."

I sat up abruptly while she clutched at the sheet, keeping it close. "You've got to be kidding me." When hurt registered on her face, I rushed on. "I mean, you got me all worked up about you having green tits, and now you tell me your breasts are a little different in size?"

"It's not only a little. And this is a big deal to me, Max."

I didn't think I'd ever seen her so vulnerable. "Okay, yeah." Before she could protest, I straddled her covered body with my naked one. I put my hands on her shoulders and leaned in, kissing across the part of her chest that was showing and onto her neck, wanting very much to kiss her on the lips but remembering that would be the end of my chances.

Instead, I leaned back and looked into her eyes. "It's true, you know. About you being my fantasy. I've had you in my dreams a hundred nights, but I know the reality is going to be a million times better." She wiggled with what I knew was pleasure, not resistance, so I went on, scooting lower to kiss her sheet-covered breasts. "There's not another woman in this town who turns heads the way you do." I inched the sheet down. "You're an awesome friend." Another half inch. "Any day I get to see you makes it a great day." Another quarter inch. I stopped pulling and looked at her. "Let me see you, Daphne. I've never wanted anything more. I want to touch all of you, to know all of you. Please."

She looked at me for a long moment. "Come here," she said finally and patted the bed beside her. As I slid under the sheet, she put her arms around me and pulled me onto her shoulder. I wished I could describe how amazing it felt. The warmth, the completeness, the safety. It was like coming home. I groaned and slid my leg across her, "Oh, damn, Max," she moaned, her hands dancing over my skin, making every nerve she touched tingle.

Carefully, I eased my hand up her belly until I cupped her breast. I thought the weight of it was the most breathtaking thing in the universe, but she tensed for a moment, and I stilled. "Does that hurt?"

"No, I'm just…sensitive."

I eased the sheet off with my other hand, gradually letting my eyes drift over her body. It was easy to keep my expression approving because it was clear to me that this was one of those things an individual might obsess about, but no one else would even notice. If she hadn't told me, it would have taken a scientific level of observation to tell the difference between her breasts.

"You're gorgeous. And I wasn't kidding about you being perfect. Whoever made you question that must have been out of his mind. And the best part is, I know how wonderful, how strong and lovely you are inside too."

"Don't," she said sternly, putting her hand on mine where it still covered her breast. For a second, I was afraid she meant for me not to touch her. "Don't make me out to be something I'm not. And don't make this out to be more than it is." She took my hand and guided it onto her pubic hair.

Apparently, some other part of my brain was in control because I lost the ability for rational thinking. I pulled the sheet away with my other hand and put my mouth on her breast, teasing my lips around the nipple until I felt her legs open wider, and I slid in my fingers in a little farther. I found her clit already hard, I straddled her leg, pressing just hard enough to ease the pressure inside me, and moved my mouth to her other breast, biting with no warning. She arched, and I eased off in both places, stroking lightly, moving my fingers slowly toward the source of her wetness. She moaned when I cupped her other breast again and moved my mouth onto her neck, alternately kissing and sucking the skin. She was letting me, wanting it even, until she gasped and wrenched away, her expression fearful as she rubbed that side of her neck briskly. "And don't you dare give me a hickey, Max Terrell," I eased my fingers back to her clit, working along it until her breathing returned to its steady panting, and her eyes closed again.

"What if I want to?" I asked while I kissed from her belly to her shoulders. "What if that's the one thing I have to do before I make you come?" I stopped moving so intently and was touching along her outer folds, teasing with quick light strokes.

"No, you can't. Please don't. Not now. Please."

My head swam at the tone of her voice. She was begging and moving against me, desperate to bring me back to where she wanted me. I gave in easily, first with touch, next with heart, as I put my lips close to her ear. "I wouldn't do anything that you didn't want, Daphne. Really. I promise, I won't ever hurt you."

Eyes still closed, she let out a shaky breath as her head lolled against me, and her arms held me tighter. Her whole body seemed to soften, and for those few seconds, I had her. Then she jerked a little, pulling herself back, her look cool. "This is only a lesson, remember?" She brought my head to her breast, her voice strict again. "Stop being such a pitiful romantic, Max. Finish me. Do it now."

I tried to follow both her instructions, but as I felt her clit swell and her body stiffen as her grip on me tightened and she cried out softly, I had to hold her afterward. For a few minutes, she let me.

When she shifted, I rolled to the side, letting my hand drift over her belly, down one thigh and up the other, carefully avoiding touching her sex. I moved slowly to one breast while I kissed the other lightly. She made a contented sound, making me believe it wasn't that bad.

I hated asking, but I had no idea what her protocol would be. In books, they sometimes talked about it afterward. "Was that, I mean, are you okay?"

Her lips curled, and she sighed. I liked that reaction. "Mmm. Very, very okay." She bit the side of my other hand before kissing the exact same spot. Involuntarily, my hand on her breast jerked. Her dreamy smile widened. "Couldn't you tell?"

"Uh, yeah, I thought I could. But, well, you didn't, um, you didn't make much noise."

"Noise? Oh, you mean like they did in that movie?"

Okay, now I was embarrassed. But…yeah. "Something like that, uh-huh."

"Life isn't like the movies, Max. Noise is unladylike."

"Sex is unladylike."

She burst out laughing. "I suppose you have a point there."

I grinned. Making Daphne laugh was my favorite thing to do. Well, now my second favorite thing to do.

She stretched and opened her eyes. That smile faded, and she stared at me for a few seconds. "How can you look like that?"

"Like what?" Worried, I started to look at myself, but she caught my chin and brought my head back up.

"So fucking sexy and so goddamned beautiful at the same time."

Heat rushed to my face, and I hoped the light she'd left on in the bathroom didn't show my blush. Caught off guard, I let her roll us over until she was on top of me. Somewhere in the process, my legs parted, and she settled her body there, still watching me. "Has anyone ever gone down on you, Max?"

I lost my breath, and with it went the ability to speak. All the blood in my body headed south as she lowered her head and sucked my breast for a few seconds. When she glanced up, her face had that powerful, confident look of a woman in total control of the situation. "Cat got your tongue?" She stuck out her own tongue and lapped playfully at my other nipple.

I groaned. She stopped licking. "I'm sorry," I said, thinking she must be offended.

"No, no, no." She nipped at my stomach, and I shuddered. I could feel her smile again. "You don't have to apologize for anything. I like the way that sounded."

"Unladylike," I managed, aware that she was making her way down my body.

She dipped her tongue into my navel before making three wet kisses across my abdomen. The last tiny spot cooled as she breathed, "But you're not a lady. You're..." She was hovering over me, her mouth teasing a mere inch away from my clit. "Max," she finished, and her lips touched me. My hips jerked hard into her.

She raised her head. "You can't do that, honey. You'll bruise me. Besides, you're not fucking my mouth. I'm sucking you off. Understand?"

Frankly, I didn't. But some message about not letting myself rear up got through, and I nodded.

"Just let me," she said. I did. Her hair tickled my thighs as she lowered her lips again, and I let her do whatever she wanted, and the better it felt, the more unladylike sounds I made. The wet, tingling sensation I'd felt while masturbating hadn't prepared me for the incredible heat building in my center. I had one brief moment of panic, where the pleasure was almost too intense, where the loss of control felt like falling. She kissed me there and lifted her head again. "It's okay, baby. You can let go. I've got you."

She'd called me honey before, lots of times. That expression was something southern women used for most occasions. But baby? She'd never said that, and it made something in me open up, reached someplace deeper and more personal.

"Yeah," I managed to rasp, and she kissed me again in that same spot before she stroked her tongue slowly across my clit. When she sucked me into her mouth and bobbed her head, I couldn't hold back, and my shoulders pressed into the bed, and everything behind my eyes and lower exploded.

"Yeah," she echoed, her lips now close to my ear. I had no idea she'd moved.

My heart was still racing, but the throbbing bliss between my legs was slowing. I realized I'd been breathing through my mouth, so I closed it and swallowed.

"Take your time," she suggested in that sultry voice. "Enjoy it." She let her hand brush over my pubic hair, and I bucked a little, amazed to realize that I was almost ready for more. Her voice indicated some gratification at my response. "We're just getting started, can't you tell?"

"Fuck," I said and immediately regretted it. I should have expressed something sweet, something romantic, or something appreciative, at least.

But she laughed. "Yeah," she said again. "Let's do that next." She relaxed and laid her head on my shoulder, caressing my body absently while I tried to memorize everything about the moment: her slight weight against me, the heat wherever her hand lay, the combination of our scents, and the incredible fact that the reality of being with Daphne was way better than my most erotic dream.

Maybe it was the orgasm that brought on my sudden burst of honesty, but as my strength returned, I rolled to the side and looked into her eyes. "Why are you marrying Bill? Would you please explain it to me?"

Her face, which had been relaxed and smiling faintly, stiffened, and her whole body tensed. "Don't start with that shit again, Max," she said through gritted teeth and pushed herself away as if to get up.

I grabbed her wrist, holding her tightly. "I'm not criticizing you, Daphne. It's your life. I just wanna understand."

"Damn right, it's my life. You got no business asking me anything. Who do you think you are? You think I owe you something because we're lying here naked together?"

She was as mad as I'd seen her in ages. I figured I had one shot at this before she walked out. "No, not because of that. I'm asking as the friend you know I am. Because that friend doesn't want to see you unhappy."

She was still staring at me, but I could see her anger leaving. Her shoulders slumped. I loosened my grip on her wrist and slid my hand into hers. *Don't say another thing. Give her time.*

Sighing, she reached over and took a sip of water. When she turned back to me, I could see tears. "I'm pregnant."

CHAPTER FIVE

1999
Age Seventeen

I swallowed, trying to keep my expression neutral. An unexpected pregnancy certainly explained her sudden return from the community college in nearby Clearmore. I waited a beat. "Does Bill know?"

She shook her head and looked away, her voice so quiet I had to strain to hear it. "It's not his."

"Okay," I said, pulling her to me. She resisted for half a second before giving in, returning to our prone position. I stroked her hair while I considered the situation. There was no point in talking about options. Daphne and I both absolutely adored kids. While I totally believed that a woman should have complete control over her body and a choice about what happened to it, and I think Daphne felt the same, in principle, I also knew that there wasn't anything on earth or in heaven that could convince Daphne to have an abortion. And even if it was 1999, for Daphne to have a baby out of wedlock would be incredibly hard on her and her family. We didn't only call it Pokeyville for its slow pace. It was also small-minded in a lot of ways.

There was no point in asking about the father either. I didn't think of Daphne as a slut, but she'd dated regularly in high school, sometimes more seriously than others. She might tell me eventually or maybe not ever. It didn't really matter. But for her to settle for Bill Polk? He was a decent-looking guy, but anyone could see he was poised to take a shortcut on the road to ruin. He'd had a reputation as a heavy drinker in high school, and that obviously hadn't changed. He had little to no ambition, seemingly content to take the owner-in-training position at his dad's tool and dye shop without benefit of working his way through the ranks. His family's other claim to fame was that the town was actually named after them, but somewhere along the line, an ignorant clerk or early mapmaker had misspelled it.

In spite of my disdain, I tried to phrase my question delicately. "And Bill Polk is your best option?"

"Yeah." She sounded so defeated, it made my heart ache.

"When..." I tried to remember the right phrasing. "When are you due?"

"October." Her voice took on a dreamy quality. "You know, I've always looked forward to having children. I just didn't think..."

I gave her a nudge. "You're gonna be the best mom ever."

She looked at me, her brow furrowed. "You think so?"

"I know so. That kid is going to be spoiled rotten. And super, super smart. And terribly good-looking, of course. And—"

She cut me off. "I want you to be a godparent. Will you come to the church for her christening?"

I had set foot in a church maybe twice, and Daphne was only marginally Catholic. But I was deeply moved by the message of this invitation. I was to have a place in her child's life. I pretended to consider. "Would I have to wear a dress?" I asked, and we both laughed.

"No, you goof. You can wear a suit."

We grinned at each other, probably both envisioning a very uncomfortable Father Waverly. Then, something else registered. "You said 'her.' Do you already know?"

She shook her head. "It's just a feeling." I glanced quickly at her abdomen. After a moment, she took my hand and laid it carefully across her stomach. "No one else knows, Max," she said softly.

I nodded, still regarding her belly as if I might develop X-ray vision and be able to see through to the life inside her. "I apologize for giving you such a hard time about Bill. He'll make a good father, won't he?"

Her voice got harder. "He'd better."

It made me laugh, her trying to sound tough. "I'll be there for you and her, in any case. You know that, don't you?"

"Babysitting?

"Absolutely?"

"Doctor visits?"

"Of course."

"Diaper changing?"

"Don't push your luck."

She smiled and pulled my hand to her breast. "Late night feedings?"

"Well, uh…" I didn't know exactly what she meant.

Without any fanfare, she straddled me, running her hands through my hair and leaning close to my face. For a second, I thought she was going to kiss me, and I was so ready, wanting to lose myself in her mouth. "I think it's time for your lesson, stud."

I'd probably never have gotten that harness on right if Daphne hadn't helped me. We'd been naked with each other for a while now, but I felt strangely inhibited standing in front of her with this foreign thing hanging in front of me. And though I'd always, always, been making love to a female form in any fantasy, I'd never imagined being a guy. But I had to admit, wearing the dildo was turning me on, especially with the way Daphne was looking at me.

"Come here." She guided me onto my back and turned on her side, running her hand along the length of it. "Can you feel that?"

I could. Besides the fact that watching her touch my accessory was about the sexiest thing I'd ever seen, the motion of her hand pressed the shaft into my clit. "Yeah," I said hoarsely. I pushed my hand through her damp curls, finding her very wet. I let the motion of my fingers match that of her hand until her hips were rocking, and she moaned softly. "Are you ready for me?" I asked, ready to hear that sound again.

"That's right, Max," she murmured, clearing her throat. "You should always ask. Sometimes, women fake it."

"Are you faking it now?" This was probably a stupid question. A woman who was faking it wouldn't admit it, would she?

"No, baby, I'm not. I'm incredibly excited." She put her arms around me and looked into my face, her lips close again. "I want to feel you inside me."

"Oh God." I rolled us over, ready to mount her, but a thought stopped me. "Daphne, this isn't…it won't hurt the baby, will it?"

She fluttered her lashes innocently. "What would you do if I said yes?"

I was indignant. "I'd stop, of course. I mean, if there's any chance—"

She pulled me close, and I could feel her heart beating. "It's fine, I promise. And stop being sweet. You're making me crazy enough as it is."

"I'm making you crazy? God, Daphne, do you have any idea how beautiful you are? It feels so damn good to be with you like this."

She pushed me back and took the dildo in hand, positioning it at her entrance. "Go slow," she whispered. "Ease in at first." I did as she asked, resisting the urge to plunge into her. "Yeah. That's it."

I couldn't speak. I was in some kind of transcendent state. I saw myself sliding into Daphne's body, and I didn't think anything in my life would ever compare to this moment. She spread her legs wider, pulling me in farther. I groaned, unable to suppress the pleasure. "Move for me, Max." I pushed my hips forward slowly, carefully rotating my pelvis slightly as I did. "Oh, that's it, baby. Just like that."

Incredibly, the throaty sound of her voice was making me more excited, and I could dimly hear growling sounds coming from my mouth. The movement, easing myself out before thrusting carefully back in, was already instinctive. Still balanced on my hands, I leaned to kiss her breast.

"Suck on it," she commanded, and as I did, her hips rolled up, and I was drawn in all the way. When our bodies met, so completely joined, sensation merged with emotion, and I cried out her name. She grabbed my ass, bringing me to a rhythm she wanted. "Yes," she panted, her voice urgent with need. "There. Right there. Yes."

Dropping my head to suck the other breast, I became aware of the hard, fast approach of my own orgasm. Following some primal instinct, I moved a little faster, and she matched me. I groaned, driving her insistently, desperate to coax the last needy sound from her throat, wanting to feel her climax beneath me even more than I wished for my own finish. At the same time, I never wanted this to be over. I wanted her cries and her grasping hands and our sweat and this compelling force between us to last forever.

But it was too late to rein myself in because she hissed, "Now, Max. Oh fuck, yes. Now. Now," and as the last word faded, her head went back, and her high keening sound pushed me over too, shouting my passion in time with the slowing of my thrusts.

For a while, she seemed to like me staying inside her. She rolled her hips, shivering and making humming sounds of pleasure. I floated in semiconscious bliss until she said, "Okay," and gently pushed me away.

I slid out easily, and she pulled me back to her. I collapsed, still on top of her, loving the contact of our bodies, loving the sweet lethargy that was creeping over me, loving…Daphne. I had lost my consciousness of who we were or where we were. I had only feeling. I stretched up and kissed her, softly and then deeper, and she kissed me back, and those few seconds were the most perfect I could have imagined and beyond anything I had ever wanted.

"I love you," I said, almost not recognizing my own voice as I admitted the rest of it. "I've always loved you." As the words left me, her eyes, which had been closed with satisfaction, snapped open with an expression so furious, her whole face was distorted.

"Goddamn it, Max. Now you've ruined everything." She shoved me off, standing so quickly that she wavered slightly.

She grabbed her clothes and began putting them on with quick, irritated motions, while I stuttered, "Wait. I'm sorry. Please, I—"

"Shut up. Just shut up." She was practically shouting now. "We had a deal. I thought I could trust you."

"I know. I fucked up. I'm sorry. You can trust me. You can. Please. It won't happen again. I promise." I was panicked, babbling.

"Damn right it won't." She was dressed now and pulling on her shoes, muttering to herself. "I must have lost my mind." She addressed me again. "You're a child, Max. And I'm about to be a married woman. So don't call me, and don't come by for a while. I'm going to have to reevaluate our friendship, and I'll need some time."

I was too rattled to react at first, nearly dizzy with the swing of emotion. I started to get up, but she held out a hand, every word she spoke completely final. "No. Don't. I'll see myself out." She pointed down. "And take that ridiculous thing off. At least until you learn how to use it properly."

❖

Two days later, very early in the morning, I heard our house phone ring. Normally, I never answered because that number was used mostly by solicitors or my dad's buddies. JT was back, but he'd gone to catch up on things at the shop, and I'd been using the excuse of a head cold to cover my frequent nose blowing and red eyes. If he suspected that me staying in my room had to do with Daphne, he was too cool to say anything. Or perhaps my one-word answers when he'd inquired about the bridal party had tipped him off.

Anyway, after a whole bunch of rings, the phone finally stopped, but then it started again. *Fuck.* I dragged myself out of bed and grabbed the extension in his bedroom. "'Lo?" I knew I sounded scratchy from not having spoken much in the last few days, and I hoped my grumpy tone would discourage any salesperson or desperate customers asking for JT.

"You gotta help me." Her voice was a muffled whisper, but I knew it was Daphne.

I was instantly wide awake and taut as a bowstring. "Of course. Anything."

There was a hiccup, and I replayed the whisper in my head. Had she been drinking? At this hour? Or was she still drunk from some premarital activities? Had thoughts of her wedding today made her forget the baby? I grabbed the water from my dad's bedside and helped myself to a big swallow while I waited.

"I need you to tell me something," she said finally.

This was more strident but still very quiet. And maybe a little slurred? "What?" The water had helped my throat recover, and my question sounded loud to my own ear against the receiver.

"Shh," she breathed urgently, as if I was in the room with her.

"Sorry," I whispered back, listening as her breathing steadied.

"You gotta do this. As…as my friend."

I kept my voice low. "Ask me. You know you can, Daphne."

"Okay. Okay." She took another breath but must have pressed her mouth too close to the mic because her words were so hurried and muffled that I couldn't understand.

"What?" Panic that I'd missed her request made me speak louder, so I lowered my voice again and went on quickly. "I'm sorry, Daphne, but I couldn't understand you. Say it again, please. Say what you just said again."

"I need...goddamn it, Max." Now her voice had an undertone of frustration, the way she talked when she was angry at herself for something. She swallowed, and her voice was almost normal. "Tell me you don't love me."

Her words ripped through me, and I answered without thinking. "No."

"Yes," she insisted, more infuriated. "Say it. Tell me right now."

"No," I growled again, still angry. "Why would I tell you a lie like that?"

"Because I asked you to. Because I need you to. Because I..." Her voice trailed off, and I thought I heard her drop the receiver. There were some other sounds. Rustling. Sniffling. A kind of choking gulp. As I was beginning to worry that she might not talk to me again, there was the sound of the phone being picked up. She sighed deeply. "Because I can't get it out of my mind." She had more composure now, but her tone was still cross.

I thought I knew what she was talking about, but I wanted to hear it. In fact, I was desperate for her to say it. If I was going to do what she asked, she would have to give me this. "Can't get what out of your mind, Daphne?" My tone was cold, but I pretended it would help us both.

"You." It was working. I could hear the incensed tenor of her voice, although she still spoke quietly. "The texture of your hair. The way you taste. The expression on your face when you were inside me. The feel of..." Whatever resentment she'd found was running out. We listened to each other breathing for a few seconds.

"Your skin," I said, not realizing that I was crying until I heard the quiver in my words. "Your scent. The way your hands—"

I heard the knock as loudly as if I'd been beside her. Someone must have spoken, but I only heard her side. Her voice was extremely cheery, exactly the fake tone I'd heard her use at school a million times. "I sure am. I'll be out in just a few."

Whoever must have been pacified by her reply because she returned to the line, crisp and sharp. "All right, Max. Now do what I asked you to do."

"I can't."

My evident despair made her turn almost encouraging. "Yes, you can. You can do this. You'll do it because it's important to me."

I hadn't meant to let her hear me crying, but I needed to breathe, and as I did, that sobbing sound came out. I covered the receiver quickly, but she must have heard it.

"It's only words, Max." She gave a sad little laugh. "Talk is cheap. We both know that."

I was shaking so hard inside, I thought I might come apart, but I wiped my face on the sheet and sniffed once. "I don't love you."

There was an intake of breath on her end. The line disconnected, and I listened to the dial tone until a loud beeping sound started. I lay down and pulled the receiver against my chest, letting each harsh tone drive my tears further inside, as if holding them there would wash away everything that had happened. But after a few more seconds, a recording instructed me in the process of making a call. If I needed help, I was to hang up and dial my operator. What would the operator say, I wondered idly, if I approached her for help with my specific problem?

For a few moments, I gave myself over to the fury that I normally feared and carefully controlled. I would go to the wedding. I would speak out when they asked if anyone had any objections. Or I would find her beforehand and say what I'd really wanted to tell her on the phone. *Don't marry him. Wait for me. Come live with us and have your baby.*

In actuality, I did none of that, and I didn't hear from her for months. While time hadn't completely healed me, I'd quelled my resentment and hardened my heart enough to respect her wishes. I avoided any places where I was likely to see her. She was probably doing the same. I heard from others about where the newlyweds were living, and by July, I heard how marvelous she looked being pregnant. On Saturday afternoon of Labor Day weekend, the phone was ringing as I came in from cruising the neighborhood. Her voice was so breathy, I had to listen hard to understand the words, though of course, I knew exactly who it was.

"Can you please drive me to the hospital? Something's wrong, and I can't find Bill."

She wasn't due for another month, I knew. I barely exhaled a yes before I was back on my bike, arriving at her house in record time. Daphne was lying on the couch with her eyes closed. Her face was covered with a sheen of sweat, and several towels nearby had splotches of bright red blood.

I knelt beside her, brushing her hair off her face. "Hey."

"Hey." Her voice was much too weak.

"Have you called your doctor?" I asked as she struggled to sit up.

"Yeah. He said to come in."

"Good. Let's go. Can you walk?"

She grimaced faintly. "Why? Were you going to offer to carry me? In my elephantine condition?"

"I probably haven't ever revealed that lifting pregnant women is one of my superpowers. It hasn't come up before, I guess."

"I suppose not." Leaning forward to stand, she abruptly made a strangled sound, grabbing her abdomen, her face ashen.

"Don't strain yourself." I kept my voice calm. "I'll call an ambulance if you'd rather."

She looked over, looking directly at me for the first time since I'd come in. "I'm so scared, Max. I'm terrified I'm going to lose this baby. I need you to get me to the hospital right now."

"Then that's what I'll do." I put my arm around her, and she leaned heavily on me after she was finally able to get to her feet. When we reached the door to the garage, she stretched out a hand to get keys off a decorative hook, gasped, and bent over, obviously in pain.

"I'm here to help you. Let me," I scolded, taking the keys and opening the door. Inside was a new BMW convertible. I helped her into the passenger seat and hurried around, starting the engine. I tried to drive quickly but also very carefully.

We'd been riding in silence for a couple of minutes when she said, "I should have brought a towel. Bill is going to kill me if I get blood on the seat."

Under any other circumstance, I would have let fly with some exceedingly specific suggestions about what the missing Bill could do, but this wasn't the time. Instead, I offered, "I suppose we should have taken my bike."

She started laughing, and then she was crying.

I held out my hand. "It's gonna be okay, Daphne. Just hang on. You and the baby are both going to be fine."

She grabbed my hand, bending again, moaning low. Fuck careful. I hit the gas, and we blew through the last few miles of town, arriving at the hospital in less than two minutes. I screeched to a halt at the emergency room entrance and threw open the door, ready to jump out of the car and get someone to help us.

She stopped me, still holding my hand. "I'm so sorry. Sorry for—"

"Shh." I touched her face. "Let's talk later. The baby might want to be in on this conversation."

People in scrubs ran out, and one of them had a wheelchair. A cop stopped me before I could follow them in. "You're gonna need to move this vehicle, ma'am. You can't leave it blocking this drive."

I was going to tell him to tow me but figured it would take them a few minutes to get Daphne checked in. I parked haphazardly toward the rear of the lot, taking two spots the way people with expensive cars did, and sprinted back to the ER. At first, they told me she was being examined, so I couldn't go in. Next, they wouldn't let me see her because I wasn't family.

Before I could lose my mind and my temper, a different nurse came into the waiting area. "Is there a Max Terrell here?"

Daphne was hooked up to an IV and all manner of monitoring devices. In spite of all the dripping going in and the beeping coming out, she looked much calmer. She was wearing a hospital gown, and though she was still perspiring, her eyes were clearer.

"Hey," I said softly. "You okay?"

She nodded. "I'm fine. They tell me I have placental abruption. The baby's all right so far, but they might have to induce labor."

"When?"

"We'll know soon." She swallowed. "Or I might need a C-section."

"Have I ever mentioned that I think scars are really sexy?" I was trying for our usual witty banter, not thinking about our last time together.

She shook her head. "You are nothing if not predictable." I was going to try for a less suggestive comeback until she added, "Thank God."

I petted her arm lightly. "What can I do?"

"Will you try to find Bill?"

I shook my head. "Not until someone else gets here for you. I'm not leaving you alone."

She looked at me for a few seconds and whispered, "Then please, keep doing that," before drifting off.

I wasn't sure how long it was before I heard the door behind me, and heavy footsteps came toward the bed. I smelled alcohol before he spoke. "What the fuck, Daphne? You're never early. In fact, you're usually late."

My whole body stiffened and Daphne's eyes popped open. She grabbed my hand where it had been touching her arm, shaking her head ever so slightly before letting go. Her voice was light, almost hiding the edge in it. "Well, you know me, Bill. I'm just full of surprises."

It took everything I had to step aside, but I'd spent the last six months learning to accept that this was what she wanted. I didn't want to look at him, so I turned the other way before I started for the door.

"Who was that?" I heard him ask, using the tone that meant the question was understood to end in some derogatory term: who was that freak? Or who was that dyke?

"That's my very good friend, Max Terrell." Daphne's response soothed my heart. "She drove me over since no one could find you at work."

"Yeah? Well, you should talk. I don't know where you are ninety-nine percent of the time." I didn't care about their domestic dispute and was already into the hallway when Bill called, "Hey, kid." I turned slowly, expecting thanks or some expression of appreciation. "You still got the keys to the Beamer?"

I dug them out of my pocket and tossed them to him. "It's parked toward the rear of the ER lot."

"Give her something, Bill," Daphne said, but I waved it away before he could react.

"It's fine. Besides, I might hang around for a while and sample this gourmet hospital food."

Bill shrugged. "Suit yourself."

Daphne's voice was a little stronger. "Thank you, Max."

He was standing between us. I couldn't see her, and she couldn't see me, but it almost didn't matter. "I'm really glad you called."

"Me too."

After getting a giant Dr Pepper and a bag of Sun Chips from the cafeteria, I called JT to let him know what was going on and sat waiting in the hallway outside the maternity ward. People trickled in, sharing concerned looks or eager conversation. I recognized Daphne's parents, but they didn't notice me. Bill eventually appeared and announced that the patient was doing fine. Apparently, he hadn't felt the need to be present for another of Daphne's exams. Everyone swirled around him in various stages of excitement or worry.

After an hour or so, Bill was summoned by the nurse and was gone for a relatively brief time. He was pale when he returned but accepted several hugs before he threw himself onto the only couch in the room and started making calls on a brick-sized mobile phone. Daphne's mother hurried past. I started pacing but couldn't bring myself to enter the room and ask what was going on. Not yet. After Bill's cronies showed up with three bottles of champagne and a box of cigars about thirty minutes later, I relaxed slightly.

After another forty-five minutes, the girls from Daphne's bridal shower—Katelyn and Jeanette and Chloe—bustled in with flowers and a bunch of balloons, the biggest of which said, "IT'S A GIRL!" I smiled and took my first deep breath in what felt like hours, stretching for a second before I started for the exit.

"Oh hi! Max, isn't it?"

It was Jeanette, waving to me from the door of the maternity waiting area. I turned toward her. "Yeah. Hey. How's she doing?"

"They're both fine. Come on in. Bill's gonna open the champagne."

"No, thanks. I've gotta get going." I looked at the balloons. "So it was a girl, huh? She was right in her prediction."

"No," Jeanette mused, frowning as she drew out the word. "Daphne told everyone she was positive it was going to be a boy. Bill already bought a toy football and one of those battery-operated trucks for his son to ride in." She looked concerned. "I hope he kept the receipts."

I cocked my head. "Well, some girls like that kind of thing."

Jeanette's eyes went everywhere but to mine. "Oh yeah. Sure."

"Tell her congratulations from me, okay?"

Jeanette nodded, and I turned toward the door again. Her voice stopped me. "You know, it is kinda funny. She already had a girl's name picked out."

I looked back. "Yeah?"

"Yeah. Guess you gotta have a backup plan, even when you're sure. Bill said he doesn't care, so…"

I had to ask. "What did she name her?"

"Lena. Lena Eleanor Polk."

Eleanor. My middle name. The one practically no one in the whole world knew, other than my father and the school district officials. And Daphne. "Cool." I grinned. "Thanks. Have fun."

She waved and returned to the increasingly noisy crowd.

I took a quick detour by the nursery. There was a man standing out front, and I slowed as I realized it was Daphne's father. He looked around and smiled. "Would you like to see my granddaughter?"

I couldn't tell if he recognized me since he hadn't seen me for over eight years, but I went with it. "I certainly would." He pointed, and we admired the sleeping infant for several minutes. "She's perfect," I whispered. "So beautiful."

"Just like her momma," he said proudly.

I couldn't have agreed more. "Congratulations," I said warmly, knowing to leave before it got too crowded.

He nodded, his gaze never leaving the baby. I told myself I should go home, but instead, I pushed the elevator button for Daphne's floor. No one was at the nurses' station, so I snuck down the hall and opened her door quietly. There was still dripping and beeping, and Daphne appeared to be asleep. I crept closer, wanting to see her face and reassure myself that she really was all right.

She shifted and moaned in obvious pain. "Nurse?" she asked. "Did you bring my baby to me?"

"Hey. It's me. I'm sorry if I woke you. I wanted to make sure—"

"Max. I need to see her. I need to feed her. All the books say—"

She was getting agitated, so I moved to her bedside and put my hand on her arm again. "Daphne, I just saw her. She's fine. She's beautiful. She's sleeping, and you should be too."

"No." I'd heard that tone before. Post-op or no, she wouldn't be deterred. "Make them bring her here, or I'll go get her myself." She put her hand on the IV as if ready to pull it out and focused on my face. "And you know I'll do it too."

I did know. The station nurse was back, and one look at her expression told me I would lose this argument. But I had to try. "Nurse Vickers?" I'd stolen a quick glance at her nametag as I tried to form a sincere expression. "We're in need of your expertise. Mrs. Polk is in pain, but she's refusing to take any medication until she sees her baby. Would it be possible for that to happen now so we can set our new mother's mind at ease?"

She glanced at her watch, appearing to be giving the matter some thought before asking the most implacable of all hospital questions. "And who are you in relation to the patient?"

Make up a quick lie or take a chance on the truth? A voice from behind me spoke up. "She's the patient's sister." I turned to see Daphne's daddy standing there, his face stern. "And I am her father. Please bring the baby immediately. My daughter needs rest."

I would have resented the effectiveness of male privilege, but all that mattered was getting Daphne what she needed. After the nurse scurried off, Mr. Kimball turned to me. "You go keep her company, Max. I'll hold the fort out here."

Daphne had turned to look out the doorway, and her face was ashen from the effort. "She's coming," I told her. "They're bringing her now." Her eyes closed for a few seconds as she nodded slightly. As much as I would have liked to take credit for everything, I added, "Your dad is out in the hall and he—"

"I need to tell you something." She spoke quickly. "In case I—"

"No." I couldn't listen to that. "There's no 'in case.' You're gonna be fine. Everyone says so."

"In case I get busy," Daphne insisted, "and become one of those crazy mothers who forgets everything."

I relaxed, too relieved to feel foolish. "Yeah, right. 'Cause we can all see that happening."

There was the sound of conversation coming closer and a weak cry. Daphne's face lit up like Christmas. It was a beautiful sight.

"Why don't you tell me later?" I said around the lump in my throat. "I think you're about to have company."

She grabbed my arm to stop me from turning away, her expression intent. "What I said to you. That last thing. It wasn't true. You were my best ever. You still are."

Before I could ask what she was talking about, the door opened, and baby Lena made her grand entrance, accompanied by a nurse, the attending doctor, and proud grandparents. I'd already had one good look, and that was all I'd needed to know I was going to love her. Plus, I could recognize a private moment when I saw one, so I took the elevator back to the main floor. Things were quiet in the maternity waiting area. Almost everyone had cleared out. A hospital helper was collecting used cups and the drooping streamers from across the furniture and the light fixtures. Bill Polk was snoring loudly on the couch.

I stepped out into the evening, stunned to see my dad's truck parked by the far curb. He leaned over to call out the open side window, "Daphne's dad called and said you needed a ride."

It wasn't until I sat in the passenger seat that I realized how tired I was. "Sorry to get you out so late." JT wasn't anything resembling a night owl.

"No. It's fine. And I was glad you told me what was going on earlier." He hesitated. "I've been kinda worried about you, Max."

"I know. But I'm...I'm feeling better lately. I'm gonna be fine, okay?"

"Okay."

We drove home in silence, but he seemed pleased that I hugged him before we stumbled to our separate rooms. It wasn't until I was lying in my room in that twilight state just before dropping into sleep that I remembered Daphne's comments: *That last thing. It wasn't true.* There in my bed, where I'd never failed to think of being with her, it all made sense. She was apologizing for the harsh words she'd flung at me before she'd left the night of her bridal shower. *You were my best ever.*

I woke up with my face aching. I must have smiled all night.

CHAPTER SIX

2000
Age Eighteen

Everything seemed to get better after that night. Since the high school had an open campus, I'd run over to Daphne's for lunch every few days, just to see the baby, of course. We talked about her endlessly, admiring her every move and sound, planning a variety of exciting futures for her. Only twice was Bill there, and those conversations were very different and somewhat stilted. He clearly didn't know what to make of me. On some level, he might have sensed that I could be a threat, but his male superiority complex wouldn't allow him to really believe it.

Daphne and I never talked about our night together or about what she had said in the hospital. She was incredibly happy being a mother, and I'd begun to branch out with interests of my own at school.

In the spring of my junior year, I auditioned for a role in the chorus of *Oklahoma!*, the yearly musical. I'd already been in the choir for a year and a half, so the director knew me. I genuinely liked Mrs. Cannon, who was the kind of teacher who got the best out of her students without threats or ragging on us. Under her direction, the choir was consistently in competition for state honors, and we were one of the few schools in the area who still put on a full musical show every year. When a family moved to town from somewhere nearby, it was often because they had a talented singer who had turned high school age and wanted to take part in Mrs. Cannon's choral program.

At my audition, after I quietly stated that I would be happy dressed in a costume of either gender and would sing the part accordingly, Mrs. Cannon didn't bat an eye. She had a husband of many years and was a proud grandmother, so her matter-of-fact acceptance was probably not from any personal experience. She was simply cool.

Right before school started, I'd gone through the ceremony of becoming one of Lena's godparents. I was so happy and proud to be standing there that it didn't bother me to hear the priest address all his remarks—except those about evil and temptation—to Bill's younger brother, who was the other godparent. It also didn't hurt that Daphne and the baby had been in the bathroom where I'd stopped off before the ceremony began.

While Lena had giggled as I'd nibbled on her tiny fingers, Daphne had looked me over and licked her lips. "You look very nice." When I'd returned the compliment, she'd covered Lena's ears carefully and added, "And you look sexy as hell." She'd leaned in and kissed me on the cheek, lingering an extra second as she caught scent of my cologne. There was the slightest brush of her cheek on mine before she'd swallowed and said, "Yeah. Now I'm going to have to ignore you for the rest of the day." And she had. But the extra baby-holding I'd gotten while she'd visited with everyone had pretty much made up for it.

I was a year older than most in my class, but it was having loved and lost—more or less—that made me feel more worldly-wise. I relished the feeling that my whole life was stretching out before me, and unlike many students who suffered from "premature senioritis," I was ready to kick back and enjoy the last of high school.

Somewhere in the process, I must have lost that "fuck off" expression because more people began speaking to me in the halls. A classmate even asked if I wanted to run for student council, a gesture which I appreciated, though I declined. I just felt like I was in a really good place, and I didn't want to upset my equilibrium.

With age, I also gained a clearer understanding of my mother's mental disorder and worked to manage any extreme emotional highs or lows, allowing the feelings but keeping my reactions as level as possible. I spent hours scrutinizing my thoughts and behavior, checking for any sign I might be motivated by delusions or responding inappropriately to situations. Such introspection might have been something that many folks did, but I had a better reason than most. Intellectually, I'd known that the mood swings of puberty were normal, but both the frequent irritation and the occasional depression terrified me. During those times, it was all I could do to keep the dreadful images of my past in that remote place where I'd carefully stored them. But now, having survived so much emotion over Daphne and coming through unscathed, I felt like I could breathe easy and appreciate life for a change.

In my new, less troubled state of mind, I was more sensitive to what others might be going through, and with that awareness came new empathy. For example, I didn't envy the politics of Mrs. Cannon's job. With so many cuts to programs like hers at the state level—because who needed the arts when you had football—she was really dependent on community fundraising. One of her *Oklahoma!* casting decisions had already ruffled significant feathers. As everyone had anticipated, the main female lead—farm girl, Laurey Williams—had gone to Maryjane Bowen, a senior who'd fancied herself God's gift to music and theater. She was accomplished enough, I supposed, but her arrogance and entitlement were nothing short of annoying. She'd been in my original class, before I'd missed a year of school, and had been super nice to me at recess after I'd returned to face a whole new group of classmates. Otherwise, I wouldn't have been able to stand her.

Everyone expected that the secondary role of Ado Annie would go to Maryjane's best friend, Katherine Hutchins. But shock waves rippled through the small but dedicated group of theater students and parents after Katherine was given the lesser role of Aunt Eller, and a newcomer to the school won the secondary lead.

That girl was decidedly playing against type. While her character was flirtatious, Sylvia Raymond was the total opposite. According to gossip, this was the first school activity she'd ever participated in. Her family had recently moved to town, and she had yet to date or hang out with anyone. She wore ankle-length, frumpy dresses or skirts and long-sleeved blouses, even in the Texas heat. She ate lunch alone. I only had one class with her, and she was very quiet, although she appeared to be listening intently and knew every answer when called upon.

Our paths intersected after the boy playing Will Parker, Ado Annie's love interest, got the flu during the first week of rehearsal. In another shocking move, Mrs. Cannon tapped me to stand in for him until his return. I'd won the role partly by virtue of already knowing practically all the lines, since *Oklahoma!* was one of JT's favorites, and because I could sing well enough for an understudy. Asking me privately if I would do it, Mrs. Cannon had also indicated that she'd needed someone whose ego didn't need to be massaged, and I'd known she was referring to a boy named Albert Fannin, who was already smarting that he didn't get to play the part of Jud Fry, another major character. I secretly thought he had exactly the right personality to play the lonely, disturbed field hand, but I accepted Will's part and ignored the stares and whispers about me playing a boy's role.

The only other openly gay person in the school, a beautiful Hispanic boy named Marcos Salazar, was playing Hakim, one of the males pursuing Ado Annie. He wasn't particularly swishy, but he knew how to add comic relief, and the theater teacher had to pull him aside on several occasions to caution him about stealing scenes. I'd known Marcos since eighth grade, where we'd frequently had classes together and were often paired in group activities—because the teachers had expected we would stick up for each other—so it had seemed inevitable that we would bond. We stood next to each other in the concert choir, where we got into trouble for chattering, as Mrs. Cannon called it, although we'd always mind her request to, "Settle down, you two."

Now, Sylvia Raymond and I would be acting as potential lovers, with Marcos on the third point of our triangle. He was usually quick in finding someone's least attractive characteristic and naming them after it—"Halitosis," "Stupid on a Stick," and "Oversized Falsies," were a few of our fellow cast members—but was strangely gracious about Sylvia. "Still Waters Run Deep," was his designation for her.

After Mrs. Cannon pulled her aside to explain the temporary change, Sylvia paled, and I could easily imagine why. There were several points in the story where Ado Annie and Will kissed or almost kissed. I had watched Sylvia during rehearsals with her male lead, and she had clearly been uncomfortable. It wasn't hard to imagine how much worse she would feel about kissing a girl.

For the first two days, we blocked out our scenes, practicing where to stand and how to move without any other actors. We rehearsed our lines in a prop storeroom across the hall from the auditorium. Whenever we got to a stage direction about kissing, Sylvia would look away, saying something like, "What's next?" or "Then what happens?"

Our new roles allowed me to notice her alluring appearance. Her eyes were a deep brown behind her glasses, which she removed while on stage, and her tawny skin seemed highlighted by the long brown hair she wore loose while in character. She was taller than me by several inches, even in flats, and I had on boots with heels, but it would be no problem when the real Will returned, as he towered over her by almost a foot. She'd evidently spent enough time in the southwest to replicate the twang needed to play someone from Oklahoma, but it was odd to hear those inelegant sounds coming from her somewhat wide, improbably sensuous mouth.

In spite of my growing fascination with her chameleon-like abilities as she shifted effortlessly from silent, drab Sylvia to bubbly, teasing Ado Annie, I'd quickly grown tired of the implied brush off regarding our so-called love scenes. I needed to clear the air. "Look, Sylvia," I said on our third day of rehearsal, "I understand if it weirds you out to kiss a girl. If it makes you feel any better, you can put your hand over your mouth, and our lips won't actually touch. But we do need to practice the move, at least."

"Thank you, but it's not what you think," she replied vaguely.

"How would you know what I think?" I asked, a little arrogantly. I hated it when people assumed they could understand anything about me simply because they knew my sexual identity.

"You think I don't like you," she answered calmly. "That I find you disgusting or perverted, and that's why I act as I do."

"Yeah, and in that case, I'll get past it, believe me. Your feelings about me won't change how I feel about myself, and that's what counts." It had taken me some thought to hone that remark, and I was damn proud of it.

A slight smirk crept across her face. "An admirable sentiment. Bravo, Max. But such a declaration is wholly unnecessary, given your confident use of such a masculine name."

Her response puzzled me. Assuming my best drawl, which I'd beefed up for our production, I asked, "Where're you from, anyway?"

The grin disappeared, and she looked down. "I used to say that I was from everywhere, but lately, I've been feeling more like I'm not from anywhere."

She sounded so sad that I took a step toward her, my hand out as my inopportune, idealistic self emerged yet again. "That means you're waiting for your true love. Because once you find that person, they'll be where you're from."

As soon as the words were out, I grimaced, trying to imagine what her reaction would be. Would she think me ridiculous? Incredibly lame? A total fool? To my surprise, I heard her take a step toward me, and I looked up to find her dancing eyes fixed on mine.

"Why, Max Terrell," she said in her Ado Annie voice. "You're a romantic."

I looked away, trying to play it off with a sniff. "No...I meant—"

"Don't try to deny it. Or I'll lose my nerve to tell you what I was going to say earlier." She was back to being Sylvia. She touched my face, bringing my gaze to hers, and I realized she'd closed the distance between us. She was near enough that I could see her nostrils flaring. "I haven't avoided dealing with our love scenes because I don't want to kiss you. I've been avoiding them because I do."

"You do?" Easily the stupidest response I could have made, but luckily for me, she smiled and nodded.

"Yes," she repeated, bending slowly toward me. "I do."

Sylvia Raymond kissed me like I had never been kissed before. When I'd kissed Daphne, it had been all heart. My body and my mind had been in a completely different dimension, so I didn't count that. With other girls, it was all experimentation and working on my technique. This was intensely physical, no tentative peck or grinding immature press. Her mouth opened just enough that I could sense the moisture on her tongue; the pressure of her lips was sweet but certain. For a few seconds, I was too shocked to react, barely aware of her holding my face and of my hand resting on the curve of her waist where it had somehow landed as she'd stepped into me. I let myself sink into that incredible mouth, and the more I let her, the more she took.

She pushed into me enough that I had to take a step back and then another. She followed until I was against the wall, and her body was flush against mine. Somewhere in the process, I put my hands on her biceps to steady myself and was shocked to find significant muscles.

"I'd like you to take your blouse off," I murmured, my voice unsteady as she had moved to my throat and was alternately kissing and biting.

Her hands moved inside my shirt. "I will if you will." She massaged my breasts through my sports bra. "These are gorgeous. Don't think I haven't noticed."

She devoured my mouth again, and I didn't ever want to come up for air. I wanted her to touch me. I wanted her to fuck me. I could feel the blood racing through my body, and I knew it wouldn't take much to get me off. I massaged her well-developed ass and was rewarded with a low moan.

Mrs. Cannon's voice boomed down the hall instructing us to return to the stage. We hastily broke apart.

"Damn, Raymond." I was breathing in short gasps. This wasn't my role. I was supposed to be the cocky, casual one, the lady-killer.

"Ray," she whispered, her hand on the doorknob. "You can call me Ray." She devastated me with a wink. "But just...well...only at times like this."

I barely managed to fumble my way through the rest of rehearsal, incredibly thankful that we didn't have any scenes with Marcos, who could detect arousal at forty paces.

❖

During our wild affair, I learned that the girl I'd thought of as dowdy and brainy could be forceful and dominant in matters of passion. If I fought her for control, she would slow and become hesitant, but if I gave in, she wouldn't stop. The lines we practiced in our prop room run-throughs led us away from the *Oklahoma!* story and into our own.

During the line where Ado Annie teased Will about the first time she was kissed, I asked Sylvia about her first time. It was a few years ago at church, she disclosed, in the choir loft after everyone else had left. Struck by an unexpected jolt of jealousy, I started a kiss that made us both want to rip our clothes off. We separated, panting, and I demanded to know if that kiss had been as enjoyable.

I sensed Ray in the responding grin, but Sylvia answered as Ado Annie. "Not hardly."

I spoke as Will, drawling, "I always thought you good girls was secretly up to no good."

Sylvia sobered. "Everyone puts their own preconceived ideas on the pastor's daughter. Especially if she acts the part. But I never claimed to be good...or a girl."

"Well, you are a damn fine actor," I said earnestly, beginning to see where Sylvia left off and Ray began.

She looked at her hands. "You have no idea."

Being with Sylvia, or Ray, made me painfully aware that I was as guilty as anyone else about stereotyping others. Those words about not being a girl echoed in my head, making me reassess the understanding I had of my own identity. I wore my hair shorter, and I liked sports and pretty girls, so as I started figuring things out, I identified as butch. But even when my body began to fill out, I was comfortable being inside it. Oh, I might have wished for more height or more strength, but the sense of wrongness and the craving to change that Sylvia felt must have been almost overwhelming.

We began eating lunch together, holding a script to make it look like we were working on our lines. But in our quiet conversations, I learned that her parents were insanely strict. They'd moved frequently because her dad was a minister, and they'd also been missionaries in Burundi for several years during her childhood, which explained her accent. She didn't talk much about that time, except to say that it was often exciting, though there had been times she'd been terribly frightened.

Her dad was now intent on getting his own church here in America, she reported, but he'd tended to go about it by stirring things up where he was an associate and trying to get enough of the congregation to split off and follow him. This approach didn't make their family particularly popular with the bigger church, which was why they kept getting reassigned, and he was increasingly bitter that things weren't working out. Her mom was fanatical, obsessed with

Biblical teaching, though of course, she deferred to her husband on all things, as a good Christian wife would.

When I asked her to go for a ride on my bike one unexpectedly warm afternoon before rehearsal, Sylvia shook her head. "You're clearly an abomination," she said with a contradictory roll of her eyes, "so I can't ever be seen with you, especially outside school. If anyone else saw and my dad found out, they'd start homeschooling me again. My attendance here is to show other parents that we're part of the community as well as a godly family. And the sole reason he's letting me participate in this musical is because I told him I had to, or I'd fail the class."

Since she'd revealed that she wasn't above lying to her folks, I was eager to help her craft fabrications that would get us alone, but it only happened a few times. Our first opportunity came after Mrs. Cannon had to cancel the rehearsal because of a short in the light board. Once everyone else was gone, Sylvia nervously agreed to come to my house. The perfect young lady I introduced to my dad became terribly anxious when we went into my bedroom and shut the door.

She looking around suspiciously, peering into my bathroom and noting the adjoining door on the other side. "What's in there?"

It could have been Adam's room. Not like I would mention that at this point. "Nothing. It's our guest room. We use it for storage, and there's some exercise equipment in there too."

Seemingly satisfied but still tense, she said, "Won't your dad wonder what we're doing in here?"

"He'll assume we're studying." I pointed to her book bag. "Otherwise, he won't think about it. He usually watches TV with his headset on, so no worries." I put my hands on her shoulders and squeezed. "Relax." I wiggled my eyebrows suggestively. "You're not the first girl I've had in my room at night."

She grabbed my shirt and backed me up until my knees hit the bed. With her arms wrapped around my back, she bent me slightly backward. Holding me off-balance, she demanded, "How many women have you kissed in here, Max?"

Damn, she was strong. "Maybe five. But one was in fifth grade."

Her expression softened, and she lowered me carefully to the mattress. Hovering over me she asked, "And did you fuck any of the others?"

"Just one. And I don't want to talk about it. Please, Ray?"

She smiled slowly. "All right. Since you asked so nicely." She brought her lips to within an inch of mine. "Do you think we could manage to make it two in the time we have left? Without alerting your dad?"

"Yes." I tried to reach for her mouth, but she held me back.

"Yes, what?"

"Yes, please." She lifted my legs onto the bed. I couldn't believe how excited I was. I was scooting over to make room for her when she lay on top of me. I fought hard not to moan, but a little whimper came out.

She bit my neck and whispered in my ear, "I've been thinking about you every night. Do you want me to show you what that's like for me?"

"Yes, Ray." I started to unbutton my jeans, but she stopped me.

"No. You can't do that. At my house, I'm not allowed to close my door, and one of my parents often walks past in the hallway. They make a point of checking on me quite regularly." Taking my hand, she guided my fingers to the crotch of my jeans. "Rub yourself, Max. But remember, you can't move very much. And you can't make any noise."

I looked back at her as she commanded me with a rough whisper:

"Hurry. Do it quickly. They might come by at any second." I swallowed and started rubbing. The center seam of my jeans was firm on my clit, and I grunted involuntarily. "Stop." She stilled my hand. "Is someone out there?"

I understood. She was not only showing me what she did but also making me feel everything she experienced in doing it. "No. They didn't hear me."

"Be careful," she said. "I'll be punished if they catch me. Then I'll never get my hands on your beautiful breasts. And God, I want to so badly. I want to watch your eyes close while I suck them. I want to feel you arch beneath me."

"Ray," I mouthed her name at less than a whisper. The warm coils of orgasm were starting deep in my groin, but I didn't want it to be like this. The thought of her oppressive home life, constantly scrutinized as a "PK," preacher's kid, moving frequently and unable to make real friends—people she could trust enough to be her true self—made me frightened for her and for the risk she was taking to be here with me now. But she had already trusted me this far, and perhaps that was the key.

I stopped my motions, though I didn't turn to look at her. "You can touch me. We're safe here. I promise."

There was no sound for a few seconds. I held my breath. I was about two heartbeats from begging her when she rolled me onto my back and kissed me. Oh God, that mouth. In a matter of minutes, we were both naked, and she was doing exactly what she'd imagined: sucking my breasts while I arched beneath her. And though she was still clearly in control, there was something immensely empowering about fulfilling her fantasy.

Abruptly, she straddled my thigh, rocking herself hard for a few seconds before sliding a finger inside me. I gasped, and she froze, holding herself still. "Is this the first time for you like this?"

I nodded, still recovering from the shock of being penetrated so unexpectedly. Daphne's words praising me for asking if she was ready threatened to surface, but I pushed them away.

Ray closed her eyes, moving inside me. "You feel incredible, Max. You're so delicate there, so tight." She rolled her hips again, and I could feel her clit, rigid along my leg. I trailed my hands down, caressing her well-developed back, pulling her harder against me. She moaned low in her throat and began moving with purpose as she thrust inside, panting quietly. I felt her body stiffen and shudder, and I tried to match her, to let her pleasure push me toward climax, but it wasn't happening. After a few seconds, she grunted and withdrew her finger before rolling onto her back, her breathing still uneven. I waited a few seconds before turning to her. She flinched when I rested my hand on her abdomen, but I felt her settle again as I stroked her lightly.

"How did you get so strong?" I asked, keeping my voice soft. Seeing her naked for the first time, I confirmed what I'd felt through her clothes. She was incredibly muscular, not as extreme as a competitive bodybuilder but with the physique of a very powerful athlete.

She breathed in, letting it out slowly. "Ever since I could walk, I worked with the villagers in the fields. Carrying tools, bringing water, whatever I could manage. Doing something physical suited me, and I truly wanted to be of service. I pushed myself, determined to lift more, move faster, eventually helping with the planting and harvesting. Farming is hard work." A corner of her mouth lifted. "My parents were busy saving souls. They had no idea what effect that kind of daily exercise would have. But I loved being strong enough to move a bale of hay or help hold a birthing cow."

After a moment, she said, "It's not enough, but it's helped me be more comfortable in my body. Since then, I've always found a way to work out, whether it was walking for miles or lifting big cans of food or jugs of water over and over. I'd give anything to dress like you do, but"—her tone changed to a serious, lower pitch—"'a woman shall not wear man's clothing, nor shall a man put on a woman's clothing; for whoever does these things is an abomination to the Lord your God.' I've worn those shapeless, long-sleeved dresses no matter the weather or the occasion because"—her voice became mocking now—"we are a plain people, for according to scripture, 'women should adorn themselves in respectable apparel, with modesty and self-control, not with braided hair and gold or pearls or costly attire.'" She shook her head and smiled contemptuously, returning to her normal voice. "The only good thing about our family modesty is that my parents haven't really seen how my body looks since I was in diapers."

I thought about the day I'd come out to JT and how his acceptance and unconditional love for me had never faltered. From the day we had "the talk," he stood up to anyone who questioned my upbringing or my appearance. He never asked me to change, never suggested I tried to be anyone but exactly who I was. Part of me wanted to go give him a hug right then. Instead, I asked, "What are you going to do after you graduate? Are you going to college?"

"No. I'm supposed to go into the mission field. And find a husband. In that order, I think."

"So will you?"

She looked at me for a long moment, as if evaluating the extent of our friendship. "I'm getting out," she said with great intensity. "No matter what. I have to. I can't remain a part of my family or my church and be myself. Or who I want to be. Who I need to be."

The ferocity in her voice worried me. I'd been born in Pokeville, and people here knew me, even if some didn't accept me. She had no such roots and no support system. "Who do you want to be?"

She'd looked away so her voice was faint. Still, I know she whispered, "Ray," as Tracy Chapman's "Give Me One Reason" began playing on my clock radio. She turned to me abruptly. "What was that?"

I thumbed it off and sighed. "I set an alarm to make sure we'd get back to school all right. That's just the song that came on."

She was off the bed and dressing before I could finish my sentence. "We won't be late, will we?"

Her anxiety made me move quickly too, as I assured her, "No. I left us plenty of time. We're fine."

Still, she was standing at the door in less than a minute, shifting from foot to foot, waiting for me to button my jeans and slip into my boots. She reached for the knob as I joined her, but I stopped her arm with one hand, touching her face with the other. "I wish you didn't have to go. I like getting to know you."

Clearly, I hadn't learned my lesson from Daphne because Ray's expression turned distant. "That's sweet, Max. But let's just enjoy ourselves while we can." Turning the knob, she unexpectedly stopped, as if she'd heard the coldness of her words. Or maybe it was how I jerked my hand from her grasp. She brought her lips softly to mine, and I wondered absently if I could learn to orgasm from her kisses. "Don't misunderstand me. I like you too, and I don't want you to get hurt, okay?"

I made a brave face. "Hey, don't worry about me. I'm tough, remember?"

She laughed and went out, making a point of saying good-bye to my dad. He insisted we take his truck, saying the temperature had dropped at least twenty degrees in the last couple of hours and that snow was predicted for tomorrow. The school building was dark and deserted, and she was clearly worried that it would look different than it had at other times. "Tell your folks rehearsal let out fifteen minutes early, and everyone cleared out because of the weather," I suggested, employing the excellent lying technique I was constantly perfecting.

She nodded, fidgeting with her book bag. "Go on, Max. Please. I'll be fine."

I drove off but turned the truck around once I was out of sight and crept closer with my lights off. Almost fifteen minutes later, as I was about to go get her out of the cold, an old Ford came slowly along the road, stopping in front of the school. I slumped down as it drove by but still tried to get a glimpse of the driver. When the door opened and the inside light came on, I could only see salt-and-pepper hair on a head turned toward his passenger, the daughter he thought he knew.

❖

"You don't look much like your father," Sylvia observed.

We were on stage waiting for Mrs. Cannon to finish working with the chorus who had missed their entrance cue yet again. I blinked a few times, apprehensive about where this seemingly casual comment might lead, trying to sort out the best response. "Yeah, but I'm a whole lot like him on the inside," I offered, and she looked pleased. I lowered my voice. "Everything okay at home?"

I truly wanted to know, plus I really, really wanted to change the subject. "Fine." She stretched, looking casually at the other students. Everyone else was practicing with Mrs. Cannon. "Where's your mother?"

I shook my head and looked away. Nobody who was from Pokeville would have asked me that question. Once I'd returned to elementary school after the disaster that had sent my mother to Rusk State Hospital, where Texas housed those who had been found not guilty by reason of insanity, my teachers had been quick to hush up any talk. By middle school, that part of my story was old news compared to my emerging butch style, but a particularly mean bully like Albert Fannin might combine a past insult with a current slur. Any new students obviously heard the story at some point, as I'd occasionally catch a questioning or pitying expression from a face I didn't recognize. No matter which groups of kids I was hanging with,

I knew Daphne had my back, and we didn't need to discuss it. We'd lived it. So it might seem strange that such a simple question could feel like someone opened a partially healed scar with a dull blade, but it did.

How Sylvia could see me bite my lip with my head turned, I don't know, but I felt her touch my shoulder. "Cough," she said softly.

I heard the shuffling of feet and Mrs. Cannon's voice. "All right, Will and Ado Annie. Let's try that again from your break."

My mind caught up. I coughed. A lot.

"Could Will go get some water, Mrs. Cannon?" Sylvia asked.

"Of course. Go ahead, Will."

I exited the stage with my hand over my mouth, taking the deserted hallway to the farthest water fountain I could think of.

There was a faintly warm homemade blueberry muffin in my locker the next morning with the word, "Sorry," written inside a heart. Sylvia had gotten the story somehow, and she didn't mention it again.

CHAPTER SEVEN

2000
Age Eighteen

My official duties as Will Parker ended, but while mentoring the recovered Will, a nice guy named Jack Mickton, I got some extra moments with Sylvia. We continued having lunch together, and there was World History, where we exchanged notes each day. It was an extra window into her soul to read the far-ranging thoughts that appeared in her neat handwriting. The next time we managed to be alone was when we skipped that class, she with a forged note and me with the bravado of someone whose dad would give them only a minor punishment if they got caught.

At her insistence, we went separate ways to a third house two streets over from the school, where I picked her up on my bike, before going to my house. Once there, however, she refused to undress or let me touch her, eventually admitting that she had her period and was suffering from bad cramps, as was usual for her. I offered to help, but she replied that we didn't yet know each other well enough for me to see her in that condition. When I didn't argue, she managed to put her talented mouth to good use, getting me off in rather spectacular fashion without taking off a single piece of clothing.

On our way back, a car behind us started honking. Sylvia was almost beside herself in terror, begging me not to stop. After a careful glance in the rearview, I told her it was a friend of mine and slowed to let Daphne pull alongside us.

"Hey, you goof." She smirked before her gaze flitted to Sylvia. "Are you skipping school again?"

"Technically, perhaps," I admitted, unable to keep from smiling back. "But Ado Annie here had one of those female accidents, so I took her to my house to get cleaned up and borrow some underwear." This was somewhere in the vicinity of the truth.

Daphne's brow arched as she appraised Sylvia's simple, unfashionably long skirt. "So you're wearing boxers under that outfit? Honey, that's what I call a fashion statement."

"Let's go," Sylvia hissed in my ear. I nodded, unable to explain that too quick an exit would make Daphne suspicious.

"How's Lena?" I asked.

"Missing you, I think." Daphne pretended to ponder her answer. "Although, I can't imagine why."

Sylvia poked me in the ribs, and I revved the throttle a few times. "Gotta return this A student to her education," I gestured toward her with my thumb. "Come see our show."

"Only if it's the X-rated version." Daphne licked her lips. "Nice sort of meeting you, Annie."

It was too late for us to use the same "separate ways" process to return, so I let Sylvia off by the athletic fields, which were at the end of the block where the school was.

She wasn't at lunch, and everyone but me was quite amused when Mrs. Cannon announced that I would be standing in for Ado Annie tonight, Sylvia having been called away for a family emergency.

She's fine, she's fine, she's fine, I repeated over and over, to the point that I missed three cues I knew perfectly well, having played the other side of them for a week. After rehearsal, Mrs. Cannon pulled me aside and handed me some sheet music.

"I'm worried about Sylvia," she said. "Her father sounded rather distressed when I returned his phone call."

"Her father called?" I asked, my reassuring internal refrain quickly fading.

"Yes. Evidently, there was a problem in some other class. He indicated she might not be taking part in the show after all." Her eyes were sad, and I knew she wasn't only upset about the musical. I couldn't manage a reply. "So…you'll need to learn these songs, and we'll get you fitted for her costume if I don't hear anything tomorrow."

My hands were shaking so badly that the sheet music was making little fluttering sounds. I tightened my grip on the pages. "But she'll be back at school, won't she?"

"I'm afraid I don't know, Max." Mrs. Cannon turned away after a few seconds. "It's too late to put you in the official program, but we'll print inserts with your name, and I'll get my second period class to staple them in next week."

"I don't care about that," I blurted, and she looked back.

"I know you don't, honey. But as they say, 'the show must go on.' I know that's not much, but it's the best I've got for you right now."

I wanted to cuss and scream and cry and hit something, all at the same time. Guilt and loss, the hardest emotions for me to deal with, drove me from the room, and I stalked through the deserted hallways until I reached the darkened attendance office. I wasn't the type to vandalize property, but I couldn't stand the thought of losing Sylvia after I'd lost Adam and had never really had Daphne. I broke the window in the door to gain access and jimmied open a drawer in the ancient wooden file cabinet where new student records were kept. I carefully replaced Sylvia Raymond's file after getting her home address and phone number.

I drove past slowly, steadily revving my engine as loudly as I could. There were a few cars parked out front, and the lights were on in what appeared to be a living room. Was there some kind of intervention going on? And if so, was it my fault? Had someone seen us? My mind went to Daphne, but I dismissed it. Even if she was vaguely jealous, which she had no earthly reason to be, I was certain she wouldn't rat us out. Then who? How had this happened?

Three times, I drove up and down her street at top speed, my engine roaring. I stopped out front and planted my foot, doing a doughnut in the street, the stench of burning rubber filling my nose.

The door to the house across the street opened and a man yelled, "Get out of here, you punk, or I'm calling the cops."

I wasn't the only one in town with a motorcycle, and there was no way he could recognize me in my leathers at night. Letting my ire dominate me for a moment, I shot him the finger, but I knew I had to go. As I turned my bike for home, I thought I saw the curtains in the Raymond house move, and a crack of light shone out. I couldn't see faces, but I stretched my arms out, palms open, in the pose of Jesus on the cross.

I'm sorry, Ray. Please forgive me.

❖

I went through the next few days in a kind of funk, screwing up so regularly that Mrs. Cannon took the rest of the crew to the choir room and left Jack and me to practice alone. He was super sweet and patient, and when we were taking a break after one of our songs, he said, "I guess you'd rather not be playing this role, huh?"

His family were ranchers, so getting into character wasn't much of a stretch for him. I managed a weak smile. "It's not a bad part. It's just—" I felt my throat start to close up.

"You made friends with Sylvia?" I nodded my reply. "She seemed nice. Sure could sing too."

It was true. Sylvia had a beautiful singing voice, too good for Ado Annie's songs, really. She would have made the perfect Laurey, but no way could Mrs. Cannon have put a recent arrival to town in the lead role.

"I guess she grew up singing in her church choir," Jack went on. "Albert told me she had a solo about every other Sunday."

"Albert?" I asked faintly, still hearing echoes of Sylvia's songs in my head.

"Yeah, he goes to that church where her dad preaches sometimes. We have gym together third period." He grinned and nudged me with his elbow. "Saw you let her off your bike a while back. Figured you went for a joyride." His expression sobered. "I told him it was probably okay for someone like Sylvia to let her hair down a little but Albert, he said…uh…"

"I know Albert doesn't like me," I assured him, trying to keep my voice calm. Jack was too much of a gentleman to say something hurtful if he could avoid it. "And I can't imagine he could think of something that I haven't heard before. You can tell me, Jack."

Jack scuffed his boot on the floor. "Oh, well, he said something about you being a bad influence, and he didn't imagine the reverend would approve of you being friends with his daughter." He gave me an apologetic look. "I think Pastor Raymond has been counseling Albert since his daddy took off last month."

The hurt inside me lifted a bit. There was plenty of blame to go around on this one, but at least I had the big picture.

Jack cleared his throat. "But you know what? Sylvia ain't here anymore, and you are. And your voice sounds fine. You know the lines, I know you do. So you gotta quit fighting yourself and let Ado Annie take over while you're on stage." He grinned and thumped my forehead lightly with his thumb. "I reckon she's in there somewhere."

I smiled at him. "I reckon you're right."

Oklahoma! went off without a hitch, on my part anyway. Other players made a few mistakes here and there, but after our last night, Mrs. Cannon gave me a warm hug and told me that our performances stole the show. At the cast party, I shared her remark with Jack and told him he was the real hero of our act.

"I honestly wouldn't have made it through this without you," I said as we embraced, causing him to swing me around and give me a substantial kiss, after which he blushed sweetly.

I looked around, seeing everyone kissing everyone else and was surprised by very nice kisses from both Maryjane and Katherine. All the cast members were laughing and hugging with a combination of pride and relief, and I was feeling better than I had in many days, until a voice beside me commented, "Don't know why you're getting all the love when you got that part by default, Terrell."

It was Albert Fannin. The room quieted as I turned to him slowly. "And whose fault is that, Albert?" He wouldn't meet my glare. After a few seconds of awkward silence, I lifted my red plastic cup and toasted. "To Sylvia. She brought us a long way in a short time."

"To Sylvia!" the room chimed in, and we drank. I left soon after, the joy of the evening having been stolen by my tribute of loss. I kept my cup, though, and snuck up to her front porch, leaving it on the railing there. I wrote the initials AA on it—for Ado Annie, of course—but left it empty. I thought that was symbolic.

❖

The rest of the school year was uneventful. My fame as Ado Annie got me a couple of dates, but my heart wasn't in it. Instead, I returned to routine visits with Daphne and Lena, amazed at how much the baby had grown and thrilled that she seemed to recognize me.

"Match," Lena exclaimed, and I looked to Daphne, waiting for a translation.

"That's you, you goof," Daphne clarified. "I'm Mama. She can't quite make that X sound yet."

"Yeah?" I made a raspberry on Lena's pudgy tummy, and she screamed with delight. "Is that right, jelly belly?"

"Why don't you take her outside for a bit?" Daphne asked, turning away. "You could both use the fresh air. But don't go far. I'm making lunch."

I walked Lena around, and we discussed names for trees and birds. When I walked her toward the driveway, she pointed at my bike. "Match bye." She waved, making me laugh and kiss the top of her head.

"Don't you get that child interested in your wild lifestyle," Daphne cautioned from the porch where she'd been watching. "Come and eat."

I started on a ham sandwich and chips while she cleaned the baby's hands and face and fed her some nasty looking stuff from a jar. "So tell me," she began with what sounded like forced indifference, "are you still seeing that Annie girl, or what?"

I shook my head, taking my time to drink my milk. "I'm sure you heard the story." Daphne was nothing if not a major link in the town's gossip chain. "Her parents took her out of school. That's why I got her part in the musical."

She nodded as if that information had slipped her mind. "You were good, by the way. Really cute. I never knew you could sing so well."

I wasn't surprised that she'd come to the musical. It was a major source of entertainment in a town our size. "How come you didn't talk to me afterward and let me bask in your adoration? We stars like that kind of thing, you know."

She ignored this. "Would you still be seeing her?"

"I'm not sure." There was no point in denying what Daphne obviously knew. "She wasn't exactly my type. Although, she was a great kisser." I threw that last part in and was pleased by her reaction.

"Was she now?" Daphne grabbed my plate abruptly and dumped it in the sink, ignoring my attempt to snag the last few chips.

"As a matter of fact, yes."

She glanced at me over her shoulder. "As a matter of fact, you're going to be late for your next class."

Shit. She was right. I jumped to my feet and headed for the door. "Thanks for lunch."

"Don't mention it." Her reply was cool enough to let me know precisely what she was talking about. But hell, she'd brought it up. As I raced back to school, I thought about Sylvia-Ray again. I definitely hadn't been in love with her. In many ways, we hardly knew each other. We hadn't shared years of memories and thousands of conversations the way Daphne and I had. But I wondered if I'd ever see her again. About three weeks into the summer, I had my answer.

❖

As JT spoke on the house phone one evening, something in his tone got my attention. I'd wandered into the kitchen while taking a break from an online college class I'd decided to try and heard what must have been the end of the conversation. "Yes, I certainly will. All right, sure. Of course not. No, I'm glad you called."

He sounded concerned and formal in a way that he rarely was, which made me think the call couldn't be anyone we knew or even a new customer. Before I could ask, he was getting his keys. "Your friend Sylvia is in the hospital. They won't release her on her own because she's had a concussion, so someone needs to watch her for at least twenty-four hours."

I moved toward the door, but he put out his hand to stop me. "Get the guest room ready, Max. She asked me to come alone. You'll see her soon."

"But—" The look on his face made me swallow everything I might have said. I simply nodded, and he left.

After two hours of intensive cleaning and reorganizing in our extra bedroom, during which I'd considered every terrible possibility and was about to take up smoking, I finally heard his truck.

I stopped myself from rushing to the door and summoned all my composure, determined not to make a fool of myself. But when she walked in, I had to cover my mouth to keep from gasping. A nasty-looking shiner had swollen her left eye almost shut, and she had a split lip. She walked carefully and with some effort, as if she was trying to avoid hurting herself any further. As I watched, I realized that I was seeing her in pants and a T-shirt for the first time. But the greatest change was her hair. Her waist-length locks were now short as a man's.

She tried to smile at me, but it looked more like a grimace. "Has anyone ever told you that you don't have much of a poker face, Max?"

My cool had already deserted me. "I'd really like to hug you, but I'm afraid it might hurt if I do."

"It might. But some things are worth the pain."

I moved close and let her lead, as she'd always done. She put her arms lightly on my shoulders, and I leaned into her, listening to her shallow breathing and feeling her trembling. "I'm so glad to see you," I whispered. She squeezed a little tighter.

JT closed and locked the door, something we rarely did while home. "Get her settled in the guest room, and let her rest, Max. You can talk all day tomorrow."

I'd laid out an extra T-shirt and underwear on the bed in our spare room. She put her hand on them, stroking lightly. "I never got to ask you about that lady in the car. When we were on your bike that day." Another smile-grimace. "How did she know you wear boxers?"

"Dad said to let you rest." I probably would have answered any other question.

She nodded. "I heard the show was terrific. Thanks for the cup. My father thought it was a message from Alcoholics Anonymous."

I laughed. She started to, but her face contorted, and she wrapped her arms around herself. A tear leaked from her swollen eye. I felt entirely powerless and enormously angry at the same time. "Oh, God, Ray. What can I do? How can I help you?"

"You can't tell anyone I'm here." Her voice was barely a whisper.

"No, of course not." I put my hand on her arm. "Did the hospital give you anything for the pain?"

She reached into her pocket and pulled out a bottle of pills. "Yeah. I didn't want to take anything while I was there because I needed to be sure I didn't sleep until I was safe." She looked toward the living room where the TV had come on. "Your dad is amazing. You know that, right?"

I nodded. "He's the best man I know."

She gestured with her head. "Tell him."

"What?"

"That's what you can do for me. Go in there and tell him how much you love him."

"Okay. And you'll sleep?"

"Yeah." She started to bend to take off her shoes and stopped with a moan.

"Sit," I ordered, pointing at the mattress. "I'll do this first."

She eased down, and I knelt to untie the men's dress shoes she was wearing. "I've imagined you on your knees in front of me, but I thought I'd feel better about it."

I slipped her shoes off and stood, smiling suggestively as I pointed toward the bathroom we would share. "I'm through there. Call if you need help with anything else." She sighed. I kissed the top of her head. "You're gonna be fine. I can tell."

JT was in the den, and I gave him a quick hug. "Thank you." I kept it simple, because anything else would have made me feel too sappy.

"I told her she had to stay with us for a month, at least," he said. "Along with that concussion, she's got two broken ribs and a host of other bruises." His face clouded. "I've got half a mind to visit that reverend fellow and give him a taste of his own medicine."

"Her father did this?" I couldn't keep the shock from my voice.

He sighed. "She told me most of this damage is from a few days ago when she tried to run away for the first time."

I was incensed. "Shouldn't we call the police or child protective services or something?"

"I suggested that. She was adamantly opposed. Said she wanted to get away, and now she has. But she needs to heal enough before she travels."

Travels? "Where is she going?"

"Some town in Colorado. Apparently, they have a facility where she can stay."

I guessed Sylvia had told him things she'd never said to me. But seeing her with her hair short and wearing men's clothes made me think of her telling me she wanted to be Ray. After I'd come to understand that meant she was planning to transition, I'd done some research and learned that Trinidad, Colorado, was considered the gender confirmation capital of the US. Trinidad was about six and a half hours north and west of us, but about six light-years ahead in terms of enlightened acceptance.

"Would you..." JT cleared his throat. "Would you ever want to do something like that?" I started shaking my head but stopped when he reached for my hand. "Because if you do, I want you to know that I'd back you one hundred percent." I looked up at him, shocked to see he had tears in his eyes. "I can't pretend to understand it," he went on, "but I want you to know you are my cherished child, and your happiness is more important to me than anything else."

I wasn't ashamed for crying, then. He hadn't said anything like that to me in years, but I knew his offer was completely sincere. For a while after I was released from the hospital and was recovered physically, I'd needed to hear that kind of thing a lot, and he never, ever hesitated to tell me that I was brave or good or loved as he sat with me at bedtime in my new room or in the mornings before school. He'd repeated it often and in so many different ways that I generally came to believe it. JT had become the constant in my life, and it hit me that I often took him for granted.

Since I was already crying, it seemed like the best opportunity to tell him that I loved him. I reassured him that I would continue to be his butch daughter, but that was as far as I needed to go. We blubbered on each other for another few minutes before he knuckled my head and said, "So you're okay?"

I swallowed my shuddering breath as I gave him one more quick squeeze. "Yeah, I'm fine. And you're okay too, right?"

He smiled. "Sure. I'm gonna live to be a hundred and fifty, remember?"

This was another of our running jokes, so I nodded dutifully and gave the expected response. "Yep. Then I can sell you to the circus as the world's oldest man."

❖

Ray ended up staying with us for three months. My dad purchased everything from underwear and toiletries to pants, shirts, socks, and shoes that fit. Seeing Ray in men's clothing had become routine by the time the bruises faded. He borrowed some paper and kept a running total of everything he felt he owed.

JT and I both used the name Ray and embraced saying "he." It was surprisingly easy to adjust my thinking, and I knew it was important to do. After a couple of weeks, he seemed to be sleeping through the night, as I no longer heard him moving around in the wee hours.

"Are you over being freaked out by me?" he asked one afternoon.

I indicated a place for him to sit on the edge of my bed. "I wasn't ever freaked out by you," I insisted. "I was just upset that you were hurt."

He gave me a doubtful look but let it go.

The house phone rang. JT was outside puttering around in the yard, so I picked up. At the sound of Lena crying loudly in the background, I knew it was Daphne. "I'm losing my mind," she announced, and from the way the words echoed, she must have been calling from the car, using the new cellular phone Bill had gotten her for Christmas. "Lena refuses to wear her left shoe, and she won't quit bawling about some cartoon. She needs a nap, and I've been driving her around, but it hasn't helped. I'm outside your house now, and I need to pee. Could I please come in for a minute?"

"Uh." I wasn't sure how to dissuade her, and I knew Ray would freak out if we let a stranger into the house. "Why don't I go with you to the Tastee-Freez and get you both an ice cream? You could pee there."

"Ew. That bathroom is the nastiest in town. Besides, wouldn't your dad like to see her? Even in her currently less-than-charming state?"

"Let me ask him." I looked out the window before glancing back to see Ray's wide-eyed, worried expression.

I mouthed the words, *It's okay*, as Daphne said, "Oh, he's out there watering the backyard. Let me go say hi."

She clicked off, and I turned to Ray. "Look, this is the lady we saw that time on my bike. She's cool, really, but I'll try to keep her outside. Why don't you wait in your room? She won't go in there."

Ray moved quickly, and I knew he was scared, but I didn't have a chance to reassure him further. I could hear them in the kitchen, Lena babbling happily now, and when I walked in and saw my godchild looking adoringly at my dad's face, I was fleetingly concerned about her potential dyke-ness. Then she saw me and reached out, crying "Match!" and I knew none of that mattered. I couldn't understand how any sane parent could shun their child. Lena wasn't my own flesh and blood, but I couldn't imagine life without her. My heart hurt thinking about Ray's parents' rejection.

Daphne took my arm. "I'm going to use your bathroom," she murmured while JT poured glasses of tea. "You can show the baby your den of iniquity."

"Uh."

She was already walking down the hall, and I followed, shrugging helplessly at my dad as we left. Daphne left the door mostly open as she peed, commenting on the somewhat messy state of the bathroom while I bounced the baby on the bed, making her giggle hysterically. "For heaven's sake, Max, you've got enough stuff in here for three people. Are you planning to open a drug store or something?"

"Come here and look at your daughter," I called, trying to sound casual. "I think she's going to be a gymnast when she grows up."

"Just a minute. I've got to change my tampon. I'm thrilled to have my period again, I can tell you."

I could only shake my head, imagining how embarrassed Daphne would be if she knew Ray was in the other room hearing every word. "Your mama's crazy," I whispered to Lena.

"Yeah, but you're crazy about me, aren't you, baby?" Daphne's voice had taken on the sultry growl that made me get tight in the pit of my stomach, though I assumed she was talking to her child. My back was still turned, so I didn't see her shut my door, but I sure as

ON MY WAY THERE

hell felt her lean against me, smiling at Lena over my shoulder. "It's summer. What are you doing home, anyway? Shouldn't you be out chasing girls? Or are you still pining over that great kisser? What was her name? Annie?"

Shit. Anything Ray heard on this topic was too much. For several reasons. "Daphne, JT could come in any second. And we shouldn't talk about this in front of the baby."

She laughed, a genuine sound that I didn't get to hear nearly often enough. "I believe your dad is already aware that you chase girls. And Lena's command of English isn't quite sophisticated enough to concern herself with the nuances of your dating preferences." She leaned in, sniffing. "I think her main concern would be getting into a dry diaper." She grinned wickedly at me. "I guess all us Polk girls need a change."

I turned my head, my mouth open slightly as a second possible meaning of her words flashed through my mind. Did she mean a change from their life with Bill? Her face was inches from mine, close enough to smell her perfume and see the perspiration on her brow. How was it possible that being a mother had made her even more beautiful than she'd been the last time we were alone together in this room?

As if she knew what I was thinking, she smiled softly, running a single finger up my neck and across my chin, pushing my jaws together. "May we use your facilities again?"

"Uh-huh," I managed.

She moved smoothly around me and lifted the baby, shushing her as she fretted faintly. I held my breath as I watched her walk into the bathroom, immobilized as my mind's eye envisioned following her and putting my hands on her waist, kissing the back of her neck as she cared for her child, our child. Would she always have this effect on me?

The water ran, and I heard her call, "You're out of washcloths in here. Are there any extras in your guest room closet?"

I opened my mouth to say yes before I remembered Ray. "Wait," I called, about the same moment I heard a thud, followed by a short scream. Lena started whimpering, and I heard my dad's footsteps in the hall.

"Who the hell are you?" Daphne's voice was a cross between anger and fright.

Hearing her question made me move. I picked up the fussing baby on my way through the bathroom and arrived in our guest room to see Daphne standing with her hands on her hips and Ray on the floor, obviously having stumbled over something on his way out of the closet where he must have been hiding.

"Dat?" Lena asked, clearly echoing her mother's question in a somewhat more genteel fashion. JT opened the hall door and stopped, surveying the scene. The two of us looked at each other and knew there was nothing to do but laugh.

Once introductions and explanations were finished, and Daphne was sworn to secrecy, she reverted to her usual technique of flirting until she was certain she'd have the upper hand with Ray, as she did with everyone else in the house. My dad had always enjoyed Daphne's company, and he seemed amused to watch her in action, but I needed to clear my head.

Once it was evident that Ray was deeply under her spell, I took Lena into the backyard so we could play in peace. The baby and I talked through the events of the day while swaying gently on my old tire swing. Well, I talked, and she babbled, obviously making more headway with her processing than I did as she fell into a quiet gurgling which soon dwindled to steady breathing.

Even the softening twilight hadn't calmed my agitation when Daphne came to reclaim her child. She walked toward me, her expression pensive before it transformed into that special mother smile at the sight of Lena almost asleep.

"That baby sure takes to you." I waited for the expected, *I can't imagine why*, or some such, but it didn't come. Instead, she asked, "So that is your great lover?"

"Great kisser," I clarified, not thinking about how it sounded.

"But not so great in bed?"

"Meh." I waved my hand in a so-so gesture.

She laughed. "Like you would know."

I was mentally sapped from the earlier tension. The unanswered pulse of arousal had left my body edgy, and I responded more harshly than normal. "I used to think I knew. But you're right. I probably haven't any idea what something real would feel like. Maybe it's time I gave up my stupid fantasy and found out."

Seemingly taken aback, Daphne blinked for a few seconds before she snatched the baby from my arms. "You do that, Max. But just be sure that anyone you bring home knows if there's someone in the next room. Some people don't appreciate an audience."

I stood and faced her, my earlier resentment flooding back. "Does that mean you've decided three really is a crowd? Is that the message I was supposed to get in my bedroom earlier tonight?"

She said nothing at first, only studied me for a moment, shifting the baby to her other hip. "You've developed a mean streak, haven't you?"

"If I have, I learned it from the master. Or should I say, mistress?"

Daphne gave a bitter laugh. "Oh, please. You're going to have to work a lot harder than that if you're trying to hurt me."

She started to turn away, but I grabbed her arm roughly, unable to bite back the exasperation, speaking through my teeth. "Is that what you want, Daphne? Is that what it takes for you these days?"

I wasn't prepared to witness the flash of tears that came so quickly, it made me catch my breath. But as hard as her voice was, it was the coolness of her words that broke me. "If that was the case, I could just stay home."

CHAPTER EIGHT

2000
Age Eighteen

My antagonism disappeared so quickly, I was inert with emptiness. Not even the powerful sound of the BMW's engine moved me from where I stood. JT called me for dinner, and I went, but only because I knew he'd worry if I didn't. I pushed my food around, working on an apology letter in my head. I excused myself as Ray cleaned up as he did at every meal, insisting it was one thing he could do to earn his keep.

I was staring at a blank page when a tap on the door of my room roused me. Ray slipped in and sat carefully on the edge of my bed. It struck me again how much more at ease he seemed. I tried to work my face into a pleasant expression. "Hey."

"That's her, isn't it?" he said without preamble.

"What her?" I was pretty sure where this was going, but I didn't want to make any more mistakes tonight.

Ray lowered his voice, though we could hear the TV faintly in the other room. "The one you had sex with. That you didn't want to talk about before."

"Look, Ray—" I started, but he cut me off with a wave.

"I'm not here to ask for details." He grinned for one of the few times since he'd taken up residence with us. "Although she is incredibly hot."

"I'm not going to—"

"Sorry," he interrupted again. "That really wasn't what I wanted to say."

"Daphne and I are friends, Ray. And sometimes, not even that."

He inclined his head in a dubious way, chewing his lip. "Did I ever tell you about living in Hugston, Oklahoma?"

Relieved by the subject change, I turned, giving him my full attention, aware that I now had the answer to that perfect Ado Annie twang. "No."

"There were several reasons why we left, but the main one was because I was having an affair with a married woman."

My jaw gaped, and I was speechless.

A corner of his mouth lifted. "Yeah, well, what can I say? Tanya was perfect. She was our choir director. Talented and passionate about her work, beautiful, sweet, and devoted to her two little boys." He'd so rarely spoken about his life that I knew not to break the spell with any inane comments. "Her husband Walker wasn't abusive or anything. He wasn't a jerk. He was simple...unremarkable...bland. And she was anything but. Still, neither of us meant for anything to happen. It wasn't like with you, where, well, we both knew exactly what was going on, didn't we?"

I nodded. Here was another thing we hadn't spoken of since he'd come to stay, but it clearly wasn't the purpose of this conversation.

"With Tanya, I just...she..."

I watched him drift into the past, seeing an expressive tenderness in his face I'd never seen before. Then, swallowing hard, he blinked back to the present. "I already knew about myself. I mean, I'd already had some brief experiences. My parents suspected, I know, since we constantly addressed"—he made air quotes—"'temptation' in our daily devotionals. Funny thing is, I'd almost convinced myself that we'd prayed it away until her." He eyed me briefly. "Obviously, you've had a crush on someone who didn't feel the same."

I wanted to tell him that my relationship with Daphne was more than a crush, but he had a point. Clearly, Daphne and I didn't feel the same, which explained why we were always fighting. Unless we were fucking.

Ray stood and looked out the window for a moment. "I couldn't stop wondering if there was anything inside her that pulsed the way it did with me when we were alone together. I was losing weight, not sleeping, letting my grades slip, generally going crazy. Finally, I was in such a state that I decided the best way to get over it would be to tell her, certain she'd assure me she had no such feelings. I hoped she'd call me terrible names, throw me out of the choir, reject me in such a way that I'd have reason to stop caring, to stop wanting her so badly."

"Oh, Ray." I put my hand on his arm, understanding completely how he felt.

He sat again, more heavily this time. "I was singing a difficult solo for Easter. I pretended I was staying after practice to work on it, but I didn't come in after she played the intro. I was looking out the window, speaking to the night, knowing things would never again be the same between us, but so close to breaking that I didn't care. I told her I had feelings for her, serious, romantic feelings. I knew it was wrong, and I knew she didn't feel the same, but I couldn't keep it to myself anymore. I told her I'd quit the choir if she wanted."

His gaze was obviously focused on the past, but I could sense his pain.

"I was practically sobbing. She hugged me gently and suggested that such 'affection' between women was normal. I pushed her away, angry that she hadn't heard or hadn't comprehended the magnitude of what I'd told her. I said that it wasn't simply affection, it was attraction, and I kissed her. I tried to keep it soft and gentle, but she made a little sound, and I stepped into her and ran my tongue across her lips. Her mouth opened, and I slipped my tongue inside. She clutched my hair and ground against me, and I was ready to come...or die...at that instant.

"She wrenched her mouth away and whimpered something. In the haze of my desire, I wasn't certain if she'd said *oh* or *no*, but my brain demanded I find out." He flushed and looked down. "I was kissing her throat, pleading with her to tell me what to do.

"The outside door banged open, and we both recognized my father's footsteps. She moved away, assuring me I had nothing to worry about for Sunday. For four nights, I barely slept, questioning exactly what she'd meant. On Easter, I put all my heart into my solo, knowing it would please her if we did well. After the song ended, the congregation did something completely unexpected. They clapped.

At most, we usually got a few amens. I took the opportunity to look directly at Tanya, only to find her staring at me with the most breathtaking smile I'd ever seen. My father seemed displeased by the congregation's reaction. I was shocked to realize I didn't care what he thought. I felt liberated, released from the weight of his expectations. It was wonderful.

"Once everyone else was finally gone, Tanya took me in her arms and told me I was magnificent. Her lips found my mouth, giving me a series of kisses that left me lightheaded as she pulled at my waist, bringing me tightly against her. I pleaded to see her alone, offered to meet her anywhere. She whispered yes so quietly, I wasn't sure what I'd heard until she said it again."

His eyes had closed, and I moved closer. I squeezed his hand, and when he looked at me, I saw tears.

"I don't know if I'll ever have passion like that again, but it was also the worst time of my life. I shared Tanya's guilt that she was neglecting her children. We struggled with religious issues and constant fears about being caught. I'd say whatever I could to convince her that her husband would be a fine father without her, and then I'd hate myself for trying to break up her family. She tried to tell me I needed to find someone my own age, but whenever I mentioned someone or if she saw me talking to someone from Sunday school, she'd get insanely jealous."

Some parts of his story described me with Daphne, almost to a T. I took a shaky breath, as he swallowed hard.

"Twice, we agreed to end it, but I couldn't get out of going to church or even quit choir after my Easter solo, which meant we still had to see each other at least twice a week. It was agony, but it was worse to see her and not…well, you know. One or the other of us would give in, and it would all start again." He sniffed. "This went on for most of a year."

There was another long pause. "What happened?" I asked hesitantly.

He grimaced. "Oh, about the worst thing possible. She agreed to leave, and we were going to run away together. That Saturday night, I managed to slip out with a few possessions. I waited by the side of the road for hours, stubbornly holding on to my faith that she would show." He sighed. "Instead, my father picked me up. Tanya had written him a letter of resignation that included a confession, along with her conviction that if I was around more people my own age, this 'issue' would resolve itself. I think that's another reason why he agreed to let me come to public high school here." He rubbed his face, shaking his head slightly. "Tanya's family had moved away that Thursday. Her abrupt departure from the church raised more than a few eyebrows, especially in conjunction with my refusal to return to the choir." He looked away. "That was the first time he beat me. I absolutely gloried in the pain. I think it scared us both…in different ways, of course."

"And you never heard anything from her?"

"Nothing. And at this point, I'm just as glad." Turning back to me, he cleared his throat. "When I heard Pokeville High was doing *Oklahoma!*, all I could think of was that 'All 'er Nothin' song. That's what I want, the romance and everything else. Maybe Tanya would have been happy with half me and half her husband and boys, but I couldn't live that way." He stretched his neck, and his voice was quiet but firm when he spoke again. "I'm not saying that Daphne is like Tanya, Max. But I'm telling you married women are trouble in too many ways to count."

Part of me wanted to argue, and part of me wanted to slap him on the back and agree. "Thanks for telling me, Ray," I finally said. As he nodded, something else occurred to me. "Did you and Tanya ever talk about…uh…about you wanting to—"

"To transition?" he asked, smiling faintly. "Yeah. We talked about it a few months before the end. She seemed fine, supportive, even. But maybe it upset her more than she let on." He shrugged. "All or nothing, Max. I'm a man on the inside, and I've got to get my 'all' from whatever modern medicine can give me."

For a time, we sat quietly. Ray seemed lost in his memories, but for me, I was redefining what it was I felt for him. I respected his courage and his determination. I should have been more like him, but I suspected I never would be. He was fearless, and I kept a constant eye on my feelings for fear I would turn into my mother. He'd learned what wouldn't work for him, and I only knew what I thought I wanted. Maybe that was why my heart had always been an off-and-on, half-and-half thing.

I invited him to stay with me that night, hardly knowing where the words came from. Heat rose on my throat as I tried to justify my proposal. "That guest bed may not be as comfortable."

Cursing myself as the stupidest person on the planet, I finally looked up and was relieved to see he was smiling. "Yeah," he said. "I think I'd like that."

Just to make sure I sounded like a complete ass, I added, "Only to sleep, I mean. We don't have to do anything."

But eventually, we did.

❖

I had started back to school, and Ray was going stir-crazy, so my dad brought a car from the shop for them to work on together. I could manage some basic repairs, but Ray caught on much more quickly than I had. He started reading manuals, and he and JT were talking over my head in a matter of days. That was probably my first clue that I'd be better at driving vehicles than repairing them.

In spite of our pleasant sleeping arrangement, I was restless too. One day, I got an unexpected call from Jack Mickton, inviting me to a party. A lot of people from the musical would be there, he added. I was undecided, but Ray urged me to go, saying he'd be eager to hear the latest gossip.

Surprised at how warmly I was welcomed, I realized I was ready to unwind. I had more to drink than I should, but I was enjoying dancing with everyone. When the music slowed, and people began coupling up, Maryjane Bowen pulled me into an embrace and began moving her hips suggestively.

"I remember kissing you at the cast party," she whispered in my ear, her words slurring a bit. "It was really nice."

"Mmm," I murmured, wondering vaguely if the slight touch of vertigo was from the liquor or because Maryjane's perfume reminded me of Daphne's. Instinctively, I shifted so my leg was between Maryjane's, not too subtly cupping her buttocks. "Wanna try it again?"

"Yeah." Her tone sounded rather urgent, and I could tell by the way she pressed against me that she'd found a spot she liked. "But not here. Come down the hall with me," she said, a coded expression for sex.

"What about Bert?" I asked. Bert and Maryjane had been hooking up for over a year. A baseball player, he seemed like a nice enough guy, plus, he was easily twice my size. I hadn't seen him there, though.

"Bert and I have an understanding," Maryjane explained, nibbling along the edge of my ear. "We both need a little more experience before we settle down."

"Oh." I was going to be her *experience*. I could almost see my ad now:

Don't go off inexperienced. Rent-a-lesbian will provide all the sexual diversity you'll need to ensure a long and happy marriage.

For a moment, it sounded like a great plan. Then fate, in the person of Albert Fannin, intervened. "Get away from her." He grabbed my shoulder and slung me against the wall, pinning me hard. "Isn't it bad enough you corrupted Pastor Raymond's daughter? You know where she is, don't you? Where's Sylvia?"

I attempted to shove his hands away, but he'd caught me by surprise, and I had no leverage. "Damn, Albert, let me go. I don't know what the fuck you're talking about."

My "date" of a few seconds ago and several other couples were watching the scene with interest. When no one intervened, Albert laughed in a scary way and stepped closer. "Oh, right. You expect us to believe that you were best friends while she was here, and now you don't know anything about her?"

Acutely aware that I wasn't going to get any help until I got them on my side, I assumed a genuinely offended expression. "I don't, and you know why. You were the one who ratted her out and got her parents to pull her out of school. You probably ruined her life, and you almost ruined our show." I had to throw in that last part since half the room wouldn't care about Sylvia's life. But the stir of conversation around me suggested my remarks had hit home.

He backhanded me hard enough that my vision blurred, and my ears rang. "Shut up, you freak."

Several people moved then, including Jack Mickton, whose flushed face and somewhat disheveled clothing suggested he might have recently been down the hall himself. Pulling Albert roughly away, Jack said, "Hey, man, this is a party. Let it go, okay?"

I slid to the floor with relief once they'd taken Albert outside. Katherine Hutchins handed me some ice wrapped in a napkin. I held it gingerly to my face while conversation swirled around me.

Maryjane sat beside me, not meeting my eyes. "I'm so sorry," she whispered.

I waved dismissively and worked my jaw a little. I'd certainly sobered up enough to ride. I patted her hand. "Maybe another time, okay? I'm gonna go now."

Several people tried to talk me into staying, offering all manner of alcohol and swearing their personal protection, but I was done. Maryjane shadowed me all the way out to my bike. While I was putting on my helmet, she asked, "Do you really not know anything about Sylvia?"

Dismayed that this was her parting question, I decided to respond differently than I had Albert. "I truly don't. But you know, she always used to talk about wanting to go to Florida. She had the idea that she could live on the beach, maybe work on a fishing boat or something. You know, the kind of dreaming we all do now and then."

On the way home, I decided to find another group to hang out with for my senior year. The time I'd spent in the hospital meant that I was older than nearly everyone else in my class. That, and the accumulation of my life experience to date, made me less and less tolerant of the immaturity and indelicacy of these peers. I'd enjoyed playing soccer in middle school, and I thought maybe athletes would have less drama than the music and theater gang. Or that it would at least be a different kind of drama.

Pastor Raymond and his wife left Pokeville for Miami about a month later. I didn't hold it against Maryjane. Ray was already gone by then, but I liked thinking that he wouldn't need to be looking over his shoulder for a while, at least.

❖

2001
Age Nineteen

One fine spring day, I'd stopped at the Sav-Mor after school to get something for dinner. I heard Lena crying the minute I walked in, so I headed straight for the baby aisle, where the sight of them stopped me in my tracks. Lena's face was blotchy, though her cries had subsided to unhappy whimpers. Daphne looked like she hadn't slept in days, her hair was a mess, and her blouse needed ironing. This was not the first runner-up to Miss Cotton Ball that I knew, the woman who wouldn't be caught dead in public without lipstick and matching nail polish.

I approached her carefully, recalling that our last parting hadn't been good. If she'd been in her usual attentive mode, Daphne would have been alerted by Lena's sudden change of demeanor. Instead, she looked around warily at the baby's burbling sounds, as if some alien had unexpectedly inhabited her daughter's body. I pretended to ponder the diaper selections.

"Max?" Daphne sounded like she was trying to remember the name of her fourth cousin's second son.

Lena echoed with something that sounded like, "Mack."

"Yeah, baby." I made sure my words were directed at the child, who reached for me so vigorously that I had to step over quickly to keep her from lurching out of Daphne's arms.

Amazed at how much she'd grown, I tickled under her fat little arms, and we played briefly with various products until she insisted on carrying a package containing a Water Temperature Test Duck back to the cart. Daphne hadn't moved, only watched us with an expression that was almost sad.

"Sorry," I said to her, pointing at the item. "But she really wants this."

"She's going through a duck phase," Daphne answered, and in a few seconds, we were both laughing.

"But other than duck appeal, why would you need this?" I asked when we'd regained our composure. "Couldn't you just feel the water yourself?"

"Of course you would, you goof," she responded. "This is merely one of the multitudes of useless baby crap that's on the market."

"Oh." We looked at each other for a few seconds until someone else came down the aisle, and we had to move aside. "I guess I should get going," I said, glancing away after the silence had become awkward.

"Please don't," she whispered. The slight tremor in her voice made me look back. She cleared her throat. "Unless you have to."

"I need to grab something for dinner."

"Come eat with us. Bill's off hunting with his buddies."

Another shopper moved past, giving me a few seconds to think. I should have said no, gone home and eaten with my dad, and done my homework. The slight pressure of Daphne's hand squeezing my arm made me look at her, and she mouthed the words, *I'm sorry.*

Me too, I acknowledged in the same way.

"It's no trouble," she said, her voice light as she continued our earlier conversation effortlessly.

"On one condition," I countered, knowing I was already giving in. She cocked her head, waiting. "You let me cook, and you relax."

Daphne gave a bitter chuckle. "Oh, what? You think I need it?"

"No, I want to show off what I've learned in Family and Consumer Sciences this year."

She pointed at me almost accusingly. "Tell me Miss Yeager isn't still there."

"Oh, she is," I assured her. Miss Yeager was about one hundred and seven and as interesting to listen to as sandpaper on smooth wood. She did, however, share her family recipes for some of the best dishes in the county.

"All right," Daphne said. "Can you shop for your ingredients while I take Lena to the restroom?"

"Done," I agreed, thinking it would give me time to get something for JT's dinner when I dropped by to tell him of the change in plans.

Lena started to wail as Daphne carried her away. "It's okay, sweetie," she soothed. "Mack will be at our house for dinner."

When she caught up to me in the checkout lane, she looked like a different person. She had on makeup, and her hair was brushed and pulled back stylishly. Her clothes looked neater. She tossed her head at my expression and whispered, "Contrary to what my mother used to tell me, sometimes, a lady does need a reason to get done up."

❖

Lena sat in her high chair, ingesting Cheerios at a stunning rate while simultaneously talking happily to the duck device that we'd forgotten to take out of the cart before they rang it up. Daphne had excused herself, and I heard water running in the bathroom. She reappeared in the kitchen as dinner was almost ready, and not even the faintly citrus scent of bubble bath was sweeter than the aroma of her clean warm skin.

"That smells good." She looked into the skillet from over my shoulder. I knew her breasts were less than an inch away, but I resisted the urge to lean into them.

"It does," I agreed, wondering if she knew we weren't talking about the same thing.

"I should have told you to save some macaroni for Lena."

I indicated the small covered pot beside the skillet. She brushed against me while she looked inside, finding the cooked macaroni inside. She dropped the lid and moved away. I peered into the pot, stirring with the other spoon to check the consistency. "I found your baby book, and it said kids her age can eat it. Was that what you meant?"

There was no reply, I looked around, finding Daphne with her head in her hands, her body rocking sluggishly. I couldn't tell if it was from anger or pain. I'd seen her angry plenty of times, but other than that horrible day in my childhood backyard, I'd only seen her come close to crying the day she'd been worried about losing her unborn child.

I quickly switched off the burners and embraced her from behind, joining in her motion. "Oh no, honey. You're tired. It must be hard, I know. But it's gonna be okay. I have last period athletics, but we don't start playing for a couple of months. I can help in the afternoons till Bill gets home."

Nothing changed for a minute. She shuddered once more, and I felt her breathe deeply before she tightened, pulling herself together. "You don't understand." She still sounded somewhat choked and bent her shoulders away from me. I let her go, but she didn't turn. She spoke to the empty living room. "This is why it's hard for me to see you, Max. Because you're so fucking wonderful. It's obvious by the way you play with Lena that you love her. If he notices her at all, it's mostly to tell me to shut her up 'cause he's trying to watch some game. You're willing to cook, and you think about things like what she might want to eat. Bill's an absolute ogre if his dinner isn't ready when he gets home at whatever time that might be. Having him here is like having two children, one of whom is usually drunk."

I took her shoulders and turned her, but she put her face in her hands again. I said what I'd wanted to say a million times. "Leave him. Come live with me. My dad loves you, but if it's too awkward with him there, we can get our own place." I pulled her to me. "You know how I feel about you, Daphne. I—"

She dropped her hands and straightened so abruptly that I almost stumbled back. "Don't, Max. Don't say it. I don't want to go through all that since we'll just end up right back here in this kitchen because nothing's going to change."

"What do you mean?" I questioned, ignoring her irritation, my own voice rising slightly with apprehension. She wasn't going to turn me down, was she? Not after everything she'd acknowledged about her life. "I asked you—"

"I heard what you said," Her tone had sharpened, although her volume didn't increase by much. "And I'm telling you that your sweet romantic ideal is exactly what you called it before. It's a fantasy."

I started pacing, unable to believe what she was saying. Hearing Lena start to fuss, I decided to try a different tack. "Okay, even if you don't want to be with me, think about your daughter." I gestured toward Lena, who was clearly reacting to our argument. "Look at her. Is this what she goes through with you and Bill? It wouldn't be like that with us, and you know it." I was getting more and more upset. "We're fighting now because you're being stupid about this."

"Stupid? I'm being stupid?" She laughed bitterly, and her voice went up. "And your plan is to get me labeled an unfit mother for taking my child to live with the town dyke and her blue-collar old man? You're worse than stupid. You're asinine."

I froze, closing my eyes so I could replay her words, thinking I couldn't have heard her correctly. I glared into the distance when I was sure, feeling like everything in me—from the heat of our argument to the slow burn of my desire—had been turned to ice.

She had her hand out. "Max, I'm sorry. I didn't mean—"

"Fuck you," I said, my voice matching my deathly cold heart. "Fuck you and fuck your drunk-ass husband—oh, excuse me—the straight white male whose built-in privilege is infinitely preferable to anything the town dyke and her blue-collar old man could ever offer you." I turned and walked toward the door.

"Max, wait."

She sounded distressed, but I didn't look back. "I'm done, Daphne. I'm done pretending, and I'm done waiting." I heard her say no, but I kept walking until I was in front of Lena in her high chair. I bent and kissed the top of her head. "Best of luck, kiddo. I'll miss you tons. Call me once you're ready to run away, and I'll come pick you up."

When I straightened, Daphne was beside me, taking hold of my arm. "You've got to listen to me. I am so, so sorry."

"I don't have to do anything. It's over." I shook her off as roughly as I could, enjoying the unfamiliar power, cognizant that I could do damage, make her hurt too. Flushed with returning heat, I understood how someone could get angry enough to hit someone they professed to love. I saw a flash of my mother's distorted face. Had an incident like this started her psychosis? The thought alone scared me enough that I swallowed hard.

"Mama, Mack. Mama, Mack," Lena wailed, reaching for us both.

I braced myself as Daphne picked up her child. Her child. Not mine. Her problems. Not mine. Ray's words echoed in my head again: "Married women are trouble in too many ways to count." I was through counting. The callous cold filled me again, and I turned away, reaching for the door. "Good-bye, Daphne."

I heard her sob first. Then Lena started to cry. Against my better judgment, I looked back. She was on her knees, tears streaming down her face. "No, Max, no." Her voice was shaking so badly, I could barely make out the words. "God, please don't say that. I know I make you crazy, but please. I'm begging you. If you leave me, I'll die. Being around you is the only thing that keeps me alive inside."

Lena was blubbering some equally sad sounds, her face pressed into her mother's neck. I'd never in all my life seen Daphne like this. As hard-hearted as I'd felt toward her seconds before, everything inside me completely melted. I dropped to my knees and put my arms around both of them. "I don't want to go. But goddamn it, Daphne, you can't talk to me like that. Because I care about what you say. Your words matter to me. You can't keep cutting me and think I won't ever run out of blood."

"I know." She repeated everything as if her speech was stuck on two. "I know. You're right. You're right, Max. Thank you. Thank you so much."

"Now, come on." I pulled her to her feet, careful not to be too forceful or squeeze the baby. "You don't have to thank me for not being a jerk."

"I do." She clung to me, tears still falling. "Because it's a rare thing, believe me." Lena was hiccupping in the fast way kids did. "Bill calls me stupid all the time, and it…it's no excuse, I know, but it just set me off."

I reached for a Kleenex on the kitchen table and blotted her cheeks. After a moment, she looked at me, her eyes still swollen. "I need to…I have to feed the baby. When she starts hiccupping like this, it's the only thing that helps. She'll make herself sick if she doesn't stop."

"Okay." She was still leaning into me, and I kept my arm around her. "Shall I reheat the macaroni?"

"No, I have to feed her myself. You know. Breastfeed her. That's what calms her down." She swallowed and took a shuddering breath. "I don't want to let you out of my sight. Will you stay with me?"

"I'd like that. Very much."

Chapter Nine

2001
Age Nineteen

We made our way into Lena's room. Along with her crib and what had to be several hundred toys and stuffed animals on shelves, was an oval-shaped infant lounger on the edge of a single bed. "Here," I said, reaching for the baby. "Let me hold her for a minute while you get set."

Lena seemed worn out, slumping while she continued hiccupping. She didn't much care about the toys I tried to distract her with, but she liked me talking to her as her bear, apologizing for the scene she'd just witnessed. "Mack is sorry, Lena. Mama's sorry too. We don't usually fight that way, do we? And we won't again, okay? We promise."

"No, no Mack," she said, her tiny fingers touching my face while she looked into my face. A wave of fiercely protective emotion swept through me, and I swore to myself that no matter what happened with Daphne and me, I would never let it hurt this child again.

I looked back. Daphne was lying on her side, facing me. Her blouse was open, and her breasts were bare. "Are you ready for her?"

"Yes."

I handed Lena over without another word, unable to take my eyes off mother and child. Daphne settled Lena on her side so they faced each other. She pulled up a mesh siding I hadn't noticed on the edge of the bed. When Lena began to suck, making soft, satisfied sounds, both of them had expressions on their faces that were almost rapturous. I thought it was the most beautiful thing I had ever seen. Daphne looked at me and smiled, gesturing carefully to the area behind her on the bed. "Would you like to come lie down with us?"

"Are you sure it's all right?"

"Yes, I'm positive." She had the slightest tease to her response.

I moved around and eased in beside her, rising on my elbow so I could watch while being careful not to crowd them. I put my hand on Daphne's hip to steady myself, feeling her tremble. I lifted my hand. "Should I not touch you while you're doing this?"

"No, it's fine. It's real nice, actually. In the video they showed during my pregnancy class, the father and mother were lying together like this. He was stroking her arm. It was sweet."

"Does Bill—" I couldn't say why I let the question start, but she cut me off.

"He wasn't at the class. And, no, he doesn't."

"I shouldn't have asked. He's got no part in what's between us."

She stared at me for a few seconds. Then she put my hand on her hip again, pushing it slowly down her leg. I took up the movement with no further prompting, As I watched Lena's mouth slow, I realized my fingers were working toward the front of Daphne's thigh. She had eased herself back, pressing her hips into my crotch. A trance-like heaviness had replaced all the other extreme emotions of the day, and we pressed against each other, moving nearly imperceptibly. I stroked leisurely over the sweet curves of her body as she breathed deeply, a soft humming sound occasionally coming from her throat. Even as I yearned to touch her, to make her come fully and powerfully, my arousal was deeper than sex. I was reminded of what I'd known all my life: we were connected at a level that defied time and transcended circumstances.

When I saw that Lena had fallen asleep, Daphne's nipple slipping from her mouth, I stretched and kissed the back of Daphne's neck, moving my lips softly to her shoulder and to her ear. "Thank you," I whispered, not wanting to awaken Lena. "Thank you for letting me be with you for that."

Daphne eased Lena into the sleep nest pillow. She rolled onto her back and ran her fingers through my hair. Her voice was quiet but intense. "This is the other reason why it's so hard to see you. I'll be in the middle of cleaning the house, and I'll remember looking into your beautiful blue eyes while I touched you. Or I'll be out shopping, and for no reason, my skin will start to tingle, and my whole body will heat up, and I can practically feel you moving on top of me, hear the way you cried out when you came inside me. The first few times it happened, I had to go into the ladies' room and relieve myself. For a while, I thought I was going crazy. Then, I decided I was being punished for not being a good enough wife." She regarded me intently. "It would be wrong, wouldn't it, Max? For us to be together? It really would be cheating since I'm married now."

There was a part of me that thought I should say yes. I could see myself agreeing it was wrong, giving her a chaste kiss on the forehead, and leaving, having stored what we'd shared tonight in the back of my mind for examination in the coming lonely years. I wasn't sure if that was the noble part or the stupid part, but the Max Terrell who was lying there with Daphne Polk had no intention of leaving unless she was specifically asked to go. "The way it feels to me..." I hesitated because I didn't have a very helpful answer. But Daphne's brows lifted, and she nodded encouragingly, so I started again, still speaking rationally. "You were my first, Daphne. I feel like you're cheating on me when you're with him."

Sadness filled her eyes, and she murmured, "Damned if you do and damned if you don't."

I didn't like it that I'd made her feel that way. Maybe good-stupid Max needed to take charge. "No, that's not true. Most anyone else you'd ask would agree with you. What I said might not be right, but it's how I feel." I touched her cheek. "I'm sure you're a fine wife. I know you're an excellent mother. And you've always been there for me. You're an amazing friend." I let my hand drop and tried for a smile. "Yeah, you make me crazy sometimes. But, hey, I'm tougher than you, so if you can take it, I can too."

I started to move away, feeling like I was pulling off a tightly stuck Band-Aid, but she grabbed my shoulders and pulled me back, hugging me tightly, her voice breathy with passion. "God, Max. That's just it. I don't know if I *can* take it. At first, I thought I felt horny. Apparently, I'm one of those women who goes that way after pregnancy. Hell, Bill and I haven't—you know—done anything, ever since I got a little bit big." She scoffed. "Not like that would help much in any case." She stopped talking for a minute, and her grip softened. She caressed my back, moving to my hips, and I became molten, ready to pour myself into her. Spreading her legs, she pressed up, ready to receive me. "It's you," she whispered into my ear. "I want you."

She'd captured my arms, but I worked one loose, slipping it down her abdomen and stopping at the elastic of her panties. "What if I…" My breathing had gotten faster in the last ten seconds while I sought some compromise. "What if I touch you like this?" I moved my fingers over the silk into the vee between her legs. "Without taking your clothes off?"

"Yes," she hissed, arching slightly. "Do that…or anything. I need you, Max. Please. I—"

She cut off with a gasp as I pressed in, fondling her rapidly hardening clitoris with the pads of my fingers. I could feel her juices through the material, and I knew she wanted me inside. As much as I wanted to be there, I needed to be sure, needed her to be sure. But good-stupid Max seemed to have left the room, so I kissed Daphne's neck, biting when I got to where it joined with her shoulder, only dimly aware I was slowly flexing my hips, rubbing my own swollen clit against the seam of my pants. She worked her hand under the waistband of my jeans, squeezing my ass in the rhythm we'd set.

"Can you…" she asked.

I grunted, "Yes. With you, yes."

She stifled a cry, working herself more quickly against my fingers while still trying not to move the bed too much. "I won't…last. Need it…so much…"

I put my lips against her ear to keep myself from shouting. "Take all you need. It's here for you."

"Yes." She was clutching at me spasmodically. "Yes," she repeated, her voice going up in pitch, though still quiet. "Oh yes. Yes, Max. Max." The second time she said my name, she tensed and began to shudder.

Currents of pleasure surged through me, and I buried my face against her, moaning into her skin. She was breathing in soft, wheezy tones while wetness flooded her underwear. I jerked against her twice, unable to control it.

Her arm around me tightened, and she kissed softly along my hairline. "The baby?" she asked after we'd both caught our breath for a minute, and I looked over her to see Lena, sound asleep in her pillow lounger, a little drool at the corner of her mouth.

"Still sleeping," I replied, looking at Daphne's face.

"Thank God," she said, her eyes still closed as she squeezed my breast through my shirt. "I shouldn't have to pay thousands for her therapy if we didn't take our clothes off."

This was the Daphne I knew. Funny as hell and incredibly beautiful. Those terrible words, *I love you*, almost slipped out again, but I'd learned my lesson. Sort of. "You're pretty fucking amazing, you know that?"

"Shh," she whispered, pulling me down. "Don't scare me, Max. Just be here for a second."

We drifted until the grinding sound of the garage door jolted Daphne upright. "Oh my God!" She had genuine terror in her voice. "Bill's home early."

"It's okay," I said, bolting off the bed and slipping into my shoes. "I'll take the baby. You…you get yourself together."

Bill banged around outside for a bit, so my superhero speed might not have been entirely necessary. Still, by the time he made his appearance, dinner was reheating on the stove, and I had contained myself to the point that Lena was giggling at the faces I was making, some of which—panic, desperation, and anger—were absolutely real.

Bill was drunk enough to do a double take once he realized I wasn't Daphne. "What the hell are you doing here?"

"Hi, Bill." I was trying for offhandedly pleasant. "Daphne and I ran into each other at the grocery store." *True so far.* "She wasn't feeling too well, and since I hadn't seen Lena in a while, I volunteered to be your cook for the evening." *Reasonably true.* I gestured vaguely toward the rear of the house. "She finished feeding the baby, and now she's…doing whatever women do after." *After they've come through their underwear.*

"Oh yeah." He looked blearily in that direction and plopped into a chair at the kitchen table. I turned to the stove, but I could feel his gaze on me. He drummed his fingers. "Remind me how it is that you two know each other?"

He sounded less drunk and more suspicious, so I looked around and smiled at him. "Our families used to live next door to each other when we were little."

He cocked his head, his eyes distant. "Oh yeah. I think Daffy told me about that."

I couldn't begin to imagine how much Daphne hated that nickname, and I sincerely hoped that was all she'd said. I kissed the top of Lena's head and sat her in her high chair, moving to stir the meat. She looked at me accusingly for a few seconds before beginning to cry. I put the spoon down and walked away from the pots, grabbing a small piece of ice out of the freezer for her to suck on and shushing her by kissing her slightly reddened face.

Lena's cries were already subsiding when a toilet flushed, and Daphne's voice came from the hallway. "What's wrong with my baby?"

"She's fine," I called. "Just momentarily neglected."

"Goddamn," Bill muttered, looking impatiently at the simmering food and then toward the bedrooms. "Are all women so fucking gaga over their kids?"

I hated him. I hated him on several levels. Beyond the obvious fact that I was in love with his wife, I hated him for being one of those guys who talks about "all women," as if we were one make and model with a small variety of optional parts. And I hated him for not realizing how spectacular Lena was. Even if he suspected she wasn't his, which he might have since she looked nothing like him, he should have loved her anyway. I did, and she wasn't my kid, either.

Rather than continue my mental list of loathing, I made my voice as cold as I could and answered, "I wouldn't know."

Something in my voice brought his attention to me again, and he frowned as if he was truly puzzled by my animosity. Then, his face changed, and he snapped his fingers, pointing at me. "Oh yeah. You're that kid whose crazy mom bashed her head in."

I couldn't move. I couldn't speak. The world tilted backward so fast that I had to squeeze my eyes shut. I grabbed Lena up out of her chair, determined to rescue her as I hadn't been able to do with Adam, but the movement startled her, and she began fussing again.

Daphne's heels clicked into the room.

"About killed you, didn't she?" Bill asked. "But she'd already killed your brother, right? Who would have thought a stand-up guy like your dad would marry a crazy bitch like her? That shit was probably the worst thing that ever happened in this town."

Glancing at my face, Daphne inhaled sharply. "Oh God," she said. "Stop it, Bill." She moved to my side, lifting Lena from my shaking arms and murmuring, "Come on, baby." She might have been talking to Lena as she lowered her carefully to the carpet, but I knew the words were for me. I couldn't look as she eased an arm around my shoulders, and we began walking toward the back door.

"You found her, didn't you?" Bill addressed Daphne as if he hadn't heard her rebuke. "And wasn't the brother some kind of retar—"

"Shut the hell up, Bill," Daphne all but screamed at him. "Everyone knows you're a dullard, but do you have to be so fucking insensitive too?"

"Mama?" Lena asked from the floor. I sensed, rather than saw, Bill start to stand, and I felt Daphne turn her head toward him. Clearly, her look stopped him cold.

"The only insensible thing I ever did was marry you," he replied after a few seconds, but she'd opened the door, and we stepped into smells of gas and tires in the garage as he yelled, "And where's my goddamned dinner?"

Daphne kept us moving. "You're not blind, and you're not handicapped. It's obviously sitting there on the stove. Get a bowl and help yourself if you can't wait thirty seconds for me to return and serve you. But mind the baby in the meantime."

"Damn right, I'll wait," he exclaimed loudly, and I heard the clink of glass from the fridge. "And you better be back before I finish this beer."

The door closed behind us, and it was quiet. She embraced me, and I waited for her warmth to push away the fearsome chill that had seeped in from Bill's words. Daphne felt solid and alive, but I was drowning like Adam, submerged in the knowledge that my life had been inches away from being consumed by the madness of a woman who was supposed to love me. "Tell me you'll come by tomorrow," Daphne ordered softly.

My teeth started chattering, and I couldn't respond.

She pressed herself closer, rubbing my arms and shoulders. "You're okay. It's over. You're safe now."

Betrayal. Death. And God, the pain. "But Adam?" My voice seemed small.

"Max, look at me. Open your eyes and look at me."

As her instruction came through, I gave her words some thought, trying to decide if I could…or if I wanted to…do what she said. I was terrified of what I might see or hear. My blood on the grass. Lots of it. A small white body floating facedown in our play pool. Mom standing frighteningly close, holding our skillet and ranting in the way she did when things were really, really bad. Pain like I'd never felt in my short life. And only Daphne between me and all of it.

"Max, baby." Into my sickening visions of that day came the sound of my name with a sweet, gentle tone that I rarely heard anymore. "Look at me." She kissed each eyelid delicately. "Come on. Let me see you."

The taste of vomit and chorine had vanished, and my head wasn't pounding so hard that I was seconds from fainting. I forced my eyes open and saw her and the garage beyond. "Shit." She held on as I staggered slightly, my mind putting the past back where it belonged. I hadn't been ambushed like that in a long time, and I could only guess it was due to all the other emotions of the day.

"That's my girl." She kissed me quickly on the mouth, and before I could react, she leaned over and pushed the door opener, and there was that grinding noise, and a light went on. Keeping her arm around my shoulder, she walked us toward the edge of the driveway where my bike was parked. "Are you going to be okay to ride?"

I blinked and breathed deeply, letting the present settle around me again. "Yeah, in a second. I need to feel…a little more like myself." She looked into my face and nodded. My heart rate quickened as I remembered her nursing the baby and us coming together. The garage door. Bill. "Are you going be okay with Mr. Polk?"

She rolled her eyes and gave a snort but didn't answer. Instead, she took my hands. "Tell me you'll come by tomorrow," she said. "I want to hear you say you will."

My throat was tight with everything I wanted to say. How much I loved her. How much I needed her. How I thought she was the strongest, bravest, most perfect woman in the world. "Yeah, I will."

She tilted her head. "That was pretty good, but I'd like to hear more certainty." I grinned as she pulled me toward her, still holding my hands. She retreated into the shadows of the side yard, looking behind her until she stopped with her back against a tree. I kept going until I was right up against her. "Max," she cautioned as I leaned in to kiss her neck. "Someone might see us." I put my hands on her breasts, and she jumped, batting me away. "Stop. You'll make me leak."

"I've been leaking all night," I growled, grabbing my crotch. "I always leak around you."

"Do you now?" I could hear in her voice that she was enjoying herself. She pulled my hand away and put her own between my legs. She put two of my fingers into her mouth and pulled them out slowly while she sucked them.

"Fuck," I gulped, sure that she could feel me thrust involuntarily into her palm.

"Yes," she said. "Bring that hostess gift I gave you, and we'll do that tomorrow." She kneaded her fingers against me, and my head went back. "You are coming, aren't you?"

"Just about," I assured her.

She laughed, giving me one last squeeze before deftly stepping around me. At my bike, she stopped and looked back. "You're certainly acting more like yourself. Okay to ride now?"

I growled in frustration and rushed over, wiggling my fingers as if planning to tickle her. She caught my hands again, and I lifted hers to my lips. I kissed each one and rubbed my cheek across them as the importance of everything I needed to tell her bore down on me. "Daphne—"

But the door opened, and Bill yelled, "Woman, you better get your ass in here right this second."

"Tomorrow," she repeated quickly and walked away.

I started my bike and sat on it for a few moments, wondering how long it would take me to save enough money to hire a hit man.

❖

I arrived the next afternoon, finding the back door standing open. I knocked on the screen, and when there was no answer, I entered cautiously, carrying the Chinese food I'd picked up on the way. We hadn't had a chance to talk about it, but I figured that if Daphne had already made dinner, I'd take the Chinese home to my dad. The kitchen was quiet, although there were dirty dishes on the table and in the sink. I yelled hello and thought I heard water running in the back part of the house, so I didn't worry at the lack of reply. The den was empty too, but I detected a sour smell which might have explained the roll of paper towels that stood among the scattered toys. I stepped into the hall and called for Daphne. There was still no response, so I checked Lena's room, finding regular towels on the floor, a stronger smell in the air. Baby puke, I was pretty sure.

I was following the sound of the water down the hallway when it stopped. Lena was crying, and I could hear Daphne's voice, although I couldn't make out the words. I turned into the master bedroom where I'd never been before. Like everything else in the house, it was nicely decorated, although the bed hadn't been made, and there were several pieces of clothing scattered on the floor.

I tapped on the bathroom door as I opened it. "Anybody home?"

She was kneeling on the bathmat; her hair and shirt were soaked. Lena was in the tub, her face scrunched up and red with crying. Daphne turned with a start. "Goddamn it, Max, you scared the hell out of me."

"Sorry. I knocked, and I hollered a couple of times."

"And how was I supposed to hear you with this water running?" she snapped and turned back to the baby, who was now blubbering in her baby language, trying to tell me what a terrible day they'd both had.

Daphne was about the girliest girl I'd ever known. In childhood, she'd hated getting dirty or wet or mussed in any way while I'd exulted in the rough-and-tumble world of the boys, never coming home without dirt, scrapes, torn clothing, or all of the above. It was also obvious at an early age that a nursing career was not in Daphne's future, as illness made her very anxious, needles made her swoon, and dealing with blood or shit was out of the question. I'd been curious to see how she might deal with the various fluids babies emitted. Her expression—a combination of despair and weariness—gave me a sense of her struggle. I stripped to my undershirt and stepped out of my shoes.

She sniffed and ran a washrag over the baby's arms. "Oh please, Max. Does it look like I'm in the mood for that?"

I knelt beside her. "Why don't you let me take over here, and you can get cleaned up?" I pointed to the shower. "I bet you'll feel better if you put on fresh clothes afterward."

She stared at me for about ten seconds, and I watched the anger fade from her expression. She bit her lip. "I don't even have dinner going yet," she said softly, her voice heavy with defeat.

"Good, 'cause I'm in the mood for Chinese, and I bet you don't know how to make a decent lo mein. But thanks to the miracle of modern takeout, there's some in your kitchen." She closed her eyes, and I took advantage of the moment to kiss her on the forehead. She sighed, and I saw her shoulders relax. "Is Lena sick?" I asked. Wrong question.

Her eyes snapped open. "No, I just thought changing her outfit five times and giving her three baths today while using every towel in the house to clean her vomit would be fun. Doesn't it sound like fun to you?"

"Shower." I pointed again. I sniffed and made a face. "And wash your hair too."

Daphne pushed the baby angrily in my direction and stood. "Fuck you."

Since she rarely used that phrase except in conjunction with the actual act, I knew she was genuinely infuriated, although I didn't think her ire was aimed entirely at me. I tried for a doubtful expression. "Maybe later."

"Mama," Lena pronounced and released a bubbly fart into the bathwater.

I tried. I truly did. I pressed my lips together as hard as I could. But after a little snort escaped, I gave up and burst out laughing. "You got that right, kiddo," I said, kissing the baby's head. "Your momma is a toot."

Daphne chewed her cheek the way she did when fighting a smile. Then, her expression shifted to that haughty look. "*Maybe* later?"

I indicated the baby. "Well, my schedule looks rather busy at the moment, but let me know about your availability, and we'll see if you can fit me in." I was grinning, mighty proud of how I'd worked that phrase in, when quick as a flash, she reached into the tub and splashed me. Not a flick of water, but a big wave that wet my hair, my face, most of my undershirt and a large part of my pants.

"That ought to cool you off, stud."

Lena squealed with delight, waving a chubby arm in my direction. "Match!"

"Yes, baby," Daphne agreed. "Max is all wet."

I growled and jerked in her direction like I was going to jump up. She shrieked and ran as far as the shower. "Lucky for you, I have my hands full with another girl at the moment."

She laughed, and it was beautiful. "Lucky for you, I like you wet."

And just like that, I was.

❖

Daphne let me watch her undress, but once her shower was done, she insisted that the baby and I leave the bathroom while she "got herself together." In the meantime, I carried Lena around in my underwear, my shirt and jeans in the dryer, while I cleaned the house. I sang all the baby songs I could think of, but she was still fussing a bit, so I found a box of chamomile tea in the pantry and brewed some for her. I cooled and weakened it with ice cubes and gave her several spoonfuls, surprised that she seemed to like it. After the dryer buzzed, I dressed and was contemplating the baby bottles in the fridge when Daphne came into the kitchen.

"She's already eaten, and she kept that last feeding down," she reported before I could ask. "Unless you're looking for a beer or something."

I shook my head and told her about the tea. She looked at me strangely. "How did you know about chamomile for an upset stomach?"

I shrugged. "I don't know. PBS, probably."

She turned her head without comment.

After a few seconds I took her plate from the oven and indicated the place I'd set at the table. "I'm glad you haven't eaten."

"You know," she remarked, studying her food. "Someday, a really lucky girl is going to snap you up, and I'll never see you again."

"Maybe I don't wanna be snapped up," I said carelessly. "Maybe I'll keep playing the field until my bones are too brittle to rub against someone else's."

She laughed a little. "That's not you, Max. I know you see yourself playing the field, but believe me, you're a one-woman woman."

"If that's true, maybe I've already found her," I murmured, knowing we were going onto dangerous ground but unable to help myself.

She started eating without another word. I followed suit, trying to maintain my cool. After a few minutes, she sighed. "That was really good. Thank you. I'd eat some more, but I need to have something for Bill."

I rose and put another small helping on both our plates, pointing toward the fridge as I came back. "There's an unopened beef dish in there. And fried rice."

She ate a few more bites, and then her gaze met mine and held it. She seemed to cycle through a series of reactions. Finally, she asked, "What do I owe you?"

Of all the things she could have said, that was so not what I expected. I tried to play it off with a shrug. "You don't owe me anything. Since I can't take you out to dinner, I thought this was the best option."

She rose and got her purse. "I noticed you cleaned too. Thank you for that." I watched silently as she pulled out five twenties and laid them on the counter. "I'm tired, and I'm going to go to bed, but I didn't want you to go away empty-handed."

Before I could get good and mad, it occurred to me what she was doing. After having known Daphne for more than ten years—although the exact nature of our relationship seemed always open for discussion—I recognized her classic brush-off technique. It was like a test that anger would always fail. "Great." I squinted, touching the money with my fingertips. "But there's one problem."

Sighing, she leaned against the counter. "What is it?"

"Our menu has recently changed, so listen carefully to these options before making your selection." I didn't look at her but studied one of the twenties while I thought fast. "If today's event featured my favorite child's hysterical bathtub fart, press one. If there was also a completely unnecessary water splashing incident that required me to walk around in my underwear until my pants finished their acquaintance with your dryer, press two."

With alarm, she looked around at the windows. "You didn't."

I went on. "If tonight's service offered me the chance to improve my stock holdings in rug cleaner and Febreeze, press three. If the occasion included me getting a chance to enjoy the Ming Dynasty lo mein, which I haven't had for a full month, press four." I risked a quick glance. She had her hand over her mouth, which hopefully meant she was smiling. "And if spending the evening here accomplishes what I looked forward to all day, press five."

The corners of her eyes crinkled, but she spoke from behind her hand. "What am I going to do with you, Max?"

"If your answer is all of the above, and you really are that tired, press six, and I'll go give Lena a kiss good night and get out of your hair."

She brought her hand down and pressed a finger into my palm. I nodded and squeezed her shoulder lightly as I went by. In the baby's room, I spent a moment watching Lena in her crib, admiring her sound sleep as I pondered what was going on in her little mind. Did she have dreams like adults did? And if so, what did she dream about? When she was sick like today, did she cry because she feared her illness or just because she was uncomfortable? Could she feel how much she was loved? Did she truly love in return, or had she simply learned certain responses, like smiling or reaching for someone, because such behavior got her the results she wanted? I knew she was as exhausted as her mother, so I didn't take a chance on waking her with a touch. Instead, I kissed my fingers and waved them over her.

I'd started toward the kitchen but stopped after catching the scent of chamomile again. Unbidden images of Adam appeared around the fringes of my thoughts, and I sighed, thinking how glad I would be when Lena made it past the age I'd been when my life had changed forever.

I often wondered if Adam had known he was different. Did he ever reach an awareness that the person who was supposed to love him most had a fearsome mental illness, the same disorder that had ultimately led to his murder? "Take care of your brother" was one of the consistent refrains from my childhood. Though he was almost two years older, I was in charge whenever mom was having a bad day, which seemed like always, practically from the time I could walk. Adam's relationship with the practical world could be frustrating, like trying to get him to eat or take a nap, but it was through our play that I'd learned to see the world in more than one way. A leaf was part of a tree, yes, but it could also be a boat or a hat for a bug. Did he know how much I missed him and how I still carried the guilt of not being able to save him like a talisman, warding off all others except the only woman whose company I craved because she was a safe harbor?

Daphne Kimball's childhood had probably been marred differently, but every bit as much as mine. After witnessing the frequent peculiarity and later, the frightening weirdness of our lives from the perspective of a neighbor, she'd arrived in our backyard that particular day to take on the role of savior. For me, that had never really changed.

Adam and I were utterly fascinated with Daphne because her occasional appearances in our lives were like a visit from an exquisite being who dwelt in an enchanted land far, far away. In her regular life, she'd attended dance lessons or cooked with her mother or played Barbies with her other friends, but when she'd joined in our play, her magical powers had included getting either of us to do anything. Adam had let her cut his hair, something he was normally terrified of, hiding if he saw scissors. She'd gotten me to eat a "pie" we'd made in the yard, which consisted of dirt, pieces of a green stick, and some grass. I'd thrown up later, never connecting that experience with the marvelous Daphne.

I'd always felt bonded to her in my thoughts. Even now, in our most intimate moments, Daphne and I never talked about that day, but I sometimes questioned what her memory might be. What had she said or done to keep my mother from striking me again with what certainly would have been a fatal blow? Perhaps, on some level, she still identified herself as a fortuitous, eleventh-hour protector in the same way that I thought of my innermost self as both a failure and a victim.

I hugged myself as I shivered. Daphne came down the hall and stood beside me in the doorway. "You learned about chamomile tea from your mother," she remarked, obviously reading my mind as we kept our voices low to avoid waking the baby. "Adam often had an upset stomach, but he refused to take medicine. I went to the library to try to find a way to help him feel better. It was the first time I'd considered that pharmaceutical drugs weren't necessarily the best idea."

"Except when they are," I answered hollowly, thinking of finding the hoard of my mother's untaken medication the morning that she...

I closed my eyes, and Daphne pulled me into an embrace. I shivered again, dreading the day she'd grow tired of salvaging me. As I laid my head on her shoulder, she ran her fingers through my hair, confirming my suspicions of her clairvoyant skills as she traced around my head to the place where my hair would always be longer, hiding the small bioabsorbable plate on the left side of my skull, just above my ear. I never, ever allowed anyone but Daphne and JT to touch that place.

"Come here," she said in her husky voice and drew me toward the small bed. "You've been so sweet to me today, and I've been such a bitch." I gave her my "what else is new?" smirk, and she replied with a warning wag of her finger. "I was going to ask you what would make you feel better, but I won't if you misbehave."

"What if misbehaving would make me feel better?" I asked, trying to put away the melancholy of memory.

She smiled, running her hands over my shoulders and down my back. "I'd be disappointed if you wanted anything else."

CHAPTER TEN

2001
Age Nineteen

Three hours and forty-five minutes later, I was sitting at my desk, doing my homework. I was having trouble concentrating, apprehensive that these daily visits would lead to Daphne tiring of me. Emptying my pockets as I got ready for bed, I found a note in Daphne's swirly handwriting. *I must be crazy, but I want to see you tomorrow. And don't leave your "talent" in your backpack. I want you wearing it all day.*

Elated, I focused on our future. She had to see we belonged together. It would surely happen soon.

The next day was a Friday, and I had forgotten it was one of those half days. I called Daphne from the school pay phone to ask if it was okay to come by early. There was no answer, but I decided to take my chances. When I saw Bill's truck wasn't there, I tried the front door. It was unlocked. The TV was on in the den, and Lena was on the floor in front of it encircled by a mound of toys. I turned the TV off and picked her up, plopping onto the couch and finding a book from the selection of options that surrounded her. "Honey, I'm home," I called, smiling at Lena because it was so cheesy and exactly how I felt.

"Match," Lena called before going on a mile a minute in her personal language while I nodded and grinned at her.

"I'll be out in a quick minute," Daphne said from the back.

I began pointing out the animals in the book as Lena dutifully made sounds for each, including the duck that sounded suspiciously like a fart. "No rush," I said casually. "I'm being entertained by a fascinating young beauty with an interest in the wild side."

"Is that a fact?" I heard her say from the doorway after we'd read a few more pages, but I didn't turn.

"Yep," I answered, deliberately not looking her way. "I'm really not sure if I can…" I started stretching, letting my head turn casually in her direction as I finished, "…tear myself—"

My mouth was open, but nothing more came out. Daphne was wearing the sexiest negligée I had ever seen, red with black accents, tight where it needed to be with see-throughs and splits in all the right places. I'd been teased several times that day at school about being dressed up since I wasn't wearing my usual jeans and a T-shirt but rather my nice black pants and a shirt and tie. My classmates couldn't know it was because of what I had on underneath. My jeans were tight enough that it would have been rather obvious, especially the way it felt now, practically coming to life all on its own like Pinocchio's nose.

"Away," Daphne said in that sultry voice.

"Huh?"

"I believe that was the end of your sentence. You couldn't tear yourself…away."

"Oh," I cleared my throat and carefully put the baby on the floor. "Did I say that? I might have misspoken." I stood, feeling unexpectedly shy, as if she was someone I barely knew. "Daphne, you look…incredible."

She walked toward me slowly, and I fought to stand my ground, knowing my knees were weakening. "You look nice too," she purred, lifting my tie and running her fingers along the length of it. "Have I seen you in this before?" Her fingers continued down the center of my body until she found what she was looking for, and she smiled. "Did you wear this all day?" We could have been talking about my outfit, but we both knew we weren't.

"Yes," was all I could manage as she closed her fingers around the strap-on she'd given me over a year ago, measuring it through my pants.

"I see. And is there someone at school you wanted to show it off to?" The fingers of her other hand rested on my breast, teasing my nipple until it was hard. "Use it on, even?"

"No." That didn't seem like enough, but I struggled to get the next words out. "There's never been anyone else."

"Never?" She leaned back to look at my face but kept her hands where they were. "I heard that you and Maryjane Bowen were an item this past summer."

I tried not to look surprised that she'd heard about that. Damn small town. "I wouldn't say that."

She let go of the strap-on and brought that hand to my other breast. "What would you say?" She squeezed, not gently.

"I'd say there was a party, and we danced some." I was proud that I didn't flinch.

"Is that all?" Her tone was almost dangerous.

"No. Albert Fannin freaked and slapped the shit out of me." I met her look as she let go of me.

We stared at each other for a few seconds until she touched my face, genuine concern in her voice. "Is that true?"

"Yes." I wanted to close my eyes and sink into her touch but worried she might think I was making it up if I did. "He got the drop on me, and it took Jack Mickton and a couple of other guys to pull him off. Fucking religious fanatic. He was going on about Sylvia too." *Oops. That might have been a mistake.*

Daphne traced her fingers across my chest and around to my back as she walked behind me. "I'm very sorry that happened to you." Her breath on my neck gave me goose bumps as she added, "Albert Fannin better never cross my path in town, or he'll be more than sorry."

"Thanks," I said, trying to swallow with an unexpectedly dry mouth.

"But...Sylvia. Or rather, Ray. Your great kisser..." Still behind me, she rested her hands on my waist and leaned her breasts against my back. "I think we'll have to talk about that another time."

Relieved, my shoulders slumped, the change in my posture brushing me against her breasts more firmly.

"I'll be back." She scooped Lena up and carried her down the hall. The vision of her bending over to get the baby about set me off. In the kitchen, I drank some water, trying to cool myself off.

I heard her return, but didn't move from the counter. She pressed her hands onto my rear. "I want to tell you what I was thinking about last night, right after I went to bed."

"Tell me." I thought my voice sounded tight, but either she didn't notice, or she didn't care.

Making small circles on my buttocks with her fingers, she leaned close to my ear. "I was thinking about your sweet butt. That got me to imagining you were a gay man, and I was too." She brought her hands around my front, grabbing my breasts and pressing her crotch against me as she pulled me to her. "I could see my dick and how hard I'd be, waiting for you to come home so I could fuck that tight ass." I felt her shudder lightly as she thrust herself against me, bringing me into her fantasy.

Without a second thought, I widened my stance and bent forward slightly, flexing my butt, meeting each thrust more actively. "Oh yeah." She growled, and I knew without looking that her eyes were closed and her head back. "Would you let me do that, Max?" She moved a little faster and then stopped to grind against me. "Would you let me fuck you in the ass?" She must have felt me tighten up because she added, "Not now. Not now. But sometime?"

Would I? I almost couldn't think for the weakness in my knees, due, at least in part, to the copious wetness that was flooding my boxers.

She bit my shoulder through my shirt, hard enough to make me grunt. "Say yes, baby. You know you want to. I can smell how much you want to."

Oh, hell. Who was I kidding? Was there anything I wouldn't let Daphne do? Would I really tell her no when she was turning me on with incredibly erotic imagery? "Yeah, okay, sure. Just…uh…just give me some advance warning, will you?"

She laughed and held me still against her. "What, like a year or two?"

I turned in her grasp, and she let me, the fantasy gone for now. Giving her a lazy nod, I said, "Yeah, that would probably do it."

We stood and looked at each other for a few seconds until Daphne took a breath. "I need a quick drink. What do you say?"

More cooling off was definitely in order. "Sure. A beer?"

"No. Not a beer. I'm making you a grown-up drink. Would you see if you can get Lena to take her nap?"

Holding her face gently, I moved my lips to within a whisper of hers. I wanted to tell her how much I loved both of them, and how happy it made me to have a place in their lives. Instead, I breathed, "Okay," and strolled carelessly down the hall.

"You know, having your mouth that close doesn't help my composure," she disclosed as I opened Lena's bedroom door.

"That's good to know," I replied from the hallway, feeling pretty damn pleased with myself.

I was even happier when Lena's eyes closed after only half a story. I watched her sleeping peacefully in her crib for a couple of extra minutes, but I was thinking about Daphne, working through everything I knew or thought I knew about her sexually. I knew she wasn't gay, and I didn't think she was bi. Maybe there was a thing called omnisexual. All I knew was, she was an incredibly exciting, adventurous woman, and the sudden idea of her being with anyone but me sent me into an emotional tailspin.

I sat on the small bed where we'd been together the last two days. Certainly, there hadn't been anyone else lately, right? But could I persuade her to embrace monogamy? After all this time, I knew that going out there and beating my chest like a caveman would be the completely wrong thing to do. Besides, nothing had been decided, at least not out loud. The thing to do was to be cool. Show her that I knew how to treat her like the fabulous lady she was. I'd pushed her a bit in the last two days. That needed to stop. Daphne had a very clear view of my emotions. She simply needed a way to find her way to the same place.

I went to the bathroom, carefully wiped myself, and checked my look. All good. I had a great plan.

I came into the kitchen, and we had our drink. She'd made something fruity but extra strong. The gasp of my reaction made her laugh.

"Beer is for pussies," she announced, making me wonder if this was her first one.

Our conversation turned kinda silly, but we eventually found our way to the couch. She undressed me—except for my tie and the other obvious portion of my outfit—and pushed me down. With the back cushions off, there was plenty of room for her to straddle me. For a minute, neither of us moved. She was gorgeous and so damn sexy in her teddy, I couldn't even blink.

"Today, we're going to fuck. Do you have any objections to that?" I certainly couldn't think of a single one. But I did have one expectation. "I closed the door to the baby's room." She glanced toward the hall, and I put my hands on her waist to recapture her attention. "I want to hear you scream."

I could tell she liked that idea. But she countered with a sneer. "I suppose you think you're gonna make me?"

I moved my hand to cup the side of her breast. "I'm gonna try." I squeezed hard, and she jumped a little.

With a piercing stare, she held the strap-on and lowered herself slowly onto it, groaning as she did so. She watched me as she rocked, grinding the base of the shaft into my clit. The movement sent sparks up my spine and a very certain awareness that much more would set me off. I put my hands on her thighs. "Easy, baby. I'm getting ahead of you. We need to let you catch up."

Daphne took hold of my chin, the gesture more controlling than tender. "Let me tell you something, stud. You caught me off guard yesterday, but the days of you taking charge are over. You're coming two for one today. I'm gonna make sure of that."

Shit. Those words alone nearly did me in, not to mention the diabolical grin on her face. I knew better than to challenge her, although that could be part of the fun. I settled for, "You're the boss."

Sometime later, the faint jingle of keys, followed by the turning of the door handle, was barely audible over Daphne's cries of pleasure that accompanied the urgent anticipation of her second orgasm. A sweep of warm air from the open doorway moved across our sweaty bodies, along with the somewhat distracted, initially businesslike tone of the familiar southern voice: "Ms. Daphne, I got my daughter Briella with me today. She got out of school early so she can help—"

Several things happened at once. With a reflexive combination of self-preservation and self-doubt, I turned my face away from the door. Daphne stilled and went completely silent.

The voice at the entryway turned to shock and horror. "Oh, my good Lord," and the door quickly shut again.

Daphne was off my lap and standing next to the couch in a matter of seconds. "Get dressed." Her voice was so flat, I wouldn't have recognized her if she hadn't been standing beside me. She grabbed her robe from the nearby chair and started toward the door.

"Hey," I said, standing and looking around for my clothes. "It'll be all right."

She looked at me with an expression that was almost kind. "No, Max, it won't. There is no universe in which this will possibly be 'all right.'" She sighed. "If you can't dress faster, take your stuff to Lena's room."

"What are you going to do?" I asked, watching her walk toward the front door, but she didn't answer. In some weird trick of perspective, it looked like she was disappearing. But that couldn't be the case, not after all we'd meant to each other these past days. She paused with her hand on the knob, looking at me again. I smiled encouragingly, but she only gave a "get going" jerk of her head. So I did.

Standing in Lena's room, I dressed and tried to get my head around what had happened. When I was fully clothed, I looked at Lena, finding her bright eyes searching my face. I picked her up, and we discussed the situation until Daphne breezed down the hall.

"Call your father and have him pick you up at the corner." She gestured toward the end of her street. "The story is that your bike wouldn't start and you left it yesterday. Have him drive you on an errand or something, and then you can come back and get it. You can't drive off on it now."

"Because?" I asked.

She looked at me as if I'd asked the stupidest question she'd ever heard. "Because I just sent Odie Mae to the Sav-Mor, but I don't know how long she'll be or if she really went. She or Briella could be watching to see who leaves here."

"What if they are? It's actually good this happened, Daphne. Now we can quit sneaking around. Bill will have to give you a divorce and we—"

"Stop it, Max! Go now before things get worse than they already are."

"But that's what I'm saying, baby. They don't have to get worse. They could get a whole lot better." I stepped toward her, and she stepped away, her palm up, stopping me cold.

"No. We're done here, and we both know it. It was simply a matter of time anyway."

"A matter of time?"

Lena started fussing. For the first occasion I could recall, Daphne ignored her. "I've got to get dressed, and you've got to get out of here."

I crossed my arms. "And if I refuse?"

Her eyes narrowed dangerously. "Don't go there, Max. We have a history together, and you know that means a lot to me, but don't push it. I'm not going to let you ruin my life. I'm warning you."

I'm not going to let you ruin my life looped through my brain. I shook my head to clear it. *Cards on the table, Max.* I spoke quickly so she couldn't cut me off. "Daphne, you know I love you. Why won't you take this chance for us to be together?"

She sighed heavily. "You're going to make me say it, aren't you?" She took in a breath. "Fine. I don't love you, Max. I never have, and I never will. We had some fun, and that was it." She leaned toward me, something in her expression I had never seen before. "Now get the fuck out of my house."

A thousand ways to confront her were dueling in my mind with the last of my pitiful misgivings. But what would I gain from any of it? Whatever else I knew or didn't know about Daphne, there was this: she was incredibly stubborn once her mind was made up, which it clearly was. Turning away, I put on my backpack. I leaned over, touching Lena's reddened face, and her whimpering stopped.

I spoke quietly, but I knew Daphne could hear. "Some people won't ever be able to tell you that they love you, Lena. I'll never be one of them. Not now and not ever."

When I straightened, Daphne was turning away. I walked past her without a word, leaving by the den door that went into her backyard. I hopped the fence and made my way to the corner 7-Eleven, but I didn't call JT. I called Maryjane Bowen. She seemed pleased to hear from me.

❖

I set out to prove to myself that I truly was a stud, which by my definition meant I could sleep with someone and be perfectly nice about it but not really care. Luckily, Maryjane was an eager participant in my learning curve. She was pretty and had a good enough body to keep my attention, but we both knew precisely what we were doing, which was basically just passing time. I passed a lot of time for the rest of my senior year, dropping enough well-intentioned lies along the way until I ultimately had to do my time passing in Clearmore. Maryjane was in college there, and I enjoyed three dates on the strength of her recommendation. Once, I passed Briella in the dorm, and we gave each other a quick nod. Thankfully, she indicated no awareness of the part I'd played in the yearly tuition funds that Odie Mae had begun receiving from Daphne.

I guess I was what someone might call heart numb. I got to a point where everything was automatic and so predictable that I'd catch myself questioning why in the world people bothered to get married. Reflecting on the question, I decided to ask JT, but the conversation never happened because that was the evening when I realized he wasn't okay. Then, through all the rest of it, I had no desire for anyone or anything.

❖

2007
Age Twenty-five

The first year of my trucking life was sorta like being a freshman again, if I'd entered Pokeville High in a fifty-thousand-pound, seventy-foot-long, eight-foot-wide vehicle. But in the same way that freshmen tried to figure out the ins and outs of their new environment, I spent that year learning my truck, my routes, and my own endurance, all while trying not to kill anyone or myself. I had a few close calls—a couple of which were my fault—and got good at predicting which four-wheelers didn't have a healthy respect for the time and distance appropriate to the road conditions.

Like the average sophomore, I was more certain of those fundamentals by my second year, so I began branching out, making frequent use of my CB and my phone to combat the lonely hours. In both cases, it didn't take long to figure out who I could talk to and who to stay away from. Before long, I came to rely on my iPod, a few select stations, and my own company.

I learned my way around truck stops, warehouses, rest areas, and the occasional Walmart parking lot. As I'd done with some of my high school acquaintances, I sometimes had to let things go and cut my losses. I sometimes didn't venture out of Nephthys for more than an hour or two in a day to stretch my legs or spend time doing paperwork. But I never once questioned my decision to take up trucking. Driving was the life for me.

In early December, I was back at my home base in Etta's parking lot when I heard tapping on the side of my rig. I wasn't expecting anyone, and there wasn't anyone I wanted to see. The small cheering section I'd had during my actual commencement was much smaller now. Oh, there were folks at Nan's who might say hi, or I might shoot the shit with the guys at my dad's shop for a while, but otherwise, my conversations were brief exchanges with strangers. The only person I saw regularly was Zelda since she'd retired back to Isabell. Her place had a spare bedroom—along with a nice parking space out front—that had my name on it, according to her.

I'd heard other truckers say how hard it was to only see their family every few weeks, so I counted myself lucky that no one was waiting on me to come home, wringing their hands when the weather got bad. I was free, and generally disinterested in the rest of humanity...or so I thought. When I opened the door and saw Daphne standing there, I was almost struck dumb.

We'd spoken casually over the last couple of years, running into each other at Sav-Mor or in line at the pharmacy. People who lived in a small town knew better than to make enemies or hold grudges. After she and Lena had helped me return to the world after my dad's death, I'd make arrangement to visit with Lena whenever I was home for more than a few days. Daphne still worked the register at Etta's, and I saw her there whenever I was in town. The threads of our friendship might have gotten frayed, but she'd still seat me at the quietest table and give me free coffee. And despite the fact that it wasn't my concern, if I saw some new driver working on getting next to her, I'd explain things to him or get one of the other decent guys to do it.

If I tired of my own cooking, I'd overtip the servers at any truck stop while never overtly flirting, even with the cute ones or the funny ones or the lonely-looking ones. I knew they got enough of that from the men. In return, I got good service and the occasional note containing a phone number or a time they got off, along with my check. The great thing about such offers was that everyone already knew the score. It was a couple of hours or an evening, a pleasant distraction, a temporary treatment for whatever ailed us, and there were never any desperate clutching embraces or tears upon parting.

I did make it a point not to hook up with any of the gals from Etta's. Don't shit where you eat, I told myself, especially when a new hire gave me a wink or an extra warm smile. I wondered if Daphne gave them the same kind of warning that I did with guys who might be after her because their extra friendliness all but disappeared by any second encounter.

I gathered myself and eyed her suspiciously. "Did you need something?"

That wasn't the best opening question, but to her credit, only one corner of her mouth lifted. "Is it too late for a tour?" My eyebrows rose in shock. "If I'm not interrupting anything," she added, giving a hasty glance around.

My current novel was lying on the loveseat. The dishes were drying on the rack. I had a done my laundry recently, so clothes weren't piled up in what passed for my bedroom. It seemed like an okay time to show her around, though I couldn't believe that was all she really wanted. Gradually, I warmed to the task, showing her all the little nooks and crannies, specialty drawers and cubes and gadgets I'd designed. I opened the divider door, gesturing vaguely at the bed. "Everything in there is pretty routine."

She took a moment to peer in before looking into my face. "That's not the way I remember it."

Turning away, I ignored the slight flutter in my stomach. I stood at the dinette, comforted by the solid expanse of table at my back. I wasn't in the mood to be toyed with. "What do you want, Daphne?"

Her eyes flitted around uneasily. "Aren't you going to offer a lady a drink?"

"That depends." I leaned away slightly.

She put a hand on her hip. "On what?"

"On what you want."

As she gave me a slow smile, I realized we were already playing. It was out of my control, obviously. Our tone, our body language, everything was as familiar as a well-rehearsed song in which we'd each memorized our parts. Still, I was determined to hold my note just a few seconds longer than she did.

When I didn't move or comment further, her expression gradually sobered. "Lena's missed you."

"She told you that, did she?" Lena was all of six years old, but Daphne had long been using her as a vehicle for things she wanted or didn't want to say.

"All right, damn it. I've missed you. Satisfied?"

Oh no. If we were going to play, I was going for blood. "Are you?"

Now she had both hands on her hips. "Not particularly. The service around here is lousy."

Determined as I was to win this round, I could at least be hospitable. I moved to pour a drink from a box of white wine I kept in the fridge. I'd learned the regular bottles went bad before I could finish them, and there was something about buying wine in a box that appealed to me. Probably because at that level, it was hard to make a mistake.

I expected Daphne make some snide remark, but instead of commenting on my lack of decorum, she came over and stood next to me at my small counter. "Are you seeing anyone?"

That was about the last thing I expected her to say, given that our conversations of the last couple of years had either been entirely superficial or about Lena. My instinct for self-protection kicked in. "Are you?"

"Goddamn it, Max, stop answering every question with a question. You make me feel like I'm in goddamn therapy."

We stared at each other for a few seconds, and then I couldn't help laughing. When she relinquished her mock anger and joined in, it felt almost like old times. I decided to risk being honest. "To your most recent question, no, I'm not seeing anyone regularly. I have a date here and there, and that's as much as I need." I handed her the wine. "Your turn. How are things with Bill?"

She sighed. "Things with Bill are about the same. We don't love each other, but we've reached a place where we are mostly civil. He's drinking less and taking a little more interest in Lena now that she's older. She would totally be a daddy's girl if they could find some common interest." She sipped her wine, obviously not really tasting it, her expression pensive. "She loves her pappy—that's what she calls my father—but he's been slowing down a lot lately. He says he's fine, but..."

She hesitated, studying me. "After your dad passed, did you ever think about—"

I knew where she was going with this, and I cut her off quickly. Whatever else she wanted, we were not going to talk about my mother. "No."

"But you know where she—"

"Yeah, I do. All that information is in a safe-deposit box. I might look at it someday."

She nodded and squeezed my forearm gently. "If you ever do, I'd be glad to keep you company."

I swallowed around the tightness in my throat. "In that case, you'd be the first—and probably only—person I'd call."

"I guess I was wondering if it was still like that for us." She kept her hand on my arm, her fingers trailing back and forth in light strokes. "I know I hurt you, Max, and I don't think I ever apologized properly. I truly am sorry."

I shook my head. "Given our childhood history, we'll always be friends." Strangely, with her simple admission of remorse, my old pain seemed to evaporate. I took a breath, ready to move on. "Look, you told me how it was between us from the beginning, but I didn't listen. That's on me. Besides, if it hadn't been for you and Lena, I'd conceivably still be hiding out in my dad's house. Except I might have a few dozen cats by now." I grinned, and her hand squeezed again.

"Well, I'm glad you don't. One is a perfectly normal number of cats to have." She had mentioned more than once that she and Lena were having conversations about pets, Lena declaring she wanted two kittens and one older rescue dog who would be gentle with them.

I loved the way Lena's vision of the world was so clear and simple. After a few seconds, it occurred to me that we were still standing at the counter. "Would you like to sit down?" I asked.

"Could we use the sofa instead of the table?"

"Sure." At my casual reply, she sauntered over and sat, taking another sip of her wine. Something about seeing her there, looking relaxed and very much at home, made me pour myself a couple of fingers of bourbon before I joined her.

"Oh good," she said approvingly, patting my knee lightly. "I hate to drink alone."

"I wouldn't think you'd have to worry about doing that. Any man who walks into Etta's would buy you a drink, and most would throw in a diamond ring if you weren't already wearing one."

For a moment, she didn't comment, her gaze resting on my face but her expression remote, as if she was weighing something in her mind. "What about you?" she asked finally.

"What about me?"

"If you'd never been to Etta's before and we'd never met, would you offer to buy me a drink?"

I waited a few seconds, trying to figure out what she was really asking. Was this an attempt to confirm that strangers would still find her attractive, or was this something more personal? I shook my head but smiled to ease my response. "I never make the first move. It saves me getting my face slapped or worse."

"So what would you do? If you were interested in sleeping with someone, but you weren't sure if they'd be receptive to a direct overture. How would you go about it?"

"Daphne..." I began, somewhat exasperated. Forgive and forget was one thing, but I truly didn't want to talk about my current sexual experiences with her.

"No, please. I honestly want to know."

"Why?"

"Come on. Humor me, Max. You don't have to tell me everything, but give me your typical approach."

I stood to pace. For one of the few times that I could recall, my current living space felt much too small. "There is no typical approach. Every situation is different. Every woman is different. Why would you think I'd use some stock pitch or bullshit pickup line?" My exasperation was verging on anger now. "I don't understand why you're pushing me on this."

She cocked her head and gave me her *if you weren't so stupid, I wouldn't have to be such a bitch* look. "Because I'm trying to figure out how to ask if you'd still like to sleep with me."

I stopped pacing and blinked at her, replaying the words, verifying what I'd heard. Her face didn't change, and when I was certain of what she'd said, I could only manage, "Oh."

She put her wineglass down and stood, smoothing her skirt before moving toward me. Her voice was bright with anticipation. "Remember my friend Chloe from the bridal shower?" I nodded mutely. "She was telling us about this couple on *Oprah* who were talking about being 'friends with benefits.' Now, Oprah didn't approve, but I thought of you. See, it's where two people—"

"I know what it means."

"You do? Oh, good. Well, don't you think you and I fit that description? We are friends, you said so yourself. And since you're just dating here and there, couldn't I be one of those dates when you're here?"

I stiffened, having absolutely no idea of how to respond. She took advantage of my indecision to move closer, her voice softer. "It seems a shame to let such a great fit go to waste. Or have you forgotten?"

I couldn't look at her. Concentrating on a spot on the floor, I let my head drop slightly as I whispered, "No. I haven't forgotten."

Her hand rested on my waist. She drew me to her, and I almost stumbled. Our faces were at the edge of focus, and her eyes held an expression of desire I remembered well. She leaned in to whisper in my ear, "You don't have to decide tonight...although Bill's gone, and I told the babysitter I might be late."

I could feel her breasts, firm against my body. Unyielding. Curiously so. Unfamiliarly solid. Bewildered, I stepped back, staring at her chest. "Daphne...what—"

She giggled like a child. "I've been waiting for you to notice." She threw back her shoulders, accentuating the body parts in question. "I had them done last year. I guess we haven't seen each other much since then." She did a slow quarter turn. "What you think?"

I knew what I was supposed to say...*they're great,* or *you look fantastic*...but it simply wasn't true. At least, it wasn't to me. But I recalled the night of that bridal shower, the very first time we'd been together, and how embarrassed she'd been about her breasts, claiming that the difference in their size was dreadfully noticeable. While I'd never found that to be the case, I knew I couldn't contradict her about it. And back then, I'd been so infatuated, it wouldn't have mattered if she'd had three tits as long as they were hers. I tried for a smile, but my response had already taken too long.

Her face fell. "You don't like them."

"I'm...surprised. I guess I was out of town and missed all the gossip about it. I bet the girls at Etta's teased you no end."

My attempt at diversion wasn't successful. She turned away, clearly distressed, with her hand at her throat. "I hoped you'd think they were sexy."

Every reply that came to my thoughts was outside the "friends with benefits" arena. *I thought you were perfect the way you were. You have always been the most beautiful woman I know.* Scrambling for a way to repair her hurt pride, I blurted something on the edge of appropriate. "You never needed any help being sexy."

She looked over her shoulder at me. "You're just saying that."

"You know I'm not." I put a hand gently on her waist. "If I don't use lines on strangers, I certainly wouldn't use one on you."

A shy smile played across her mouth. "Which is another reason why we're here talking about being friends with benefits."

As tempted as I was to get a look at the new Daphne, I didn't want to fall into my old bad habit of making us into something we weren't. "I'm gonna need some time to think about this, okay?" Seeing her smile disappear, I decided to go for total honesty. "You're too important to me to let this turn into a mistake. My head will need to be in the right place before I say yes."

She looked into my face for what seemed like five minutes. "What about your heart?" she asked finally.

I swallowed. "That too."

She did something she hadn't done since we were youngsters living next door to each other. She kissed me on the lips. It started off soft and sweet like those childhood kisses, but there was such a promise of heat behind it that it quickly escalated into much more. In less than a minute, neither my head nor my heart had any more say in the matter.

CHAPTER ELEVEN

2007
Age Twenty-five

Daphne stood at the door, smiling while I buttoned my pants in preparation for seeing her to her car. Moving to her side, I tucked a strand of her hair back where it belonged, and she caught my hand and kissed it. "Are we good?"

I liked that she asked, and I liked her tone in doing so. It was as if she truly cared. "Absolutely. The whole taking time thing is clearly overrated."

Her smile grew. "So how long will you be here?"

"Another couple of weeks. Things tend to get slow around Christmas. I could get a call, though. If I do, I'll let you know." She'd already redone her makeup, which meant more kissing was out of the question. I ran my hands up her arms before helping her with her coat. "Otherwise, since you'll be the one with scheduling issues, I'll wait till I hear from you. All right?" I might have known what friends with benefits meant, but that didn't mean I knew the proper conventions.

She turned and ran a finger down my cheek. "Thank you for this. My life isn't the same without you in it."

The old Max would have said something stupid about her always being in my heart or us finding a way to be together. Instead, I nodded. "Can I see Lena soon?"

"Of course. Let me call you when I've had a chance to check our calendar."

"I'd like it if you'd call me anyway. Just to let me know you made it home okay."

She laughed. "Is that gentlemanly, or are you mothering me?"

"You know the answer to that without even thinking." We smiled at each other, and I walked her to her car.

Afterward, I lay on my back, staring at the ceiling, trying to find exactly how to think about all this. The sex had been better than ever. Replaying the evening, I couldn't get over the way Daphne had started everything off. There had been a couple of occasions in our inglorious past that I'd tried kissing her first, always with disastrous results. There was no telling what had changed her mind or how she'd come to the idea of including kissing in our repertoire, but whatever it was, I'd certainly enjoyed it.

Everything had happened quickly after that first kiss, and I hadn't considered getting the strap-on. I hadn't used it since we'd been together anyway. After our terrible parting, I'd gotten a weird attitude about it, wanting to ensure that the women I slept with truly wanted me and not just some device. I'd mainly use my hand and was fine with the same in return. Only on those rare occasions when a woman had gotten me really worked up did I go down on her. There was something uncomfortably intimate about oral sex, and it wasn't an intimacy I'd desired. Until now.

Tonight, Daphne had come quickly around my fingers, so I'd kept them inside her and eased myself lower, taking her in my mouth to bring her off a second time. After she'd recovered, she'd matched me in every respect. As great as it had felt to have her stroke me to orgasm with her fingers, when her lips had touched my clit, it took everything I had not to come that instant. Even trying to hold back, I'd quickly reached the point of no return. Worse, I'd yelled loudly and long at the peak of my climax, becoming extremely self-conscious… once I was able to think rationally again.

I'd gradually become aware that Daphne was running her fingers through my hair while she kissed my face softly. "You are something else, Max Terrell," she'd whispered. Or maybe it had sounded like a whisper by comparison.

"I…" My throat was hoarse from the shout. I'd swallowed and added, "I was just thinking the same thing about you."

She hadn't seemed displeased with that exchange. In fact, she'd seemed okay with everything, except for the fact that I clearly didn't enjoy her new equipment. I'd tried not to be obvious, but I'd paid her breasts much less attention than I normally would have. It was a thing that couldn't be undone, and I supposed I'd adjust, sooner or later. She was probably thinking the same thing.

Turning onto my side, I closed my eyes, still catching a whiff of our scents in the air. Eventually, I admitted that whatever this new chapter with Daphne was going to be, I'd missed her too. It seemed that we were destined to be in each other's lives. I simply needed to leave love out of it this time.

❖

Actually, when it came to authentic, abiding feelings, Lena was the Polk who held my heart. I'd adored her from the first moment I'd seen her, and I still found her wonderful company whenever I got to spend time with her. And the best thing was, unlike her mother, she clearly loved me back.

Daphne watched us with fond amusement, but she usually stayed out of our games or other entertainment. After the first day, we both begged to have another playday and Daphne, acting as if she simply couldn't withstand two sets of pleading eyes, agreed.

It was a strange week that followed. I saw Daphne, my friend with benefits, twice. I also saw Daphne, Lena's mother, on two separate occasions. Knowing Zelda's insistence on snail mail, I wrote her a long, rambling letter in which I asked more about Janey, her longtime companion. I was probing for a way to make sense of what I had and-or figure out how to get more.

To my great surprise, Zelda called me a few days later, and in her typical no-nonsense way, told me I needed to fish or cut bait. Somehow, she'd read between the lines of my questions and had figured out that I was, in her words, "Hanging my wash on someone else's line." I tried the "it's complicated" dodge, but she was much too wise to let that lie. Part of me thought that all the world's problems could be solved if every leader on the planet could have a nice long sit-down with Zelda. Accompanied by a decent bottle of whiskey, of course.

But since that hadn't happened yet, I phoned Daphne again at the beginning of the second week to ask if I could take her and her daughter to lunch. I could hear Lena crying in the background.

Her voice was curt. "No. This isn't a good time."

"Later today?" I asked.

She lowered her voice significantly. "Not today, Max."

Lena's vague sobbing increased, and I heard her call my name.

"What's wrong, Daphne? Just tell me that." Before she could answer, I heard a male voice increasing in volume, although she must have had her hand over the receiver because I couldn't make out the words. "Call me tonight," I whispered, as if he might hear me. "Say yes if you promise you will."

"Yes, thank you. Good-bye."

She didn't call, though. Late that evening, I rode my bike to their street and peered at her house. It was dark. I was nearly overwhelmed by a terrible sensation, remembering Ray's story of his lover Tanya, who had moved away without a word. But Pokeville was their home, both hers and Bill's. Surely, they wouldn't…

I returned to my truck, but I was too restless to stay there. I went to Etta's, slipping my cell phone in my pocket where I hoped I would feel it ring over the racket around the TV. I sat at the bar and sipped a beer, watching the men watching a football game. I liked football, but it didn't make me crazy the way it did them.

Katie was working, and she poured me a second beer without asking. "You look like your dog ran off."

"Why are people so complicated?" I wondered aloud.

"Oh, honey. There's nothing complicated about people. Most of us aren't willing to put in any effort to understand 'em. If they came with a set of instructions, you'd probably lose interest real quick."

I sighed. "I'm not convinced that's true."

A man stumbled up. I had to push off from my seat to avoid the splash of remaining liquid in his glass as he all but threw himself against the bar. I was about to say something when I caught Katie's "stay out of it" look.

"Where's your buddy tonight, Ken?" she asked him, taking his glass and starting him a new drink.

"Fucking the wife for a change." He sneered. "Says she's been making noises about wanting another baby. Said he was taking her to that fancy motel north of town." Snorting into a handful of pretzels, he added, "I think he has frequent flyer miles there." He looked around, his bleary eyes landing on me. "Ain't it enough that he's married to the best-looking woman in town?" he demanded. "Plus, his daddy's money gets him all the loose pussy. Can you blame me for hanging around him? Sloppy seconds ain't all bad, you know."

I reached for my wallet. "What do I owe you, Katie?"

"Let's call it six dollars even, Max."

"Max?" boozy Ken asked. "Are you that lesbo trucker?"

That he'd obviously been talking about Daphne already had me simmering. The rest of it brought me to a full boil. I slapped a ten on the counter. "Ken? Are you that drunk they call Dinky Dick?"

Katie started laughing, but she was also reaching for Ken's arm. I knew it would take him several seconds to figure out my retort, and Katie's interference would probably save my hide, so I said, "Keep it," and hit the door.

I was angry at myself and at Ken and Bill and Daphne. Of course they had sex. They were married, right? And of course Bill was an asshole, which was why Daphne kept reappearing in my life on those occasions when she couldn't take it anymore. There was nothing new here, but somehow, it hit me differently, hearing details from Bill's drinking buddy. Maybe I was at the point where I couldn't take it anymore. On my way across the parking lot, I noticed I had a voice mail. After I got inside, I listened to Daphne's message:

"I'm sorry I had to be rude. Everything is fine. I'll call you in a day or two, okay?"

Sure, everything was fine. For her. She'd gotten what she wanted from me, and now she was working on getting what she wanted from Bill. As she had over the years, she'd given just enough to make me believe it could work between us. Her offer of "friends with benefits" was obviously a new name for the same pastime, which meant neither my head nor my heart would get the "benefit" from this arrangement.

When I was younger, the doubts I'd had during these rough patches seemed like minor skids from which we'd always recover. But the pileup of bruises and scars from her insensitive behavior was making our carrying-on look like a painful wreck. I sat on my loveseat, feeling like I was seeing an updated map that showed a familiar location in astounding new detail. Was it possible that what I'd valued as important history between us had become a weight that was only slowing me down? Daphne wasn't strictly to blame. I'd willingly taken this path countless times before. But maybe I needed to find another road.

Since I had apparently started thinking like a trucker, I needed to act like one. Shaking off my romantic revelations, I emailed a few of my business contacts. The next morning, I had three job offers. I accepted them all, scheduling through what would have been my Christmas break. I called Daphne from the road, pretending a bad connection and shouting my change of plans. Ignoring the hint of disappointment in her tone, I added that I'd send Lena's present at my first opportunity. Then, I lowered the phone to where she'd hear nothing but the roar of my engine for a few seconds before I hung up.

❖

I had a fine first run, and someone was going to be very happy with the lovely bedroom suite I'd picked up from the custom furniture maker in Austin for delivery to a ritzy home in Albuquerque. Equally interesting was the brief conversation I'd had with the woman whose striking creations were exactly what I'd want to have in my own home if I ever stopped driving.

It was hard to determine her age because she was usually wearing sawdust-covered overalls and a skullcap. I imagined her in her late thirties or early forties because I doubted that many woodworkers in their twenties had this kind of successful business. Her eyes, which were a kind of gray-green, held the sharp, focused expression of a woman in charge of her own life. This was my fifth job for her, and we were always on a tight schedule. During our brief conversations, her focus was on the care I took in padding and strapping down her precious cargo, and mine was on our payment arrangements. I guess she'd come to a point where she trusted me enough to think about something else because once everything was loaded, she stopped my progress toward the cab with a hand on my arm.

"It's Max, right?" I nodded, surprised. "I'm Risa. Risa Lavoie." I knew this, of course, from her invoices, which was certainly how she knew my name. "I dig your truck name." I'd had *Nephthys* stenciled on both doors in a kind of scripty-looking font that looked Egyptian to me. "I bet there's a story there."

I gave her a vague smile. "Yeah. But it's not a quick one."

She acquiesced, taking my meaning. I was on a job and time was money. "Do you work all through the holidays?"

"It depends," I answered, shrugging. "When there's a job I want, I take it. If not, I take a break."

She grinned as if flattered I'd taken her job. "I'm asking because I'm having a New Year's Eve party. Consider yourself invited. If you can make it, maybe there'll be a chance for you to tell me the tale."

Now it was my turn to be flattered. I imagined she'd have a gathering of Austin's artists and intellectuals, probably a very interesting scene. I'd often wished the rest of Texas would catch what Austin had. "That sounds nice. Do I need to let you know how my schedule shakes out?"

She gave my arm a little squeeze before letting go. "Not at all. Just come if you can."

"I will. Thanks."

We nodded at each other, and I let that nice, warm feeling percolate inside me for several hundred miles.

❖

Since that haul went extremely well, it figured that the next run had to be a clusterfuck, which it was. I was moving some equipment for a Houston-based band who was going to have a weeklong show at a dance club in Oklahoma City. I'd been reluctant to take the job because when I'd hauled for them before, it had taken me over six months to get paid. Sure enough, about halfway there, I got a call saying the gig had been canceled, so I turned around and started back. About halfway back, I got another call saying the job was back on, that it had all been a mix-up. I turned again and began retracing my route, cussing a blue streak the whole time.

Turning a semi was a pretty big deal. Luckily, I was on a well-built stretch of highway, but still…between finding good exit and entrance ramps, gearing down, and then gearing back up to speed, I estimated I lost at least a half hour to forty-five minutes each way. Then, when I was about fifty miles from OKC, I got another call. The band was breaking up, and I needed to return to Houston with their stuff.

"I tell you what," I said, really tired of their bullshit. "I'll send you a bill for what you owe me now. You pay me now, I'll turn into Santa Claus and bring you some nice, slightly used equipment. Otherwise, I'll give you until April, when the Easter Bunny and I will sell everything for whatever we can get. Till then, Merry Fucking Christmas."

I disconnected in the midst of his protests and rolled on to a familiar truck stop on the outskirts of Oklahoma City, feeling better when I got a great parking space thanks to the light holiday traffic. Being a woman, and frequently the only one in an area, I didn't like being too close to other trucks. Somehow, a lot of guys had the idea that simply because you had a vagina, you wanted them in it. And when I got tired of being hassled and explained why my answer was no, that could be much more hazardous. Like many things in life, it was a balancing act, but I was in good shape this time. I got cleaned up and unloaded my bike, ready for a drink and perhaps more.

A couple of beers and a couple of dances later, I met a really nice woman. Stephanie—"call me Steph"—was a high school biology teacher. She had a pleasant face with a great smile and kind eyes. I liked the way she moved on the dance floor, and from what I could see under her winter sweater and jeans, she had a nice body too.

"If I was in your class, I'd beg to sit on the front row," I told her as we started getting acquainted.

She laughed but sobered quickly. "I know you're kidding, but I take my position very seriously. The relationship between teacher and student is like a sacred trust, and I would never—"

"Oh no," I cut her off. "I didn't mean to suggest—"

"It's cool," she jumped in, saving me from a stammering apology. "I just thought you should know that about me."

I nodded, leading her to a small table as the next song started. "May I buy you a drink?"

When I returned with two beers, she was talking to someone else. I tried not to appear territorial. She wasn't my girl or even my date. At this point, I'd leave my alcohol investment and walk away rather than get into a squabble. But the woman gave her a quick pat and left when I approached with the drinks.

"That was my friend, Janis," Steph explained. "She was checking on me."

I watched as Janis joined another woman at a table near the front of the room. She inclined her head in greeting, but the other one's head was turned in the direction of the restroom, probably checking for a line. "It must be nice to have friends like that. I usually have to take care of myself."

"It is nice," she agreed. "So why isn't someone looking out for you?"

It felt like this conversation was taking a quick turn toward serious. "I guess because I'm not from here," I explained.

Her expression blanked. "So you're just passing through?"

"I haven't decided yet. Tell me something else I should know about you." I was hoping to lighten things up.

"I take all my relationships as seriously as I do those with my students. I don't have casual friends, and I don't have casual sex. Does that make your mind up?"

It did, actually, but there was still something intriguing about this intense woman. "How's that working out for you?" I asked, not answering her question.

She gestured in the direction of the nodding woman's table. "I have two very good friends who I absolutely love, one of whom I've known since high school and one I met in college. And I loved my ex until she cheated on me with a guy."

I could see the hurt in her eyes, and it made me sad for her. She told me her friend who had just left was the one who'd enlightened her about her ex's extracurricular activities. She hadn't wanted to believe it, then had all but caught her in the act. Understandably, Janis felt terrible, but Steph was glad not to go on being a fool for years.

"Do you think you'll ever be able to trust someone again?" I was genuinely curious, though I hoped I wasn't picking at a wound that hadn't healed yet.

She took a drink. "I want to. I'm guess I'm a hopeless romantic, but I can't imagine having a relationship where we weren't able to be open and honest and completely available to each other."

To my dismay, I felt the prick of tears. She'd named exactly what the romantic in me wanted and the very thing I'd never had with Daphne. And what I secretly suspected I'd never have with anyone. "Would you excuse me a moment?" I stood. "I need to check out the facilities. I'll be right back."

It didn't take me long to pull myself together, but I assumed Steph would be long gone when I returned. She wasn't. There was even a small bowl of nuts on the table. "Sorry," she said, chewing as I sat. "I haven't had dinner yet, and it's not wise for me to drink much without eating."

"You know what? I haven't eaten either. If you know a decent place nearby, I'd really like it if you'd join me for dinner. I'll bring you back here when we're done." Uncertainty flashed across her face, and I added, "I promise I'm not a serial stalker or a psycho bitch. But I usually eat alone, and you're nice company." While she considered, I suggested, "Why don't you ask your friends to join us? If they're friends of yours, I bet they're great too."

That seemed to do it. "Would you mind if we took my car?"

"Sure. I have a motorcycle, and it's kinda chilly right now."

She smiled in a way I hadn't seen from her, a kind of teasing, fun look as her gaze traveled over my body. "So does that mean you're not really into leather?"

"Not full-time, no. Why, would you not have talked to me without it?"

"Truthfully, I almost didn't talk to you because of it. Some of the leather women are a little too...hard-core. You know?"

I rose and offered my hand. "When you know me better, you'll know I'm a big softie inside."

On the ride to the restaurant, we started a conversation that seemed to flow for the next two hours without stopping. When the check came, I grabbed it quickly. She protested, but I insisted, saying I wanted to return the favor of the ride.

The drive back was quiet as she concentrated on the road. After she parked at the bar, but before she opened the car door, I said, "Hey, I'm sorry if my paying the tab upset you. If it makes you feel any better, I promise, you can get dinner the next time."

That brought her head around sharply. "Will there be a next time? I thought you were just passing through."

What if I told her that had been a line in case I decided I didn't like her? Or what if I suggested there might be a chance for us, and we ended up in bed? Don't be a shit, I told myself. "I am passing through, but I might pass through again. And if I do, I'd like to see you. That's all I meant."

She studied me for what seemed like a long while. "How about one more dance before you go?"

Inside the club, the mood had changed as well. It was getting later, and the DJ had begun mixing in a few slower tunes. I took her in my arms on the dance floor, and we moved together, finding our rhythm easily. Would sex with her be like the rest of our evening had been, nice and easy? *Stop. You're not going to find out, so don't think about it.* But when I felt her relax against me, a strange yearning reared up inside. I thought of the old expression, "If you keep on doing what you've always done, you'll keep on getting what you've always got." That summarized my experiences with Daphne for most of my life, and I considered that Steph, or someone like her, would be what I needed to get me out of my deeply rutted life. I closed my eyes and let the music and her body guide me, while I pushed away the yearning, forcing myself to keep my mouth shut from something I might say that either or both of us would regret.

When the music ended, she kept her arms around me, putting her mouth against my ear. "Thank you, Max. You've given me more hope than I've felt in months. There's someone out there for me. I just wish it could be you." She kissed my cheek and was out the door before I could even ask if I could call her.

I saw Janis join her at the exit. I looked for her other friend, thinking maybe she would give me Steph's number, but I couldn't pick her out in the dim, smoky lighting. My phone buzzed, and I pulled it out. A message. Lena thanking me for the new toy truck and the accompanying stuffed cat I'd sent her.

Why was I thinking that I might be available? Daphne and Lena were my only family, and I wasn't going to leave them, no matter how fucked-up my association with Daphne might be.

I went to the bar for a double shot of bourbon to chase away the night's chill before I got on my bike and returned to my home on wheels, alone. I'd been sitting and nursing my drink for about ten minutes when a voice behind me asked, "Did you like her?"

Without looking around, I muttered, "Shouldn't you be sticking to your knitting?" Steph being an educator must have reminded me of Mrs. Williams, my third-grade teacher, who would offer that advice to any kid who got overly inquisitive about my being absent for a whole year.

The person laughed and slid onto the stool beside me. Though I'd struck out with Steph, I wasn't in the mood for any more company, so I decided on the direct approach. I got as far as "Why don't you—" before my eyes focused on her face. I stopped right before the "fuck off" and couldn't seem to make myself say anything else.

"Yes?" she asked, one brow raised. I'd always envied people who could do that.

Her face seemed a little thinner, and her hair was longer, but I would have known her anywhere. I tried to regain my cool, but it was long gone. In its place was my own personal version of shock and awe. "Thrill," I finally said, stating the obvious while I grappled with how long it had been and how we'd last parted.

Daphne would have enjoyed my mortification, but Thrill took pity on me. "Hello, Max. How have you been?"

I was willing to engage in polite small talk, but I had to know one thing first. "What are you doing here?"

She inclined her head toward the door. "Steph and I went to high school together. She's one of my dearest friends. My parents went on a cruise for Christmas, so I came to visit her and Janis for the holidays."

My mind replayed the woman sitting at the table with Janis, recalling how she'd been looking away. "You've been here the whole time?" I heard myself sounding like someone who was overdrawn at the memory bank, but Thrill gave me a hard look.

"Yes. Now you answer my question. Do you like Steph?"

"I like her fine." *But not as much as I like you* materialized unexpectedly in my mind. I welcomed the appearance of smart Max, who suggested that such a response wasn't the best choice when the image in Thrill's mind could very well be me slow dancing with her best friend. Thankfully, I had another truth to make use of. "But I told her I was only passing through. She's looking for something more permanent."

Thrill nodded. "She messaged me that you said so, and she didn't think it was a line." I tried not to flinch under the scrutiny that followed. "So you're still driving?" she finally asked.

"I am." Anxious to move the conversation away from Steph and more into her, I asked, "What are you doing now?"

"I'm looking out for my best friend."

Apparently, we weren't done with that topic. "Yeah, okay. But could we possibly go somewhere else to finish this interrogation?" I asked. "This music is starting to give me a headache."

"You didn't seem to mind it earlier." Her tone was cooler than a cast-iron commode, and a new thought occurred to me. Could she be a tiny bit jealous?

I gave her my best smile. "I wish I'd known you were here. I would have asked you to dance instead."

She stood and crossed her arms. "Steph has had a rough time lately. Janis asked me to talk to you after I said I thought I knew who you were. And I see I was right. I know exactly who you are, Max. You're still trying to seduce any woman who comes within three feet of you."

Shit. "No, I didn't…I mean, I thought it would be nice to get to know Steph better. But I respected that I couldn't give her what she wanted. She asked me for that last dance, not the other way around."

Thrill pulled out her cell and touched the keys furiously for a moment. I heard the faint ding of a reply, and she gave a slight nod before putting her phone away. "Does this mean you've found honesty to be a better route to a woman's heart—or I should say, to her bed—rather than lying about who you are or who you're seeing?"

I guessed I owed her that, and I got the sense she was gearing up to exact more repayment. Now I really was getting a headache. I stood, rubbing the bridge of my nose. "Look. I've had a shitty day, and I mainly wanted to relax and maybe have some conversation. If it led to something more, that would be okay too, as long as we both knew the score."

I thought I detected a slight softening in her posture and in her eyes. "And what is the score, Max?"

"That I'm here for the night, and I'm not available beyond that." I grabbed my jacket off the bar. "And since you know I'm being honest these days, I want to add that it was very nice to see you again, and I'm genuinely sorry you don't feel the same. Good-bye, Thrill."

I was outside putting on my helmet when I felt a tap on my shoulder. "You're the only one who calls me that, you know. The only one who ever has." The puffs of her breath in the cold air suggested she might have hurried to catch me.

"What does everyone else call you?"

Biting her lip, she looked away. I could almost hear the wheels turning in her head. Clearly, an important decision was forthcoming. After what seemed like at least half a minute, she said, "Do you like pie?"

I laughed. "Wow. And I thought Trillian was kind of a weird name. With a name like Do You Like Pie, you could have a symbol, like the Artist Formerly Known as Prince."

I sketched a circle in the air and was making cut marks in it when she pinched my arm. "I don't want anything else to drink, and it's too late for coffee, but there's a pie shop a few blocks from here. It's open late."

I met her eyes, feeling a twinge stirring somewhere other than between my legs. It felt closer to my heart. Maybe that was why I put more emotion into my response than was warranted. "I really love pie."

She might have blushed, but it was hard to tell in the parking lot lights. Eying my bike, she asked, "Can I ride with you?"

"It'll be cold. Here." I took off my jacket and held it out.

"Won't it be cold for you as well?"

"Nah. I'm used to it."

Jacketless and trying not to freak her out, I was going a careful speed, but after about a block, she yelled, "Go faster." By the time we roared up to the place she directed me to, Baby Pies, my tits were freezing, but my backside tingled from where she'd pressed against me. "God, that was fun."

I tried to control my shivering as I put down the kickstand and turned to her. "You look good in leather. I'd let you keep it, but that would mean we were going steady."

After the words were out, I worried I'd overstepped, so I was relieved when she laughed and shucked off the jacket. "Well, we can't have that, can we?"

CHAPTER TWELVE

2007
Age Twenty-five

Once inside, I learned Baby Pies were, as the name implied, palm-sized individual pastries filled with assorted flavors. They looked delicious. I wanted to order a dozen to take on the road with me but thought it might seem weird, so instead, I ordered a peach, she ordered a cherry, and we got a chocolate to split. Thrill didn't seem to notice when the guy behind the counter gave her a once-over and then lost interest when I insisted on paying. A group of frat boys stared for a few seconds, nudging each other and murmuring as we passed before going back to their pies. Thrill had the kind of look that could pass in any world; she'd fit in at a NASCAR race or at the opera. In this case, her outfit of light-wash jeans and a beautiful, black patterned V-neck sweater over a green T-shirt was perfect for a lesbian bar or a pie shop.

I directed us to the most private booth available, forgetting any other patrons once we started talking. "You're out of school now, aren't you?" I asked, wanting to start the conversation by learning more about her. Besides her name.

She gave her head a shake, chewing. "I'm through with college, but now I'm in law school."

"Really? Where?"

"Houston."

"Ugh. Terrible weather, worse traffic. And home to a band I genuinely hate."

She laughed. "You're right about the first two, but I couldn't speak to the band. I don't get out much."

I tasted my pie while I pondered that information. The pastry was delicious, but it didn't distract me from wondering about her social life. I wanted to offer that, in spite of my previous statement, I'd be willing to come to Houston and take her out somewhere nice, but it was hard to tell how that would be received, given how she'd seen me with Steph. *Probably best to stick with the topic at hand.* "Do you have a specialization in mind?"

"I'm planning to go into health care law. I think I could do some good there." While I chewed, she added, "My older sister is a doctor, and I've heard stories."

"How many sisters do you have?" I didn't usually get into family stuff, but I wanted to know everything she was willing to share. Spending time with her felt really great.

"There are three of us. I'm the baby." She rolled her eyes. "And totally spoiled, so the other two tell me."

I grinned. "I'll reserve judgment on that until I know you better."

She raised that eyebrow again. "Is that your plan?" Before I could decide how to answer, her cell went off. An old telephone-style ring. It fit her somehow.

"Saved by the bell," I stage-whispered, taking another bite.

"Excuse me." She walked toward a small hallway in the back. I liked it that she didn't sit there and have a conversation in front of me while I tried to pretend like I wasn't listening. I finished my pie but waited on the chocolate one in case she had a special splitting method. Families with an odd number of people likely did.

She gave me an apologetic smile when she returned a few moments later. "I'm sorry. That was Janis, and I didn't want her to worry."

"Do you need to go?" I asked, hoping she'd say no.

"Not yet. I want to hear about your family first."

I hid my grimace with a drink of water. "Nothing to tell there. Besides, you haven't explained about your name yet. Or do I have to keep calling you 'Do You Like Pie'?"

"No sisters?" Her persistence reminded me of someone, but I was too busy planning a quick change of subject to get my mind around who it was. I shook my head, opening my mouth to ask something else about school. Or Houston. Or whether she preferred cats or dogs. Anything but this. "No brothers, either? You're an only child?"

Go on. Tell her, a Max I didn't recognize urged. Sure, why not? I could do this. "I had a brother but he..." Shit. It was simply words. I didn't have to witness it all again, right? "He died." I picked up my glass again, but the tremor in my hand made some water slosh out. I tried to put it down quickly, but she'd already seen.

"I'm so sorry. Was this recently?"

My hands were flat on the table. She wouldn't know I was holding on, would she? "No, but it was...bad."

Something warm was grounding me. I hadn't realized my eyes were closed until I opened them to find her holding my hands. "Pokeville isn't that far from Lubbock. I was surprised you didn't have anyone at the NTDS ceremony. Are both your parents gone too?"

A cascade of guilt sloshed in my gut. I hadn't been to my father's grave since the day I'd put him in it, but we'd never been a grave-visiting family. I had a vague idea of where his parents were buried, but we never went. Death hadn't been something we'd ever discussed, and now, it was too late. Not long after he'd died, I'd catch myself talking to him in my mind, but I'd cut it off, scared it was another step along the road to psycho-ville, where my mother still resided, for all I knew. I'd forced myself not to honor a special man and a great parent, either in my head or in my heart, thinking it would keep me from being sad. Thrill's prompting had me wondering if he would approve of my life now and what advice he would have given regarding Daphne. Would he still love me for who I was?

It was too much. "Listen, would you excuse me for a minute?"

I felt her hold on for half a second longer before she replied, "Of course."

I made it to the back hallway and found the women's restroom. I leaned against the sink, running water so no one would knock, though Thrill struck me as the type who would come looking for me after a few minutes. I pushed the one on my phone. Four rings later, a sleepy voice answered.

"Call me in one minute," I said.

"What?" Daphne asked.

"I need a favor. Just do it, okay? One minute." I ended the call without waiting for a reply, flushed the toilet, and turned off the water. I took a few extra seconds to check my face. Not bad. As I'd planned, my cell rang right as I returned to our booth. I glanced at the readout and rolled my eyes. "This is my version of Steph," I explained. "A friend going through a hard time. Give me a minute more, will you?"

Thrill nodded, and I made my way to the hall again. "This better be good," Daphne griped.

"I need an excuse to leave," I whispered.

"Someone getting overly personal?" Daphne asked.

I couldn't imagine how the fuck she knew that, but I chuckled. "Thanks for calling. Sorry I woke you up."

"Is she cute, at least?"

Damn. Thrill's persistence had reminded me of Daphne. In my view, that characteristic was the best and worst of them both. But unlike with Thrill, I knew what Daphne wanted me to say. "Not as cute as you."

"Great answer." She sniffed, and hung up.

And that, I realized, was how I'd learned to talk to women. Simple flirting and appropriate flattery. Sweet little lies here and there. None of this deep sharing shit. I tried not to equate this shallowness with a less than stellar mental condition. When I returned to our booth, she was standing. "You need to go, I take it."

"Yeah, I—"

She handed me my jacket, and we walked toward the door. "Don't explain, Max. I'm sorry if you felt pushed into talking about something uncomfortable." I had a feeling she knew the call was a setup, and she was trying to spare me another falsehood. The Max I didn't recognize wanted her to call me on it. Wanted her to stay after me until I got through the past and made a new, different future. "I've just…I've always been curious about you." There was a hint of sadness in her smile.

Wanting to cheer her, I gestured at my bike. "Can I give you a ride to…to wherever you need to go?"

She shook her head. "I've already called Janis to come get me. You go do what you need to do."

"Thrill, I—"

"It's Elise. My middle name. That's what most people call me. Of course, you're not most people."

"Right now, I wish I was." That reply was the most straightforward thing I'd said all night. I fought the feeling of something important slipping away. "Can I call you if I come through Houston?"

A car was coming down the deserted street. Probably Janis. "Sure. You can find me through the school." Thrill spoke absently as she watched it approach.

Determined to have one last instant of her attention, I touched her hand. We looked at each other for a few seconds, then moved as if in sync. It was an incredible hug, my leather jacket creaking in the cold and her breath warm on my neck. "Be careful," she whispered, her lips brushing mine so quickly that it didn't seem real except for the sudden acceleration of everything inside me. She turned and made her way to the car without looking back.

I revved my bike as they drove away, the sound of the engine matching my emotional state: gratified that I'd gotten all I could get from her at that moment. On the way to my truck, I began thinking about my schedule and when I might next get to Houston. Back in Nephthys, I was hanging up my jacket when I noticed the weight of it felt off. Feeling in the pocket, I discovered the chocolate pie wrapped in a napkin. I realized I hadn't gotten anything more at all. I didn't even know her last name.

❖

I did two short runs, the last of which ended in Dallas, where I dropped off the cargo for an upcoming trade show before helping out the Marines with the annual Toys for Tots pickup and delivery—that one for free, of course. Afterward, I sat in a nearby Cracker Barrel, sipping coffee with my truck idling outside. It was after two o'clock in the afternoon on December thirtieth.

Interestingly, the distance between me and Etta's and me and Austin was almost exactly the same. If I went home to good ol' Pokeyville, I could hang out at the sports bar or see if Maryjane or any of her friends were around. I might get in a quick visit with Lena, but Daphne would certainly be busy with Bill, a concept that would apparently make me forever dejected. I toyed with the idea of going to OKC and trying to find Steph. Maybe she'd give me Thrill's number. But the odds were better that I'd wander around the city for a while, get frustrated, and end up with some strange woman, which on the night before New Year's Eve sounded like all kinds of desperate. I called Zelda, thinking she might be available but got no answer. Risa's invitation was starting to sound like a saving grace. I hoped she wouldn't mind if I arrived a day early.

Her house and workshop were set well back on an oversized lot. When she opened the door, I nearly didn't recognize her in jeans and a tight, faded T-shirt with a band name on it. Her short, reddish-brown hair was curlier than I had known, and bangs hung above her eyes.

"I know I'm early. My schedule—"

She squeezed my arm and began pulling me into the house, evidently glad to see me. "This is perfect timing." Glancing at my rig idling at the curb, she added, "Oh, leave it by the shop where you always do. I'll tell everyone else to park in the yard or on the street, so you'll be fine."

Risa was waiting when I climbed down from the cab. After confirming that I'd never been inside her home, she offered me a tour. I stopped in each room, trying to take it all in, while she walked ahead, trying to guide me forward with things like, "And this is the den," or "Over here is the kitchen." Finally, she stopped, amused by my gawking.

"Your home is stunning," I said. "I'm at a loss for words, except to say that it's exactly what I'd expect from an artist."

She moved to where I was standing and took my hand. "How come you never hit on me, Max?"

That was honestly about the last thing I'd expected her to say, and my response was awkward enough that it must have showed. "Well... um...because I...I work for you, and it's not my habit to hit on my boss." Relieved when she laughed, I shrugged. "And I didn't know if you were..."

"Available?" she finished, and we smiled at each other.

"Yeah, that." Interested was more like it, but I didn't correct her.

Apparently satisfied we'd gotten through that issue, she kept hold of my hand and led me back outside. We spent the next several hours doing various chores to get ready for her party. She kept thanking me, but actually, I was glad to have something physical to do. I tried to exercise every chance I got, but there was no denying that I sat on my ass for up to twelve hours a day when I was working. Plus, it gave us a way to spend time together without the typically uncomfortable, getting-to-know-you chatter. I was about to suggest we order a pizza when she disappeared into the other room for a bit. She returned with two beers and gestured to the glider on her patio.

December in the Texas Hill Country could be downright cold or mildly temperate. This day had been of the mild variety, and sitting outside, sipping a beer at dusk, was particularly pleasant. She settled in next to me; her usual woody scent combined with perspiration and something spicy made for a very appealing fragrance. "Dinner will be in about forty minutes. Is that okay?"

"That's great, but I was going to offer to take you out. To thank you for the invitation," I added, in case I'd sounded too forward.

She waved, indicating I shouldn't worry. "It's nothing fancy. Vegan lasagna. Salad and bread."

"Sounds delicious."

She looked at me appraisingly for a moment. "You know, you're not exactly what I expect of a truck driver."

I laughed. "I've been told that before."

"How did you decide to do this? Do you like it?"

"Most days, I like it very much. Some days, it gets kinda routine, but then another day comes, and I get to hang out with someone like you, and it's terrific. It appealed to me at a point when I didn't know what else to do with myself."

"And Nephthys?"

"Ah." I took a long pull on my beer, surprised to see I had almost finished it. "Do you know who she is?"

"An Egyptian deity who's over death, right?"

"Death, service, lamentation, nighttime and rivers," I clarified, and she nodded. The soft twilight and her calm presence made it easy to go on. "I bought the truck after I finished high school. My dad had passed away, hence the death and lamentation aspect. Rivers because that's what he loved, more than a lake or even the ocean. Fly-fishing was his way of relaxing, and he was always saying stuff like, 'No one ever steps in the same river twice, for it's not the same water, and you're not the same person,' or 'You drown not by falling into a river, but by staying submerged in it.'"

In that moment, I could hear his voice so clearly that it made me both sad and comforted. But maybe it wasn't a bad idea to put him back in my thoughts, to restart those mental conversations. Leaning her head against my shoulder, Risa put her arm through mine but said nothing. It was nice, and I let myself relax into her. "And night because that's when I prefer to do a long haul, like a lot of truckers do. The image of people sleeping while I drive past is a lot more soothing than dealing with road rage or traffic jams. I'm kind of a loner, I guess."

"So there's no woman waiting on you in Pokeville?"

I shook my head. It was the truth. None of the women there were waiting on me.

"And your dad's passed on, but what about your mom?"

I stood without much warning, startling her a bit. "She's not in the picture. Could I trouble you for another beer?"

She stood too. "Come into the kitchen with me, and we can check on dinner."

Because she looked good in her jeans and because I wanted to apologize for being so abrupt, I tucked a couple of fingers into her empty belt loop. "Don't lose me."

She glanced at the house and then brought her eyes to mine. "I thought I might have there for a minute." I started to apologize, but she put a finger on my lips. "Let's eat."

On barstools at her kitchen counter, she talked about growing up in Austin and laughed at her folks' predictable reactions to the idea of her becoming a furniture maker. Her dad: "You'll starve." And her mom: "What if you cut off a finger?" She'd worked for others, honing her craft and developing her style, and when her folks had died within months of each other, she'd taken over their house and remortgaged the property to build her workshop in the back. "At that point, I knew I'd have to make a go of it. I love this place, and I couldn't lose it."

"You're brave," I said.

She shrugged. "Life either means something, or it doesn't. I've never been able to stand the mediocre or the commonplace. What about you, Max? What philosophy guides you through life?"

We'd finished dinner and were sitting on the comfortable couch in her den, nibbling fudge that a neighbor had brought over for Christmas. She was having a glass of brandy, and I was having water, feeling the need to keep my wits about me. "On any given day, I'd probably give you a different answer, but right now, I'm going simple. 'Fill what's empty. Empty what's full. And scratch where it itches.'"

She looked at me for a second and burst out laughing. "That's priceless. Did you make that up?"

"Oh no. I think it's a quote from Teddy Roosevelt's daughter."

She was still smiling, but her eyes had grown still. "Well, we've emptied, and we've filled. Was there a particular itch you had in mind?"

I hadn't intended for her to take it that way. "Risa, I didn't mean—"

She leaned forward and kissed me lightly on the mouth. She tasted like chocolate and liquor. "I like you, Max. Would you care to join me for a long hot shower?"

Damn. An offer of a long hot shower with an interesting woman who liked me? Was this a trick question? "Absolutely."

In her bedroom, she handed me a thick terry cloth robe and said, "Give me a minute," before disappearing into the bathroom.

When I heard the water running, I knew it was on for real. I stripped and put on the robe, aroused by the idea of something I'd never done before.

Risa called for me, and I swallowed. The bathroom was already warm and steamy, exactly the way I liked my encounters to be, and I gaped at the overly large enclosure that ran along most of the wall. Dropping my robe, I opened the opaque door, finding two shower setups about a foot apart, both with detachable heads connected by long silver hoses. Risa apparently enjoyed bathing for two.

"Wow," I said, trying not to sound like the hick I was. "This is incredible."

She favored me with a *just wait* kind of smile. "Thanks. Hot water on demand is one of civilization's greatest accomplishments, don't you think?"

"I hadn't thought that, but you do have a point." I tried not to focus on her sinewy body, but the streams of water sluicing over her breasts and between her legs were hard to ignore. I stepped under the spray and groaned. She laughed, pointing to a liquid soap dispenser and a nearby loofah tucked into a niche in the wall. "That's yours. It's new."

I thanked her, trying not to let my mind contemplate how many guests got offered bath strips in a month. I started scrubbing, appreciating the clean scent of the soap and enjoying the invigorating feel of the loofah. I'd about finished when I looked over and found her watching me. "Want me to do your back?" I offered.

"No, I want you to do something else." She moved closer and kissed me. The wetness of her mouth seemed multiplied by the steam, and I stepped into her body, finding myself genuinely ready for more. She was taller and leaner than I was, but I stretched into her, making our breasts meet in a most pleasurable way. We spent several minutes in soggy foreplay, but I didn't want to get pruney, so I reached between her legs, thinking to move things along.

"Wait." She stopped my hand. "There's something else I want to show you." She indicated the showerhead I'd been using. "These have a variety of settings." She turned the outside ring, and the shape of the spray broadened; another option turned it into mist. "This is my favorite." She turned it once more, making the water into a pulsing jet.

"Oh, for massage," I said, and she smiled again.

"Uh-huh." She turned the head upside down and directed it between my legs. The stream hit my clit with a wallop, and I shouted and pushed her hand away. "Sorry." She pointed to the control knob, placing the device in my hand. "You can make it softer or cooler if it's too hot."

She stepped away, making adjustments to her own showerhead. Seeing my confused expression, she nodded encouragingly. "Try it. Find what does it for you." Resting her back against the tile wall, she aimed the spurting water between her own legs and closed her eyes.

I decided this was a "when in Rome" situation and fooled around with the knobs until I'd gotten the pressure to a gentle pulse. After a couple of different positions, I unexpectedly hit the perfect spot, and at my moan, Risa turned to me, reaching out to caress my breast with her free hand.

"That's it," she assured me, and it damn sure was. In about twenty seconds, I went off like a rocket. I managed to lean into her, putting my mouth to her breast, before I heard her rising cry of orgasm.

She helped me turn my control until it was a mist, and I imitated her motions as she sprayed herself with it. "Wow," I murmured a minute later.

She grinned before coming over to kiss me. When she pulled back, there was a gleam in her eye. "Wanna go again?"

I hadn't been with anyone since Daphne, so I was pretty confident my clit could rise to the occasion. Now that I knew what to expect, I was able to draw out the buildup to my second orgasm a little longer, but when it hit, it was over faster than double-strike lightning. This water play was fine, but I was ready to get Risa into bed and go for some full body contact.

But she stopped me as I reached for the knob to turn off the water. "Now try a fantasy. Something new and different."

I drew out my, "Okay," long enough to let her know I wasn't totally into it. I didn't practice any BDSM in real life, but it sometimes made for effective stimulation when I was alone. I tried imagining Risa on her knees, lapping at my cunt. When I felt her finger stroking the muscle of my anus, I knew I wouldn't last much longer. I held her head still as I worked myself against her mouth. I heard myself groan loudly as I came.

Still shaky, I fumbled for the controls, but she beat me to it, taking the showerhead from my limp hand once the water was off. "I take it you're done," she said, and I nodded weakly. I managed to pull myself together enough to towel off before collapsing next to her on the bed.

❖

Risa was gone when I awoke. Dressing in yesterday's clothes, I followed the lingering scent of coffee but found only a note on the counter. *Need to work for a while before the party. See you later.*

Was that a brush-off, or did she feel awkward about me still being here or what? Maybe we hadn't had full-on sex last night, but we'd spent the day together and had shared some meaningful conversation last evening. I'd expected at least an in-person hello, but maybe things were as the note implied: she needed to get things done, and we would have a chance to talk later. I looked up a nearby coffee shop as I changed and put on my leathers, and after adding a brief reply to her note, I rode over for breakfast. But not even the strong coffee cleared my confusion at Risa's lack of hospitality. Maybe I should have tried to talk with her before I left, at least to say thanks for letting me stay the night.

Pushing my breakfast around, it gradually dawned on me that what I'd experienced was exactly what I usually gave my own "dates." A little cozy conversation to gauge our mutual interest, perhaps a meal or a few drinks to add a suggestion of intimacy, followed by sex, in which my involvement could practically be called rote. And if she was awake when I departed, there was at best a "see you around" farewell.

Unable to sit still with such uncomfortable thoughts, I left a large tip and went to renew my acquaintance with Austin. It was a fine town, and I could almost imagine settling down here, but I wouldn't want to be alone.

Daphne had a portion of my heart, simply because she had literally saved me during the worst times of my life and had been physically present—and often naked—in some of the best times. She also knew the real me because for the first few years of our relationship, I'd eagerly told her what was on my mind and in my heart. But gradually, she'd trained me to keep what was most intimate between us on a superficial level. Now that I was driving, my personal world was increasingly solitary, and I'd became more self-contained in my thinking and even in my society. I could flirt, and I could fuck, but when somebody like Thrill asked questions, seeking to hear my real-life experiences, to know who I really was, I closed up like an eyeless needle.

Thinking of Thrill made me ponder if I could ever change my ways. To be able to truly love, I knew I would need complete commitment, someone I could count on to tell me the truth and call me on my shortcomings in a way that made me want to be better. But I suspected that to find such a relationship, I'd have to offer the same, and I wasn't sure I knew how to give faithfulness or honesty on a regular basis. I was an expert at what I considered harmless untruths, while guarding my feelings like a sentry at Fort Knox. Perhaps my recurrent returns to Daphne demonstrated a kind of warped loyalty, but what would it be like to care enough about another person, and about myself, to exchange the off-and-on crap that Daphne and I experienced for steadfast devotion and dependable permanence?

On the UT campus, a group of students were throwing a ball around. Remembering the flag football game at Texas Tech and Trillian and the bees made me smile. Thrill had crossed my mind more than once as I'd regretted the abrupt ending to our evening at Baby Pies, but I knew I was at fault there. I'd chosen to withhold the secrets of my fucked-up life, unwilling to believe that Thrill wouldn't be scared off by hearing them. For a moment, I imagined getting the opportunity to really get to know her and opening myself up in return, and the feeling was as buoyant as it was fearsome. Unexpectedly, I heard a bell, but it sounded very far-off. Was that sound what Zelda had talked about? Was Trillian the one who got away?

At a stoplight on Guadalupe, a couple walked past me on the crosswalk, the man behind the woman, his hands moving ever closer to her breasts and practically dry fucking her as they walked. The back of the man's T-shirt read, "You're not in love, you're just drunk." They turned at the sidewalk and were walking in my direction, so I could see what was on the woman's shirt. "I think I'm in a love triangle. I love myself. Myself loves Me. Me loves I."

Weren't they the perfect couple, I thought, jeering at myself and the preposterous turn I'd taken into romantic daydreams. That chiming sound was merely from somewhere on campus. And I hadn't let Trillian get away; by not giving me her last name or her number, she'd run like any sensible woman would. Even Risa, who barely knew me, was keeping her distance. Something like what I had with Daphne, for all its difficulties, was the best I was going to get. Normally, thinking of her and Lena improved my disposition, but my life felt timeworn and lacking. Not even the beauty of Austin soothed my discomforted spirit.

When I got back to Risa's, the party was well under way. There were probably plenty of good people and interesting conversations, but I couldn't get into any of it. It didn't help that Risa was hanging on some guy with a goatee and made no effort to introduce me to him or anyone else. I wandered around for a while, sipping a beer, declining multiple offers of smokes or powders or pills. I couldn't have said what I wanted, but I knew this wasn't it. The party was still going strong when I climbed into Nephthys, where the only sure things in my life—nighttime and the road—were waiting.

CHAPTER THIRTEEN

2007
Age Twenty-five

I dozed for a couple hours before leaving, not looking back to see if my departure disturbed Risa or any of her partiers. I was in an unusually foul mood where nothing satisfied me. Not NPR, not an audiobook, not any one of the hundreds of satellite radio stations, and not silence.

I started a conversation with myself, but that wasn't going well either. Anxious Max cautioned me against this negativity, certain that my mother had felt it too. Then bad Max wanted to stop off in Pokeyville for a quick fuck with Daphne or at least a visit with Lena, while good Max said to put the pedal down. Knowing I wouldn't be suitable company for either of the Polks, I decided to make it to a favorite pullout between Amarillo and Dumas to take my usual sleep break before driving on to Pueblo, Colorado. I was scheduled to pick up replacement parts for a dozen wind turbines, but since they wouldn't be open on New Year's Day, I had plenty of time to get there. Being at Risa's must have gotten me off my routine, or maybe I'd needed some extra rest because despite my plan to drive through the night, I didn't wake until dawn.

Life was marginally better once I was clean and full and caffeinated, but I still felt a sense of desolation. It was as if the solitude I'd been so comfortable with had, without warning, become like a vast wilderness with no familiar trail. My anxiety level ratcheted up, and I put on Vivaldi's 'The Four Seasons' but was unable to find the serenity it usually gave me. Had my mother's derangement started this way?

Lost in my worst-case scenario, I automatically made the turn for Raton Pass. The part of my mind that was still driving helpfully assured me that the mild winter meant there'd be no snow or ice on the road. It was still early enough that there wasn't much traffic, but the wind got stronger as I climbed. My attention turned to fighting the gusts, working hard to keep in my lane. When I thought to check my gauges, I saw that Nephthys was overheating. Shit. She'd been so trouble free, I'd lost the habit of regularly looking at the instrument panel.

The instructors at NTDS warned us repeatedly about problems coming when you least expected them. Or in my case, when you were distracted or complacent. Now I was at loss for my best course of action. Pull over and let her cool off? There was an old weigh station with plenty of parking coming up, though it wasn't manned since the measurements were mostly done by electronic sensors these days. But what if she didn't cool off, and I was stuck on the top of the pass? I knew I could call Zelda, and she'd come get me, but I wasn't in the mood for the lecture that would accompany her rescue, deserved though it might be.

I thought some more about my route. Once I was over the pass, it would be mostly downhill to the next town, Trinidad. Like most truckers who made this run, I used that momentum to shoot me on down the road, but given their location, Trinidad was bound to have a diesel mechanic. As I crawled toward 7,800 feet, I used my phone— something I very rarely did while driving—and found a number and address for a shop just off the highway. Decision made, I stroked the steering wheel. "Come on, sweet girl. Get me over this hill, and I'll get you fixed up."

By the time I rolled into the oversized parking lot of Jackie's Repair and Towing, I was almost trembling with relief. Getting gingerly out of the cab, I stretched and tried to shake the tension out of my body. I looked toward the shop and saw a man about my age making his way toward me. I hoped we wouldn't have too many of the "where's your husband?" or "we don't see many women drivers" type comments, and that whatever was wrong could be easily fixed.

"Hi. Welcome to Jackie's," the man greeted me in a pleasant tenor. He stopped his approach and pointed at my truck. "That's quite a rig you got there. You having trouble or just need a break from the wind?"

I walked closer, pulling on my jacket as I went. "She started overheating on Raton Pass. We've made this trip a lot, and that's never happened before. Do you have a few minutes to take a look at her now? I need to be in Pueblo by—" I cut off as the man cocked his head, his wide mouth dropping open as he pulled off his sunglasses.

"Max?"

After a few seconds, the bleakness I'd been feeling since Austin abruptly fell away like the sun coming out from behind the clouds. "Ray. Oh my God!"

We hugged for what must have been a full minute, both of us near tears. Actually, I was closer than near, and I think Ray was too.

When we finally pulled apart, we both started talking at the same time. "How long have you been—" Ray was asking as I said, "So you never left—"

"Wait." Ray held up his hand, taking charge as usual. "One, would you come to the office where we can get out of this wind, and two, how badly do you need your truck fixed right away?"

"Yes, and I'll have to make a call and let you know."

Ray put his arm around my shoulders, and I leaned into his sturdy warmth. With my hand around his waist, I could feel that the rigidity that had so often been present in his body when having to pass was absent. From up close, I could see the skin on his face was rougher, like he might be shaving at least every other day. His smile was genuine, and his warm brown eyes lacked the wariness that I'd grown accustomed to when I'd known him before.

We made our way to a tidy lounge area that featured a newish couch and a couple of comfortable-looking chairs with a small table between them, along with the usual short counter and cash register. A man and woman sat on the couch, and Ray asked if they'd talked to Bailey. They nodded, and the woman replied they were told it should be about ten minutes more. I veered toward a chair, but Ray shook his head, escorting me along a short hallway to a tidier and more comfortable office. Unlike many mechanic's shops, where I was hesitant to even breathe, Ray's place was so clean, I was not only willing to sit down, I would have willingly eaten off the side table or slept on any of the couches or chairs. There was the faintest hint of grease in the air, and I noted at least two air purifiers humming away. I couldn't wait to see the shop itself, but I was more interested in hearing Ray's story.

Gesturing at the phone on his desk, Ray said, "Make whatever calls you need to. That's our 800 line, so you won't have to call collect or run up your cell phone bill." I stared dumbly, and he added, "Is it okay if one of my people takes a look at your truck?"

"You have people?" I asked, somehow having thought this was a one-man show.

He grinned. "Three. Transmission specialist, engine repair, and tires. But they all know their stuff."

"Sure. That would be great, Ray." I handed him the keys.

He started out and stopped in the doorway. "I understand if you need to hustle, but if there's any way for you to get an extra day, it would be wonderful to get caught up. And you'd be more than welcome to stay over in our guest room."

I liked working for Verwinday, the wind turbine folks, but I would have turned down the next five trips to be with Ray, his people, and whoever the "our" was that he had a guest room with. Luckily, the company wanted to make some adjustments to the order I'd be transporting, so they gave me three extra days. Alone in the office, I examined the various framed certificates for mechanical training classes, all made out to Ray Sylvan. Seeing the name warmed me. I was making my way to the photos on the bookcase when footsteps sounded in the hall.

Not wanting to be caught snooping, I met Ray in the doorway. "I've got three days before I have to be in Pueblo."

He grinned broadly. "Fantastic. Are you hungry? Thirsty?"

I requested a water, which he pulled from a small fridge in the corner. "Let me show you the shop."

I nodded enthusiastically, and as we crossed an enclosed walkway leading to the shop, Ray took my arm and pulled me close. "I'd love for us to spend time together, Max. I've thought about you so often.

You and your dad saved my life, you know. I sent him a check for all my expenses, but it came back undeliverable."

I'd been ready to ask a hundred questions, but as had often been the case, Ray caught me off guard. I swallowed, trying to keep my voice level. "Yeah, he passed away the year after my graduation. Cancer. I started driving soon after that, and I'm renting the house to a new teacher in town and her family. But I can always live there again if I get tired of the road."

Ray stopped, bowing his head for a few seconds. When he looked at me, there were tears in his eyes. "I'm really sorry. He was such a fine man."

I nodded, thickness in my throat making my voice low. "He was. The best."

We stood in silence for a few seconds before Ray said, "If it's okay with you, I'd like to talk more about him after our tour."

"Sure. Yeah. That would be fine."

It wasn't like I had to fake being impressed. There were four bays for semis, one of which now held Nephthys, opposite four bays for regular cars. Bailey turned out to be the transmission specialist, and I also met Knox, who worked on engines, and Kinsley, who did mostly tire work. Kinsley was a muscular woman but not butch at all. The guys seemed genuinely nice, and I liked it that Ray had a woman in his shop too. Knox assured me that Nephthys had most likely blown a gasket, which would be a fairly quick repair, but he'd do a thorough check just in case.

"This is an amazing rig. Do you live in it full-time?" Kinsley asked. I'd heard other women with low voices like hers, but knowing Ray made me give them all a second, casual look.

"Yeah, pretty much," I told her. "Unless I'm staying with friends." I grinned at Ray, sure I now understood something about his people.

"Speaking of which," Ray said. "Let's get you settled in."

Everyone offered a friendly parting, and Ray and I walked out into the gusty wind. He pointed to a good-sized, beautifully landscaped home across the street from the shop. "We're right here."

I gave him a look as we reached the front door. "You've got a fantastic setup here, Ray. But I have one question."

"Yes, they're all trans like me." He nodded slightly.

"Yeah, I figured. But that wasn't what I was going to ask."

"Oh?" He seemed surprised. "What did you want to know?"

"The name of your shop. Who's Jackie?"

His smile returned. "You're about to meet her. Jackie is my wife." Closing the front door against the wind, Ray hollered that he was home. In response, two children's voices, yelling, "Daddy, Daddy," grew louder, as did the din of footsteps. A brown-haired girl of about six leapt into Ray's arms while a younger one, maybe four, danced around his legs. The little dancer continued the "Daddy" chant until Ray picked her up too, giving an exaggerated grunt as he did.

"Who's been best girl today?" he asked, looking expectantly from one to the other as they both repeated, "Me. Me. Me," until the sound of another set of footsteps quieted them both.

"I swear, Ray Sylvan, if you don't teach these children to tell time, I'm going to send them with you to the shop tomorrow." Despite the implied threat, I could hear the teasing tone in her words, and Ray's grin suggested he might have heard this before. "No matter how often I said—" She came into view and seeing me, cut herself off, blushing slightly. "Oh, excuse me. I didn't know you were bringing company."

"I'm sorry, baby. We got busy talking, and I didn't get a chance to call you." Ray put the children down, keeping a hand on each one's shoulder. "Jackie, Roxanne, Paige, I want you to meet someone very special. This is my friend, Max."

Three pairs of eyes stared at me, and I sketched a quick wave. "Hi. Nice to meet you."

Jackie turned to Ray. "Is this…*the* Max?"

Ray nodded, and I could hear the emotion in his voice when he added, "She's driving a semi now and just happened to stop in at the shop."

Jackie's face lit up, and she squeezed Ray's arm. "Another miracle."

The older girl, Roxanne, tugged on my pant leg. When I looked at her, she asked, "Are you a boy or a girl?"

"Roxanne," Jackie cautioned in the tone that all mothers had and all children recognized as "you're in deep trouble."

"No, it's fine," I assured Jackie, hoping to spare Roxanne any punishment while simultaneously thinking it had been too long since I'd seen Lena. "I'm a girl, Roxanne. How about you?"

She nodded vigorously. "I'm a girl too. So is my sister."

"Girls are great, aren't they?" I asked.

"Hey, now," Ray countered, smiling. "Boys aren't bad."

"Some boys," I corrected, and Jackie laughed.

"You got that right," she said with conviction. I couldn't wait to hear their story.

❖

In the two days and three nights I stayed with them, I learned that Jackie had been Ray's nurse during his major operations. She'd been married during his top surgery, but her husband had left her before Ray began the bottom procedures. Paige was a baby then, and Roxie had barely turned three. Ray told me he'd fallen in love with Jackie from the start, but he knew she would need to recover from the desertion by a man who had vowed "till death do us part," but then only honored the "parting" concept.

"I took my time courting her," Ray explained. "And improbably, I learned more about myself that way. I guess the best things can take a while, but when you're both sure, it's totally worth it."

I thought of all the years I'd spent courting Daphne, believing she was my best thing, convincing myself that whatever I could have of her was enough. Maybe subconsciously, I had considered myself unworthy of anything other than whatever she could spare, or else I depended on her to continue to protect me from what I feared I might become. I'd had my disconnected flings along the road, but being with Ray's family was altering my outlook. With unexpected clarity, I understood that to have a life as full as his, I needed to accept the painful reality that my own choices were holding me back and stop pretending otherwise.

As if reading my mind, Ray asked, "You still seeing the married lady? Darlene, was it?"

"Daphne," I corrected. "And, yeah, sometimes. Or I don't know. Lately, I…"

I trailed off, and he waited. When I didn't finish, he said, "Think you might be about done?"

"Maybe," I conceded slowly. "But…she and her daughter are like family to me."

"You could be in a relationship with someone else and still have them as your family," he suggested. "But it's pretty clear that nothing's going to change on her side of the equation. Seems like if you want something else, something better, that'll have to come from you."

When I thought about moving on to something better, an image of Thrill popped into my mind. I was about to mention her, but Paige had joined us, so I set it aside for later consideration.

Being with them also reinforced how much I liked being around kids. Lena had always been and would always be my favorite person in the world, but Roxanne and Paige were delightfully entertaining too. While Roxie could talk a mile a minute once she got going, Paige was quietly observant. She came through with some zingers, though. When I went to check on Nephthys after Ray's crew had finished with her, Paige was waiting for me when I climbed down. "Are you compensating for something?" she asked.

"What?" I nearly choked.

"Mama says that sometimes about people with big cars or trucks," she explained, cocking her head. "What do you think that means?"

Given their circumstances, I didn't think I should discuss male anatomy, so I went with, "I think it means, if you don't have much of something, you try to make up for it with more of something else."

"Like what?" Paige demanded.

"You're in kindergarten, right?"

"I'm homeschooled, and I'm reading on a third-grade level," Paige replied proudly.

I knew Ray and Jackie were homeschooling her, and I knew why. They'd told me about the trouble with her kindergarten teacher, which was not only sad but also surprising in an open and accepting town like Trinidad. Meanwhile, I was stalling while my brain was trying hard to supply a suitable example. Thinking of Lena and her crayons, I said, "Suppose you knew someone who wasn't very good at coloring, but they tried to cover for it by hogging all the Legos. That would be compensating."

Paige nodded slowly, obviously considering my explanation. Her serious face propelled me into my secondary go-to move, the one for the younger set: I started tickling her. She shrieked with delight, and we chased and rolled and laughed all over the parking lot.

That third morning, when I came downstairs with my small travel bag, Ray was explaining to the girls that I had to leave. Paige's eyes filled with tears, and her bottom lip stuck out in the cutest pout I had ever seen. Even better than Daphne's.

"Hey, I'll come see you again before long, okay?" I offered, but she shook her head and crawled into her mother's lap.

"We've had folks stay with us before," Jackie explained as she rubbed Paige's back, "who promised they'd come back, but they haven't." She regarded me steadily. "We'd love to have you any time, Max, but if you don't think you'll be stopping by again, please don't say so."

Ray picked up Roxanne, who was starting to sniffle as well. "Listen, everyone. Max is different. Max is a special friend, and she only says what she means. Isn't that right, Max?"

I swallowed, feeling the significance of the moment. Ray and I had talked into the wee hours last night, and after hearing of his journey to the life he'd always imagined, I'd heard myself confessing how I envied what he had. "You've got it all, man. A steady living doing something you love with a good woman who obviously adores you, great kids, and decent standing in the community."

He'd smiled, but the whiskey I'd consumed showed me a flash of sadness in it, the kind I'd seen often when we were younger. "Your father and I talked a lot about life and how to go about living it. While I was staying at your house, I read a lot of things that had been forbidden by my parents. I encountered views from different religions and philosophies, and sometimes, I didn't know what I believed. JT said he'd gone about finding bits and pieces that resonated and created his own way of dealing with the world. He mentioned a quote from Rollo May that said while physically surviving is living, for a good life, you have to figure out what really matters to you. The more I thought about that, the clearer it became. I'd done so much research on the physical changes I needed to ensure my survival, but I hadn't begun to figure out what I cared about outside myself. I spent days sorting through different visions of what I wanted my life to be. In the end, it was simple. I knew I needed love and stability. The family part was a surprise, but it's completed me in a way I never could have imagined."

Bitterness had shot through me, the feeling as unwelcome as a porcupine at a nudist colony. I'd taken another drink, the burn of the liquor helping pinpoint the source of my resentment. It wasn't Ray's home or his wife or family or business that I coveted. It was the hours he'd gotten to spend with JT, time I hadn't taken and would never get to have. Before I could find my way out of my regret, the earnestness in Ray's next words had taken me by surprise.

"I can't tell you how much I envied what you had. Your father was very clear on what he cared about. It was you. He didn't just care, he adored you, and did everything in his power to make up for what happened with your mother. He told me he'd never forgive himself for working so much those first years after you were born. Not being around enough to know what was happening with your mom was the biggest regret of his life. But he hated the repair chain he'd started working for—saying they overcharged and underserved—so he was desperate to open his own shop, but he didn't know how to start. That's why, once he believed your mom was doing better on her new medication, he began taking those business classes at night while still working during the day. You always seemed fine, and he was especially pleased with how well she did with Adam, despite his being…differently abled."

I had taken a longer drink, trying—unsuccessfully—to swallow the acrimony. "She didn't do well with him. I did." Ray had frowned. "I've not spent much time trying, mind you, but I can't remember my mother ever saying a kind word to me. Or about me. Nothing but, 'Get your brother a snack,' or 'Help your brother get dressed,' or 'Take your brother outside to play when you go.'"

"That must have been hard, having all that responsibility at such a young age." Ray's expression had been gentle. "Did it make you resent him?"

I put my glass down so hard, he'd flinched as I'd practically shouted, "No, I didn't resent him. He was my best friend. I loved him." I'd struggled to resume my normal speaking tone. "But it was pretty damn overwhelming being in charge of another person. I wasn't 'fine.' Even at that age, I knew Adam was different, and I worried

I wasn't taking care of him the way he needed. Though he always seemed happy, it was really hard. If I resented anyone, I resented her. Why couldn't she have been like other moms? Why didn't she bake us cookies or drive us to the park or sit with us and watch TV? She was a terrible mother and probably not much of a wife. Why the hell did my dad have to marry her?"

I'd read enough psychology to know that my antagonism was partly anger at my father for dying, but I'd trusted Ray to recognize the truth behind my temper. I'd been about to apologize and head off to bed, waving my whiskey glass in the air as an excuse for my inexcusable rudeness, when Ray had put his hand on my arm. I resisted the urge to pull away. "I think he was waiting for you to mention it, believing you'd ask when you were ready to know."

When it became obvious that JT wasn't going to get better, the overwhelming sadness I'd felt had included deep regret for all the questions I hadn't asked, even if some of the explanations he could offer might shatter me. Now, hearing something that sounded so much like my father, my eyes had filled with tears. "But he told you?"

"Some."

I knew Ray was giving me the chance to end the conversation here. He'd clearly idolized my father as much as I had. Sitting with him now, all the things I'd been afraid to know had seemed safe to hear. "Would you tell me?"

Ignoring the tremor in my voice, Ray had begun filling in the blanks, sketching in missing parts of my history. "Your mother moved to town to live with her aunt during the middle of her senior year in high school, an occurrence so uncommon that everyone suspected something was off. Well, everyone except your dad, who said he was smitten with her from day one. Lisa Collins was new and different, and he told me she had a way about her that was exceptionally compelling. While not completely innocent, your dad wasn't prepared for the full-court press she gave him. 'The onslaught of a woman on a mission,' he told me. Apparently, this included activities other girls wouldn't consider, at least not before being engaged." Ray swallowed. "You know that his dad, your grandfather, passed away from a heart attack when he was ten, so JT didn't have much male guidance in his life."

I'd nodded, easily imagining my mother offering sex to an innocent, honorable boy, with the understanding that he would care for her regardless of her mental state. "I get the picture."

Ray had inclined his head. "She announced her pregnancy just before their graduation, and your dad told me that once he got over the shock, he was truly excited about being a father. But the baby came prematurely. After a difficult birth, Adam had to spend over three months in the neonatal unit. Those bills left them deeply in debt, and your mom was suffering from what they thought was postpartum depression." Ray had sighed. "He did what he could for her, including giving her what she said she most wanted, another baby. In thinking about it later, he realized she only wanted to prove she could have a normal child, that Adam's issues weren't the result of her illness. After everything went perfectly when you were born, he was sure she would get better."

The rest of the story had been almost predictable: JT coming home to crying children and a practically comatose wife, repeated trips to the family doctor until a specialist was recommended, various prescriptions and misdiagnoses, Mom angry one day and sad the next. All the while, Dad tried to keep from losing the house to bill collectors.

My childhood memory had kicked in. I'd remembered being sad and angry myself, not understanding why he was gone so much and why he'd insisted on leaving us with someone who was menacing one moment and vacant the next, though I didn't have the vocabulary to express those thoughts at the time. "I suppose he didn't notice that both Adam and I clung to him like honeysuckle vines whenever he did come home. Or he didn't care." At the resentment in my words, Ray had looked down, clearly dismayed but not wanting to say anything. Shame had flooded me. My father was a fantastic, supportive man who I'd loved with all my heart and missed every day. "Shit," I'd murmured as my tears started to fall. Slamming what was left of my drink, I'd put my head in my hands, my words almost unintelligible through the sobs that alcohol hadn't drained. "Oh God, I didn't mean that. I'm sorry, Dad. I love you so much. Shit, shit, shit."

Ray didn't say another word until we'd said good-night. He'd just held me while I'd relived the anguish of losing Adam and the pain of my own injury. But gradually, I'd come to understand that nothing that happened before could outweigh the life JT had made for us afterward. His love and compassion had created all the family I'd needed, and not even his death could take away the love I'd felt for him or diminish how incredibly grateful I was to have had him in my life.

Before Ray walked me back to the shop that next morning, I knelt to hug Paige and Roxanne, having given my solemn promise to visit again. Before Jackie and I embraced, I saw the look of a mother bear in her eyes. Good. Ray and the girls deserved her protection. As I powered my way through my multiple gears on Interstate 25, I thought about family and about love. But what struck me more than anything was how incredibly powerful the truth could be.

❖

Nephthys and I got a workout that lasted into the new year as we were busier than ever. A couple of new routes kept my attention, but on the familiar roads, I thought about my choices, examined my decisions, and worked toward conclusions about the results of it all. Most nights, I was too tired to look for company, but that was fine by me. The temporary pleasures I'd turned to in the past seemed empty now. When I had the energy, I wrote to Zelda, who still refused to have anything to do with email or any kind of electronic communication, even a mobile phone. It was nice to find replies from her whenever I arrived at Etta's, which I'd given her as my home address.

When I finally had a moment to breathe, it seemed life had muddled on for another nine months. To mark my fully mature entry into the second quarter of life, I sat at Etta's and got drunk with a few of the locals. Not Daphne, who had a PTA thing she absolutely had to attend. She'd missed my birthday plenty of times before, so the only difference this year was that I was actually relieved she wasn't there. I couldn't quite envision how she would react to my decision that our relationship was going to shift to "friends without benefits." Not that I would make that announcement publicly, but still.

Though I was genuinely appreciative of the off-key singing and the beer can with a candle on it, I soon reached the apprehensive stage of inebriation where I couldn't shake the sense that some essential element had been overlooked, like starting off on a trip without checking the tires or fluid levels. Unlike many folks in Pokeville and beyond, the life I was living was entirely of my own making, but it was possible that my recent decision regarding Daphne's role in it would be something like the butterfly effect. Altering the nature of my relationship with her wasn't exactly a meager change, and it might result in a major transformation for me. Beyond that theoretical prospect, I had no idea what kind of difference I was expecting, only that losing contact with Lena would be the one thing I couldn't stand. I had to believe that even at her worst, Daphne couldn't be that cruel.

Shuddering at the thought, I reassessed my plan. Was comparing my life to Ray's what had made me certain that something was lacking? And if I didn't know what that something was, how would I know when I found it? Since our talk, I'd gradually resumed my one-sided conversations with JT. Back in my truck, I let myself wonder if he would have been pleased with my life since he'd been gone. In my stupor, I asked for a sign, some indication of his approval...or disapproval.

CHAPTER FOURTEEN

2008
Age Twenty-six

When my cell rang the next morning, I almost didn't pick up. A Houston number showed on the screen, and I thought that it might be the suck-ass band who still owed me money. But right before it would have gone to voice mail, my foggy brain reminded me of someone else who lived in Houston.

"Terrell's Trucking," I answered, trying to pitch my hungover voice in the professional range.

"Max? Oh, thank God. Hi, it's Elise. Uh…Thrill. Are you busy? I'm calling to ask a huge favor, but you can say no, okay?"

Three thoughts hit me at once: one, she was babbling, which had never been a feature of my limited encounters with Thrill. Two, short of committing murder or possibly robbery, I was going to say yes to her favor. And third, I was so pleased to hear her voice that I felt practically giddy. I took a quick sip of water and deepened my voice into my best John Wayne impersonation. "Well, howdy there, little lady."

"Max?" she said again, sounding uncertain.

My John Wayne wasn't that authentic. Clearly, she was worried about something. "Yeah, Thrill. Sorry, I was playing. What do you need?"

In the same rushed, anxious tone, she told me how she was mentoring a mock trial team at a local high school there in Houston.

They'd qualified for the state competition in Dallas, which was great, and had even secured additional donations to fund the trip. When a nearby Ford dealership had come through with the use of a transit van, the last piece had fallen into place. "The school district requires someone with a commercial license to transport students, and we had a bus driver lined up, but he's come down with the flu." She stopped for breath—finally—and added, "I know you're probably working somewhere hundreds of miles away but…"

I waited for a second after she trailed off. "But what?" I asked, unable to keep the smile from my voice. Knowing that I would have this chance to be there for her, it was hard to keep any semblance of cool.

There was a silence on the other end. I was about to give in, thinking she was too agitated to play, but then she whispered, "I need your help, Grand Master."

Tickled, I went to my Yoda voice. "Help you, I will. Yes. Certain can you be of that." Her laughter made me feel like Super Yoda, but I spoke normally after that, believing we'd fooled around enough. "When do you need me and for how long?"

Apologizing for the short notice, Thrill told me they were due to leave Houston in two days. It would be a long weekend, and I'd be driving ten students, a parent who would help chaperone, and Thrill. "Sounds like we'll get to have our dream date," I said. Another silence suggested I'd crossed a line. Again.

"Max, I'm not out to these people. Not to the kids or the parents or anyone in the school district. Being a mentor was something I very much wanted to do, and I was afraid that if I told them—"

I cut her off, not wanting her to regret asking me. "Oh no, hey, I was joking, Thrill. I'll be on my best behavior, scout's honor."

She sniffed suspiciously. "Were you ever really a Girl Scout?"

"I've been girl scouting all my life."

She giggled, but it took another few minutes of reassurance before I got more details. Once I'd secured Thrill's phone number and home address, I was in high cotton. I'd already planned to take my birthday week off, so I didn't need to cancel any runs. But I'd scheduled some much-needed maintenance for Nephthys, and if I didn't go ahead with that now, it would cost me next week's job. I considered taking my bike, but it was almost six hundred miles to Houston. She'd obviously been desperate to reach out to me, which meant this was probably my last chance to look good. Grimy and road tired was not the way I wanted to arrive. Mulling over other options, I only came up with one.

I chained my bike to a tree in Daphne's side yard. She lived on a fairly busy street that was often used as a cut through between two major roads. There had been a rash of robberies in the neighborhood lately, and Bill was concerned about his tools to the point that he'd started leaving the garage door down. Since I couldn't judge who was home, I politely rang the doorbell. Daphne answered with a folded dish towel in her hands.

"Max, what the hell? I thought you were one of those religious crazies who have started coming around." She turned away, and I followed her into the house.

"Why are you being visited by religious crazies?" I watched as she opened the dish towel, revealing a Bible wrapped inside.

"Oh, Bill thought it would be real funny to tell them how much his wife needed saving, and they've been here practically every week since." She laid the book on the coffee table.

"What were you going to do, whack 'em with the Good Book?" I secretly thought the whole thing was pretty funny, but I couldn't let on.

She glared at me. "I'm going to prove that I'm a virtuous Christian woman who reads her Bible faithfully between cooking and cleaning and taking care of her husband and child, so they can leave me the fuck alone."

I did laugh then, and after a few seconds, she did too. She sat me down with a glass of iced tea and caught me up on all the clever things Lena was doing in school. I was getting ready to ask for my favor when she said, "Oh!" and jumped up like a scalded cat. She scurried into the back of the house and returned with a wrapped gift. "Bet you thought I'd forgotten your birthday, didn't you?"

By the feel of it, I had a pretty good idea that it was a photo, but I acted surprised and pleased and tore off the paper to find a photo of her and Lena, grinning like two possums and waving at the camera. Of course, knowing that I hadn't taken the picture meant they were waving at Bill, which soured things somewhat, though I tried not to let it show. Instead, I gave her a quick hug and promised their picture—minus the frame—would have a place of honor on my dashboard. "Speaking of which," I began, warming to my request.

"I can't see you tonight either, Max," Daphne interrupted, referencing my usual birthday visit. "I'm sorry, but it's my book club night, and we always go late."

Her book club was really a wine club where everyone talked at once and very rarely on any literary topic, but I didn't bother to make the correction. "That's okay. I actually came by to ask..." I stopped as the perplexed expression on her face made me aware of my mistake. I was supposed to be devastated, angry, or hurt that she couldn't come by. It was such a revelation to realize that I felt none of those things but rather something resembling indifference. Or release?

I tried to cover for us both. "I mean, I know you enjoy your book club. Plus, it would be weird if you didn't show."

As she collected the discarded birthday wrapping paper, I could almost hear the wheels turning in her mind. "So you just came by for your present, is that it?"

Now or never. I needed to suck it up and hope for the best. "No, I came by to ask if I could borrow your car." She frowned slightly. "A friend needs someone with a commercial license to transport a bunch of kids, and I offered to help out. But I need to get down to Houston first."

"And then where?" I couldn't tell by her tone if she was genuinely curious or looking for a reason to say no.

"I'm taking them to Dallas for some kind of competition."

"When?"

I felt like a trap had been laid, and I already had my foot in it. "I'm leaving tomorrow."

"Great," she said briskly. "I'll go with you. I've been needing to hit the big city myself and get some Merle Norman."

"That won't work, Daphne. Once I get to Houston, I'll be driving kids and parents and a teacher to Dallas in a fifteen-passenger van." Thrill wasn't technically a teacher, but fudging the details was easier than the complicated explanation.

"I could drive with you and follow you to Dallas."

Daphne hated distance driving, which meant she was either desperate or trying to see if I'd change my story. I stood to pace, gesturing in the direction of the highway. "And follow us back to Houston after the weekend so you could bring me home? Look, Daphne, this thing is already last minute, and there are lots of moving parts. And since it involves school kids, I have to look like someone responsible and dependable, not someone who brings a married woman along for a good time."

Daphne's glare held me in place. "You've got an answer for everything, don't you? Which one of these people is your 'friend'? The teacher or a parent? Or is it one of the kids?"

She put air quotes around the word friend, and when the list of possible interests included a kid, I got steamed. "I should have known you'd give me shit when I asked you for a favor. Especially since it's one where there's nothing in it for you. But contrary to the way you work, there's no hidden agenda here. If you don't want to loan me your car, just say so." I turned away, not wanting to see her expression, and headed for the front door. As my hand touched the knob, I heard a familiar jingle.

"Here," she said. I turned to see a wad of keys flying toward my head. Thankfully, my reflexes were quick enough to catch them before they smacked me in the eye. She opened the door to the garage, letting the outside door up. "Bring it back full. And not a scratch. Bill babies that car though it's technically mine." Before I could reply, she turned sharply toward the hallway, calling over her shoulder, "Lock the front on your way out."

Clearly, I was not forgiven, but it didn't seem to affect me like our quarrels usually did. I was going to see Thrill, and I intended to make a positive impression for once.

I whistled as I carefully backed the BMW out of the driveway, but when I started to pack, it became painfully obvious that I hadn't updated the wardrobe in my small closet since God was a boy. It would be warm in Houston—it was almost always warm in Houston—and Dallas might not be much better. But if I was going to hang out in the hotel where the competition was being held, the air-conditioning might make it chilly. Even so, a sweater would be ridiculous in May, and a sweatshirt was probably overly casual. But was a blazer too dressy? A vest too butch? Breathe, I told myself. It's only two days. I settled on khaki pants, black jeans, and blue chinos as my starters. I would wear my usual jeans and T-shirts while driving, but I made sure my choices were nonpolitical. A couple of polos with a long-sleeved denim overshirt, and one nice Oxford with a blazer in case I got to take Thrill out somewhere rounded out my selections.

What should have been an eight-hour drive to Houston became ten when my extra-cautious driving in Daphne's Beemer combined with a traffic jam that stretched for several miles prior to the city limits. At the nine-and-a-half-hour mark, I came to a complete stop for the umpteenth time behind twenty jillion cars trying to get around seven hundred cones leading to two guys leaning on a shovel next to another guy smoking beside a highway department truck.

I texted Thrill a lengthy rant about my extreme loathing of all things Houston, especially their inability to understand how traffic flow and highway construction didn't mesh at 4:00 in the afternoon. I finished with the threat that if I had to sit for another ten minutes, I either needed her to talk me down or I was going to change my mind and go home. She must have been busy with something else because there was no reply at first. Things finally picked up, traffic-wise, and when I was about six blocks from her address, a sudden flurry of text alerts began to sound on my cell. I didn't stop to read, but my cursory glance at a red light revealed a large quantity of exclamation points on the screen.

I pulled up in front of the address she'd given me, got out of the car, and began stretching. I was stiff and still kinda fussy, so I didn't acknowledge the sound of footsteps. But when Thrill said my name, I turned just as she launched herself at me, throwing her arms around my neck, burying her head in my shoulder.

"Oh, Max. I'm so glad to see you. I'm sorry I didn't text sooner. I was in a meeting and then I saw your message, and I thought—"

She cut herself off, and I noticed something about her body where it pressed against mine...something besides how amazing her body felt pressed against mine. She was trembling, and unfortunately, it didn't feel like passion was the cause. "Hey, hey." I chanced rubbing her back lightly. "I'm sorry about the rant, but you had to know I was never not coming."

"I...putting all this together has been extremely difficult and if you..."

Thrill trailed off again, and I got the picture. This girl was wound tighter than a two-dollar watch, the folks at Etta's would have said. I continued my soft caresses on her back. "I know you've been working overtime to make this happen. But I'm here now, and I want to help. Let me take some of the load, okay? If there's something you need besides driving, tell me. I'm pretty good with kids, you know?" I'd actually been worrying about how to be cool and get Thrill's students to like me so that Thrill would like me. But as her trembling eased, I kept talking. "I don't know much about this mock trial business, but that can work in our favor. As the kids tell me about it, they may get a clearer picture for themselves." She nodded against me. "And listen, I've had several lucrative months on the road. I've got extra funds available. Let me buy snacks or spring for a sharp tie for your lead attorney or whatever you need."

I felt her take in a breath. Reluctantly, I stilled my hands. "Win, lose, or draw, everything is going to be fine," I told her. "We'll make sure of that."

She moved a half step away and wiped at her face. I dropped my hands to my sides, but she caught one and shook it slightly. "I come from a family of huggers, but I don't know what came over me." I was shaking my head as Thrill sniffed and let go of my hand. "I was watching for you but I didn't think this car would be yours, and this wave of despair hit me really hard. Then I saw you get out, and it was like..."

"Christmas?" I filled in when she didn't finish. She laughed, and I sensed she was coming back to herself. It was funny how we didn't know each other that well, yet there had always been a feeling of connection between us. She awakened a warmth and caring in me that was different from what I felt around Daphne or any other woman, for that matter. Thinking of Daphne reminded me of how Thrill felt about honesty, so I quickly added, "This car isn't mine. I borrowed it from a friend."

She eyed the Beemer. "Must be a really good friend to loan you such a nice car." I nodded mutely, seeming to have reached the end of my candor for the moment. "We'll put it in the garage while you're here and leave my junker on the street. This isn't a bad neighborhood, but there's no point in tempting someone."

"That would be great, thanks."

We stood looking at each other for a few seconds. There were a thousand things I wanted to say to her, but I had no idea where to start. I only had two seconds to wonder if she could possibly feel the same before she said, "Get your stuff, and let's go inside. Are you hungry?"

"Yeah, I am. But I thought maybe I could take you out to dinner?" I had visions of a relaxing, romantic meal in a neutral territory where we'd have a chance to catch up.

Thrill smiled and shook her head. "I'm betting the last thing you want to do is get back in the car and fight the traffic to wait in line for a table at some crowded, noisy spot. Besides, Raquel has been working on dinner while I've been in meetings all afternoon. Her cooking is absolutely worth staying in for."

Raquel? "Oh, okay. Sure. Whatever." My thoughts crashed into each other as if they were in a demolition derby. Thrill had a roommate; why should I be surprised by that? She was in school, after all. The question was, what kind of "roommate" was this? Like in a dorm or like, sharing a bed? It made sense that she was closeted with the mock trial kids, but she'd been open about her friends, Steph and Janis. Was that why I hadn't expected Raquel?

I grabbed my bag and followed her up cracking cement stairs. In the next moment, I was busy swallowing as my mouth watered at the delicious aroma of spicy meat cooking. I looked toward what must have been the kitchen.

"I guess you should meet Raquel before we discuss the bed situation." Thrill's words distracted me from thoughts of sustenance, and I almost stumbled.

"There's a bed situation?"

Thrill turned to me, wiping her brow in mock relief. "Whew. I was worried there for a minute that you'd truly changed. But of course, you'd find the question of sleeping arrangements more intriguing than food."

"Hey, now, Counselor. You began your testimony in a highly intriguing way. I believe that could be considered entrapment."

Laughing, she pushed through a swinging door—when had I last seen one of those—and motioned me into the source of the marvelous scents. A dark-haired woman wearing an apron turned to us. She gave Thrill a fleeting smile before fixing her gaze on me. "You must be the mysterious Max."

"And you must be the ravishing Raquel," I responded, stepping forward with my hand extended. "It's nice to meet you." She was an attractive Latina, a few years older than Thrill. Her striking face was all sharp angles, and it conveyed the confidence that women got when they'd reached an understanding of what they wanted and how to get it.

"Ah," she said, transferring a spatula into her left hand so she could shake with me. "And you are every bit as charming as Elise has implied."

Her grip was firm, and I let her determine the length of our greeting. "And I suspect you are an even better cook than Elise has suggested."

It was strange to call Thrill that, but I had no idea if they'd really talked about me or if this was all a test. Raquel seemed to be waiting, assessing me, but I stayed still. Once upon a time, I would have continued flirting, maybe made a pass. But my experience with Ray's family had settled somewhere between my heart and my gut, and temporary pleasure had pretty much lost its appeal. For now, at least.

I could feel Thrill watching us, but I probably couldn't have read her expression, even if I'd turned to see it. After regarding me for another few seconds, Raquel let go of my hand. "Dinner will be ready in a few minutes." She nodded at Thrill. "I'll leave everything else to you."

Leading me upstairs without a word, Thrill opened the first door, revealing a tidy, comfortable-sized room with twin beds on either wall. The colors on the matching bedspreads brought out the gray blue of the painted dresser that stood at the head of one bed and the dark wood desk at the other. Rich, emerald green curtains framed the window between the beds, adding to the blend of young girl and multifaceted woman that the room projected. Best of all, it smelled like Thrill. "This is my room." She gestured, apparently unaware she was stating the obvious. "I brought this furniture with me to college, so if it looks like a child's dorm room, that's why. It's definitely seen better days."

Without thinking, I declared, "Those curtains make me think of your eyes."

"My mom made them," she said, sounding pleased.

I turned to look at her. "She did a great job on both."

She blushed and gave me a little push. "All right, you." Pointing out the bathroom across the hall, she led me to the next door. "Raquel told me she hadn't had much time to clean up. She had classes this morning and then with cooking…" This room was of similar size but held a queen bed that had clearly been hastily made. A desk piled with books and papers was angled in one corner; the chair beside it had two blouses draped over it. The blackout shade on the window was slightly askew. Hints of a bold, peppery perfume lingered in the air.

"That's it." Thrill gestured between the two doors. "We don't have a guest room, and the couch is terrible, but we have several options. You can share my room, or I can sleep with Raquel, and you can have my room to yourself. Or Raquel and I can sleep in my room, and you can have her bed." She looked down the hallway. "Of course, you can sleep with Raquel if you prefer. I'd need to confirm that with her, but I'm pretty sure she'd be okay with it, based on the way she made eyes at you in the kitchen."

"You lawyers sure make everything complicated. But you left out one option." Thrill waited, her one eyebrow raised. "Raquel could sleep in your room, and you and I could share her bed."

"Would that be your first choice?"

"Yes and no. Yes, because…because it's you, Thrill. But no, because I'd truly like to know you better before we share a bed. So I'll take your first offer. And my libido and I promise to behave."

She took a step toward me. "You actually have changed, haven't you? What happened, Max?"

I opened my mouth to respond, but Raquel's voice boomed up the stairs. "If this food gets cold, you'll both be sorry. Come to the table now!"

I tossed my bag into Thrill's room, and we dashed downstairs. "I want to tell you. I do. But later, when we have time."

She nodded and showed me into the dining room where we were met with a beautifully set table. The meal was incredible, and we managed to get in some interesting conversation between bites and moans...from me, at least.

I learned that Raquel's family had owned a restaurant, and she'd learned to cook as a young girl. But mostly, she'd hidden secret places, reading anything she could.

We dined on enmoladas—rolled corn tortillas filled with shredded chicken and cotija cheese, bathed in black mole and sprinkled with sesame seeds and crumbled cheese—and Mexican street corn salad with avocado. I was ready to bust when she mentioned dessert, but it was mangonada sorbet, which was light enough to enjoy while still packing an amazing punch of flavor, at least some of which was tequila.

Afterward, we sipped our carajillo cocktails on the back porch, where the weather was warm but not unpleasantly so. As Raquel and Thrill discussed their upcoming assignments, I drifted, extremely full and remarkably content. My visit with Ray had reminded me that there were humans who made for good company, and these two were now on my list. When I heard the sound of a soft kiss and Raquel's voice saying something about a big day tomorrow, I struggled to sit up straighter, realizing I'd almost fallen asleep.

"Wait." I cleared my throat. "Let me do the dishes. It's the least I could do for such a fantastic meal."

"If you think I'm going to let you scrub my seasoned skillet with soap and put my casserole dishes in the wrong place, you're crazy. But you can keep me company while I clean up. A few wild stories of your life on the road would be the least you can do."

When Thrill protested that cleanup was her job, Raquel wagged a finger at her. "You won the bed lottery. Go get yourself ready."

I was glad it was dark enough that neither of them could see me blush. Thrill mumbled something about a shower and left.

Raquel suspiciously accepted my offer to dry. Predictably, it didn't take long for her to start grilling me on my intentions toward Thrill. I pushed back, asking, "Are you her fairy godmother? Or are there plans for a three-way?"

She tossed her sponge in the sink and frowned at me. "Elise tells me you're someone who doesn't speak willingly of their feelings. Why is that, do you think? Is it fear that you'll be found too shallow? Or too deep?"

Obviously, my usual flip remarks weren't the way to go here. "Before I answer, can I ask you a question?" She inclined her head, so I jumped in with both feet. "What's your relationship with Elise?"

She leaned against the counter. "Strictly by chance, I sat next to Elise in our very first law school class. We were both writing in notebooks rather than typing on a laptop. When she noticed too, she gave me a shy smile, and it warmed me all over. We had coffee afterward and discovered we were both looking for a place to live." She sighed. "Elise's absolute humanity is a rare and precious quality, but she doesn't take risks willingly. Our living arrangement is exactly what you saw upstairs. We're roommates and friends. The kind of friends who look after each other." Her dark eyes narrowed. "Now, tell me. What are you offering?"

I shifted nervously. "Thrill…uh…Elise and I don't know each other well, but I'd like to change that. And I do know that being around her makes me want to be a better person."

"Are you not a good person now, Max?"

I couldn't look at her. "Not as good as I should be."

Footsteps came down the stairs as Raquel said, "Try harder. She deserves it."

❖

After I was rescued from Raquel's third degree, I showered and found something to wear that would serve as pajamas, the one thing I'd forgotten to pack. Thrill's room was already dark, and I tried to move quietly in the event she was asleep. Her lack of snoring would be a plus, but I hadn't asked which bed was hers, and there was no sound to guide me. Taking baby steps in my sock-clad feet, I kept my hands outstretched, hoping to avoid knocking into something unexpected. My shin brushed something firm, and I bent to feel if it was indeed the bed, as I hoped.

When my hand found something warm and soft, Thrill's voice murmured, "I thought you and your libido were going to behave."

I jumped at least a foot. "Shit, Thrill. I'm sorry. I couldn't tell where I was."

"Left shoulder, about three inches from my breast."

Oh, God. "No, I…I meant where I was in the room." She started to giggle, and I realized I was being teased. "I don't suppose turning on a light is an option."

"Heavens, no. Where's the fun in that? It's much more enjoyable watching you walking around like a blindfolded kid playing *Pin the Tail on the Donkey.*"

The amusement in her voice charmed me. But I couldn't let her know that. Not yet. "I see how it is. Fine. I'll find my own way."

I made as if to turn but quickly reversed course and—now that I had some idea of her position in the bed—reached out and began to tickle her. "But first, I'll show you my idea of fun."

As I'd hoped, she shrieked with surprise, followed by squirming and breathless laughter. People might exist who aren't ticklish under their armpits, but I'd never met them. She was trying to catch my hands to stop me, and I was laughing too, telling her to say uncle, until a sharp banging on the wall made us both freeze.

Raquel's voice was only slightly muffled. "All right, you two. Don't make me come in there."

This made us laugh harder, though I did stop tickling. As our hilarity wound down, Thrill took my hands again, though not with the same intent of a moment before. Now her touch was gentle and compassionate. "Tell me now, Max. What's changed you?"

There in the dark, I sat on the edge of her childhood bed and talked about finding Ray and how seeing his life and spending time with his family made me reconsider what was possible.

She lay quietly, making occasional humming noises to let me know she was listening. I finally stammered to a stop, and she didn't comment at first. I opened my mouth to suggest we should get some sleep when she said, "But, Max, how could you not know you could have that life too? I don't understand."

What could I tell her? Because I was the lesbian daughter of a murdering psychopath? Because my sole experience with a long-term relationship had been with a married woman? Because my dad was the only person who'd really cared about me, but any thoughts of him were now accompanied by a stab of guilt when I recalled how rarely I'd told him I loved him? I stood, missing the touch of her hands but unable to tolerate their tenderness. The comfortable feeling I'd had earlier was replaced by a sourness in my stomach that wasn't indigestion. Despite my intention to be more forthcoming, I reverted to John Wayne. "Well, little lady, I reckon that's a story for another day."

After a short pause, she asked, "Would you like the light on?"

"No, thanks. I know where I am now." It was true. My eyes had adjusted to the point that I could see her examining me before I turned and made my way over to the other side of the room, looking at her as I settled into bed.

"Just because you know where you are doesn't mean you have to stay there," Thrill said before she turned her face to the wall.

CHAPTER FIFTEEN

2008
Age Twenty-six

When I awoke to the sound of Thrill moving around, I recognized the gray light. I knew what barely dawn looked like, having driven through the night many, many times. "Should I get up?" I asked. My voice sounded scratchy.

"Yes. I'll use the restroom first, if you don't mind. Raquel will drive us to get the van, but she doesn't have to get up until the last minute."

"Sure." After watching Thrill turn away last night, I'd mentally beaten myself down until I was lower than a gopher hole. What was I doing, tickling a grown woman? I'd begun contemplating a serious relationship, one where I could find love and commitment and a family of my own. Thrill's laughter was lovely, but I should have been trying for passion and romance, not making a woman giggle like a child. And from what I knew of her, Thrill was much too intelligent and sensible to accompany me on the trip down Loser Lane, especially given all the baggage I carried about my mother and my brother and Daphne and JT. I rose quickly and had dressed as far as my chinos and sports bra when Thrill returned.

"Sorry." I reached for my shirt before putting my back to her. "I'm almost ready."

Warm hands, fragrant with scented lotion, grasped my shoulders, and she turned me to face her. Her gaze flitted briefly to my breasts before she met my eyes. "I'm the one who should apologize. I meant it when I said I was glad you were here and not only because you're helping me out. I don't know why I always seem to ask for more than you're ready to give, but I appreciate what you told me about Ray. I know that wasn't easy for you."

A surge of desperate longing welled up inside me. "It's not that I don't want to. I just can't—that is, I kinda lost the habit of—I mean, I'm alone a lot, you know? I usually drive at night, and there aren't many folks who are interested in conversation at two o'clock in the morning. Inside my own head, I'm yakking away, which probably isn't terribly healthy." I swallowed, pushing aside the frightful image of my mother ranting and raving at her internal demons. My heart pounded as I tried to imagine telling Thrill that part of my history and how I was doing everything in my power not to make it my present.

She must have sensed my anxiety because she took my hands again. "I know how it is. My father drove for years, remember? And when he'd come home, it would take a while before my mom could get him to start talking to us again."

Her eyes went distant with memory. I squeezed her hands, and her focus came back to me. "I'm really happy to be here. Being around you makes me feel good, you know? Like, normal."

She squeezed back. "You are good, Max. And you are normal, whether you're with me or not."

"Don't be so certain, Counselor." I tapped my head. "Sometimes, it feels like I've lost my vertical hold."

She laughed and looked me over again. "Better finish getting dressed, or I might check out your horizontal hold, just to be sure it works."

I moved toward her. "Promise?"

Raquel called that she was ready, and Thrill eased back. "I'm sorry, but we need to go."

I sighed. "We need to work on our timing, don't we?"

"I couldn't agree more."

❖

The van was ready for us, and Thrill directed me to the school. On the way, I learned that the Sarah T. Hughes Magnet School was for law and justice studies, offering incredible curricula, from criminal justice to emergency services, to government and public administration, and of course, legal studies. My Pokeyville was too small to have any kind of similar programs, but I couldn't help wondering if my path would have been different if I'd grown up in a big city. I actually felt myself mellowing toward Houston.

The building looked new, a modern design with lots of glass. Thrill directed me into a semicircular drive at the front and told me to wait. She grabbed a clipboard, hopped out, and hurried in. I sensed the excitement of the kids milling about inside. Thrill gathered them close like a mother hen with her chicks. At some point, she must have mentioned me because all heads turned in my direction. After a few seconds, all but two or three of them turned back to Thrill. I decided meeting them from the driver's seat would be awfully casual, so I got out and walked around to the passenger door. I needn't have worried, as Thrill's kids walked out in single file.

"Hi, I'm Max." I offered a lame wave. Thrill moved beside me as the first student approached. "This is our lead prosecuting attorney," she said, and the girl offered her hand, giving her name as Perla Munoz. Two other prosecuting attorneys followed, one boy named Arturo and a girl named Jelani. Each greeted me solemnly, and I doubted I'd ever remember all their names. Two defense attorneys followed, then the witnesses, and lastly, a timekeeper named Juan.

"It helps build confidence for them to make eye contact, introduce themselves, and shake hands," Thrill explained once everyone was seated.

"Oh, sure." I hadn't thought of that at all, but something else occurred to me. "Isn't this your last year in law school? Do you think you'll stay in Houston to practice?"

Her voice sounded flat. "I haven't decided yet."

It seemed I'd touched a nerve, but I could tell this wasn't the time to pursue it, as she was looking around somewhat anxiously. "What are we waiting on?" I murmured.

"Juan's father, our parent chaperone, and Aiysha, our lead defense attorney." Thrill lowered her voice. "Aiysha's one of the best speakers on the team and a great closer." She looked around at the van where some of the students were watching us. Speaking louder than her usual volume, she remarked, "Aiysha has late arrival because her mom brings her when she gets off work. She'll be along any minute."

Two girls asked if they could use the restroom. Thrill sighed and nodded. They'd just returned when a car parked behind the van and a stout woman rushed over, closely followed by a thin, anxious-looking girl.

"We're here, we're here," the woman gushed, and Thrill smiled warmly.

"It's nice to see you, Ms. Lott. Aiysha, please go have a seat. We hope to get going in a few minutes." Mother and daughter gave me a wary look, and Thrill gestured in my direction. "Oh, this is our driver, Maxine Terrell."

I bobbed my head in greeting. "Ma'am."

Ms. Lott didn't respond, only looked toward the van where Aiysha was now sitting next to Perla. Sensing her apprehension, Thrill stated, "We'll have another chaperone, Ms. Lott. Juan's father is coming along. Between us, we'll take care of them, I promise."

Ms. Lott sighed and said, "Well," and that one word seemed to carry a great deal of weight.

I freaked out whenever I heard about a school shooting, so I had some sense of what it was like for parents these days. I didn't see Lena walk out the door every morning, but I still worried that a crazy asshole with an assault rifle would appear in Pokeville.

Ms. Lott scrutinized me for a few seconds. "You've got a commercial driver's license?" I nodded and produced it from my wallet. Mrs. Lott studied it carefully. "How long you been driving?"

"A year after high school, I trained at Nationwide Truck Driving School in Lubbock." I carefully didn't look at Thrill. "I've been driving my own eighteen-wheeler since then, and I've probably logged about ninety-five thousand miles a year."

She handed me back my license, making a little *humphing* sound. Before I could add anything more, Juan had appeared on the steps, cell phone in his hand. I couldn't tell if he was upset or angry. "My dad can't come, Ms. Adams. He got called into work after all. I'm really sorry."

Thrill's shoulders slumped, and my brilliant mind came to two conclusions simultaneously. One, the lack of a second chaperone didn't bode well for Ms. Lott's peace of mind, and two, Adams was Thrill's last name. If she hadn't looked so dejected, I would have laughed out loud and teased her about having the same last name as the author of *The Hitchhiker's Guide to the Galaxy* when her real name, Trillian, was one of the main characters in that story.

"Can one of the school staff come instead?" I asked.

Thrill shook her head. "I asked them before I started trying to find parents. They're preparing for a Texas Education Agency Accreditation Review next week. They can't spare anyone."

"Any other parents?"

When Thrill shook her head, Ms. Lott cleared her throat. Sensing that all the hard work Thrill and her kids had put into preparing for this competition was about to go down the drain, I carefully sidled a bit closer to Ms. Lott, though I directed my comments to Thrill. "This is the state tournament, correct? What do you think your chances are?"

Thrill hesitated, obviously trying to put aside her chaperone concerns before glancing back at the van. "I sincerely think this team's chances are excellent."

"I'm sure colleges look favorably on participating in mock trial, but winning state would really stand out on an application, wouldn't it?"

"Oh yes, it would. And if we win here, we'd go on to Nationals in Little Rock, Arkansas."

"Wow. Isn't that where President Clinton's library is? That would be quite the experience for your team, wouldn't it?"

"Yes. And it's only six and a half hours away from here, so we wouldn't have to fly."

In the pause that followed, Ms. Lott nodded slightly. "You gonna drive them there too?"

I gave her my most humble smile. "I'd be honored. But I'm just a substitute. Ms. Adams can probably find someone from the district for that trip." I glanced at my watch. "What time is registration in Dallas, Ms. Adams?"

Thrill didn't answer for a few seconds. I couldn't tell if she was surprised by how I'd addressed her or by Ms. Lott's lack of protest. Finally, she shuffled some papers on her clipboard. "Uh, we should be getting under way."

Waving as Thrill and I boarded, Ms. Lott called, "All of you, you bring me a trophy, hear?"

The van rocked with cheering.

Once we were on the highway, the swell of excitement from my passengers quieted somewhat as they chatted and compared their cell phones. Thrill, now also known to me as Ms. Adams, was in the passenger seat next to me. She'd been texting madly, informing the principal or someone like that of the change in our situation, I assumed. Sighing, she turned toward me and touched my arm.

"Please don't distract the driver while we're in motion," I told her, my tone clearly teasing.

"Max, I know you didn't agree to be a chaperone, but there will be times—"

"Hey," I cut her off. "I signed on to help you. Whatever you need me to do, just say the word."

"God, I could really kiss you right now," she murmured.

At that, I did something I rarely did. I took my eyes off the road and looked at her. "That could be arranged."

She sighed again, and I put my attention back on the highway. "It's not that they're bad. Not at all. But I can't watch ten kids at once. They'll naturally divide into friend groups or when we're working, into their trial roles. Sit wherever you feel most comfortable in the restaurant or whenever we stop, but when we're practicing, I'll take the defense. They need the most work."

"Gotcha," I said, nodding.

Giving me a long look, she murmured, "You might indeed have me if you keep this up," and I grinned all the way to Centerville, the aptly named town halfway to Dallas, where Thrill had agreed to my suggestion about stopping for lunch at the Pecan Corner Café, a small, family-owned restaurant where I'd eaten on several occasions.

The restaurant didn't have a table for twelve, so we chose two six seaters next to each other, me at one and Thrill at the other, a setup which was clearly going to be the way of it for the duration of our trip. Lorna, our server, chattered away as she brought us water and menus.

She turned to me. "So, Max…it's Max, right?" I nodded, and she went on. "Don't tell me you're hauling these fine young people in that fancy rig of yours."

I laughed. "No, ma'am. We're in that van out there."

"Well, good. I'll give you a chance to look at the menu while I get some hot rolls out."

"Order anything you want because this lunch will be my treat," I announced after Lorna departed. Smiles and excited chatter followed my announcement.

As we were finishing our meals, one of the kids asked me what Lorna had meant by a rig. When I told them about driving a semi, from the looks on their faces, I could have said I was a professional magician. I talked about what the job was like, and then Juan asked, "How do you know Ms. Adams?"

Lorna came by again, and I encouraged everyone to order dessert, mostly hoping they'd forget the question. They didn't. After all the orders were taken, I was still confronted with expectant expressions.

I wasn't sure if Thrill had heard the question, but I knew looking at her could very well give too much away. I also knew not to lie. In my limited experience with kids this age, they might not have always known what was true, but most of them had excellent bullshit detectors. So I explained how I'd been in truck driving school while Thrill was in college in the same town. I left out meeting her and her fellow bees at the flag football game and instead talked about how she'd come by the school because her dad used to teach there, and she still knew some of the instructors. Since there weren't many other women in my class, the two of us had started talking and became friends. I added that we hadn't seen each other in a while, but I was glad she'd called me for this job because they were a great group, and I was having more fun than I normally had while driving.

As Lorna began distributing the desserts, Thrill announced, "Let's not linger. We need to get on the road soon," loudly enough for our table to hear it too.

I waved in acknowledgement, taking a sip of tea.

Juan apparently wasn't through with the topic. "I think she's started dating someone," he announced, "because she's smiling more today." It took everything I had not to do a spit take, or worse, to start choke coughing.

Five pairs of eyes were fixed on me, so I knew I had to say something. "Maybe she's smiling because we're going to State."

"I heard her humming too." Juan shook his head while the other kids protested.

Swallowing, I tried for something neutral. "I don't think I should discuss Ms. Adams's private life."

Juan glared at me until Marlene teased that she thought his crush on Ms. Adams was probably safe for now. A small squabble started up, and Thrill came over to quiet things down. I excused myself and went to the restroom, hoping a break would assure the end of that topic.

❖

Things went smoothly at mock trial registration in Dallas, which unfortunately proved to be the last time such was the case. Through some electronic screwup, Thrill's reservation at the host hotel was short two rooms. I held off volunteering to share a room until she'd sorted one room's changes with the girls. When she turned to me, I merely nodded, and the relief in her expression made me want to hold her the same way I had when I'd first arrived at her house and found her terribly stressed. Feeling such tenderness toward someone, a woman I hadn't even had sex with, was so new for me that I stood immobile for a few seconds, trying to absorb it. I couldn't help doing a compare and contrast between Trillian Elise Adams and Daphne Kimball Polk.

Daphne had saved me, literally and figuratively, and I'd loved her for that. But in my recent reflections, I'd come to see there was—and seemingly always would be—something unyielding in her...other than her new tits. Perhaps the same desperate event that had forged us together as children had created a barrier inside her that kept her from being able to fully give herself to anyone. For years, I'd wanted her to keep saving me, which included wanting me in the way I wanted her, but after I'd finally accepted that would never be, it became just sex with a friend. After my time with Ray, I wanted to see if I could create something more and make it count, to be with someone because we cared about each other and both wanted a chance at a meaningful future together.

With Thrill, the starting point was almost the opposite. I wanted to save her. Not that she needed saving. She was a strong, capable person, but I got the sense she was accustomed to taking on the whole world all by herself, not quite trusting anyone else as she waded fearlessly through the bullshit while seeking the Holy Grail of good things like truth and honor. In a burst of stunning clarity, I realized that I wanted to offer her those things, to stand beside her and let her know she wasn't in it alone. The idea of being that person made my heart feel like it was expanding.

Ironically, the discovery made me take a step back, turning away as if casually surveying all the comings and goings of the State Mock Trial Tournament. But inside, I was in unfamiliar emotional territory, a place that included attraction but didn't stop there. I genuinely liked Thrill and had from the first time we'd met. After being around her and watching how she interacted with not only the kids but with everyone else, from the mock trial coaches to the hotel clerks, I'd witnessed what Raquel had meant about her humanity. Now, I had no idea of how to proceed, how to pursue her without coming across as the same hound dog I'd always been. I wanted there to be something more between us, and recently, I'd gotten a few hints that she might feel the same. I just had to be careful not to blow it again.

Unfortunately, things went from bad to worse when Thrill's team tied with a school they should have beaten easily, according to her. For whatever reason—nerves about the competition, worries about the room snafu, or trying too hard to make Thrill proud—they stumbled and stuttered their way through the first round. As the students made their way into an empty conference room afterward, I saw tears of anger. Thrill paced outside for a few minutes, listening to sounds of blame and accusation. I stayed clear, knowing I had no place in this situation.

When the volume rose, Thrill moved to the doorway and demanded, "What is the name of this group?"

Silence fell for several seconds until one of the boys said, "Sarah T. Hughes Mock Trial."

"Sarah T. Hughes Mock Trial what?" Thrill asked.

After a longer pause, Perla ventured, "Sarah T. Hughes Mock Trial team?"

Thrill nodded. "That's right. Sarah T. Hughes Mock Trial team. We win as a team, and we lose as a team. If you think your teammate needs help, give it to them. Don't blame them afterward for what you didn't do for them. And if you need help, ask for it."

Aiysha stood. "We're sorry we let you down, Ms. Adams."

"I appreciate the thought, Aiysha, but you didn't let me down. You let yourselves down. If you want to sit here tomorrow and watch another team advance to Nationals, one that you know you could have beaten, that's fine with me. If you're okay with going home tomorrow and making up stories for your friends and your family about how the judging wasn't fair, or someone kept coughing, or the room was too cold, go ahead. There are plenty of ways to lose but only one way to succeed, and that's to do your best. Then, no matter what the judges or your competition or your classmates say, you'll know you're a winner."

You could have heard a pin drop. I was ready to take the field or storm the castle or go fight Rocky Balboa for the heavyweight championship of the world, and every kid in there looked like they would join me. After making eye contact all around the room, Thrill said, "Now, if you're ready to go to Nationals, let's figure out how we're going to sweep this next round."

You could feel the energy surge as they began digging in backpacks and taking out papers. Juan stood. "Can I please say one thing, Miss?"

"Go ahead," Thrill agreed.

"That room really was cold."

I could tell by their laughter that Thrill had her team back together.

She warned me afterward that they'd be working for several more hours. My offer of help was gently declined. "You'll be driving us home tomorrow whether we win or lose," she reminded me. "Please get some sleep."

Up in the room, I tried to stay up for her but woke to her kiss on my cheek. When I asked about the time, there was a yawn in her reply. "Way too late. It's a good thing young people are resilient."

She showered while I prepared myself for our second chaste night together, determined to be as resolute as her teenagers. But once again, falling asleep to the sound of Thrill's soft breathing proved to be no hardship at all.

❖

The ride home was quiet but not gloomy. The team had done incredibly well in their next round and had finished in second place overall. I was elated for them until Thrill told me that only the first-place team advanced.

She looked drained. I asked, "Is that the good news or the bad news?" She looked shocked for a few seconds and then started laughing. I was so glad to hear that sound that I didn't even try to dodge the playful pinch she gave me.

The kids were worn out too, and most were asleep before we hit the highway. Thrill told me we wouldn't stop unless they needed or wanted to, and I glanced around once or twice to see that she'd dozed off as well. We were almost to Conroe when Marlene tiptoed up and whispered in my ear that she needed to stop for personal reasons. I nodded and pulled in to one of the big new gas stations. While the team made their way into the station, yawning and stretching, I told them to hurry out because we needed to keep moving. Once they were all inside, I headed over to the Marble Slab Creamery across the street, leaving my credit card for the rush to come. As they reappeared, I directed them to the ice cream shop.

"But we lost," Aiysha said. "We don't deserve ice cream."

"Here's the way I see it," I told her. "You didn't lose. Someone else won." When she didn't look convinced, I added, "Seriously, you came from behind, and you pulled together as a team. And you certainly made your competition sweat, even in a cold room. That makes you winners in my book."

She grinned at me. "Thanks, Ms. Terrell."

"Please, call me Max, Aiysha."

She nodded and lowered her voice. "I think Ms. Adams would like to date you, Max."

I knew I was blushing, but I had to ask, "Why do you think that?"

She leaned into me ever so slightly. "Because I would if I were her." She scampered off to get her ice cream. I hoped Aiysha would be able to defend her case to her mother when the time came.

❖

We arrived at the school, and after lots of hugs and a few more tears, Thrill and I drove to the Ford dealership.

"I'm afraid if I sit, I'll fall asleep until morning," she said, eying the Coke machine as we waited for Raquel inside the customer lounge. We'd barely made it before they closed the service area, and we were the only ones there. "But I don't think I could find the words to tell you how much this has meant to me, even if I wasn't exhausted,"

"I could say the same," I told her, hoping she could hear my sincerity.

"So was it your dream date?" She turned toward me, and I smiled.

"Just about."

"What was missing?"

I didn't ask if she really wanted to know before taking her in my arms and kissing her. I knew she was tired, so I tried to keep it sweet, but she pressed against me, and the passion of her lips raised me from the one sweet kiss I'd planned to two much more urgent ones. Her mouth was as incredible as I'd imagined. I was working my hands toward her ass, which I'd also admired, when she pushed her fingers through my hair. I wanted her touch so much, I forgot my usual defenses until she brushed across the plate in my skull. The word "no" didn't make it out of my mouth, but I stumbled away from her, the loss of contact unbalancing us both. I could see the question in her eyes, but I only shook my head. She moved toward me, opening her mouth to speak just as Raquel appeared in the doorway.

"Hey, how'd it go?" she asked brightly. I turned away, coughing to hide my misery. Thrill said nothing, and after a few seconds, Raquel's smile faded. "That good, huh?"

Thrill shook her head, and I followed them to Raquel's car, throwing myself into the back seat before there could be any conversation about who was sitting where.

Raquel wisely avoided any obvious questions and instead discussed their schedules for the coming weeks. "You're clearly exhausted," Raquel stated. "We'll eat, and then both of you rest tonight. Monday will come soon enough."

All of that was true, but I knew I couldn't stay. Thrill would ask, as she had reason to, and I'd be unable or unwilling to tell her, and we'd fight. Or more accurately, she'd be disappointed, something I couldn't face right now. As soon as we pulled up in front of their duplex, I got out, pulling keys from my pocket, jingling them nervously, and looking everywhere but at Thrill. "I need to return the car to my friend tonight. But thanks, both of you, for everything."

"You can't mean to get back on the road now?" Raquel's tone conveyed her disbelief. "You've been driving for four hours, and I'm confident you haven't had anything decent to eat."

"Ice cream," Thrill murmured. Raquel's brows raised, and Thrill's voice was soft, as if in memory. "She bought us all ice cream in Conroe."

How could the echo of something sweet hurt so much? I tried to wave it away, focusing on their garage where Daphne's car was parked. "Four hours is nothing. I drive for a living, remember? And I know all the best places to grab a bite. I'll be fine."

Raquel looked between us for a few seconds before fixing me with a glare. "Work it out, but don't you dare leave without letting me pack you some food. There's nothing but fried fat and empty calories along the highway, and you know it."

She disappeared into the house. "I'm sorry," Thrill whispered in the same soft voice that made my heart ache.

"Oh no. Please don't say that." My words shook with unshed tears, but I pushed them back. "I'm the one who should be sorry. It's… you're beat, and I need…it would take a lot of time for me to explain. Time we don't have."

She closed her eyes briefly and took a deep breath. "Okay, but please don't go yet." She pointed at the box of mock trial paperwork and our bags. "If you'll help me get this stuff upstairs, Raquel can fix something for you to take with you. I'll feel terrible if you just run off."

Whether intentionally or not, she'd hit two of my three big buttons. Of course I'd help her with stuff, and the last thing I wanted was for her to feel terrible because of me. "Oh sure. Okay."

I grabbed the box and my small bag while she wheeled her suitcase up the walk. She called to Raquel, asking her to pack my dinner. Something that sounded like, "Good," came from the kitchen. I followed Thrill upstairs and into her room where she sat heavily on her small bed. "I know you don't want to talk, but if you can spare a few more minutes to listen, I'd like to tell you something about me. Would that be okay?"

"That would be great. I'd love to know more about you."

She smiled indulgently. "Maybe not this. But we need to reach an understanding if things are going to go anywhere else between us." She patted the bed beside her. "Please sit." I did, leaving a little space between us in case she wanted it. She scooted back until she was leaning against the wall. When I did the same, the space got lost, and our thighs were touching. "I don't mind if you don't," she said, and I couldn't help grinning. Maybe she wasn't only being nice. Maybe she really didn't want me to go.

CHAPTER SIXTEEN

2008
Age Twenty-six

She squared her shoulders. "I told you I have two sisters."

"And you're the baby," I confirmed, wanting her to know I remembered.

"Yes. They're eighteen months apart, but I'm younger by almost six years."

"Oh. I didn't realize how much time there were between you and them."

Thrill sighed. "They used to tease me about being an accident. I didn't know what it meant, but it sounded bad, so I'd cry. When I was older, my mom explained that she'd had two miscarriages after my middle sister, Reid, was born. She said it simply took her a while to be willing to try again."

"I'm sorry your mom went through that." After a pause, I asked, "Is Reid a family name?

Thrill laughed. "No, she's named after the actress Kate Reid, who played a scientist in the movie *The Andromeda Strain*. And my older sister's name is Corrington, after screenwriter Joyce Corrington who wrote *The Omega Man*, among others. My folks are huge sci-fi fans, obviously."

"Obviously, Trillian."

She gave me a long look. "You don't usually call me by my real name. Would you keep using it if I asked you to?"

"Of course. Or I'll call you Do You Like Pie or Elise or Ms. Adams, whatever you prefer."

She touched my knee. "No, thank you. I like it that you call me Thrill. I hope to live up to that name someday."

I grinned. "So I shouldn't tell you that you already have?" It was getting dark outside, but I could still make out her face. She was smiling, which softened her features and made her even lovelier. The way she was looking into my eyes was making me think seriously about kissing her again. Since we were on her bed, that could be risky...in a desirable way. But she had something to tell me, so I forced my gaze away from her mouth. She took in a shaky breath.

"Before I get any further along, I should tell you that my sisters and I have a passable relationship at this point in our lives. We're not super close, but we get along fine at family gatherings." She rubbed her hands together. "Mom made us start hugging each other years ago, and it helps."

"Who's the doctor?" I asked.

"You have a good memory," she said.

"Yeah, for things I care about." Apparently, I was going to blurt out whatever came into my head, like someone who'd just fallen off the turnip truck. To my surprise, she reached for my hand, asking shyly if it was okay. Okay? It felt so nice, I got a lump in my throat and could only give her a squeeze by way of reply.

"Reid is the doctor—a gerontologist—and Corrington is a cop. Well, a detective, I should say. The two of them are and always were very close. Being similar in age, they were like a bonded pair, and when I came along, they didn't know what to do with me. I mean, I get it. Suddenly there's this squalling, smelly thing that's getting all the attention and from their perspective, all the love. I have no memory of it, but there are a few pictures where you can see scrapes and bruises on my arms and legs. My mother told me later that she'd thought I'd scratched myself, so she'd cut my fingernails almost to the quick."

This seemed beyond the typical sibling rivalry. "And the bruises?"

She must have heard the edge in my voice because she rubbed her thumb over the top of my fingers. "They thought I had a vision defect, like farsightedness, which made me run into things when I crawled. At that point, Mom started watching me more closely, and the damage faded, so their plan backfired in a way. Though the whole family still laughs about the night my mom and dad had company over when I was first learning to walk. Everyone was watching the baby, the way people do, and I began taking those half walking, half running steps. The grown-ups were oohing and aahing, and Corrington apparently had enough of it. She stuck out her foot and tripped me. Even though everyone saw it, Corrington was able to play it off like an accident, like she didn't mean to. Or that's how they tell it."

I shifted uncomfortably. She put her head on my shoulder.

"The older I got, the worse it got. Not physically. They'd learned their lesson about that. But Reid and Corrington were expected to include me in their games and adventures, which was the last thing they wanted. So they'd make up horrible, scary stories about things that would happen to me if I didn't do what they told me or if I told on them for something. They'd lie about where we were going or what we were doing, and when I questioned them, they'd tell me I misunderstood, that I was being silly or just wrong. Once, they told me we were going to play hide-and-seek and left me for hours in a place I hadn't been before. I didn't know how to get home, and when they finally came back, I was hysterical. They belittled me and insisted it was my fault for being good at hiding. The few times I got upset enough that I did tell, they were able to convince Mom and Dad that I had an overactive imagination. I mean, it was two against one, and I was too young to express exactly what happened, so it probably did sound like I was making things up."

Her voice had taken on a tremor of emotion. I put my arm around her shoulder, pulling her closer. "I'm not telling you all this to garner sympathy," she said. "I need you to understand why honesty is extremely important to me. And why, once trust is broken, it's very hard for me to be okay around that person." She pulled away and looked at me. "I've been attracted to you from the first moment I saw you. But I have to be able to believe you, Max. I need absolute confidence in what you say and who you are. If you're not ready to tell me something, that's okay. But please, don't lie to me. Not again."

I hung my head, hating the things that I'd written off as little fibs, meaningless fabrications. I was so ashamed of myself, my stomach hurt. "I'm sorry, Thrill. Really, really sorry. I don't deserve your forgiveness, but I'd give anything for another chance."

She lifted my face and kissed me softly on the lips. "In case you haven't noticed, you're getting that chance now."

The truth of what I'd told Raquel struck me hard. Trillian Elise Adams made me want to be a better person. I put my forehead to hers, and we stayed like that for a few minutes. It occurred to me I hadn't heard the end of her story. "Can I ask you something?"

"Yes."

"When did it stop? With your sisters. When did they stop tormenting you?"

It was completely dark now, and though my eyes had adjusted as the light had left us, her face was partly in shadow. When she didn't respond right away, I thought I had overstepped. "You don't have to tell—"

"I had a breakdown." She cut me off. "I became so confused about what was true and what wasn't that I disassociated from reality. I spent three months in a treatment facility under the care of a kind, very competent woman psychiatrist. When I first heard the term 'gaslighting,' and learned what it meant, it resonated with me like nothing ever had before."

A breakdown? How was it possible that I was interested in a woman who had a mental disorder? I suppressed a shiver, forcibly reminding myself that this wasn't my mother's story. "How old were you?"

"I'd just turned ten."

"Oh God, Thrill." I turned my head away, feeling her pain and my own coalesce.

"No, therapy was exactly what I needed." She blew out a breath. "I think it was harder on my parents. My dad quit driving and started teaching to spend more time at home. I'm not sure my mom has ever forgiven herself."

I turned to her, my voice tight. "And your sisters?"

"What about them?"

I wanted to scream that being grounded for life was only the start of the payback I envisioned. I took a second to calm myself. "Did they understand what they'd done?"

"In some ways, yes, and in some ways, no." She stifled a yawn. "We don't talk about it."

She had to be exhausted, and I needed to process what she'd told me. "What I meant to ask is, would you mind if I stayed a few more minutes while you get ready for bed?"

"That would be nice. Thank you."

She stood, and I stood with her, taking her hand. "No, Elise. Thank you."

❖

It didn't take long for her to drop off as I massaged her back and shoulders, relishing her soft sounds of pleasure. When her breathing evened into sleep, it almost took me with it again. I felt an almost primal urge to stay, but Thrill had her world to get back to, and I had mine. No amount of pushing or pulling could force our lives to mesh at this moment. Oddly, instead of feeling disappointed or resentful, I was filled with understanding and an unexpected sense of peace. Even if we could be right for each other, it also had to be the right time. Holding to this new insight, I went to the kitchen and found a full grocery bag tied up on the counter. I called softly for Raquel and heard her answer from the dining room.

In place of the elegant settings from our previous dinner, books and papers covered most of the table. I asked the obvious: "Studying, huh?"

She rolled her eyes. "I thought you might be spending the night."

"I can't say I wasn't tempted. But I really do need to get going." I lifted the bag. "I assume this is for me?" At her positive gesture, I added, "It feels like it will feed half of Pokeville." That got me a grin.

"If that's what you want to do with my superb cuisine, go ahead." She paused. "She knows you're leaving?" I nodded. "Will you be returning anytime soon?"

"Maybe? It's hard to say what our schedules will allow. But I'd like to leave a note. May I borrow some paper and a pen?"

"Yes, since I applaud your gesture." She provided both, and I went into the kitchen to write.

❖

When I arrived back in dear old Pokeyville, it was way too late to return Daphne's car. Etta's was about to close, seeing as it was Sunday night, and even God needed rest at that point. I didn't mind either situation because I wasn't really in the mood for a drink, and I definitely wasn't in the mood for Daphne. What I was in the mood for, I'd left over five hundred miles southeast of my current parking spot.

My body was still buzzing from my time with Thrill, but my mind was worn out from replaying the story about her breakdown. I knew I wasn't the only person with childhood trauma, but I hoped someday to hear more about her mental state. Maybe it would help me understand what my mother became, as well as giving me some comfort about myself. I imagined meeting her sisters and beating them within an inch of their lives, and it amazed me that Thrill held no grudge against them. Then again, it seemed she held no grudge against me, either, so I couldn't protest.

Too wired to sleep, I called Zelda, hoping she'd forgive the hour. Her voice sounded rusty, either from just waking up or from not having spoken much during the day. Rather than nattering on about myself as I usually did, I asked how she was doing. She griped about the usual aches and pains, chastising me for being too young to understand and adding her usual warning to take care of my knees. She told me she'd lost her balance on a familiar trail and had skinned an elbow on a protruding rock.

"Damn thing still hasn't healed, and I'm not going back until it does."

I chuckled, trying to figure out whether she was punishing the trail or her body for the injury. I told her she should fill the recovery period with a visit to Pokeville. She said she wasn't comfortable making that drive right now as her vision had gotten worse, and yes, before I could nag her about it, she already had an appointment with the eye doctor. Zelda wasn't usually the type to complain, but her mood was probably due to the late hour. When I calculated that I hadn't seen her in person in almost a year, I felt like the worst friend ever.

"I'm sorry it's been so long, Zelda. The next time I call you, it'll be to say that I'm coming for a visit, okay?"

"Not on that crotch rocket, I hope."

"Oh, come on. You know you want a ride," I teased.

"Couldn't I have a poke in the eye with a sharp stick instead?"

No one could out-Texas Zelda when it came to colorful language.

I got in bed, sleepy now but making a mental note to put a gap in my schedule for a visit. Zelda helped me get through driving school without punching my touchy-feely instructor, and she'd talked about her long-term relationship in a way that made me believe such love could actually exist. She'd become a true friend, and I owed her a great deal. I fell asleep thinking how I'd like to take Thrill with me for that visit since they both had a history with NTDS.

Though I was going to start another run that afternoon, I wanted to be sure I got up early enough to see Lena on her way to school. Since Daphne was one of the champion grudge holders of all time—another way that she and Thrill were different—there was no telling if she'd give me permission to see Lena again tomorrow or if I'd be banned until her graduation from college. That thought hurt my heart, but since Daphne herself had taught me the fine art of sneaking around, I'd figured a way to see Lena somehow.

She was walking the three blocks to school as I pulled alongside her. She gave the car a puzzled expression before looking in at the driver's seat.

"Want some candy, little girl?" I stage-whispered in my best weirdo voice.

"No, you freak. Get out of here before I call the cops."

I laughed, having taught her that line. "Perfect delivery, Jodie Foster. Now get in here and let me save you the six-hundred steps to your fine educational institution."

She hopped in the passenger seat and hugged my neck. God, I loved this kid. "Thank goodness you're back with mama's car. She's been fretting about it all weekend."

"Well, it's got a full tank of gas and not a scratch on it. Therefore, the fretting will officially end in less than thirty minutes."

She eyed me in the way kids had when they suspected something was amiss. "Did y'all have a fight?"

"Not exactly. She wanted to come with me, but since it wasn't that kind of trip, I told her no. She might have been kinda miffed about that."

"Where did you go?" she asked, the question missing the suspicion Daphne's voice would have contained. Rolling toward the school at less than the twenty mph required, I told her about the trip and the students on the mock trial team. She wanted to know more about the competition, and I explained as best I could. She was quiet for a few seconds, taking it all in like the adorable sponge she was. "Maybe I'll be a lawyer when I grow up," she said thoughtfully.

"Maybe you will. If you want to know more about it, you can ask my friend who mentors the students. She'll officially be a lawyer in a few months, when she graduates from law school."

Lena's eyes got big. "That would be so cool. Will you bring her here? I can't wait to tell Mama."

Well, shit. If my brains were ink, I couldn't have dotted an i. When I started to ask Lena not to say anything, Thrill's words about honesty came back to me like a kick in the gut. "I'll bet your mama would be happy to have a lawyer in the family."

A bell rang in the school, and I checked my watch. "First bell?" I asked, and she nodded.

"Will you still be here when school gets out?" she asked anxiously.

"'Fraid not, jelly belly. But I'll come see you as soon as I can."

"Will you take me to see a movie?"

"Sure. What do you want to see?"

She wiggled excitedly. "It's called Happy Feet. And it's about..." She stopped, biting her lip as another bell rang. "I've got to go. I'll tell you later."

Lena threw open the door and jumped out. "Hey, chicken licken?" I called. She turned. "I love you."

She ran around to the driver's side and hugged my neck again. "I love you too, Max."

Now I had all the ammunition I needed to face her mom. Or so I hoped.

❖

The garage door was up, and since Bill's car was gone, I parked there before letting myself into Daphne's kitchen, calling, "Is this the Polk Car Rental Drop-off Center?" The house was clean and cool and very quiet. Maybe Daphne was out, and I could leave the car and go. "Hello?" I called again.

"Come on back, Max." Daphne's voice sounded distant.

When I found her naked on top of the covers in the master bedroom, I knew things weren't going to go well. They never did when situations didn't play out Daphne's way, and this, obviously, was going to be one of those times. I didn't turn away, but the lack of enthusiasm on my face must have been enough to clue her in. "What?" she asked as if trying to salvage the moment. "Has it been so long since you've seen a grown woman naked that you don't know what to do with her?"

"No, I just...I can't, Daphne. For one thing, I gotta get on the road."

She rose and put on a robe, leaving it open and taking a half step toward me. "I thought the point of being your own boss was so you could work whenever you wanted and play whenever you wanted."

I shouldn't have reacted, but I wasn't in the mood for one of her verbal attempts to push me into a corner. "It might work that way for your husband, but since my daddy isn't around to bail me out on the regular, I've got to work when my clients need me."

She sinched the robe tightly. "I see." Her voice had turned icy. "You said, 'For one thing.' What's the other? Did you put all that mileage on my car to go fuck someone else? Was it your teacher friend or one of her students?"

I tried to rein in my temper. "Let's not do this, okay? I care about you, and I think you care about me, but this"—I flicked my hand back and forth—"this part of us hasn't been working for a while."

"It seemed to work pretty well the last time I gave you an orgasm."

If she was going to go low, I could go lower. "And when was that, Daphne? Before Christmas, before you and Bill decided to try for another baby? I guess his little swimmers didn't make it since you're clearly ready for your consolation prize again."

Her face flushed. "Get out." I was almost to the front door when she added, "Does your new girl really know anything about you, Max? Or are you going to lie about who you are and who you've been fucking all these years, like usual?"

I didn't turn. "Since you asked, I'm gonna try to unlearn everything you taught me about lying and cheating and try the real thing for a change."

She yelled something else, but I'd already closed the door.

I'd just gotten my bike unchained when a squad car came squealing around the corner. Daphne was apparently madder than she'd ever been, since she'd not only called the cops on me but refused to open the door to vouch for the fact that I was not the garage-tool-stealing thief. After my ride to the police station, I answered questions for half an hour before Katie, the server from Etta's, showed up to testify on my behalf.

Katie drove me back to Daphne's to get my bike, but now both my tires were flat. She was kind enough to take me to my dad's shop so I could get some help. We'd just loaded the bike onto Pete's truck when another cop car showed up. After providing my license and registration, I pulled the new lady cop aside. "Look, Officer Ruiz, I'm not saying you're gay or anything, but I am, and the lady in this house is mad at me for personal reasons, and that's why she keeps calling you."

"Hell hath no fury?" she suggested, barely concealing a grin.

"Yeah, that."

She didn't take me in, but I had to get new tires since the old ones had been slashed. By the time I got Nephthys ready for the road, it was early evening, but I was so ready to get out of town that even a hundred miles might be sufficient. About full dark, I was thinking to pull over for a catnap when my cell chimed. Apprehensive that it would be someone telling me my credit card had been canceled or a Netflix account which I hadn't applied for had been approved, I was almost afraid to check. My heart did a little jump when the screen showed Thrill's number, but I still answered with my professional voice. "Terrell's Trucking."

"Oh, good evening." Thrill's tone was professional too, but it had a warmth to it that made me smile. "One of your employees left me a really nice note asking me to call, so I thought I would."

"Why, that's very nice of you, ma'am. We at Terrell's Trucking certainly appreciate your prompt response." The lousy parts of my day, which was pretty much all of it except Lena, faded away, and I wanted nothing more than to keep Thrill on the line. "How are you? How was your day? Tell me everything."

She laughed, and we started a conversation that lasted another hundred miles. "I guess I should let you go," I said when I heard her yawn for the second time.

"No, don't do that." Her tone was playful, but I heard something more in it too.

"Would you like me to tuck you in and tell you a good-night story?" I asked, keeping it light but adding wistfulness to my tone.

"I'd like that more than anything. Well, maybe not *anything*," she amended, and we both laughed.

"Will you call me again? Like, tomorrow? Or whenever you can." I tried not to sound needy.

"It's not dangerous for you to talk on the phone while you're driving, is it?"

"No, I promise. I have headphones, and I'm on a sparsely populated stretch of highway at the moment. If I was in town or in traffic, I'd let you know."

"Okay, then. If you promise, I'll call you tomorrow," she agreed.

"I absolutely do. I…I really enjoyed talking to you, Thrill. You made the miles fly by."

"I wish those miles were headed my way."

"Me too."

We were quiet for a few seconds. Then she murmured, "Get some rest, Max. And pleasant dreams."

"You too, peach." *Peach?* I tried to figure out where that had come from. The scent of her lotion, maybe? Her auburn hair and creamy skin? I held my breath.

She giggled. "My dad used to call me that when I was little. Only he said sweet peach."

"He was right. And you are." I was so relieved she hadn't thought me ridiculous that I almost couldn't breathe.

"Max?"

"Yeah?"

"I'd very much like to see you again. I'm sorry my schedule will be crazy until graduation. But maybe after that?"

"No maybe about it. 'Cause I'd like to see you again too."

"Good night."

We talked nearly every day for the next few weeks, our conversations long or short, playful, sometimes serious, and once, extremely erotic. It was oddly pleasing to learn the fun things, like her favorite color—green—and favorite sports team—Cowboys, yeah—and even hearing school horror stories—starting her period in gym class—and more about her family, including the sisters—who I mentally referred to as "those bitches." She asked me similar questions, and I did okay on everything but family.

After the third week of talking with Thrill, I called Ray. He was delighted to hear about the new person in my life, who I introduced as Elise, and when I told him about our phone chats, he said, "You're dating, Max. In a weird way, granted, but that's what happens when people date. They get to know each other."

I was quiet for a minute. "How can I tell her about Daphne without sounding like a total schmuck?"

"A totally immoral schmuck," he corrected.

I groaned. "Yeah, that."

"Hmm." He sniffed. "Have you talked about her...uh... experiences yet?"

"Not really. Mainly because I've changed the subject whenever it comes up," I admitted.

"Everyone has a past. Maybe she's got a deep dark secret too."

I started to laugh, but then I thought about her mental breakdown. It was one of those things that if I didn't know, I would never have guessed. Thrill was smart and thoughtful and kind, and unlike me, she gave no evidence of being damaged. Was there a way to talk about Daphne that followed a similar route? I swallowed when I realized where that path began. "Did you tell Jackie about Tanya?"

"Of course. She knows everything about me. As I do about her."

It hadn't dawned on me that Jackie might know the short physical history between me and Ray. She'd been nothing but gracious and warm the entire time I'd been with them. Although, there was that one moment before I left..."Did you ever consider saying you just didn't want to talk about something?"

"Nah, man. That kind of evasion always comes back to bite you in the ass. If you're really getting another chance with Elise, don't let that be how you start it. I mean, how would you feel if she told you that?"

"I'd feel like she was hiding something terrible. And like I couldn't trust her until I found out what it was." Which meant that approach wouldn't work, for sure.

We were both quiet for a few minutes. "Would it help if you practiced? Like, told me the story as if I were her?" Ray asked.

"No, I…" My first instinct was to say it wouldn't work.

Reading my mind as he often did, Ray said, "Hold off. Think about it. Give it a couple of days or whatever you need. And call me either way, okay?"

"Yeah. Thanks, Ray. You're a good friend."

"I want to see you happy, Max. Not only because I'm your friend, but because you deserve to be."

It was hard to talk around the sudden lump that had formed in my throat. "'K. 'Night."

"Be safe out there."

"Yep."

❖

Two days later, I was still thinking about it. Little by little, I'd been working out the words in my head. It was like trying to pull a splinter that had been buried for so long, it had become petrified. I wasn't sure which scared me more: that I'd finally get the damn thing out, or that it would break off and continue festering the way it had for most all of my life. But the image that tormented me most was that once it was out, Thrill would take one look and run, never speaking to me again. Not that I would blame her. What did the daughter of a murdering psycho have to offer?

We continued chatting, though there must have been something different in my tone because twice Thrill asked me if this was an okay time. With someone else, I would have fabricated some story about being tired or busy. For her, I gave as much truth as I could find at the moment, apologizing for being distracted, and saying I had something on my mind that I hoped to talk with her about soon. She was quiet for a while. "Is it a, maybe you don't want to do this with me, kind of thing?"

"Oh, God no, peach." It slipped out again, but I kept going. "It's a, you shared a really significant part of yourself, and I want to do the same for you, kind of thing. But I…it doesn't…" I tried to give her my authentic intention, but all I could come up with was, "Your story is better." I was glad she couldn't see me roll my eyes at how poorly I finished that statement.

Toward the end of the month, a text came from a number I didn't recognize. It was Raquel, telling me that Thrill would be working around the clock with her study group and wouldn't be available for a couple of days, other than to text good night. I laughed but was exceedingly pleased that she cared enough to let me know.

I have something to ask, Raquel's next message said. *What have you done to that girl?* Was she genuinely perturbed, or was there teasing in her question? *She hums...hums, mind you...all day long. Happy little tunes that make it impossible for me to concentrate.*

That answered my question, and I smiled, even as I knew I had to play my role. *I'm sure she's simply reveling in my lingering mystique and charm*, I replied. *Which brings me to the question, ravishing Raquel, why are you not humming as well?*

My cell rang, Raquel's number on the display. She didn't bother with a hello. "I'm not the type to hum along with someone else's fantasy, thank you." I laughed, but when she cleared her throat, I knew there was more. "Tell me something, Max."

"Sure." I sensed this was serious but tried to sound nonchalant.

"You're not going to break her heart, are you?"

I swallowed hard. "I'm going to try not to."

"No. That's not enough. Not for Elise. What does the *Star Wars* creature, Yoda, say about trying?"

We recited the famous line together. It was good counsel. But like all advice, easier to give than to take.

CHAPTER SEVENTEEN

2008
Age Twenty-six

One useful thing I did get from Raquel's call was the exact date, time, and location of the law school graduation. Since Thrill had kindly attended my ceremony at the truck driving school, I intended to return the favor. Plus, her family would be there, which was both a chance for me to make a positive impression or an opportunity for me to blow it completely. No pressure there. At least I had the better part of a month to improve my wardrobe and possibly my manners. I did some shopping and practiced imaginary conversations with Thrill's parents.

I also practiced talking through the childhood incident that had scarred me in every possible way and its link to my sordid relationship with Daphne. Speaking the words out loud still felt like torture, so I started writing them instead. Ray encouraged me, telling me to pretend like I was telling someone else's story. It was working pretty well, and I was thinking about how to frame the next paragraph as I pulled into Etta's with only a couple of days before my trip to Houston.

I'd decided to drive Nephthys there for several reasons. One, there was no chance in hell I'd get to borrow Daphne's car again, and two, I figured Thrill's dad would like to see my rig. Okay, I wanted to show her off to the whole family. And three, I wouldn't have to worry about getting a hotel room. Since anyplace I could park would be a ways outside town, the downside was that I'd be riding my bike to the various events. But they might as well get to know the real me. That was a majorly different kind of thinking for me when it came to someone I was dating.

I'd gotten settled in for my stay at Etta's when my cell buzzed. I was shocked to see Daphne's number and considered letting it go to voice mail. But hell, if she was calling to cuss me out, I might as well get it over with.

"Where are you?" she demanded, with absolutely no prelude.

She couldn't be working, or she would have seen me. "I've just parked at Etta's."

"Oh, thank God," she said before I could add anything more. Her voice was quaking.

"What's wrong, Daphne?"

"Lena's been in an accident."

My heart stopped. "Is she—"

I couldn't finish, and Daphne's voice hardened. "Some contemptable asshole sideswiped her when she was riding her bike, and she fell and broke her arm."

I felt like I could breathe again. "When?"

"Three days ago."

Blood pounded in my head. "And you're only calling me now?"

Daphne sighed. "She's started asking for you. She wants to know when you're coming to visit so you can sign her cast."

None of this answered my question, but I supposed she was making the point in her usual, roundabout way. She wouldn't have called me at all, given our last encounter, but Lena wanted to see me, so…

"Tell her I'm on my way. Oh, and…uh…I'll be riding my bike, and I'd like to ride it away when our visit is over."

"Shut up," she said, which I translated as, "Your bike will be safe this time."

I was surprised to find Bill there, and while his anxiety level was considerably lower than the lady of the house, he seemed relatively sober and creditably concerned. He gestured angrily after letting me in. "It's a damn shame when a kid can't ride her bike on her own street without worrying that some speeding fool is gonna—"

"I know Max agrees with you, Bill, but let me take her to see Lena before that pill takes effect." Daphne's interruption was more even-tempered than usual.

"Oh sure, yeah. Okay." He plopped onto the couch, staring at the muted television screen where a baseball game was on. I grinned when I saw the remote firmly ensconced in the pocket of Daphne's slacks.

She whirled to face me outside Lena's room, speaking in an angry whisper. "Before the accident, she was carrying on about going to see a lawyer with you. What the hell was that about?"

Shit. "I saw Lena on her way to school the morning before I brought your car back, and we chatted for a few minutes. She asked where I'd been, and I told her about driving the high school kids to the mock trial competition. She seemed really interested in the legal stuff." I carefully didn't reference what had happened between us afterward.

She narrowed her eyes. "So where does the lawyer come in?"

"The woman who mentors the students is a friend of mine. She's about to graduate from law school, and I told Lena she could talk to her sometime about what it's like to be a lawyer. It's never too soon to get her started on a meaningful career path, you know."

Daphne was giving me the look that meant she knew I was leaving something out, but before she could analyze what it might be, Lena called for her in her sleepy voice. "I'm here, sweet girl. And someone special is here to see you." To me, Daphne said, "Don't keep her awake for too long."

Lena and I had a careful hug, and we both teared up. "How are you feeling, skinny Minnie?" I asked, handing her a Kleenex and taking one for myself. I'd given up on crayon names and was now simply grabbing any silly rhyme that came into my head.

She sighed dramatically. The apple didn't fall far from the tree on that one. "I feel okay, mostly. But I'm sad because I don't know when I'll get to see your friend, the lawyer. I was excited about that, but when I told Mama, I guess I didn't explain it right because she didn't look very happy." She looked so dejected, it hurt my heart.

"I'll talk to her later and try to explain it better."

"Please, Max. And tell them I'm tired of being in bed all day."

"Okay. Now, you tell me what happened,"

"I was being careful. Really. Riding with the traffic like Daddy told me. I could see a car coming alongside of me, you know? They were going fast, so I kept real steady, but then they swerved. That's the last thing I remember until Daddy was putting me in the car, and Mama was crying, and my arm hurt something awful, so I was crying too." She looked at me with her beautiful brown eyes. "And I was scared."

"Oh, baby, I would be too. In fact, I think I'm kinda scared just hearing you talk about it." She nodded. "But tell me, does your arm still hurt?"

"No, not hardly. But I need to keep it propped up like this as much as I can." She indicated the pillows under her arm before she grinned and pointed with her good hand. "There's markers on the bedside table. Do you want to sign my cast?"

"I sure do." After noting Daphne's signature of "Mom" with a heart where the O would be, I put a rainbow border all around my name. It took a while, and I thought maybe Lena had fallen asleep. But when I looked over, there were tears on her face. "Oh, Lee, did I hurt you?"

"No, but I was thinking about that car, and I realized that I'm afraid to ride my bike anymore. Daddy already got me a new one, but I don't think I want it."

"Aw, honey. It's only natural for you to feel that way. We need to do something about those fast cars, so you don't have to be scared anymore."

"How can we do that?"

"I've got some ideas, and I'll talk to your Mama and Daddy about it."

Lena's bottom lip came out. "They'll get mad and yell. Or Mama will cry. She's even more scaredy than I am."

"It might seem that way sometimes, mellow yellow, but your mama can be really brave when she has to." At Lena's skeptical look, I squeezed her shoulder. "It's true."

"How do you know?"

Well, there it was. The challenge to see how brave I could be. "I'll tell you, but can I ask you to keep it to yourself for now? Maybe later, you and your mama can discuss it, but for now, it needs to stay between you and me, okay?" She nodded solemnly. "You know that your mama and I used to live next door to each other when we were kids?"

"Yes, she told me. I wish I had someone my age living next door."

"Maybe someone new will move in," I suggested, but she shook her head.

"People drive too fast, and families won't want to live here."

I could see she was stuck on this point, which was probably valid, but I needed to distract her. "Well, when I was about your age, your mama saved my life."

Her mouth opened a little. "Really?"

I swallowed, trying not to get overly emotional. "Yeah. Someone bad was trying to hurt me, and she stopped them."

Lena's eyes were round as dinner plates. "How?"

"You know, I don't remember exactly because I was scared like you were, but I bet she just got her big voice and told them to stop." My mouth was getting dry, so I rushed to finish. "And that's what we're going to do out there on that street, mug bug. We're going to get big and tell those cars to slow down."

Lena nodded, then yawned. "I think I want to sleep now. But come tell me good-bye if you need to leave before I wake up, okay?"

"Anything you want, henny penny."

She smiled and closed her eyes.

Both Daphne and Bill pounced on me the minute I came back into the den. I waved them onto the couch and told them about Lena's fear of the cars going fast. I warned them not to push her about riding the bike again anytime soon. "But you need speed humps on that road," I said, shaking my finger at the street like I was scolding the source of Lena's fears. "And soon."

"You know what this city's budget is like. How do you suggest we go about accomplishing this miracle?" Daphne asked, although her tone wasn't as sarcastic as her words intimated.

I started pacing as my plan took shape, telling them to get one of those radar guns from Bill's buddies at the police station and clock the speeds of the cars. I suggested Daphne could canvass all the neighbors and gather stories and ask them to sign a petition, maybe start a neighborhood page on social media. Have a neighborhood gathering, a pleasant social event with their local councilperson. "Oh, and take pictures of Lena's arm and her damaged bike. Blow them up and take them to the meeting. And raise hell when you get there."

They stared at me as if I'd grown another head. After a few seconds, Bill asked, "Well, what if we do all that, and they still say no?"

"You go to the next meeting and the next one and the next one. Get your hands on the real budget and get an estimate of how much speed humps would cost. Demand to know how the council could justify spending money on widgets when a little girl was scared to ever ride her bike again."

Daphne was nodding. "I think this could really work. Bill?"

"Hell, what have we got to lose except some time? Yeah, I'm in."

"Good. And there's one other thing you need to do," I said.

"Name it," he stated, with the kind of bravado I planned to make him regret.

"You need to let me take Lena with me to Houston when I go in two days."

"What?" Daphne jumped up like something bit her. "No way. That child is bedridden."

"That child is sick of being in bed, and she wants to meet my lawyer friend. She needs a change of scene, and she doesn't need to sit here watching trash TV while you start on the speed hump operation. It'll make her nervous at best and scare the bejesus out of her at worst."

"She has a broken arm," Daphne declared.

"She's not going to do any heavy lifting," I countered. "But her spirit is shaken. Let me take her somewhere different and restore her confidence in herself and in the world."

"And you think Houston is the place to do that?"

She might have been putting two and two together, but I pressed on. "I think it will be very positive for her. Maybe I could even take her to Galveston too."

"That's a terrible idea. She can't get her cast wet. It'll make her sad not to get to play in the waves."

I gave an inch. "You may be right. But maybe we could drive by, and she could get a sense of the ocean. Then if she likes it, you all can plan a beach vacation after she heals up."

Bill's head had been swiveling between us like he was watching a tennis game. "Where will you be staying on this trip?"

"We'll stay in the truck." I had to address him now, but at least it was on a subject I felt confident about. "The cab is like a compact RV. It's got a fridge and a stove and a microwave, so food will be no problem. The passenger seat makes into a single bed. I'll sleep there, and she can have the bigger bed. That way, we can keep her arm propped up at night."

Bill scratched his head. "I think I've seen it. You park that thing at Etta's, don't you?"

I swallowed. Had he ever seen Daphne coming or going from Nephthys? "Yeah, usually. You're welcome to come check it out if you have any doubt about Lena staying there."

He looked at Daphne, whose expression was almost frozen. "Maybe we should let her go, Daf."

Her grimace broke the ice. At least it wasn't Daffy anymore, I thought. Turning to me, she put her hands on her hips. "You categorically cannot take my child on your motorcycle."

"Yeah, I know. I'll rent or borrow a car when I get there." Her protests were getting weaker, but I kept my expression serious.

"You know she'll tell me if you don't."

"I know she will." Lena had long been my standard for honesty.

"I'm going to talk to her. Make absolutely certain this is something she really wants and that she understands what all will be involved."

"Sure, I think that's a fine idea."

"I'll bet you do." The sarcasm was back, but it lacked bite. Daphne went to check on Lena, and Bill, finding himself in the unfamiliar role of host, surprised me by offering me a beer. I surprised myself by accepting. How weird if the two of us ended up as friends after all.

❖

My feelings about taking Lena to Houston were a tad mixed. As much as I wanted to cheer the kid up, I'd also been looking forward to whatever alone time I could get with Thrill, though with her family attending, such moments would undoubtedly be scarce. Generally, I was pretty excited to have Lena along, and her eagerness was next level. She called me twice that night, once to thank me again for offering to take her, which she'd already done before I'd left the house, and again to ask if she could bring her drawing supplies, which I agreed to without a second thought.

But when I returned to the Polk household the next day and saw two duffle bags and a large suitcase that she and Daphne were busily packing, I suggested that a trip to Nephthys might be in order, so "they" could see how much space there was. Of course, Daphne knew exactly how much space there was, but we both understood the parts we were playing.

As we got under way Friday morning with one duffle and a much smaller suitcase, Lena eyed the multiple gauges with great interest and watched my every move with the intensity of a driving instructor. Once we reached highway speed, there was less going on, so we talked about school and other places I'd been and almost everything else. We stopped to eat lunch at Mama's Daughter's Diner because I'd heard good things about it and also because of the name. We got so full, we had to get dessert to-go. After about an hour, Lena said she was hungry again. I told her that if she was careful, she could get her dessert from my fridge. Making her way carefully across the floor, she declared, "This is really cool, Max. I think it's better than a regular house."

We discussed the pros and cons of life on the road. I hadn't had a travel companion before and hadn't realized how agreeably it made the miles pass. Of course, Lena was great company in any case. She called her mom when we got to Houston, and then I got her settled in the bed with her arm on a pillow. I gave her part of a pain pill to help her nap while I went to get the rental car at a place that would store my motorcycle for the duration.

Raquel had told me that Thrill's family would be gathering at their duplex for dinner the night before graduation. She'd invited me to join them, and I'd sighed deeply. "As much as I hate to miss your cooking, I think I should give them family catch-up time. I would like to come by later in the evening, though. Do you think that would be okay?"

"I think our little hummingbird would be delighted to see you whenever."

I'd grinned at her reference to Thrill's new musical practice, but that had been before Lena's accident. Still, I was ninety-nine percent certain that Thrill would accept Lena's presence in the same way she warmly accepted her students. I didn't have the guts to consider how she might feel if she knew of my relationship—at least, my former relationship—with Lena's mother.

Lena was refreshed and chattering excitedly as we drove to Thrill's house, completely unaware of the knot of anxiety residing in the back of my skull. I questioned, too late, if Thrill liked surprises.

And how would her parents react to me dropping in unannounced with someone else's kid in tow? I didn't give a shit about the sisters, but Thrill would care about their reactions because she was that kind of person.

At their door, Lena edged behind me. "Hey, I was planning to hide behind you," I said.

She shook her head. "No. You go first."

Raquel answered my knock, giving me a flash of a smile. "Max," she announced in mock surprise. "How lovely to see you."

"Hello, Raquel. Is Elise in?"

"Why yes, the Thriller is in residence."

I grinned and shook my head, wishing I'd gotten to hear Thrill explaining that nickname. Lena peeked out, and Raquel's eyes widened. "Oh my. Who is your darling friend?"

I introduced them, and Raquel lavished attention on Lena, chatting with her encouragingly. When Lena began standing taller and speaking more confidently, we started toward the living room. As we approached, I could hear the sounds of conversation, accompanied by occasional laughter. "Elise, you have visitors," Raquel announced from the doorway, and the room went quiet as everyone turned.

I'd taken a breath, prepared to introduce us, or at least to offer Thrill congratulations, but when our gazes locked, my mouth went dry. She rose, the expression on her face one of pure amazement. "Max. Oh my God. What are you doing here?"

She took one hesitant step, and when I began, "Well, you came to my graduation, so I thought—" she was in my arms before I could finish. She didn't kiss me, but her embrace was close and warm.

She murmured against my neck, "It's wonderful to see you," and every inch of my skin tingled.

Tell her, smart Max urged. "It's really great to see you too. I…" Rather than babbling on about how right it felt to hold her, it occurred to me to acknowledge the other people in the room. "I hope we're not intruding."

Thrill seemed to focus on the "we" and stepped away, almost wary.

A quick look around the room at the reactions of her family confirmed that nothing seemed terribly amiss. I knew from one of our many conversations on the road that Thrill was out to her family, and they were fine with her sexuality. I gestured at Lena, who was now glued to Raquel's side. "I'd like to introduce you to my goddaughter. Lena Polk, meet Elise Adams."

I saw Lena swallow before she stepped up next to me. Bravely, she extended her good hand. "How do you do?"

Thrill smiled sweetly. "How nice to meet someone with such splendid manners. It's my pleasure, Lena."

"As you can see, Lena had a little accident, and I...well, her parents and I, thought a trip might cheer her up," I explained. "Plus, I told her about the mock trial group, and she's very interested in hearing more."

Lena stared. "Are you the lawyer?" When Thrill nodded, Lena breathed, "And you're so pretty," and the room filled with laughter.

Lena blushed, and Thrill said, "Raquel is a lawyer too."

Eyes wide, Lena breathed an "Oh, wow" and a man, who I assumed to be Thrill's father, stood. "I think further introductions are in order, Elise."

Holding Lena's free hand and with Thrill on my other side, I met her family: Ben and Arlene Adams and their daughters, Corrington and Reid, who I tried not to glare at. No one offered to hug me, which worried me a bit. Thrill's mother rose shakily, extending her hand, palm toward Lena's face, but not touching her. "What happened to you, sweet girl?"

"I was riding my bike on our street, and a car was going too fast and hit me, and I fell and broke my arm, but they didn't stop, so I went to the hospital and got this cast, and Mama and Daddy both cried, and I did too." Lena ran the words together quickly, like a jerky, old-time movie. Finally taking a breath, she held her arm up.

"Oh my," Arlene spoke softly. "Who would do such a terrible thing?"

Lena lifted her chin. "Mama said it was some bastard, but Daddy said we don't know it was a guy, so he said we should just call them a contemptable asshole."

Someone—it might have been me—took in a shocked breath. One of the sisters snorted, and Ben burst out with a loud laugh. The rest of the evening was delightful as Lena sat with Raquel and Arlene, clearly enjoying the undivided attention of attractive, sweet-natured adults. I kept an ear out for any signs of distress in Lena's voice, but all I heard was the grown-ups oohing and aahing over everything she told them.

Meanwhile, Ben and I swapped driving stories, and Corrington added tales of her early years as a traffic cop. Thrill flitted from group to group, refilling drinks and offering additional desserts. We made plans to meet at graduation, and everyone wanted to see Nephthys afterward. When I saw Lena's eyes start to droop, I stood. "We should get going. But it was great to meet all of you. Thank you for letting us crash your evening."

I waved good night, and everyone responded graciously. Ben insisted on carrying Lena to the car, saying he hadn't helped put a little girl to bed in far too long. I kissed Raquel's hand, pleased to see her blush, and put my arm around Thrill as we walked out. "I'd always planned to come, but Lena's presence was kind of a last-minute thing."

"She's fantastic. And I can tell she thinks the world of you. You'll have to tell me more about her another time."

Cowardly Max cringed. *Definitely another time.* "Your family is great. I'm glad I got to meet them."

Ben was easing Lena into the back seat, taking extra care with her injured arm. He patted my shoulder on his way to the house. "Tomorrow," he said.

"Yes, sir," I agreed.

As soon as he went inside, Thrill moved swiftly, pinning me against the car, her hands on either side of me, her body pressed against me. "Admit it," she murmured. "Lena is part of your secret plot to make me fall in love with you."

My body jerked, and the possibilities of our position almost made me miss her declaration. When it registered, I wet my lips. "Busted. I kidnapped this strange child and broke her arm, certain it was the way to convince you I was a good person."

She traced the curve of my cheek, and I tried to keep from closing my eyes and leaning into the touch. Everything in me surged toward her, attraction and yearning combined. "I already know you're a good person, Max. I'm just trying to figure out if you're my person."

Unable to stand it another minute, I grabbed her and kissed her, the same combustion that was smoldering in my abdomen, heading south. She moaned into my mouth and was reaching for my ass when a small voice from inside the car cried, "Max? My arm hurts."

We sprang apart as if a bucket of cold water had been poured on us.

"Okay, Lee baby, okay. I'm sorry. We'll go right now," I babbled, fumbling for my keys. "Timing," I muttered to Thrill, and she kissed me softly.

"I couldn't agree more."

❖

Another great thing about Thrill was her last name. At graduation, Lena sat patiently through Adams—at which point, we cheered wildly—but by the time we got to the C's, she was fidgeting pretty badly. I knew Lena wanted to cheer for Raquel too, but when I showed her Ochoa in the program, she looked almost despondent. Thrill's family assured her they would yell loudly for her, so Lena and I sat outside the venue and talked about graduation and what it meant and how some people had their hats decorated and how cool the professors' robes were. After about ten minutes, Reid came out. She pulled out a pack of gum and offered a piece to Lena and me. We both thanked her and chewed quietly for a minute.

"So how long have you known my sister?" she asked.

I deliberated whether someone in the family had sent her to do the interrogating or if this was on her own. "Actually, we met when she was in college, but we lost touch for a while."

"Uh-huh. And when did you reconnect?"

I already had reason not to like her, and I really wasn't interested in playing twenty questions. "Maybe you should ask Elise about this."

Reid laughed. "Don't get sensitive. You know how Elise is. We didn't even know she had a girlfriend. She clams up if any of us asks the least little thing."

"Funny, she and I have had lots of informative personal conversations."

"Well, she and I wouldn't be indulging in pillow talk."

I lowered my voice, watching Lena stroking the flowers that were landscaped along the walkway. "We're not sleeping together."

She studied me for a minute. "That's probably wise on your part. You may or may not know that she's had some—" She stopped, glancing at Lena, who was now following a trail of ants along the sidewalk, still within hearing distance. "Issues," she finished, pointing at her head.

"With good reason, as I understand it." I lowered my voice. "You've got some nerve to be out here talking about her like this. She's the best person I've met in a long time. Maybe forever. I think you need to back the fuck off." As I'd talked, I'd balled my fists, ready to take a swing if she didn't shut up. I didn't know if Lena saw, or her judgment was better than mine, but the next thing I knew, she was back, tugging at my sleeve.

"I'm hot and thirsty, Max. Can I take a nap in Nephthys?"

I stood, still facing Reid but trying to shake off my fury. "Don't bother to join us if it interferes with something else in your day. Like pulling the wings off butterflies."

As I took Lena's uninjured hand, she turned a horrified expression to Thrill's sister who, from what I could hear, was chuckling as she made her way back into the auditorium.

On our drive to the truck, Lena informed me that she'd heard me say a bad word.

"Yeah, and I'm sorry, Lee. But sometimes, bad people need a bad word. Like what you said about the person who knocked you off your bike."

Lena looked concerned. "Is Reid a bad person?"

I waited a beat, knowing I had to be careful with my answer. Lena was at such an impressionable age, and my anger stemmed from what I knew of young Reid. "I don't know if her heart is bad, but she was saying something kinda bad about Elise, and I wanted her to stop."

Lena eyed me. "You like Elise, don't you?"

"Yes, I do. She's a very nice person."

"I saw you kissing her." Lena singsonged. For a second, I contemplated asking her not to tell her mother. But that would have been the old Max's way. Instead, I grinned sheepishly. "You like her," she sang again, and I laughed.

"Yeah, I do. She's kind and she's smart. And you know what? I think she likes me back. And that's really important."

Lena nodded like the wise old sage she was. "Probably the most important."

God, I loved that kid.

❖

By the time Thrill's family arrived for their tour, Lena and I had Nephthys clean and tidy, and we'd set out soft drinks and snacks. Since it wasn't enough room for everyone to be in at once, they toured in shifts, with Raquel, Thrill, and Arlene getting the first look. I noticed again that Thrill's mom was sorta shaky, but she seemed to enjoy my narration of my rig's various features.

Apparently, the sisters had decided to skip the tour, as they chatted outside before taking Arlene and Raquel home in their car. I gave Ben a more extended look at both the inside and outside, and Thrill followed. "Now I'll have a clear picture of where you are when we talk," she said, taking my hand. As Ben inspected the engine and Lena looked on, Thrill murmured, "I need to tell you something. I've accepted a job with a firm in Lubbock."

"The pull of home, huh?" I asked, meaning to tease.

Her eyes filled with tears. "Yeah. Reid thinks Mom may have Parkinson's. There's no test for it, other than a brain scan that helps with diagnosis, but I think Mom doesn't want to know. I just…I want to be around to help Dad and all."

I pulled her closer. "Oh, peach, I'm sorry. But hey, on the bright side, I'm more likely to come through there than I am through Houston."

Daphne would have made some snide comment about me calling myself a bright side, but Thrill sighed and squeezed my hand. "That's fantastic. You'll be my silver lining." Leaning against my shoulder, she added, "But the next month or so is going to be terribly hectic. I have to move, start my new job, and study for the bar."

"We'll keep talking whenever we can, and you'll let me know when it's a convenient time to come visit."

"You're wonderful. Do you know that?"

Was it possible that I made her feel as good as she did me?

CHAPTER EIGHTEEN

2008
Age Twenty-six

When I dropped Lena off at the Polk residence, she was half-asleep and full of junk food from our stop at Buc-ee's, sporting six new signatures on her cast. I'd miss her company on my next run, but I was excited about the job, the biggest I'd ever done. The two largest school districts in Denver had hired me to haul almost forty tons of old cable to the industrial recycling plant in Colorado Springs, where it would be turned into ninety-nine-percent pure copper. If the timing went well, I could stop and visit Ray and his family on my way up before dropping in on Zelda on my way back.

I was planning my route and the timetable when there was a tap on my door. Daphne was standing there with her hands on her hips. "You've got a lot of nerve taking my daughter to meet your new lover."

She sounded truly pissed, so I invited her to come in. She shook her head, obviously preferring to yell at me in full earshot of everyone at Etta's. "I knew you were a lying fool, but I would never have let Lena go with you if I'd known—"

I cut her off. "Now wait a minute. Elise is my lawyer friend I told you about. Everything I said regarding that trip was true."

"Yes, I'm quite aware that Elise exists. She and Raquel are practically all Lena has talked about since she's been home. But tell me, do you make out with all your friends? Or do you even have any other friends?"

I tried not to let her rattle me. True, I only had a few good friends, but that wasn't really her point. "It's true that Elise and I kissed. We're exploring possibilities in our relationship. But we're not lovers."

"Which is your way of saying she's not putting out yet. What's the matter, Max? Lost your touch?"

She still knew exactly how to push my buttons. Anger buttons, in this case. I pushed back. "What bothers you more, Daphne? The fact that your daughter had a positive experience with an authentic, healthy grown-up, or the idea that I might have met someone decent who cares about me?"

She reddened, and I knew I'd hit a nerve. "Don't plan on seeing Lena or me anytime in the near future. We're both going to be busy with real life, not fantasy."

I ignored both the threat and the insinuation that what Elise and I had was illusory. "Speaking of real life, how's the speed-hump issue working out?"

"It's…going well, thank you. Your ideas were very helpful." I had her there, and we both knew it. "Look, just…goddamn it, Max." Seeing her speechless was quite a treat, and I was admittedly reveling in it. Finally, she went with a vague flit of her hand, accompanied by, "Just get lost, will you?" which we both knew was monumentally weak for her.

"Well, I'm leaving in a couple of days, going on a new run, so that's always a possibility."

She sighed and mumbled something that might have been, "Shit." After a pause, she added, "Be careful doing it," letting me know she wasn't really that mad.

❖

My conversations with Elise had gotten shorter. I would have worried, but when she once fell asleep in the middle of her own sentence, I understood our lack of conversation didn't mean anything was wrong. I'd offered to help with the move, but she'd already hired someone. Her concern for her mother meant she'd moved into her family home, with all the weirdness that entailed. After only a week to settle in there, she'd started a new, intensely demanding job, and the pressure for her to pass the bar exam was extreme. I tried not to be another source of stress for her, and though our talks were brief, she was always sweet and encouraging.

"This won't last forever, Max. And you still want to come see me, don't you?"

"The minute you say the word, peach. I'll take you to the best hotel in town, and we'll have room service. I'll even let you catch up on your sleep…for a while, at least."

"Promise?" she asked wistfully. "That sounds heavenly."

"Which part?" I was nervous to hear her response, but she giggled.

"All of it. But especially what happens after the while."

Yeah, that was what I wanted to hear. I decided a slight detour though Lubbock could be in order on my way back from the next run. I'd check with her first, of course, and we might not have our next "dream date," but at least I could see her for lunch or coffee. As much as I wanted all the rest of it, I also wanted to hold her hand and look into her eyes and know that she was not totally stressed from work or freaked out from living in her childhood home. I tried not to overanalyze everything as my feelings for her grew and deepened. Believing we both wanted the same thing, I found myself enjoying the pace, bringing things to a slow boil between us. At least most of the time.

When I was younger, Daphne had made me burn, but after the fire, there was nothing left. I could see the possibility of building something lasting with Thrill. Most importantly, I liked who I was when I was with her.

I put in my headphones, eager to talk this out with one of my best friends. When a strange voice answered, I asked for Zelda. "Who's calling?" the voice asked.

Zelda lived alone, and it seemed strange to me that someone visiting would be screening her calls. I decided to play it cool. "This is a colleague of hers from the Nationwide Truck Driving School. Is she available?"

"Just a moment." The voice sounded suspicious, but after some shuffling, Zelda came on.

"Hey, it's Max. Who was that?"

"Oh hey, Max. You remember my niece Lantana?"

I surely did. Or what I remembered was that Lantana was actually Janey's niece, but Janey and Zelda had adopted her as a teenager after her parents had died in a gas explosion at their home. Lantana had become convinced that she had been spared because she was one of God's special angels on Earth. And that same God had apparently told Lantana to treat anyone who didn't grovel at her specialness like dirt.

"Oh, yeah. Uh-huh. How's she doing?" What I really wanted to ask was, "what the hell is she doing there?" but I refrained, though I kept my opinion that Lantana made a hornet look cuddly.

"She been real nice. Going to take me to my doctor appointment tomorrow." Her voice was slurred, like she'd been drinking, which was exactly what I'd have been doing if Lantana was visiting me. I heard a telltale click. Zelda was one of the few people I knew who still used a landline, and I suspected that Lantana had gotten on the extension.

"I'm planning to come see you before long. Think you'll be around?" I was being intentionally vague, hoping the avenging angel would be gone soon.

"As long as I'm looking at the grass from the green side, I'll be around." That was the Zelda I knew and loved.

"I'm counting on it. Is it okay if I just stop by?"

"Sure, Max. You know I always want to see you."

That warmed my heart. "I'm looking forward to seeing you too. Got something good to share with you."

"Can't wait. See you soon." She hung up. Zelda hated good-byes. There was a second click before I heard the dial tone.

❖

My body schedule had gotten all out of whack again, so when I found myself yawning after only six hours, I decided to pull over for a rest stop catnap. Thirty or forty minutes later, I was in that dozy state when my cell rang. I needed a few seconds to orient myself, but once I saw the name of Mr. Vittum, my lawyer, on the readout, I answered without thinking about it. Occasionally, there was paperwork, but since signatures were increasingly done electronically, I figured this was probably a "keep in touch" call.

"Max, I have important news. Can you talk now?"

"News" could have meant anything from local gossip to an actual update on my financial situation. "Yeah, I'm stationary. What's up?"

He cleared his throat. "We got word this morning from the Rusk State Hospital. Max, your mother's passed away." He paused.

I felt inert, unable to speak or process the conflicting emotions that roared through me.

After a few seconds, he went on. "She left a will, and based on the testimony from the staff at Rusk, the court will likely uphold its validity. I need to know how you want me to handle it."

I knew what he meant. With my father, I'd wanted to drag things out so I could pretend it wasn't over. This had been over many years ago. "I'd like everything taken care of as soon as possible. Just let me know when you need me to come in."

He may have been surprised, but he said, "All right," a couple of times. Another silence stretched out between us. Finally, he took an audible breath. "Saying I'm sorry doesn't quite seem fitting, but..." He trailed off, maybe hoping I'd contradict him. Or possibly agree. I felt like I'd forgotten how a conversation was supposed to go. "There's one other thing, Max."

I couldn't imagine what, but I made a little humming sound for him to go on.

"I wanted to be the one to tell you about your mother because, well, you and your father and I, we all go back a long way. But I retired about two months ago, and my wife and I have planned a European cruise that starts next week. I won't be able to handle this one for you. Do you know another lawyer?"

It seemed to be taking me twice as long to comprehend, like I was translating from another language. "Another lawyer?" I repeated stupidly.

"Yes. Your mother had her documents stored at the Rusk facility. They're sending them over, but I may be gone before they arrive. Is there someone here you'd trust to receive them?"

"Daphne Polk." Her name came out without me thinking twice.

"Fine." I could hear the scratching of a pen. "I know Mr. and Mrs. Polk. That won't be a problem." He sniffed. "I don't anticipate anything too complicated. There are no other next of kin, and I assume you'll want her remains taken care of at the facility?"

He posed this like a question but there was only one answer for me. "Uh-huh."

"So then you'll need someone to represent you at the court hearing."

I tried to imagine what he was expecting me to say. I came up with, "Okay." Fucking brilliant.

"Text me the contact information for your new lawyer so I can update him on the case."

"Right. Thanks for calling, Mr. Vittum." I muttered, and broke the connection.

I made coffee and sat at my table to drink it, trying to wrap my head around what had just happened. In a sense, nothing had changed. What I had of my mother were tragic memories, and those would still be with me. As a person, she'd been dead to me for years. I didn't think about her, unless someone like Thrill asked directly. Was there anything wrong with that, given that the last thing I could remember of her was that awful day in the backyard? After I'd gotten home from the hospital, JT had explained to me that she'd been sent away to Rusk State Hospital, having been found legally insane. He promised me she'd never come back, and sure enough, she'd never reached out to me in any way, and I'd had no desire to communicate with her. Was I supposed to feel something else now, something more?

Though Daphne and I hadn't spoken since her snippy farewell to me, she was the one person who would understand my ambivalence. Knowing she was careless about her cell phone, I called their landline. When a voice mail message came on, I almost hung up. But Daphne often screened her calls, so I cleared my throat, waiting for the beep.

"Hey, uh. If you're not still hopping mad or maybe if you are, I need to tell you something, so—"

Her voice came on the line, a bit breathless. "Is there a mother in the world who hasn't fallen for the old line, 'Please, Mom. I'll take care of her. I'll do everything.' And let me tell you, there's nothing in this wide world that stinks worse than a litter box that hasn't been emptied in a week. I swear, when that child gets home, I'm gonna snatch her bald-headed." She stopped for air, and I realized that Lena must have gotten her kitten.

Daphne starting up in the middle of a conversation with me, even though our last exchange had been somewhat disagreeable, was also good news. But I'd called her because no matter what else happened in the world, we couldn't stay out of each other's lives indefinitely. I hoped to make Thrill understand, once I started on my story, that Daphne was an ex, but she was also a friend. And at this moment, I really needed to connect to our shared history. "My mother died," I blurted.

There was a sound that might have been her sitting down. "Did you even know she was still alive? Before she died, I mean?"

That made so little sense except in Daphne-speak, that I started laughing. I could hear her saying my name, saying, "You know what I meant," and other protests, until she finally said, "Max, baby, stop laughing. You're worrying me."

I hadn't been "Max, baby" for a long while, and hearing that helped me get a grip on myself. "I think…I think I'm worrying me too," I managed after a bit. "Daphne, I…I don't know what I'm supposed to feel."

"I don't think there's any 'supposed to' in this situation. Except to maybe feel whatever seems genuine to you."

"What if I don't feel anything?" I asked.

"Give yourself time, sweetie. You're probably in shock." As I was considering this possibility, Daphne shrieked. "Shit! Now that damn cat is tearing up my couch. Get out of here, you." There were quick footsteps and a yowl that might have been her or the cat. Daphne panted into the phone, "Listen, hon, I'll call you later. Or call me back in a while if you want. It'll be okay, hear?"

The call ended before I could say anything more. I hadn't told her about the paperwork that would be arriving at her address, but when she saw where it came from, she'd figure it out. I sat and drank more coffee, staring into space, my mind somehow simultaneously busy and blank. After a time, my eye fell on the notebook where I'd been writing my story. The one I was preparing for Trillian Elise Adams, law school graduate, who would certainly pass her bar exam in another couple of weeks and would then be officially able to practice in the state of Texas, thus becoming another lawyer I knew. If I'd been in my right mind, I would have hesitated, but I wasn't, so I didn't. As her phone began to ring, I had the contradictory wish that it would go to voice mail. But she picked up, and the warmth in her voice when she said my name almost made me cry. Instead, I started babbling.

"Hi. Remember when you needed me to drive your kids to Dallas for the mock trial thing, and you starting by saying that you were going to ask me a big favor, and it was okay if I had to say no?"

She took a few seconds to digest this. "Yes?" She said it like a question. "Are you okay, Max? You sound a little…off."

"No, yeah, I mean, I found out I'm gonna need a lawyer pretty soon, so I thought I'd ask if you'd do it. Not for free, though. I'll pay you, of course."

"Did you have an accident?" Her voice was tight. "Are you or is anyone else injured?"

"No, no. It's nothing like that. My old lawyer retired and…" I gathered myself. "I'm going to need someone to represent me at probate court." I didn't want to go on, but I didn't want to make her drag it out of me either. "I just learned that my mother died, so… yeah."

"You just learned—" After a few seconds of silence, her voice was harder. "You told me both your parents were dead."

"No, I think you made that assumption because no one came to my NDS graduation. And I didn't correct you." My recollection of the conversation we'd had at Baby Pies was quite clear.

"Why not?"

"It's a long story." At her impatient sigh, I added. "And one that I'd really prefer to tell you in person."

"There have been several instances when we've been together in person that you could have told me."

I was confused by her tone until I realized she thought I was lying. "It's…" I trailed off, trying to think through it all, something I obviously should have done before I called her. Oh, hell. She was going to find out sooner or later. "My mother has been in an institution for the criminally insane since I was eight years old. In a very real sense, she has been dead to me all this time. This is merely a formality."

"Oh."

I waited, but she didn't go on. "I'm sorry if this freaks you out. It freaks me out to say it on the phone, and I want to tell you the rest of it face-to-face. In some ways, it's hardest to think about going through the legal parts, and I could use a friend. But I understand if it might feel weird and you need to say no." I could hear her breathing. After a minute, I added, "And I don't mean to give you extra pressure to pass the bar exam."

She cleared her throat. "Maybe it gives me extra incentive, so I'd get to come see you."

Hope rose in my throat, and I felt like a kid who was wishing upon a star, still believing in possibilities. "Yeah?" was all I could manage.

"Yeah." She sounded more like herself now. "But you must promise, Max. Promise me that you'll tell me the whole story when I see you."

"I promise. Absolutely."

❖

Initially, I'd planned to keep working as if nothing had happened, but after driving for an hour, I knew my mind was wandering too much to be safe on the road. The lady at the Denver school district was sweet and sympathetic about my "death in the family" excuse. I wasn't ready to go back to Pokeyville, where gossip was the only thing that was quick. News about my mother would already be out, and I'd have to deal with well-intentioned folks coming by to offer support or sympathy. I was already carrying groceries, but once I rolled into Clayton, New Mexico, I stopped to buy booze. Making my way into Clayton Lake State Park, a place I'd long wanted to check out, I knew my rig might look out of place, but there were a few scattered RVs that were about the size of Nephthys. When I found an available site at Peach Point, I knew I was in the right spot.

I texted Thrill and Daphne that I was going dark for a few days but that I was parked and safe and not to worry. I told Daphne that some mail would be coming and to set it aside until I got back and to give Lena a hug and kiss for me. I wished Thrill good luck on the bar and asked her to let me know how it went, along with telling her I hoped her mom was doing okay. I didn't wait for replies before shutting off my cell.

A week later, ninety-six percent of the booze I had was still unopened. During the days, I started my story again, ripping out the pages of weakness and excuses, pouring out my heart in those new lines, finding comfort in the brutal honesty about my past and hope in what could lie ahead. I also tried to envision my mother as a person. What had she been like as a little girl? Was she ever in love with my father? Did she ever feel anything besides harried disinterest in her children? When had the seed of her schizoaffective disorder been planted, and would it ever bud in me? Throughout my life, I'd searched myself for signs of her. I'd found her anger on occasion, as well as her despondency, but I'd had no idea of who she'd really been.

Fear that psychotic behavior would one day explode out of me as it had with her had kept me sheltering with Daphne, the only person I'd believed capable of understanding who I was and what I most dreaded. But now there was Thrill, easy to talk to and sweet-tempered but also aware of the dangers of living with lies and deceptions. She'd fought the dragon others had placed in her mind and won. That was a woman I could believe in, a woman I wanted to believe in me.

When I fired up Nephthys and turned on my phone while she idled, I found twenty-seven texts and over forty emails. I read Thrill's texts first, which began with a professional report. *Passed the bar. Can get time off for your probate. When do you need me?* Next was, *Miss you. Worried you're not all right. Want to talk ASAP.*

Of the twelve voice mails, one was also from Thrill. "I feel terrible about how I reacted to the news about your mother. It took me by surprise, and I'm sorry I wasn't more sensitive to how you must be feeling. Please forgive me, and call me soon."

Daphne's number showed up four times, and her messages were predictable. She cussed me a blue streak for the first two before her tone became more fretful. "I swear, Max Terrell, you better call me the minute you get out of wherever you are. I mean it." Then, "A big envelope with your name on it came to my address." There was a pause. "And I wanted to tell you that whenever you're ready to go to whichever lawyer you decide to use, I'm coming with you." Given my plan to use Trillian Elise Adams, if possible, that should be entertaining.

I called Thrill once I got rolling. She answered immediately. "Are you okay?"

"I'm fine. Terrific, actually. And I have a proposal for you."

She laughed. "Well, this is rather sudden, but…"

"Oh, uh, I meant…" I stuttered, realizing I'd used the word "proposal" rather than "proposition," which might not have been any better, come to think of it. I liked how she teased. It was a light tickle, fun and amusing. Daphne teased for sex or to gain the upper hand by embarrassing me. At the moment, it was hard to stop comparing them, but I was looking forward to becoming so much more familiar with Thrill that any resemblance would fade. "The paperwork from my mother has arrived, but I haven't seen it yet. Could I pick you up on my way to Pokeville, and you could look it over when we get there?" She didn't answer, and I added, "You told me you could get time off. I wasn't sure how much, but I thought—"

"Yes," she said.

"Yes? Yes, you'll let me come get you on my way home?"

"Yes," she repeated. "Are you truly all right, Max? I should have told you that I'm sorry—"

"I am. And there's nothing to be sorry about. I just needed to get my head around some things. Now I want to share those things with you."

"I very much want to hear them. When will you be here?"

I checked my mileage. "How does four hours sound?"

"It sounds like you're a mighty fast worker."

It was my turn to tease. "Well, we agreed we needed to work on our timing."

She was quiet for a moment, and I worried I'd been too offhand. "Is that what we'll be doing?"

I sighed. "Unless it'll be business before pleasure."

"I'll let you know after I see the paperwork. I'll be taking this seriously until I'm off the case. How does that sound?"

"Perfect, peach. Listen, I'm coming into Texas, and the traffic is picking up. Do you want me to call again when I'm closer?"

"Not unless you need to. Otherwise, be careful. I'll be watching for you."

I called Daphne's home phone once I'd made the turn to Dumas. Bill answered, and I was thrown for a few seconds. Once upon a time, I would have hung up rather than talk to him. New, grown-up Max decided to give it a try. "Uh, hi, Bill. It's Max. Is Daphne there?"

"Oh yeah, hi. No, she went to Houston with Lena. They'll probably be home in a day or two." Well, that was weird. Daphne wasn't the type to just up and go somewhere. Especially somewhere seven hours away. And with Lena? "Oh, and you've got mail here," he added.

"Oh, right. Will you be going to Etta's anytime soon?"

"Maybe," he hedged as if this was a trap. "Why?"

"Could you bring that mail and leave it with Katie?"

"Oh sure, Max. I'll run it over there in a little while."

I thanked him and called Daphne's cell. It rang twice before announcing that the voice mailbox was full. Daphne was negligent with her phone, not keeping it charged or leaving it on mute or forgetting where she'd left it. I was a few miles outside Lubbock when it occurred to me to call Lena's phone, but the traffic was such that I needed to concentrate, so I made myself a mental note to buzz her later.

Thrill and I were on our way to Pokeville after a nice lunch with her folks. I got the impression they really liked me, which made me feel fine as frog fur, as I'd once heard Zelda say. As we were settling ourselves in the cab, she told me that she'd called the county clerk and identified herself as my lawyer. "We have an appointment for your probate hearing the day after tomorrow. Will that work?"

"Sounds fine." I reached for her hand. "I'm really glad you'll be doing this with me."

"Me too."

I knew I should talk to her about my mother and that whole part of my life, but I didn't want to be driving when I did. Plus, I was enjoying just being with her. She seemed to feel the same, and we kept the conversation light until we pulled in to Etta's. Thrill asked if I was going to give her a tour of the town. She laughed when I told her this was it, but eventually, I was persuaded to get down the bike and ride her around, narrating the highlights of my life as we passed them: the house where dad and I had lived—which I was currently renting to a teacher and her family—Pokeville schools, Nan's Coffee Shop and Bakery, the Sav-Mor, and my favorite Chinese restaurant.

I judiciously avoided Daphne's street, even though she wasn't home. It was somewhat unscrupulous, but I wanted to have Thrill in my bed, showing her how much I wanted her and learning if she felt the same before revealing my deepest, darkest secrets. I was still afraid that hearing about my childhood horrors and my connection with Daphne would give her second thoughts, and I at least wanted to show her what she'd be missing.

Back at Etta's, I showered before treating Thrill to my signature shish kababs for dinner. When I realized we had no dessert, Thrill produced a package of M&M'S for us to split, and we both giggled as we fed each other the green ones. Everything with her felt effortless, including the little touches and special smiles that we shared throughout the evening. I hoped that she was genuinely comfortable with the physical part of our relationship because I intended to take that to the next level.

"Are you aware that we have a bed situation here?" I asked as she stepped out of the shower wearing an oversized sleep shirt.

She covered her mouth with her hand, and I knew she was trying not to laugh. "You don't say."

"Oh, but I do. So here are your options." I pointed to the queen-sized bed in what I considered my room. "You can sleep in here with me, where I'd really like there to be some intense misbehavior." I paused.

"Or?"

"I don't suppose I could convince you there are no other options? Because anything else will break my heart."

She moved until we were face-to-face. Her breath was fresh and cool on my overheated skin. "Well, we can't have that." She kissed me, her arms around my neck drawing our bodies close. Even fully clothed, I savored the way she moved, and I could feel her rhythm building inside me. "Besides, I don't want any other options, Max."

"Good." I moaned, keeping her against me with my hands on her waist. "Because I want to have all of you tonight."

She stilled. "Just tonight?" The tenor of her question was light, but I replied with all seriousness.

"No. Not just tonight." Grinning, I added, "I thought you'd stay tomorrow too."

She pinched my shoulder, but I didn't move away. Instead, I ran my hands up her sides, pausing at the swell of her breasts. "And maybe the day after?" I suggested.

She swayed a little. "Uh-huh?"

I kissed her neck, working my way to her ear, whispering, "And maybe even longer."

"I think I'd like that," she murmured, slowly moving her hands until she was pulling my hips toward her. I shifted until my thigh was pressed into her center, and her breathing quickened. "Oh, Jesus, Max. I've made myself come so many times, thinking of you. I don't know how much longer I can wait for the real thing." Well, that did it. I lifted the hem of her shirt as she teased open the tie on my sweatpants. "I want to see you naked." She panted.

I could only mumble, "Yeah."

Once our clothes were off, we couldn't keep our eyes or our hands off each other. I didn't appreciate what was happening when Thrill sat me on the edge of the bed until she dropped to her knees in front of me, moved my legs apart, and without hesitation, took me into her mouth.

Utterly surprised, I shouted, "Oh fuck," and she looked into my face. Her tongue swirled through my most sensitive parts for a few seconds before she moved her mouth away. I whimpered slightly, and she smiled. "Would you rather do something else first?"

I barely had enough presence of mind to ask myself where I'd gotten the idea that Thrill might be a bit shy sexually. I shook my head, and she ran her hands across my breasts.

"Do you remember when we had our sex talk on the phone?"

I felt heat coming to my cheeks. "Yeah. I had to pull over after about five minutes."

"That's right. And you told me you didn't go down on a woman unless you were really into her."

"Uh, yeah." All I remembered of that conversation was needing to get my hand into my pants because Thrill had been surprisingly explicit.

She lowered her mouth toward my pulsing clit. "I want you to know that I'm into you. And I intend to be, in all ways possible, while we figure out about our days."

I came so hard, I saw stars. When my breathing calmed, she maneuvered us fully onto the bed, and I rested my head on her shoulder, drifting in total bliss.

"Max," she whispered after a few minutes. "My image of you will totally shatter if I find out you're a pillow princess." That was enough to bring me back to life. I was eager to explore the body I'd first seen at that long ago flag football game. I slipped my hand between her legs, exhilarated when she moaned and thrust against me.

"Don't you worry, sweet peach. I'm gonna enjoy every drop of your juice." As soon as the words came out, I felt myself flush with embarrassment. How fucking hokey was that? But she grabbed my face and kissed me, hard at first, and then we softened into playing tongues as I continued to stroke her with my fingers.

"I like to hear you talk. And I love your touch." She panted, and I kissed my way along her throat, her collarbone, and down to her breasts. As I started to suck her nipple, she grabbed my wrist, stopping my motion. "That feels fabulous, but I want to come in your mouth."

"Can't we do both?" I murmured, nipping at her belly as I made my way lower. She writhed with each contact, lifting her hips to meet me as my lips reached her clit.

"Oh, God. I won't last. Max, yes."

I told myself I would tease her another time, that I'd draw out her release and make her beg me later tonight. As she climaxed against my tongue, I doubted if I'd ever be able to do that because she knew how to direct me to what she wanted in a way that really turned me on.

CHAPTER NINETEEN

2008
Age Twenty-six

If it hadn't been for the legal hearing, we might not have left the truck at all. I wobbled over to Etta's for coffee and sweet rolls the next morning, my mood wilting when Katie handed me the large manilla envelope that had come from Rusk Hospital. It gave me an eerie feeling to think that my mother had probably touched this paperwork. I wasn't anxious, exactly, but I was apprehensive about what might be in there. Upon my return, I found Counselor Adams fully dressed, damn it. She informed me she needed at least an hour of uninterrupted time to read over the estate information and make notes. I explained that I found the studious lawyer look extremely sexy, and I couldn't make any promises.

Thrill carefully removed the contents of the packet, placing them on the table. There were several legal looking documents, and one regular white envelope which she set apart from the rest. I sat on the couch, pretending to read the *Dallas Morning News* I'd bought at Etta's. Because JT had taken that paper for years, I couldn't resist picking it up, but my ulterior motive was to watch Thrill surreptitiously from atop the pages. Once she caught me, and the smile reached her eyes over the top of her reading glasses. Both the smile and the specs were unaccountably stimulating.

"You're not helping," she intoned.

"I'm reading," I crooned back, snapping the newspaper to prove it.

She made a doubtful hum and returned to her work. A few minutes later, she said, "I'll need to read over the will now, but the rest are documents like Power of Attorney and Medical Power of Attorney, which are not viable after death. But there is this." She held a white envelope, which was marked *Private-Confidential. For Maxine Eleanor Terrell only.* "It looks like a message for you. But would you mind if I read the will first? The letter may be referenced there, and context always helps."

"Sure. I'm in no hurry."

"You're not? Don't you have plans for later today?" Her voice had dropped into the seductive range that I'd heard a great deal of last night.

It was enough to make me aware of the dampness in my boxers. "Actually, yes. I do have plans. I need to finish the sports section before I start on the crossword." I rattled the paper again.

She laughed. God, I loved that sound. "Well, don't let me keep you."

I temporarily satisfied myself with a fantasy that involved fucking her on the table, right on top of all the paperwork and her legal pad, while she talked dirty between begging me for more. I was pretty into it, so much that I didn't notice she had gotten up from the table and was standing directly on the other side of my newspaper.

"That must be a really interesting article. You haven't turned a page for five minutes."

"Well," I replied, having glanced at the headline before lowering the section. "Who wouldn't find the stats of the Texas Rangers' newest closer fascinating?"

She straddled my lap, her breasts brushing mine as she leaned in to whisper, "How fascinating are they?"

She wouldn't let me fuck her on top of the paperwork, but we did reach a compromise. We moved the documents to the couch.

Later, when we'd made it back to the bed, I told her I was ready to read the letter. She sat up, her expression solemn. "Would you like privacy? I could take a walk."

"No. I want you here." As I said the words, I realized how true they were. I wasn't simply trying to be nice. I did want her with me and not only at this moment. In these two days, I'd gotten a glimpse into what my life could be with Thrill in it, and I liked what I was seeing and feeling. I more than liked it. "I want to live in Colorado eventually," I blurted out. "I really love the air in the mountains, and my friend Ray is there. But Lubbock is fine while you take care of your mom."

She turned in my arms, looking at me with wide eyes. "What?"

I recognized how presumptuous my comments sounded. "Nothing. Just thinking out loud."

She put her hand on my cheek. "I like it when you do that. I want to know what's in here." She tapped my forehead. "And in here." She brought her hand to my chest. I wondered if she could feel my heart rate increase. "By the way, the will didn't mention anything about your mother's letter."

"Okay." I sighed. "Guess I should get to it." While I was fully expecting some rambling, bizarre message, I couldn't suppress the part of me that wanted a message begging for forgiveness and offering words of love. Thrill snuggled against me, and I ripped open the envelope.

❖

I visited JT's grave for the first time since he died, spending the afternoon sitting beside his headstone, talking and listening. Thrill didn't question me when I got back, only kissed me and let me hold her without speaking for a few minutes.

I'd stopped by Ming Dynasty on my way back, getting some lo mein for me—though I had no appetite—and a few other dishes I thought Thrill might like. She had an odd expression on her face as I apologized for being gone so long as I put the food on the counter. "Are you hungry?"

She shook her head. "Max, I have a confession to make."

How ready was I for this? Not at all. "You're married? You're working for the CIA? You're really a country music star who's looking for material for her new album?"

She smiled, but it didn't reach her eyes. Putting the food in the fridge, she pulled me over and sat me on the couch. Pacing in front of me, she said, "I have no excuse other than being worried about you. And I'm probably more than a little meddlesome at times. I guess lawyers are that way by nature. But I sincerely apologize and if you want me to leave, I can call Steph in Oklahoma City, and she can be here in a couple of hours."

"Okay." I waited.

She looked around as if trying to decide the best place to be. Finally, she sat beside me. "I..." She sniffed. "I googled your mother's name and Pokeville. I know what happened. Well, what Google says happened to you." She laid her hand on top of mine. "God, Max, I'm sorry. But I wasn't sure if you would ever tell me, and I wanted to know so I could...help you."

"You think I need help?" My voice was flat. Since I'd never looked myself up online, I had no idea what the internet had to say about the worst day of my life.

"No, not like that. I meant, help you be able to talk about it."

I went to the fridge and got a beer. I held one out to her, pleased when she took it. I got another for myself and drank a hefty swallow before sitting down again. "And what did Mr. Google have to say?"

"All I read was an article about her hearing. But in it, they reviewed her case and the c...crimes."

I'd never heard her stutter before. "And what did you think, Counselor? Was the sentence fair? Was justice done?" I turned to look at her, finding tears welling in her eyes.

"You know much better than I that 'fair' and 'just' don't apply here. But I keep thinking about a quote from Adolph Kolping: 'No true love without justice and no true justice without love.'"

I stared at her, resentment accelerating inside me. "Love? You think there was love in that backyard? Let me tell you what there was. There was eight-year-old me, watching my mother come screaming out of the house with a cast-iron skillet in her hand." The shuddering in my body felt like a dam breaking, and all the awfulness came spilling out. "That morning, after I'd found the stash of pills she was supposed to be taking, I made my brother Adam come out to the backyard where we could hide if we needed to. I didn't totally understand it, but I already knew that without those pills, she could get hysterical, like, frenzied. When I saw her coming, I knew it was bad, and I wanted to run, but Adam had gotten in the play pool, and I knew I couldn't get him out in time."

I reached out my hand, wanting Adam to take it so we could get away, but instead of his cold, wet skin, a soft, warm hand grasped mine. My vision wavered, and I realized I was looking at Thrill through tears. "I never understood why she wanted to hurt him. He was the sweetest soul that ever drew breath. But she was holding him under the water and whispering in that scary, scratchy voice. He was struggling, and I knew I had to help him." Thrill took my other hand, and I choked back a sob. "I tried. I tried really hard, but she was too strong, I couldn't make her stop. All I could think of was to start yelling, so I did. I screamed at her, and I cried for help. That's when she turned and…and she…"

I knew my mouth was open. I could hear my own raspy breathing. But words wouldn't come out.

"She hit you with the skillet, didn't she?" Thrill's voice was soft, like she was telling a secret.

I nodded, moving my hand to the bioabsorbable plate in my skull. If she hadn't said it, I might never have been able to. "God, it hurt so bad. It knocked me over, but lying on my side meant I couldn't see Adam, so I got to my knees. And then, and then…"

Thrill pulled me into her arms. "It's okay. It's okay. I know the rest. You did everything you could."

I knew my tearstained face was making splotches on her blouse. Now I should tell her about Daphne, how she'd appeared from nowhere and stood between me and my mother like a superhero or an avenging angel, which was the last thing I'd seen before I'd passed out. Somehow, she'd stopped my mother from hitting me again, and though that first glancing blow had still sent me to the hospital with a skull fracture, there had been no brain damage. I'd talked to the police once before my surgery and once afterward when they recorded my testimony. The next thing I remembered was JT telling me my mother was far away and never coming back, and that was enough for me. It still was. I felt myself sag against Thrill, completely empty and desperately tired.

"Come on, my sweet love. Let's rest a minute before I tell you all the ways I'm so proud of you."

Something in those words got me to move, and then I was lying with Thrill's living breathing body next to me, which was the best thing I'd ever felt in my life. I wanted to tell her that, but the only word that came out was, "You."

I could hear a smile in her voice when she said, "You too," but before I could figure out what that meant, I was asleep.

At one point in the night, I awoke while spooning her. I sniffed, and she stirred slightly, pulling my arm tighter around her and snuggling her hips into my crotch for a few seconds as if it was the most natural thing in the world. Normally, such a gesture would ignite my sexual attention, but when her breathing evened out again, I felt a different kind of passion. I wanted Thrill in my bed, yes, but I absolutely wanted her in my life. When we weren't together, she was consistently in my thoughts, and when we were, my life was better than good. Was this love?

❖

We slept all night with our clothes on, and after waking, each spent about five seconds trying for some semblance of grooming, before we burst out laughing. It was fun to be with someone who wasn't fussy about their appearance. However, Thrill flatly rejected the idea of Chinese food for breakfast, so we cleaned up and walked over to Etta's, where I had to introduce her to half the town's population. When I indicated she was my lawyer, I got the, "Oh yeah, how is Max doing now that her mama's gone?" look, part curiosity and part pity. After a while, I started saying she was my friend. Finishing yet another brief conversation with a stranger, Thrill turned to me. "Friend?"

"Well, I didn't want to assume," I hedged.

She considered this and looked at her watch. "I'll be your friend or your lawyer for another three hours or so. Then, I want more. Maybe we should both start assuming."

"And I assume that's a good thing?"

"I assume so." Thrill smiled, turning as Katie stopped at our table with the coffee pot.

"I assume y'all want a refill?" she said, eyes twinkling.

I laughed along, though I shifted uncomfortably, feeling the confines of my small town. The closeness that had once been comforting and kindly now seemed intrusive and overfamiliar. I knew I'd always keep in touch with Daphne and Lena, but having Thrill in my life made it clear it was time for me to move on.

When the will was read at the probate hearing, I was surprised to learn that my mother had left me almost twenty thousand dollars. Among the wild, often incoherent phrases in her note was something about money from her family that was for Adam's college fund. I fought back tears again. I didn't need her money, and more importantly, I didn't want it, so I donated half to Pokeville's General Hospital and half to the Mental Health Association in Texas. Then, the life of Lisa Collins Terrell was officially over.

Outside the courtroom, Thrill asked, "How are you feeling?"

I turned to face her. "You're the only one, you know."

"The only one?"

"The only one who knows how this part of my life experience ends." She nodded. "But that's not what makes you special." Thrill gave me the shy smile that made my heart race. "Now that I don't have to explain or hide the past anymore, I want to take you back to my home on wheels and talk about the present and the future. And that's unique."

Thrill held my hand and kissed me right there in the Shackelton County courthouse. There was something different about being with her after that. I couldn't keep my eyes off her because I didn't want to lose our connection. Not while we ate or washed dishes or took the trash to the dumpster. Our intimate caresses that night were slower and more intense, though filled with tenderness. It was that shift from sex to making love that I'd hoped for but never really had. The mood between us seemed filled with a powerful assurance. She was everything I wanted, and I'd never been so happy.

❖

Loud banging on the door of my rig made us both sit up. I jumped out of bed, grabbing my boxers and a T-shirt. "Stay there." I motioned to Thrill. "I'm sure this is nothing."

I opened the door, and Daphne slapped me across the face. I staggered, and she pushed inside the cab. "Where the fucking hell have you been? Goddamn it, Max. Don't I have enough problems without putting your miserable ass into the mix? Do you know I went all the way to Houston looking for you?"

I rubbed my cheek, trying to position myself between her and the bed. "Yeah, I tried to call you, but your voice mail was—"

"I don't want to hear your bullshit excuses. That Raquel girl wouldn't tell me a damn thing over the phone, which meant I had to drive myself and my child to that godforsaken place, only to find you weren't there. Lena was upset, so I had to take her to that trashy Boardwalk place for two days. Oh, Raquel did say your little wannabe girlfriend moved to Lubbock, but it would be a cold day in hell before I'd go to that shithole, even for you, you contemptible pond scum."

"How did you get Raquel's number?" I was stalling but also truly curious.

"Evidently, she bonded with my child on your pussy scouting expedition and put it on her phone, something my Lena happened to mention when I told her I was worried about you. Someday, that child is going to learn what a deceitful skank you are."

Daphne was clearly walking the line between being really angry and being relieved that I was okay. I wanted her to settle on the relieved side but to do it somewhere else. "Listen, I know I owe you an explanation and a big apology. Let me take you to breakfast for a start. Meet me at Etta's in ten minutes?"

"Meet you? You must be out of your fucking mind if you think I'm going to sit alone at Etta's waiting for you like a desperate prom date. Go ahead, make yourself presentable. This won't be the first time you've gotten out of bed and dressed in front of me."

Daphne moved around the divider to gesture at the piece of furniture in question. I watched as she blinked, and her mouth formed into a perfect O. I followed her gaze, even though I knew what she was seeing. Thrill was sitting up with the sheet pulled to her shoulders. Her face was expressionless, though I couldn't help noticing that she was holding the notebook in which I'd written about my life.

Daphne turned back to me. "Obviously, you forgot what I told you about some people not appreciating an audience," she snapped.

"You didn't give me much chance to inform you," I mumbled.

"So this is my fault?" she asked.

Apparently, Thrill had had enough. "No, it's mine. I should have made my presence known once it became clear that you two have a lot to discuss."

Daphne sneered. "Don't bother with introductions, dear. Mine is the only name she remembers anyway."

Worst moments of my life? Seeing my brother die and now. "Please, give me a minute," I pleaded, but Thrill shook her head.

Addressing her next comments to Daphne, she said, "Since you haven't seen *me* get out of bed and dress, would you mind…"

It would have been amusing to see Daphne flustered if I hadn't been petrified with fear that Thrill was going to leave before I could explain. At the stricken look on my face, Daphne's expression changed to something between resentful and penitent. She opened the door. "I'll wait for my explanation and apology until a more opportune time."

I could hear Thrill moving behind me, dressing, I assumed. Once Daphne was completely out the door, I began to beg. "Thrill, please—" I began, but she lifted the notebook and started reading aloud.

"*I think I fell for Daphne because she was safe, and yet being with her was a forbidden thrill.*" Her lips were pressed together so hard, they were almost white. "Don't you ever, ever call me Thrill again. Correction, don't ever call me again, period."

She couldn't mean that, my heart asserted. But I honored her wish, name-wise. "Th…Elise, if you'll read the next part, you'll see—"

"I don't want to see. Even thinking about it makes me sick." She dropped the notebook on the floor. "That's Lena's mother?" I nodded, staring at the page where I'd written about growing up in love with Daphne. "And she's the one who loaned you her car before?" More nodding. "The one you said was a 'friend.'" She made air quotes around the last two words.

"She is a friend," I tried, my words sounding pathetic to my own ears, even though they were true.

"And obviously so much more." I opened my mouth to protest, but she went on. "She's married, I assume."

"Yes."

"And has been all along."

I pitied anyone facing Counselor Adams on the witness stand. "Pretty much, yes."

She let that go, although her mouth curled derisively. "Tell me her husband isn't involved too."

"Oh no. God, no. I wouldn't—"

"Well, I just don't know, do I? I thought I knew you, but I obviously don't. Having had other girlfriends is one thing, but I never dreamed you'd be in an ongoing affair with a married woman. A married woman with a darling child who adores you. Do you not have any morals at all?"

I hung my head. I'd kept my silence too long, and now any explanation would sound like added deception. But I had to try. "It's not ongoing. After you, it stopped."

"After me? After me when? Not when I met you at Tech, obviously. And not when I saw you in Oklahoma City, right?" She closed her eyes for a few seconds. "She called that night, didn't she? Oh God, I can't believe I've been so stupid."

I pressed on, desperate to make her listen. "When I came to Houston after I'd seen Ray, and we came back from the mock trial competition, I started feeling something I never felt before, about truth and about what was possible for me. For my heart. How different my life could be. But I wasn't sure I'd be able to get it all out, you know? Explain the whole story. So I wrote it." I gestured to the notebook again, and for one second, the anger and hurt left her face.

"I wanted it to be you. The person for me. But I can't tolerate—" She cut herself off. "I'm certain I don't have to explain. If you value anything that was between us, please step outside and let me get myself together."

I moved, trance-like, pulling on sweatpants and making my way to the parking lot, pacing in my bare feet and trying to find the words that would undo what Elise had seen and heard. Short of having Daphne give sworn testimony about our recent status, I was at a loss. The worst part was that I couldn't really dispute anything Daphne had said. I was all the things she'd had accused me of being, and even her remark about dressing in front of her was legitimate, though it didn't depict the truth of our relationship now.

If only Elise would read on to the end of my story, to the part where I acknowledged I had fallen in love with her, for her strength, her goodness, and the integrity in her every word and gesture, the situation might be salvaged. We were each drowning in a sea of our own remorse, and I kept pushing the notebook toward her like a life raft. But I understood why she was rejecting me and my offer of deliverance. To have this happen now, after the intimacy we'd shared, had to seem like the worst kind of betrayal.

Time passed. A lot of it, I thought. Maybe enough? I tapped on the door. "Elise? May I please come back in?"

"I'd rather you didn't." I wasn't sure if her voice was muffled from the rig or by the emotional walls she'd put up. Probably both. I continued to pace as minutes ticked by. Maybe I could try starting with something less invasive.

"Would you come out here and sit with me?" I opened the compartment where I kept my camp chairs. "We don't have to talk."

"I can't see much point in that."

Shit. I put my head in my hands. "Yeah, I guess that doesn't make sense." I paced some more. "But can I please tell you one thing?"

"No, thank you. I don't believe I can stomach anything more from you at the moment."

Was she offering the slightest shred of forgiveness? "Just at this moment? Like, maybe later you could?"

"I'll let you know."

That didn't sound as positive as I'd hoped. "Okay. I'll be here when you're ready."

I heard something that sounded like a sob. "Thank you."

Moving to the door, I pressed my face against it. How could I let her sit in my truck and cry? How could I let her walk away and not do something about it? I tried the door, but it was locked. I felt heavy with dread, envisioning my inability to get in as a sign that there was no way out for us. From a place inside me that I'd never acknowledged, I could hear a scratchy, scary voice: *There are times when it'll never be okay. That's when you might as well give up.*

I shook my head, trying not to let the words penetrate, not willing to acknowledge where they came from or the possibility that they could be true. "Shut up," I said out loud.

And when you're scared? You should be. Because it will always get worse, much worse, the voice informed me. Had my mother had been waiting inside me all my life for this exact moment, when hopelessness would push me into the pit of despair where she'd lived most of her life?

"Go away and leave me alone! I've lived through enough shit because of you. I'm not like you!" I hadn't realized I was yelling until the cab door opened.

Elise stood there holding a tissue, her face blotchy. She looked around, cell phone in her other hand. "Who are you talking to?"

"No one." I bounded up the stairs. "Listen, I understand if you don't want to see me or talk to me, but I need to get dressed and…" *And get away from my mother's words.* Elise's suitcase was packed and sitting by the door. "Aren't I taking you home?"

"No, that's not a good idea." She looked away from me. "I…I've made other plans."

"Oh. Okay, sure. I understand. I just—" A sense of panic was starting to overtake me. "Could you please wait until…" I trailed off, grabbing clothes from a drawer. What was I going to say, wait until the sound of my mother's voice goes away? I changed quickly in the bedroom. When I came out, she gave me a long look. "What?" I asked, looking down at myself. "Is my shirt on backward?"

"You're pale. Like you're scared or something."

I sat on the couch, rubbing the bridge of my nose. "I am scared, Elise. I'm scared that I'm never going to see you again, and the rest of my life is going to be one long what-if. Like, what if I'd dared to explain about my history with Daphne at a moment when we weren't both so flustered? And what if you took the time to really understand what had happened and why I would do such a thing? And what if we both had the guts to give what's between us another try?" I couldn't look at her, but I had to keep pushing. "Aren't you a little scared too? Isn't that why you're running away? Because you're scared to admit we have something that you don't want to lose? Scared that if you sit and listen, you might learn you've misjudged this situation? I think both of us are scared of feeling something we're not used to feeling." I stopped to take a breath. "What do you think?"

A horn sounded outside. "I think we'll never know." When she stepped out the door to wave to whoever was picking her up, I slipped the notebook into the front flap of her suitcase. She turned and picked up the bag. "Good-bye, Max. Take care of yourself."

I couldn't speak, so I nodded. I followed as far as the doorway of the cab, watching Steph give me the finger as Elise put her bag in the back seat. She must have broken lots of speed limits to get here that quickly. I waited until they drove off to unload my motorcycle. I'd have to be extra careful, but I needed a friend whose counsel was just a couple of hours away.

❖

Riding instead of driving kept my focus from drifting to Elise, and the sound of my engine obscured my mother's voice. I usually preferred the scenery of the back roads on my bike, but I was desperate to talk with Zelda. Had either she or Janey ever handled something so badly that it broke them up? How did things between them get fixed? Only the belief that it was possible to mend things with Elise kept me going.

It had been more than eighteen months since I'd been to Zelda's house, and I almost passed it. Her immaculately tended yard was overgrown, the shrubs and potted plants dead or dying. Best-case scenario: she was on a long trip, and the person she'd gotten to care for her home was doing a piss-poor job. I couldn't let myself think about the worst-case.

I knocked louder than usual, calling her name. After a few seconds, I tried the doorknob. It turned. "Zelda?" I called again, stepping into the house. I stopped to listen; there were no signs of life. After finding half-packed boxes in the kitchen and the living room, I was about to venture into her bedroom when I heard a car door slam. Lantana, Zelda's faux niece, was making her way up the sidewalk. The bitter twist to her mouth gave me a feeling this encounter could be even worse than any of our previous meetings.

"What are you doing here?" she asked, her snappish tone proving me right.

"I came to visit Zelda. Where is she?" If she wasn't going to bother with niceties, neither would I.

"She had a stroke about two weeks ago." Lantana pushed past me as I sagged against the porch railing with a mix of relief and worry. "She's at a rehab place in Lubbock."

"Why didn't you call me, Lantana?" I tried to soften my voice, hoping to appease our usual antagonism.

"Why would I? You ain't kin." She crossed her arms over her ample chest.

Family was much more than blood, and I couldn't understand why she wouldn't acknowledge that or didn't care. "Yes, but we're friends, and I'd like to visit her. Would you mind telling me the name of the facility?"

"Won't do you no good." She moved into the hallway, calling over her shoulder, "She won't know you."

"Yes, but I'll know her." I swallowed hard, knowing what I had to do next. "Please, Lantana. Allowing Zelda visitation would be the Christian thing to do."

She stopped and snorted. "Like you'd know anything about that."

Fine. At this point I wasn't above resorting to brute force. I took a deliberate step toward her, figuring to snatch her purse and go through it until I found Zelda's contact details. A purse that size must contain encyclopedic information. She must have seen the look in my eye because she put out a hand. "Don't you come near me, Max Terrell."

Recalling Lantana's assumption that single lesbians were sex-crazed creatures who would jump on any available female almost made me laugh. In point of fact, Elise's parting comment had shriveled my libido to the little end of nothing. "Then tell me the name of where she is." I could have added, "That's all I'll ever want from you," but it would be counterproductive.

With a deep sigh, she dug into her purse and read from what looked like the bottom page of a multi-copy contract. "It's the Traditions Nursing Care and Rehab Center in Lubbock."

"Thank you." I cleared my throat. "So what are the boxes for? Are you taking Zelda some of her stuff?" I put out my hands in what I intended as a conciliatory gesture. "I can bring my truck and help you."

She rolled her eyes, as if my offer was the stupidest thing she'd ever heard. "No, I'm clearing out all this junk so I can try to sell this place. Those nursing homes ain't cheap. She won't ever be coming back here, and I can use the money."

I was about to offer help with expenses, positive that my friend's recovery would be bolstered by having her things around her, when smart Max advised me that nothing would melt this coldhearted woman. I'd save myself a lot of oxygen and aggravation by buying Zelda's house myself. I could use the same real estate agent who managed the rental of my home in Pokeville and require that all furnishing and decorations remain. I hoped that step wouldn't involve hiring a new lawyer, the thought of which added fuel to the hurt burning inside me. "Okay, Lantana. I'll see you around."

"Not if I see you first." She smirked, probably having waited half a decade to use that line.

CHAPTER TWENTY

2009
Age Twenty-seven

After parking at the Traditions Nursing Care and Rehab Center, I booked a room in a decent motel nearby. I figured I wouldn't be in any shape to ride back to Pokeville after taking care of Zelda.

The facility was exactly what I'd feared: understaffed, with dark, reeking halls leading to small, sparse rooms. Two men at the front desk grudgingly looked up from their card game when I announced I was here for a visit. When I questioned how often the doctor came, one stared blankly until the other finally said, "Whenever we need him."

"How about rehab?" I asked.

They looked at each other. "Once," the same man began, and the other one agreed. "Once a week, yeah." That lie smelled as bad as the rooms we passed.

The only surprise was finding Zelda in a room by herself. "Her roommate just passed," the man who showed me in explained. "She'll probably get another one by the weekend."

I didn't bother to tell him that she'd be long gone by the weekend. After he made his escape, I sat in the rickety chair beside her bed and took her hand. It worried me that she hadn't opened her eyes when we came in. "Hey, pal," I said softly. "It's Max." Her lids fluttered, so I kept talking. "What are you trying to pull, slacking off like this?"

When her hand trembled in mine, I gave it a gentle shake. "Whatcha say we get you into someplace swankier. Like with a bar?"

She squeezed my hand once. "Is that a yes?" Another squeeze. "Do I need to tell Lantana?" Two squeezes. *No.*

By the next afternoon, I had her in the top-rated place in town, where she was bathed and given a change of clothes. After a short walk in the hall, assisted by a genial patient care assistant, her eyes stayed open, but I wasn't sure how well she was focusing. I stage-whispered, "Better looking nurses too." One squeeze.

I canceled all my jobs for the next two months. My birthday came and went without anyone noticing—not even me. Caring for Zelda during the day kept me off the highway, where I'd have hours of nothing to do but think of Elise. The sheer anguish of everything that had happened between us ebbed and flowed but seemed to be perpetual. In the evenings, I ran on the treadmill or did laps in the hotel pool until I collapsed onto my lonely bed, my mind still trying to find a crack where I could have pushed through an excuse or an explanation that she would have accepted. In the end, the best I could hope for was that she was doing well and that maybe someday, she'd forgive me. Knowing Elise and I were in the same town was extra hard, and when Zelda was resting or between appointments, I searched the personnel pages of local law firms to see if I could find her.

No one questioned me about my "aunt," beyond asking for medical information, proving again that it wasn't what you knew, it was how you signed the big checks. I also kept the nurses' station supplied with fun-sized candy and treated the therapists with gift cards for movies or dinner out. I'd already slipped each of her doctors a nice bottle of scotch and was currently awaiting the arrival of a specialist who hadn't seen her yet. As Zelda napped, I was absorbed in my usual internet prowling of Lubbock lawyers when a throat cleared nearby. I looked up to find Elise's sister Reid standing in the doorway, staring at me.

She seemed as surprised as I was, and we each took a few seconds to recover—she by looking over Zelda's chart and me by putting away my phone and standing. "Dr. Thornton," I said, staring at her name tag. I hadn't known she was married.

"Max. How nice to see you." Smooth and very professional. "So this is your aunt?"

"Mmm." I tried to make a vaguely affirming hum that wouldn't be a total lie.

She focused on Zelda. "She looks familiar. Has she been here before?"

"No, I'm sure she hasn't." It didn't seem wise to offer more than she asked.

Reid made her own humming sound as she studied the chart some more. "It seems she's making good progress, other than the aphasia."

I nodded, having been around enough medical people in the last few weeks to know that aphasia meant loss of speech. There were no guarantees Zelda would speak again, and it wasn't lost on me that the words of wisdom I'd sought from her might never be forthcoming. Moving to the side of her bed, I gently touched her shoulder. "Hey, pal. Your doctor's here. Can you show her some of your best dance moves?"

Her eyes opened, and the corner of her mouth turned up when she focused on my face. Then she pointed at me with her middle finger. Reid and I both laughed.

After the exam, Reid suggested we discuss Zelda's treatment plan over coffee. For about ten minutes, she told me mostly what I already knew: after six months, any other improvements in her condition would be much more gradual. "She's welcome to stay here, but depending on the pace of her recovery, you might also want to think about taking her home or looking into someplace less costly."

"It wouldn't be practical for her to live with me in my truck, but if she's fully recovered, she can go back to her own home. If she needs help, there are funds available." I'd already set aside a chunk of my capital for Lena. I had no qualms about spending whatever I had left on Zelda's recovery.

Reid raised an eyebrow. Must have been hereditary. But the gesture was so much like Thrill's that I looked away, the distant ache sharpening. Reid noticed, shifting in her chair. "Part of me thinks I should take you out back and beat the shit out of you," she said by way of subject change.

Given my emotional state, the thought of brawling in the alley with her was rather appealing. "You could try," I offered, puffing up a bit.

She laughed. "Unfortunately, I don't think that would solve either of our problems."

"What would, do you think?" I was bantering automatically, not really expecting her to answer.

"Once you came into the picture, my sister was the happiest I'd ever seen her. And I thought you might be a keeper since you passed the test. But now she's miserable, and you look like shit. So it must be love, huh?" She laughed and finished her coffee.

I liked thinking that I'd made Elise happy. "Wait. What test?"

"Oh, you know, at graduation. When I referenced Elise's 'issues.'" She pointed to her head like she had that day. "I was glad your young friend was there since you looked like you were ready to punch me out right then." She sighed. "Elise hasn't had much luck with the ladies. Her first love, a high school girlfriend, decided she was bi and started dating guys. When her college girlfriend was trying to get into the Secret Service, she dropped Elise because she thought that being with someone with a record of a nervous disorder would hurt her chances." Reid's voice softened. "Elise is like our mother. She doesn't recover from emotional damage very quickly."

"Oh." My heart hurt. Sweet, sexy Elise didn't deserve any of that. "Well, her breakdown didn't matter to me. There's a history of personality disorder in my family too."

"Boy, I'll say," Reid snorted. When I gave her a look, she added, "What? You think I'd let my little sister go off with some trucker without checking them out first?"

I stood. "Thanks for the coffee and for looking in on Zelda. I'm sure I'll see you around."

Reid rose slowly, and I could see her thinking something through. "Trucker…Zelda…" She snapped her fingers. "That's why she looked familiar. She's Dad's friend from NTDS, isn't she?" I was formulating my response when she cocked her head. "And not your aunt."

"She's family in every way that counts," I said, gearing up for a fight.

"Okay, okay." Reid waved her hands and moved a step away. "I was simply thinking that Dad would love to see her, and it would be good for her too."

"Sure. Just please, don't tell anyone else. She's got crazy in her family too."

Reid studied me for a few seconds. "You might want to know that Elise isn't with a private firm anymore, so you can stop looking on your cell phone." I felt a blush climbing my throat. "When she came back from your place, she quit that job and accepted one with the state. In fact, she left for Austin this morning for a one-day training workshop. She'll be home tomorrow." She tapped her finger on her lip as if deliberating something important. "She'd like to see Zelda too, I bet."

My heart leapt for a few seconds before I came crashing back to reality. "I should probably be gone when she comes by, right?"

Reid rolled her eyes. "Only if you're as stupid as you look." She gave me a half wave on her way out of the cafeteria.

Was it possible I unexpectedly had two things going for me? Elise would be taking that suitcase on her trip, and while she'd obviously been too upset to notice the notebook before, she might now. If she'd cooled off enough to read my story, I might have another chance with her. Or I could throw myself on her mercy when she came to see Zelda. Even if Elise was still angry, she might at least speak to her desperate former lover in the presence of her ailing friend.

My renewed thoughts of Elise evaporated when Lantana's name appeared on my phone as I walked toward Zelda's room the next day.

"What have you done with her, you disgusting pervert?"

The screech of her greeting bled through the phone and made a couple of heads turn at the nurses' station. Just for fun, I decided to play dumb. "Who is this?"

"You know perfectly well this is Lantana Foster. Where is my Aunt Zelda?"

"You mean she's not where you left her three weeks ago? Maybe she recovered and checked herself out? Miracles happen, you know."

I could almost hear her grinding her teeth. "I know it was you because I asked those nice young men at that place if a mannish looking woman came and got her, and they said yes."

That was probably supposed to hurt my feelings, but it only made me roll my eyes. "What do you care where she is, Lantana? I'm picking up the tab now, so you can get back to your life."

"Shows how much you know about anything. Her house sold, and I need her signature on some paperwork. I'm going to court to become her legal guardian since I forgot to get that powerful attorney before I took her to Lubbock."

Powerful attorney? When I realized she meant power of attorney, I had to put the phone on mute while I laughed for a full ten seconds.

She was yelling for me when I caught my breath. "Sorry, I think we might be getting a bad connection," I said. "I'll call you later with an address where you can email or fax the paperwork."

No way in hell was I giving her the address of Zelda's new location. Lantana was likely to drag her off to another awful place just to spite us both. But after she sent the contract, I could pick it up from my real estate agent in Pokeville and then drive back to Lubbock in Nephthys, thus getting both our homes back. Then I had another thought. If Lantana became Zelda's legal guardian, I'd have no say in her care or anything else.

Besides all the things I needed to tell Elise about how sorry I was and how I felt about her, I also wanted her professional expertise. If I became Zelda's "powerful attorney," would that override Lantana being her guardian? Zelda had always been so independent; she'd probably hate either one, but if I could explain what was at risk, maybe she'd agree. I needed to ask first in any case, or I'd be no better than Lantana, and that was definitely not something I wanted to believe about myself.

Zelda was improving every day, in spite of the time she'd lost in "God's waiting room," as I'd come to think of that first place. She now nodded or shook her head instead of relying on hand squeezes, and she cocked her head when I asked if she was okay to discuss something. I assured her I'd phrase things for a yes or no answer.

When I told her that I heard from Lantana, Zelda didn't move. "She wants to become your legal guardian, and I was thinking maybe I should get power of attorney for you instead."

She blinked.

"See, I've got no lawful say in your business because we're not related. If push came to shove, Lantana would be recognized by the courts before I would, especially if she was your guardian." I leaned toward her. "You know I don't want anything from you except for you to get better. I don't think that's true of Lantana. She wants to sell your house and the stuff in it." Zelda started shaking her head. I touched her hand. "It's okay, I've taken care of that, but for whatever comes next, I need a way to legally show that I'm the person doing what you want."

When a tear rolled down her cheek, I knew it was too much. "Hey, I'm sorry. Let's talk about this later, okay?"

She nodded.

"Listen, I'm gonna run over to Pokeville this afternoon and get my rig. I'll should be back by lunch tomorrow, okay? Do you need me to bring you anything?

She looked away, and I felt like shit. After she'd fallen asleep, I called Lantana, absurdly grateful when it went to voice mail. I left her the Pokeville real estate company's numbers.

I zigzagged my way along the small state highways, passing dying towns and struggling farms on my way to pick up Nephthys. I'd started this journey wanting to talk to Zelda about Elise, but now I wanted to talk to Elise about Zelda. At a break outside the Dixie Maid Drive-in with my root beer float, I about dropped my phone in my drink when I saw a text from Elise. It was like I'd conjured her with my yearning, but then I saw the message was over an hour old. *I'm here in Pokeville, knocking on your door, but there's no answer. I thought we should talk. Are you hiding from me or entertaining yourself somewhere else?*

My hands were shaking so badly I backspaced mistakes more than I typed. *Hey! It's really great to hear from you. I've been out of town—long story—but am heading to Pokeville now. Hate that I missed you because I've really missed you. Please let me know another time that you'd be able to talk, and I'll do my very best to be available wherever you are.*

That struck the exact balance between pathetic and desperate, but I didn't care. I would have rented a billboard or hired a skywriter if I thought it would persuade Elise to give me another chance.

Typically, time in Pokeyville went slowly, though checking my phone every two minutes probably didn't help. In between, I checked with the real estate office—nothing from Lantana yet—and called Pete at my dad's shop to come over and check Nephthys out since she'd been sitting for a while. I read Elise's message over and over until the growling in my stomach got so loud, I might not hear my phone if it did ping. I made my way over to Etta's, where a small group of men were standing around outside the front door, the tones of their conversation jovial. When I saw Bill Polk among them, I waved, and he waved back.

"Hey," he called, stepping away from the group. "They put those speed humps in last week. Thanks for, you know, talking us through the idea."

"I'm glad, Bill. That's great." Last week's news didn't seem to merit the celebratory mood, however, so I waited in case he had something else to add.

"Daphne's inside." He grinned like a Cheshire cat. "Why don't you go say hi?"

Okay, that was weirder yet, unless he was trying to get rid of me so as not to look too chummy with the local lesbian in front of his buddies. I nodded. "I'll do that."

Daphne was sitting at the cash register, but customer service was clearly suffering as Katie and three other waitresses were circling around her like water going down a drain. They looked over when I came in, and Katie said, "Well, hey there, stranger. Haven't seen you in a month of Sundays."

"Yeah, I've been in Lubbock, taking care of a sick friend."

Daphne gave the fake giggle she often employed around her friends. "Oh, I saw that lovesick little friend of yours earlier today." She pursed her lips coyly, and everyone else laughed. "Love 'em and leave 'em, right Max?"

I hadn't seen Daphne since she'd burst into my truck and ruined everything between Elise and me. I'd been willing to forgive that because she had no way of knowing what was happening at the time, but I wasn't going to tolerate her talking bad about Elise. "I thought that was more your style, Daphne. Except you don't know squat about love, and you won't leave even this dump."

The other women gasped, and to my surprise, Daphne's eyes filled with tears. Katie tried to cover for my offensive comeback, clearing her throat in the stunned silence that followed. "Have you heard Daphne and Bill's news, Max?"

Hungry and not interested in their gossip, I scanned the menu I knew by heart. "Yeah, the speed humps. Great. The kitchen's still open, isn't it? Can I get a BLT to go?"

Daphne straightened. "Get her the damn sandwich, will you please?" She hadn't addressed anyone in particular, but the whole group scurried off. When she turned to me, the wounded look was gone, replaced by something I couldn't quite decipher. "We're immensely relieved about the speed controls, and thank you for your guidance on that. But there's something else you should know before you dash off to wherever it is you're hiding these days. I'm pregnant."

My mouth dropped open, making me look even more foolish than I felt. "Wow," I finally managed, exhibiting my brilliance yet again. "Does Lena know?"

Daphne gave a little huff, smiling in spite of herself. "You and that child, I swear." She lowered her voice. "We didn't want to say anything until we were positive it was going to take, you know?" I nodded. "I'll see the doctor next week, and then we'll have the talk." I smiled, and she leaned toward me. "I'd like you to be there for that. And promise me you'll be around in about six months because you're my good luck charm where babies are concerned." I hugged her, apologizing for my earlier snarkiness.

She waved my repentance off. "Who was that girl, anyway?" she asked.

"Elise."

"Oh, no. I…I'm sorry, Max honey. The things I said…Oh Lord, I thought she was just some random thing you were doing."

"It's okay. It was on me to tell her about you. But I'm still hoping that things can work out with her."

She looked at me for a long moment. "I hope so too, baby. Though I'll miss us."

"We'll always be us, Daphne. Only a different us."

Katie came in with my sandwich. "Keep it between the ditches," Daphne said.

❖

Elise hadn't responded, and I was feeling increasingly anxious about not being with Zelda. When the contract finally arrived the next day, I motored toward the Lubbock KOA faster than a sneeze going through a screen door. I rushed into her room and found her sitting up in bed with a sad look on her face. "I'm sorry I was gone so long. Are you okay?"

She shook her head. The nurse came in, looking rather grim, and handed me a note. Lantana had stalled me long enough to find Zelda and get herself appointed as her legal guardian. The message informed me that she'd be there tomorrow to take her aunt someplace where she'd be "safe." It also cautioned me that if I tried any more "funny business," I'd find myself in court. *Shit shit shit.* The CNA came in with lunch, bringing me an extra plate as she often did. "Oo, that other lady, she mean," she said in her musical accent. "You keep her away from our sweet Zelda, hear?"

"I'll do my best," I assured her, but I had no idea how.

We'd just finished lunch when another woman's voice called Zelda's name. I looked over to see Elise's mom in the doorway.

"Arlene," Zelda said, clear as day, although her voice was soft and hoarse. Before I could react, Elise's father came in, and Zelda's face brightened. "Ben," she said, and I felt like crying. They both greeted me warmly, which made me want to cry even more.

"I guess she was waiting for someone special to talk to," I suggested, after explaining about Zelda's aphasia. "So y'all visit, and I'll go tell the nurses about this wonderful development."

All of the sweet staff members were every bit as excited as I was about Zelda's improvement. As I grabbed a Coke in the cafeteria, I felt certain that Zelda regaining her speech was a big step toward getting her back to her own home. In spite of my worries about Lantana, it seemed like the day couldn't get any better, until I got off the elevator and heard the voice from my dreams saying, "Well, I'll try again tomorrow and see if I can catch her then."

I sprinted down the hallway, calling, "Elise! Elise, wait. I'm here."

She stepped out of Zelda's room, and I stopped two doors away. She'd cut her hair into a chin-length, stylish look and looked fantastic in her skinny jeans and faded Red Raiders T-shirt. I had to remind myself to breathe. Straining to think of something reasonable to say, I came up with, "Uh, hi. Hi. I was just letting your folks visit with

Zelda. I didn't know you were coming, or I would have, you know, been here." Okay, that wasn't too bad.

While her folks were making explanations about their forgetfulness, I resumed my approach at a reasonable pace, stopping a few feet from her. "I dropped them off and went to park," she said. "They were supposed to tell you."

"Well, we had some excitement, so maybe they can be forgiven?"

She shrugged. "I suppose." I couldn't stop looking at her, but she seemed ill at ease, unwilling to meet my eyes.

"Are you worried I'm going to beg for forgiveness too?" I hadn't meant to just blurt that out, but she looked at me for the first time.

"Maybe I should be the one begging."

Carefully, I took a step toward her. "You look really good. How's your new job going?"

She looked surprised for a few seconds before smiling, almost to herself. "Reid told you."

"She also offered to beat the shit out of me, if that makes you feel any better."

She blinked and then started laughing. "That sounds like Reid." After a moment, she added, "She told me you've been here every day."

I looked toward the room. "If it weren't for Zelda, I probably wouldn't be driving today. She's special to me, but I haven't kept up with her the way I should have. There were warning signs and, I didn't—"

Her touch on my arm stopped me. "She also said Zelda was in another facility, an awful place, but you brought her here and you're paying the bills."

"Reid has a big mouth," I murmured.

Ben and Arlene appeared at the doorway. "We should go, honey. Zelda's had a big day."

"Oh, sure." Elise had moved her hand away so quickly I almost thought I'd imagined her touch. "Let me go get the car."

"May I walk with you?" I asked, sounding way too hopeful. But she nodded, so I put my head in Zelda's room. "I'll be back in a flash, Miss Chatterbox." Zelda laughed, and the sound lightened my heart. Once in the elevator, I gathered myself. "I don't mean to pester you, but things are going to get dicey with Zelda, legally." I proceeded to explain about Lantana, hurrying to finish as we reached Elise's car. "So," I said, knowing my time was about up. "If you have any thoughts about the best course of action for me, maybe you could text them or something."

She pulled out her phone, typing furiously. A few seconds later, mine pinged. I grimaced, expecting a nice brush-off, something like, *Call my office*, or, *Sorry, but I'm really busy*. Instead, her text read, *If you'll take me to dinner tonight, I think we could figure it all out.*

All? I texted back.

Let's find out.

❖

As it turned out, legal guardianship could be terminated once the other person regained the ability to manage their affairs, including caring for themselves. Zelda fit that bill in less than a month, and Counselor Adams made certain Lantana was out on her ass. It also turned out that Elise had read the rest of my journal, and she especially liked the ending, where I talked about knowing her had led me to understand what true love was, and I thought she was exactly the person I'd spend the rest of my life with.

We discussed the parameters of that idea during our abbreviated dinner before renewing our acquaintance with Nephthys's bed, where we talked some more and then, not so much. But the moment where she took my face in her hands and told me she never wanted to be without me again was engraved onto my heart. I knew I'd never stop trying to show her that I felt the same. Elise filled my sad, empty spaces with gratitude, bliss, hope, and contentment, and I adored her profoundly and completely.

When Zelda was ready, Elise and I found a place with an extra bedroom and bathroom in the suburb of Shallowater, not far from Ben and Arlene's house. Elise was usually able to spend afternoons with her folks before coming home to us. I taught part-time at NTDS, and Zelda accompanied me whenever she could, scaring the daylights out of the rookies with her stories of near misses and friends lost. She passed quietly in her sleep two years later, and Elise's mom went a year after that.

Elise's older sister Corrington announced she was tired of working in the big city and took a job in Shallowater. She and her lover bought our house, and Elise and I relocated to Colorado. I went to work for Ray, and Elise found a job working cases for trans clients at a small firm in Trinidad. Lena, eager to escape "that pesky kid"— my second godchild—stayed with us in the summers and learned to ski during winter breaks. Daphne kept promising to come and bring Chip sometime, but I wasn't holding my breath on that.

I could tell by watching Elise around Ray and Jackie's kids that we were going to have the baby discussion soon. Thinking about my mother used to make me anxious about being a parent, but being around Ray helped me remember the unconditional love and affection I learned from my dad. And when I envisioned a little Elise running around, I knew I'd love her or him as much as I did the original version.

Since we've been together, Elsie and I have had our share of joy, along with doses of sorrow. There would be more of both to come, but every day was something new and wonderful in what our life was and what it was becoming. *They say that love is a journey, not a destination, and I'm just happy to be on my way there.*

About the Author

Jaycie Morrison traded her big city home of Dallas, Texas, for the cool beauty of a small Colorado mountain town and hasn't regretted a moment of it. She lives with her wife of several decades, their spoiled cattle dog Tilley, and whatever wild creatures visit them from the forest.

Her first three novels—*Basic Training of the Heart, Heart's Orders*, and *Guarding Hearts*—make up the Love and Courage series. Set during World War II, they combine Jaycie's love of the written word and of history. Goldie finalist *The Found Jar*, her first contemporary romance, was followed by *A Perfect Fifth*, a story of love, music, and coming to grips with who you really are. *On My Way There* is a personal journey romance that contains humor, drama, and a search for something real and lasting.

When not writing or reading, Jaycie may be hiking, traveling, experimenting with gluten free cooking, or pretending to be a rock star. Email Jaycie at jaycie.morrison@yahoo.com

Books Available from Bold Strokes Books

A Degree to Die For by Karis Walsh. A murder at the University of Washington's Classics Department brings Professor Antigone Weston and Sergeant Adriana Kent together—first as opposing forces, and then allies as they fight together to protect their campus from a killer. (978-1-63679-365-8)

A Talent Within by Suzanne Lenoir. Evelyne, born into nobility, and Annika, a peasant girl with a deadly secret, struggle to change their destinies in Valmora, a medieval world controlled by religion, magic, and men. (978-1-63679-423-5)

Finders Keepers by Radclyffe. Roman Ashcroft's past, it seems, is not so easily forgotten when fate brings her and Tally Dewilde together—along with an attraction neither welcomes. (978-1-63679-428-0)

Homeland by Kristin Keppler and Allisa Bahney. Dani and Kate have finally found themselves on the same side of the war, but a new threat from the inside jeopardizes the future of the wasteland. (978-1-63679-405-1)

Just One Dance by Jenny Frame. Will Taylor Spark and her new business to make dating special—the Regency Romance Club—bring sparkle back to Jaq Bailey's lonely world? (978-1-63679-457-0)

On My Way There by Jaycie Morrison. As Max traverses the open road, her journey of impossible love, loss, and courage mirrors her voyage of self-discovery leading to the ultimate question: If she can't have the woman of her dreams, will the woman of real life be enough? (978-1-63679-392-4)

Transitioning Home by Heather K O'Malley. An injured soldier realizes they need to transition to really heal. (978-1-63679-424-2)

Truly Enough by JJ Hale. Chasing the spark of creativity may ignite a burning romance or send a friendship up in flames. (978-1-63679-442-6)

Vintage and Vogue by Kelly and Tana Fireside. When tech whiz Sena Abrigo marches into small-town Owen Station, she turns librarian Hazel Butler's life upside down in the most wonderful of ways, setting off an explosive series of events, threatening their chance at love…and their very lives. (978-1-63679-448-8)

Broken Fences by Jo Hemmingwood. Former army sergeant Seneca Twist has difficulty adjusting to civilian life until she meets psychologist Robyn Mason and has a place to call home. (978-1-63679-414-3)

Never Kiss a Cowgirl by Ali Vali. Asher Evans dreams of winning the National Finals Rodeo in Vegas, and Reagan Wilson wants no part of something that brings back the memory of what killed her father. (978-1-63679-106-7)

Pantheon Girls by Jean Copeland. Cassie Burke never anticipated the detour life was about to take when a meeting with a prospective client reunites her with a past love and reignites the star-crossed passion they shared twenty years earlier. (978-1-63679-337-5)

Roux for Two by Aurora Rey. For TV chef Chelsea Boudreaux and hometown boy Bryce Cormier, love proves as tricky as making a good pot of gumbo. (978-1-63679-376-4)

Starting Over by Nance Sparks. Jennifer has no idea if she can mend Sam's broken soul after the sudden loss of her wife, but it's never too late for starting over. (978-1-63679-409-9)

The Accidental Bride by Jane Walsh. Spinsters Miss Grace Linfield and Miss Thea Martin travel to Gretna Green to prevent a wedding, only to discover a scandalous passion—for each other. (978-1-63679-345-0)

Three Wishes by Anne Shade. A magic lamp, a beautiful Jinni, and a cursed princess make for one unbelievable story. (978-1-63679-349-8)

Undiscovered Treasures by MJ Williamz. For Cyl and her friends Luna and Martinique, life's best treasures often appear when you're not looking. (978-1-63679-449-5)

Curse of the Gorgon by Tanai Walker. Cass will do anything to ensure Elle's safety, but is she willing to embrace the curse of the Gorgon? (978-1-63679-395-5)

Dance with Me by Georgia Beers. Scottie Templeton mixes it up on and off the dance floor with sexy salsa instructor Marisa Reyes. But can Scottie get past Marisa's connection to her ex? (978-1-63679-359-7)

Gin and Bear It by Joy Argento. Opposites really can attract, and as Kelly and Logan work together to create a loving home for rescue cat Bear, they just might find one for themselves as well. (978-1-63679-351-1)

Harvest Dreams by Jacqueline Fein-Zachary. Planting the vineyard of their dreams, Kate Bauer and Sydney Barrett must resist their attraction while battling nature and their families, who oppose both the venture and their relationship. (978-1-63679-380-1)

The No Kiss Contract by Nan Campbell. Workaholic Davy believes she can get the top spot at her firm if the senior partners think she's settling down and about to start a family, but she needs the delightful yet dubious Anna to help by pretending to be her fiancée. (978-1-63679-372-6)

Outside the Lines by Melissa Sky. If you had the chance to live forever, would you take it? Amara Rodriguez did, and it sets her on a journey to find her missing mother and unravel the mystery of her own heart. (978-1-63679-403-7)

The Value of Sylver and Gold by Michelle Larkin. When word gets out that former Boston homicide detective Reid Sylver can talk to the dead, the FBI solicits her help on a serial murder case, prompting Reid to assemble forces once again with Detective London Gold. (978-1-63679-093-0)

When It Feels Right by Tagan Shepard. Freshly out of the closet Marlene hasn't been lucky in love, but when it comes to her quirky new roommate Abby, everything just feels right. (978-1-63679-367-2)

Lucky in Lace by Melissa Brayden. Straitlaced stationery store owner Juliette Jennings's predictable life unravels when a sexy lingerie shop and its alluring owner move in next door. (978-1-63679-434-1)

Made for Her by Carsen Taite. Neal Walsh is a newly made member of the Mancuso crime family, but will her undeniable attraction to Anastasia Petrov, the wife of her boss's sworn enemy, be the ultimate test of her loyalty? (978-1-63679-265-1)

Off the Menu by Alaina Erdell. Reality TV sensation Restaurant Redo and its gorgeous host Erin Rasmussen will arrive to film in chef Taylor Mobley's kitchen. As the cameras roll, will they make the jump from enemies to lovers? (978-1-63679-295-8)

Pack of Her Own by Elena Abbott. When things heat up in a small town, steamy secrets are revealed between Alpha werewolf Wren Carne and her human mate, Natalie Donovan. (978-1-63679-370-2)

Return to McCall by Patricia Evans. Lily isn't looking for romance— not until she meets Alex, the gorgeous Cuban dance instructor at La Haven, a newly opened lesbian retreat. (978-1-63679-386-3)

So It Went Like This by C. Spencer. A candid and deeply personal exploration of fate, chosen family, and the vulnerability intrinsic in life's uncertainties. (978-1-63555-971-2)

Stolen Kiss by Spencer Greene. Anna and Louise share a stolen kiss, only to discover that Louise is dating Anna's brother. Surely, one kiss can't change everything…Can it? (978-1-63679-364-1)

The Fall Line by Kelly Wacker. When Jordan Burroughs arrives in the Deep South to paint a local endangered aquatic flower, she doesn't expect to become friends with a mischievous gin-drinking ghost who complicates her budding romance and leads her to an awful discovery and danger. (978-1-63679-205-7)

To Meet Again by Kadyan. When the stark reality of WWII separates cabaret singer Evelyn and Australian doctor Joan in Singapore, they must overcome all odds to find one another again. (978-1-63679-398-6)